WHAT'S PAST IS PROLOGUE

By

Deborah Fezelle

Whereof what's past is prologue;
What to come in yours and my
Discharge.

THE TEMPEST, Act 2, Scene 1

Cover Design

By

Wendy Prince

For the kids who don't have a voice
in this fight.

Also for Cathy Shincovich,
a psychologist who made a difference.

Published 2022 by Shorehouse Books

Printed in the United States of America

Cover by

Wendy Prince

ISBN-13: 978-1-7372746-7-4

The Rose
Music & Lyrics by Amanda McBroom

Not While I'm Around (Sweeney Todd)
Music & Lyrics by Stephen Sondheim

ACKNOWLEDGMENTS

Heartfelt thanks to my publisher, Donna Cavanagh, for her unwavering support and compassion as I tackled this difficult subject.

I owe a lifetime of thanks to Joshua Grenrock and Cynthia Dickason-Scott. They were with me from the beginning as I sketched out and filled in this manuscript. Josh's point-of-view was invaluable as I strove to write an intricate relationship between two complex males

A huge thank you to Nancy Sonner, Marilyn & Kevin Wells, Kelly Kerry, Kate Fasbender-Bos and Alfrika Williams for their support and insightful feedback. And a long overdue thank you to Wendy Prince, who somehow manages to crawl into my head when she creates her perfect cover designs.

Inspiration comes from a million places, often out of the blue. PROLOGUE is a collision of my need to tell an important story and the chance viewing of a video on Facebook. As I watched a British singer/actor perform a concert in his youth, a lightbulb went off in my head and a new character was born.

"Music was my first love
And it will be my last
Music of the future
And music of the past
To live without my music
Would be impossible to do
In this world of troubles
My music pulls me though"
Music and Lyrics by John Miles

PROLOGUE

Fifteen Years Earlier
Sarasota, Florida

Tess Cavanaugh sat with Father Locato in the front pew of St. Sebastian's. The church was quiet. Very few signs of the funeral service that took place earlier that morning. Only the lilies on the altar and the scent of incense in the air.

Tess wasn't here to pay her respects to the young girl who died. No, Tess met with Father Locato every Monday for counseling.

"So sad," Tess remarked to the elderly priest. "That girl dying reminds me of—"

"Drugs. The plague of the young." Father Locato turned to her. "So tell me. How's Henry doing?"

Tess's husband was inconsolable since it happened. Never leaving the house, he spent all day in their garage carving furniture. What had been his hobby was now his entire world. "The same."

Three months ago, Henry and Theresa Cavanaugh's son Frank was killed in Iraq. Frankie was their only child, their surprise package late in life. He was their blessing from God. Until he died in a desert halfway across the world.

"And your diary? Are you still writing in it?"

The priest had recommended Tess write down her feelings, expressing her grief on the page. He said it was a productive way to work through Frankie's death.

"Yes. You were right. It helps.

"Good." Father patted her hand. "Come. I'll walk you out."

Tess took the priest's arm as they made their way down the wide main aisle. "You're coming for dinner Thursday night?"

The priest grinned. "Don't I always?"

1

"Father Locato?" A voice from above. The choir director stared down at them. "I was putting away the music and— Could you come up here for a moment? There's a ... Well. See for yourself."

Tess followed the priest up the rickety stairs to the choir loft.

In the side room where music and robes were stored, a child sat on the floor. A little boy, not more than two-years-old. Wrapped in a worn blanket, a post-it note was pinned to his shirt:

Patrick

The child had soft blond curls and the most unusual eyes. Large, oddly shaped and a vibrant blue.

They seemed to see right into Tess's soul.

*

The Present
New York City

Nick McDeare clipped along East Seventy-Fifth Street on a sunny September day. The trees lining the picturesque street were beginning to show hints of autumn colors. Central Park rolled into sight, as did the slate gray brownstone Nick called home.

It had been a successful day. A meeting with the screenwriter who was turning Nick's last suspense novel *THE SILVER LINING* into a feature film. Followed by lunch with his agent Liz to deliver his current novel, *BLEEDING BURGANDY*. Liz was shocked the manuscript came in under the deadline. So was Nick. That's what happened when you were separated from your wife and had time on your hands. Of course he didn't say that to Liz. She'd been trying to get him into bed for years. Along with half the female population out there.

Nick turned the locks and pushed into the vestibule. He was met by deafening music and a voice all too familiar. Striding down the hall, he glanced into the pristine living room on the right, the gothic dining room on the left, past the staircase to the second floor and the bathroom tucked beneath it, all the way to the study in the back of the house. The source of the ear-shattering noise.

His thirteen-year-old daughter Kat sat on the leather sofa watching the television intently. A young man's face filled the screen, his magnificent voice echoing throughout the house.

"For God's sake," Nick shouted, "turn that down."

Kat jumped at the sound of his voice and did as she was told. "Isn't Uncle Andrew fantastic in this show?"

Nick's brother Andrew was fantastic in every Broadway show he did. But there was no need to shake the walls with his baritone voice.

Nick glanced up at the huge oil painting hanging over the fireplace. Nick McDeare and Andrew Brady in tuxes eying each other. A study in contrasts. Andrew fair with sandy hair like Kat. Nick dark with ebony strands spiking his forehead. But they both had the same large amber eyes that dipped at the outer corners, the same easy smiles, the same strong noses and dimpled chins. The Saint & The Sinner. Nick's title for the painting. Andrew, the golden boy, beloved by all. Nick, the dark horse, the loner with a chip on his shoulder.

Actually, it was an exquisite painting, considering the artist used two photographs to put it together. Nick and Andrew never met in person, thanks to a twist of fate and their heartless 'male sperm-donor,' Nick's term for their natural father. Nick was adopted at birth. Andrew was raised by their mother when she refused to give up another baby. Just when the two grown brothers finally found each other, Andrew Brady was murdered.

"Don't you have your writing class tonight?" Nick asked, heading across the hall to the kitchen.

Kat shadowed his steps. "Yep. And I know what I want to write about next. Uncle Andrew."

If this home had a heart, it was the kitchen. A large island with comfortable stools ran down the center, pots and herbs hanging above it. An old-fashioned breakfast nook nestled beneath a picture window in the corner. A second set of stairs led to the upper floors. A walk-in pantry, hooked rugs, potted plants and polished wood floors gave the space a homey feel.

Mary Bodine put a glazed chicken in the oven. Mary was a stunning black woman who ruled the McDeare home. She was tough but had a heart of gold. Mother to them all. "Thank you for making her turn down that TV. She's been playing that same song for the last two hours. You know how much I loved Andrew. He grew up in this house, and I loved him like a son. But even I can't deal with a song stuck on repeat."

"I need to study Uncle Andrew." Kat stole a cucumber from the salad on the island.

Nick poured some coffee and leaned against the counter. "Use your laptop or iPad. Up in your room."

"But all of Andrew's shows are stored in the study's TV."

"That's an easy fix." Nick, too, picked at the salad. "Anyway, why Andrew?"

"Because I want to know more about him. I get bits and pieces from everyone but not the whole story. I need to sit down and grill you about him. Both of you." Kat was new to the family, the result of an affair

Nick had years ago. He only learned of her existence last year when her mother died. Ultimately, he brought her to New York. After a rocky start, Kat settled into the household.

"Jessie's the one to talk to." Nick watched Kat's face fall.

Jessica Kendall McDeare. Nick's wife and Kat's stepmother.

About to star in a new Broadway musical about Diana, the Princess of Wales. Currently living in a swanky midtown hotel.

Nick and Jessie separated in August.

*

It was an excellent rehearsal today. Jessie should be in a good mood. She wasn't. Part of it had to do with missing Nick. The other part was missing Andrew.

She stepped into the shower, allowing the warm water to cascade over her blond hair, over her tired blue eyes. Washing away the day's exertions was soothing. If only Nick was standing beside her, skin against skin, his gentle hands roaming— Jessie shook off the memory.

This separation from Nick was taking its toll. Their young marriage had been so happy. Until Kat was thrown into the mix, reminding Jessie of Nick's wild bachelor days, of his life before they met. Until Jessie made a fatal mistake while performing *DIANA* in London over the summer. A mistake that revealed hidden chasms between husband and wife. So now Nick lived at home, and Jessie lived in the Galaxy Hotel attached to the theater where *DIANA* would perform.

Their separation was supposed to be temporary, but they weren't doing anything significant towards getting back together. Their public pretense that everything was fine between them became more difficult with each passing day. Jessie was supposedly staying at a hotel because her house was too hectic. Because she needed to focus on the monumental role of Diana right now.

No one bought it.

There were daily items in the gossip columns about their marriage. Hints and innuendos that the famous couple was heading for divorce. The press was convinced from the beginning that Nick's old habits would eventually return. No matter what went down in London a divorce would be pinned on the roaming eye of Nick McDeare. Jessie stayed quiet, not wanting to poke the media rattlesnake. And of course Nick said nothing. He loathed the rags and their moronic mouthpieces.

As for missing Andrew, Jessie was rehearsing in the Crookston Theater where she and Andrew performed their signature musical *HEARTTAKES.* That must be why he was constantly on her mind. She missed working with him, singing with him, seeing those amazing eyes next to her on the stage. They'd been partners both onstage and off, married for over five years until Andrew was murdered. Which brought Nick to town. To find Andrew's killer. Although she fought it, Jessie fell in love with Nick. With Andrew's blessing.

Jessie smiled at the memory. As crazy as it sounded, Andrew's spirit hovered over the family since his murder. Maybe his sudden death was what caused him to cling to this world. Jessie didn't try to explain it. She just knew it was fact. She felt him near when rehearsals started, giving her strength. But lately he was silent.

Where was Andrew? Was he still around, watching over them?

CHAPTER 1

"Hey, Dad." Nick's nine-year-old son Anthony peeked into his second-floor home office. "Busy?

"Nope. What's up?" Nick swiveled as Anthony plopped down on the chair next to the desk. His thick mop of dark curls almost obscured his penetrating blue eyes. Monty, a Portuguese Water Dog and Anthony's constant companion, nuzzled Nick's hand.

"Kat's been asking me questions about Andrew. Which got me thinking. He hasn't been around lately."

"He comes and goes. You know that."

"I'm afraid he's gone for good."

Nick rubbed Monty's soft fur. "He wouldn't go without saying goodbye."

Anthony and Andrew had a special relationship. Years ago Jessie found herself pregnant by Gianni Fosselli, a young Italian owner of a fleet of cruise ships. When Gianni was forced to return home to Italy, not knowing about the baby, Andrew stepped in. He married his lifelong friend and secret love so Jessie would have a father for her baby. Also to protect Jessie, to prevent the powerful Gianni from ever thinking Anthony was his son. It didn't work. Andrew's gesture got him killed by a vengeful Gianni. Which resulted in Nick putting Gianni in his own early grave.

While investigating Andrew's death, Nick discovered his brother was responsible for Gianni abandoning Jessie. Andrew's intentions were justified – He knew what a despicable creature Gianni was and wanted to get him away from Jessie – but his devious actions weren't. Andrew ended up setting off a chain of events that left more than one person dead.

Andrew's halo was tarnished a bit in Nick's eyes after that. But not Jessie's. She felt Andrew was trying to protect her from a man she should have avoided from the start. Saint Andrew's record was intact.

Anthony loved Andrew, the dad who saw him through his first five years. But he also loved Nick. When Nick married Jessie, he adopted Anthony, and a special bond formed.

"We'll hear from him, Bongo." Bongo. Both Andrew and Nick's pet name for the boy. "Hang in there."

*

Nick breezed through the master bedroom to the enormous walk-in closet. Which was more like Jessie's dressing room with Nick's clothes stuffed in the back. But with his wife gone, the place was his. In other words, a pigsty. Mary refused to clean in here unless Nick picked up his clothes. A boycott of doing Nick's laundry was also in place until Mary could see the hardwood floor again.

He kicked off his shoes and tossed his socks into the mess. As he stripped off his shirt, Nick tripped over something. Pain shot through his big toe. Wincing, he dropped down on the stool of Jessie's vanity. What was so bulky it could cause this kind of agony?

Andrew's dance bag. What in the hell was it doing in the middle of the floor, buried under yesterday's clothes? Pulling the large leather shoulder bag closer, he unzipped it. Yep. Andrew's journals were still tucked inside. The last time Nick saw this bag was when he was chasing down Andrew's killer. Nick pulled a few books out and ran his fingers over them.

"Dad?"

"In here, Kat."

Kat paused in the doorway. "What are those?"

"Your uncle's journals."

"You're kidding." Her face lit up.

"Did you want something?"

"I want to jog with you in the morning, so wait for me, okay?"

"Sure."

Kat was laser-focused on the items in Nick's hands. "Can I read the journals? They could help."

"I don't think so. You're a little young."

"Did you read them?"

"The later ones. They helped implicate Gianni in Andrew's murder."

"How far back do they go?"

"From the time he was thirteen."

"Then I'm not too young. I'm thirteen."

Going on thirty. And how did she always do that? Come back with the perfect retort? She should be a lawyer, not a writer.

"Please, Dad. Let me read them. Especially the early ones. There's a lot on the internet about Andrew in his later years, but not much about when he was younger."

"I told you. You should talk to Jessie."

"No." She flung her shoulder-length sandy hair back and folded her arms. The picture of obstinance. "She wouldn't be honest with me. And we'd just end up fighting again."

Kat had a point. Jessie was protective of her history with Andrew. She would never open up to Kat about him. Jessie and Kat were like Anthony's dog and Kat's Siamese cat. Claws unsheathed. Fangs bared. And a migraine for Nick.

"Then talk to Abbie. Abbie and Andrew met when they were seven. She was his best friend."

Kat stared at him, thinking. "Yeah. Abbie. Thanks, Dad." She bounced out of sight, happy again.

Nick rubbed his throbbing toe.

She was back. "I still want to read those journals."

Nick swiped a hand through his thick hair and counted to ten. "Tell you what. Let me scan them first."

"You're going to censor the sex, right?"

"Good night, Kat."

*

A Few Days Later

Abigail Forrester dragged home. It had been a long but productive day. After a career as an actress and lipstick model, Abbie's new job was publicist/assistant for her old pal, Jessie Kendle McDeare. Surprisingly, she not only enjoyed her new position, she was good at it. As opening night loomed, flattering publicity for Jessie was vital. Which meant squashing the divorce chatter. Abbie's goal was to fill the press with photos of a happy Mr. and Mrs. McDeare.

Willie Bodine waited for her in their kitchen. Willie. Mary's nephew and Abbie's fiancé. Her Denzel Washington look-alike and the love of her life.

"You made dinner." Abbie smooched his cheek, inhaling the faint scent of the cologne she gave him for his birthday. "If I didn't love you before, I certainly do now." Abbie dropped down in their breakfast nook and swept her hair off her face. She spent the morning at the hairdresser's, adding ashy highlights to her layered mahogany mane.

"I knew you'd be tired." He ran his fingers through her hair, admiring it, and joined her.

They lived on the first floor of the brownstone behind the McDeare home. The two parties came and went through the back yards.

"And what did you do today? Besides preparing this amazing meal." Abbie surveyed the table. Grilled steaks. Baked potatoes. Sauteed mushrooms. Yum.

"Not much. The kids never left the house, and Nick hoofed it on his own somewhere." An ex-cop, Willie was both driver and security detail for the McDeare family. Nick and Jessie's celebrity demanded protection. Willie also helped Nick at times on investigations. Besides being a best-selling suspense author, Nick was also a Pulitzer-Prize winning investigative reporter.

"How about you, Abs? How was your day?"

"Hectic. Too many questions about Jessie's marriage." Abbie closed her plump lips around a bite of steak.

"How's she doing about that?"

Abbie shrugged as she swallowed. "The same. She's waiting for a move from Nick. Andrew seems to be more on her mind these days. Probably because of working in that theater again."

"Speaking of Andrew," Willie helped himself to some mushrooms, "Kat came by. She wants to talk to you about him."

"Why?"

"She didn't say."

"It's a busy week, but I'll make sure I find the time."

*

Sitting at her bedroom desk the next afternoon, Kat was on her cell with Bertie Castro. Multi-tasking was a snap for her. She held up her part of the conversation while reading a tidbit about Andrew on her laptop and continuing to organize her stacks of research.

Bertie was her best friend and pas de deux partner in ballet class. Also her boyfriend. Well, kind of. That side of things was new.

Of Puerto Rican descent, fifteen-year-old Bertie had dark close-cropped curls, long cheekbones, gray-green eyes and a wicked sense of humor. He was also a brilliant dancer and had a strong singing voice. Because of those gifts, Bertie was cast not only in the chorus of *DIANA*, but also had a small featured dance. The director of the production, Quill Llewellin, met both Kat and Bertie at a party here at the house last January.

Impressed with their talent, Quill wanted to cast them both in the show, but Kat declined. She hated the theater with its phoniness and backbiting and jealousy. Jessie was the epitome of that world in Kat's eyes. No, despite her own talent as a dancer/singer, despite her love of the piano, Kat dreamed of being a writer like her father.

"I gotta tell you, Kat. Jessie's going to be awesome in this show."

Kat rolled her eyes. "I saw her performance in London, remember?" Jessie's talent was the ONLY thing Kat begrudgingly afforded her stepmother.

Her dad knocked on her open bedroom door.

"Dad just came in, Bertie. I'll call you back."

"I have something for you." Her father dropped a stack of little books on her desk. "You can read these." Uncle Andrew's journals!

Kat grabbed the top book and opened it. "Which ones are these?"

"From the beginning to a little past his Juilliard years."

She gave him a cynical look. "Did you black-out all the sex?"

"There was nothing too objectionable. Back then, I think Andrew just wanted to record events for his future autobiography."

Kat laughed. "He knew he'd write an autobiography?"

"See for yourself. Andrew believed he was going to be famous."

"There's something to be said for self-confidence."

Her dad snorted. "More like ego."

"Actors need ego. If they don't believe in themselves, no one else will."

"You sound like Jessie."

Kat hated being compared to her stepmother.

Her father wandered around the room, surveying Kat's stacks of printouts. "I just ordered you a printer for up here. Anthony says you're using up all the ink in the downstairs computer." He joined her at the desk. "How's it going?"

"Good. Except when Hamlet goes on a tear through my papers."

Hearing his name, Kat's Siamese cat yowled and stretched every inch of his sleek body. With a yawn, he curled back around Kat's desk lamp and closed his turquoise eyes.

"You're certainly neater than I am."

"Everyone's neater than you are."

"Smart ass." Grinning, Nick headed for the door. "Dinner in an hour."

Kat opened the first journal and began to read. She forgot about dinner, about Bertie and her dad, about everything but the life of Andrew Brady.

It was almost dawn when she finished the last journal. Climbing into bed, she hoped to catch a few hours sleep before Finn, her home-school teacher, arrived. As she closed her eyes, she heard rustling. What was Hamlet doing now?

Lifting her head, she glanced around the dark room.

One of the journals was open, the pages fluttering back and forth.

*

Jessie sat in her dressing room at the theater as Maggie Mann of *The New York Times* finished interviewing her.

"The score and songs are from a new British composer, Randall Richards," Maggie said, consulting her notes. "How do you feel about his work?"

"I love him. So did the critics in London."

"One last question," Maggie said, closing her notebook. "Andrew Brady. You still miss him onstage?"

"I'll always miss Andrew." Jessie could still see Andrew onstage. How he looked as he sang to her. How easily tears spilled from his gorgeous eyes. How he'd lean back when belting a high note, his magnificent voice filling an entire theater. His theatrical vulnerability and fearlessness.

Jessie snapped back to the present. "Don't get me wrong. I adore working with Oliver Farrow, who's playing Charles. He also played the role in London." Ollie was gay, hilarious and one of the few people Jessie respected in the cold and bitchy cast of London's *DIANA*. Ollie and his partner Rafe got her through some tough times across the pond.

After Maggie left, Abbie joined Jessie. "Anything you need before I head home?"

"No." She wished she, too, was going home instead of back to the hotel. "Feel like getting some dinner?"

"I'd love to, but Kat wants to talk to me about Andrew."

Jessie frowned. "Andrew? Why?"

"She's writing something about him and wants background."

Nora, Jessie's dresser, sped into the room. Nora Connor was a gem of a woman with a silver topknot and half-glasses attached to the bridge of her nose. She'd been Jessie's dresser since her debut on Broadway. Anyone who wanted to get to Jessie had to go through Nora. Currently, the same rules applied at the hotel as Nora was staying with her charge. "Ready to go?"

*

"So what else do you want to know?" Abbie sat on the cushioned window seat in Kat's bedroom. She'd filled Kat in on growing up with Andrew.

Kat opened a journal. "Andrew worked at a lot of regional theaters before he and Jessie hit it big on Broadway. Musicals, Shakespeare—"

"He and Jessie also did a club act. And earlier Andrew did a solo act. A highly successful solo act."

Kat flipped through the journal, looking for something specific. "Do you remember when Andrew went down to Florida to do *LES MISERABLES*?"

Abbie nodded. "At the Asolo Theater in Sarasota. He played Marius. I was working at a theater in Jacksonville at the time and got to see a performance."

"So you were actually there—"

"Just for one night. I had my own show to do."

"Do you remember a girl he got involved with down there?"

Abbie squinted. "What do you mean, involved?"

"According to this journal, they slept together a couple times. She was in the chorus. Apparently, she reminded him of Jessie."

Abbie wandered around the room, thinking. "This is ringing a bell. What was her name?"

"Heidi." Kat used the journal for reference. "When the Asolo season ended, Andrew came back to New York to start his fourth year at Juilliard. Heidi tried to reach him, but she didn't have his home address so she—"

"—called Juilliard and kept leaving messages. It's coming back to me now. He finally called her back and—"

"—she told him she was pregnant," Kat finished.

Abbie shot Kat a sarcastic grin. "Is that why you're asking about this? You think this girl got pregnant by Andrew? Kat, she was lying. She was a local Sarasota girl who thought she found her ticket to New York with Andrew Brady."

"That's what Andrew said in this journal."

Abbie leaned against the desk. "You have to understand something about your uncle—" She straightened up. "On second thought, I feel a little uncomfortable talking about this with you—"

"Why? Because I'm his niece?"

"And very young."

"I'm thirteen. And I'm not stupid about boys. Men. Even Dad is starting to trust me with mature subjects. Think of me as a writer researching my subject."

Abbie turned away. "Forgive me, Nick," she whispered before looking back at Kat. "Andrew was hot. Really hot. Every girl wanted him."

Kat sat back, picturing Andrew. "It's odd. I don't think of him that way. Andrew had this boyish, jokey quality. He was the boy-next-door."

Abbie laughed heartily. "Beneath that wholesome, all-American look was a sexiness that can't be defined. You had to see it in person. And what made it even more potent was that Andrew was completely unaware of it. Add his brilliant talent into the mix, and that's catnip for women." She shook her head. "He had no idea how he came across to the opposite sex. He was only interested in—"

"—Jessie."

"Don't get me wrong. Andrew didn't sit around waiting for Jessie. He was a guy, after all. Doing what all guys do." She chuckled and rolled her eyes.

"Did Jessie know? About Andrew and other women?"

"She wasn't interested. She was involved with other men back then."

As usual, Jessie was all about Jessie. "Were Andrew and Jessie lovers? Before they got married?"

"You mean when they were younger?" Kat nodded. "When they first got to Juilliard they were an item. But then Jessie got involved with— Well, that's not important."

Kat could picture it. Queen Jessie got bored with her lapdog Andrew and moved on. But back to the subject at hand. "I tried to research Heidi. The Asolo website doesn't list the chorus members that far back, only the major roles. I need to know her last name."

"You're wasting your time, Kat. There was no baby. This girl's plan to trap Andrew didn't work. That's the REAL story about that period of Andrew's life."

*

Nick sat with Mary at the island in the kitchen, sipping brandy and catching up on today's *New York Times*. He wasn't used to having free time and was bored. The book tour for *BLEEDING BURGANDY* wouldn't start until late November.

"Did Maddie and Ethan get away okay?" Nick's half-sister and half-brother flew to San Diego that morning to begin a long legal battle. Maddie was suing for access to her sixteen-year-old daughter Christine. It wouldn't be easy. Maddie's ex was an attorney himself. Ethan took a leave from his professorship at Columbia and went with her. Also his young son Charlie. Ethan would serve as a character witness and would be there for moral support. Ethan not only loved his sister, he owed her.

"Yep. Maddie called when they arrived." Mary looked up from her puzzle book. "They could be gone for months. I know they haven't been around long, but I miss Maddie already."

Madison and Ethan were new additions to the family, courtesy of Kat. She discovered them on one of those ancestor sites. After impregnating Nick and Andrew's mother twice, Nick's 'sperm-donor

13

father' moved on to another woman, giving her fraternal twins. Not bad for a guy who hated kids.

Kat came down the stairs. "Mary, did Uncle Andrew save mementos from his productions? You know. Programs and things like that?"

"He saved everything. I didn't have the heart to throw it all away."

"Where is it?"

"In the fourth-floor storage. The boxes are marked with plays and dates. Andrew's doing, not mine. He was organized. Unlike your father." She shot Nick a look before going back to her puzzle.

Nick let the dig pass. "What are you looking for, Kat?"

Kat plopped down beside him and told him about the Asolo and Heidi. "I need her last name. If she had a baby, there'll be a record of it somewhere."

Mary removed her glasses. "Andrew was always pursued by young girls."

"Since when?" Nick asked.

"You think you got all the charm and Andrew got none? Your brother had women falling all over him. And claiming pregnancy was used more than once. But he only had eyes for Jessie."

Nick didn't want to talk about Jessie. Or Andrew. Or Andrew and Jessie. "Come on. Let's find that program."

Finally. Something to do.

*

"Nothing?" Kat watched her dad on his laptop in his office. "There's really nothing about her anywhere on the internet?"

"Not under Heidi Breen." Nick picked up the program for *LES MISERABLES* and stared at the picture of Heidi. No wonder Andrew noticed her. Blond hair and blue eyes. Alabaster skin. Etched cheekbones. So reminiscent of Jessie. Nick's wife was more beautiful, of course.

"Maybe Breen is a stage name." Kat bit at a hangnail.

"She was in the chorus, Kat. You don't change your name for the chorus." He tossed the program on the desk.

"You do if the chorus is just the beginning for you." Kat paced to the windows. "Or if you want to disown your past." Spinning around, she grabbed the Asolo program. "Her bio says she was born and raised in Sarasota. Went to Lincoln High School. Pull up their website."

The site materialized on Nick's screen. "Horrible website." He scrolled through the options. "Where are the archives?" More scrolling. "Nothing, not even under ALUMNI." He sat back. "This is a waste of time. There was no baby."

14

"Abbie said the same thing. And it's what Andrew wrote in his journal."

"End of story."

"Not for me. I want an answer. Was there a baby?" She sat on the desk, her legs dangling. "Would you feel differently if Andrew was involved?"

Nick's eyes narrowed. "What do you mean?"

"Last night when I was going to sleep, one of the journals' pages started flipping back and forth. Now, I had my bedroom windows open, and it was breezy, so it could mean nothing. BUT when I checked it out, the diary was open to the page about Heidi."

Nick suddenly remembered the dance bag appearing in the middle of the closet. The dance bag which housed the journals. Andrew? "Let me think about this."

Which he did.

All night.

*

"She's nice, Kat." Bertie Castro and Kat warmed up at the barre before ballet class. "You'd be surprised how nice Jessie is to everyone in the cast."

"Enough about that woman." Kat re-pinned a strand of hair that came loose from her tight chignon.

"Okay, what's wrong?" Bertie watched his arm elongate towards the ceiling

Kat dipped into a graceful plie. "Dad's going to Florida tomorrow."

"That's it?" She nodded. "Is this about Andrew's supposed baby?"

"Don't make fun of this, okay?"

"Sorry."

"Dad's going to do some snooping. I should be going with him, but he won't let me. He doesn't want me to miss school or my outside classes. But this is my project. I'm the one writing about Andrew. I should be the one to research it."

"He'll keep you in the loop. Let him do what he does best."

"Oh shut up, Hubert."

"Don't tell me to shut up. And stop calling me Hubert!"

Kat kissed the tip of his nose and grinned before moving into position for class.

"By the way," Kat whispered, "don't say anything about this Andrew thing to Jessie, okay? Dad wants to keep it quiet unless something comes of it."

"When would I talk to Jessie at rehearsal? She's the star. I'm in the chorus."

"Trust me, stars and the chorus get together. Some of them even have babies."

*

Nick went to the closet to grab an overnight bag. He halted in the doorway when he saw the pristine condition of the room. His mess was gone. The wooden floor shone like glass. The dressing table was cleared of his half-empty water bottles and scraps of paper. Even the dust disappeared. "What the hell happened?"

"I happened."

Nick swung around.

Mary stood a few feet away. She tossed a large basket on the bed. "Here's your clean laundry. What were you planning to take to Florida? A satchel full of dirty clothes?"

"Uh, thanks, Mary."

"You owe me, Nicholas McDeare. But if you come up with a child for Andrew, I'll consider your debt paid.

"I'm not a miracle-worker. There probably is no baby."

*

Jessie spotted Nick in the back of the Crookston Theater just as rehearsal ended for the day. He trotted down the aisle, his leather jacket reflecting the stage lights.

Jessie met him halfway, giving him a kiss. Besides putting on a show for the cast and crew, she was thrilled to see him.

"I brought your mail." He handed her a stack with a rubber band around it. "How's the show going?" Nick glanced over her shoulder.

They were both aware of the whole company watching them.

"Night and day from London."

His eyes darted to hers. "The show was a hit in London."

"You know what I mean."

He seemed to look everywhere but at her. They were still being watched.

"Feel like grabbing some dinner, Nick?"

He paused. "I can't." Again, he glanced at the mob on the stage. "Come on. We're on display here." He took her hand and led her to the back of the theater.

*

"Have you given up on us, Nick?" They were out of earshot of the others.

16

"Of course not." Nick didn't want to have this conversation. Not here.

"So why can't we have dinner?"

"I'm leaving for Florida very early tomorrow morning."

"What's in Florida?"

"Just something I need to look into."

Jessie paused. "Another investigation?"

He shrugged. "You have your work. I have mine."

"Right. Well, have a good trip." She spun on her heel.

He grabbed her hand. "Jessie, part of our problem is your refusing to accept my investigative work."

"And your refusing to understand I work with good-looking men. That I can separate my career from my private life."

"Not always."

"Don't, Nick. Let's not rehash all that."

They stared at each other.

"I'll call when I get back. We'll have dinner and talk. Promise," he whispered. "I have to run." He glanced towards the stage. "Should we give them a show?"

Jessie looked like she was about to cry.

Feeling like a shit, Nick pulled her into his arms, staring into those blue eyes and bringing her soft lips to his. He hoped the crowd was watching.

For a moment Nick forgot he and Jessie were pretending.

For a moment he didn't want to stop.

For a moment, and against his will, his body responded.

Time to go …

17

CHAPTER 2

Nick flew down to Sarasota in his private plane and rented an SUV. After checking into a beachfront hotel on Longboat Key, he called his daughter, as promised, and headed for Lincoln High School.

Mrs. Platt, the principal, shook his hand as they sat down in her office. "You've caused quite a stir around here, Mr. McDeare. You have a lot of fans."

"Seems so." He showed her a picture of Heidi Breen in the Asolo program. "I'm trying to locate this girl. She was a student here maybe seventeen, eighteen years ago. I don't think Breen is her real name."

"Which means searching through hundreds of student pictures. We're computerized, but with the size of the classes it would take me forever."

"I'll do it."

She led him to a computer in a back room and got him a cup of mud. Literally. If he had an ulcer it would rebel. "Best of luck, Mr. McDeare."

Two hours later he found her.

Heidi Barstow.

*

Mary took lunch up to the kids and Finn, the home-school teacher. As she came back downstairs, the doorbell rang.

Brianna Fontaine stood under an umbrella in the pouring rain.

"Come in, come in." Mary swung the door wide.

A Pulitzer Prize winning reporter for *The New York Times*, Bree was a longtime colleague of Nick's, going back to their early days in Hong Kong. She was also an ex-girlfriend and had the distinction of being the only past amour to remain friends with the man.

Mary admired Bree's style. Her dark auburn hair hugged her face, and her hazel eyes bore little traces of makeup. She wasn't a beauty, but she had a look that made heads turn. Today she was dressed in dark slacks and an avocado turtleneck.

"Nick's in Florida," Mary supplied.

"What's he doing there?"

Mary led the way down the hallway. "Tracking down something or other." Nick had sworn both Mary and Kat to silence about what he was up to. The last person Mary would tell was Bree.

It wasn't that Mary disliked the woman. She respected Bree and the work she did. And Bree was close with Kat, having a positive influence on the girl. What Mary didn't like was Bree living with Nick's half-brother Ethan when she was still in love with Nick. "I'm surprised you didn't go out to San Diego with Ethan. At least for a little while."

"I'm working on something big for *The Times*. Bad time to leave. I'll go for a short visit soon." Bree perched on a stool at the island. "When's Nick due back?"

Mary handed her a mug of coffee. "Not sure. You know how Nick is. He doesn't say much. Is there anything I can help you with?"

"I'm taking Kat to the newsroom at *The Times*. She wants to see what working at a newspaper is like."

"She should be down soon. Sometimes her home schooling runs over." Mary sat across from her. "You must miss Ethan and Maddie." Bree lived in a rented brownstone on the Upper West Side, a place she shared with Ethan and Maddie.

"They haven't been gone long enough for me to miss them. And I'm not home much. This thing I'm working on— Actually, I wanted to talk to Nick about it. Maybe I'll call him in Florida."

Mary eyed the woman.

With Ethan out of town, Brianna was a shark on the loose.

*

Back at the hotel Nick went for a run on the beach. The sun was low in the sky but still hot, the humidity stifling. He was sweating in no time. Still, it felt good to work his muscles after sitting on his ass for a few days.

After a quick swim to cool off, he ordered dinner and parked himself at the table on his beachfront terrace. While he filled his empty stomach with grilled snapper, he pulled up one of his bookmarked websites.

Of course there was no phone listing for Heidi Barstow. Of course.

However, there were seven Barstows listed in the Sarasota area. He called them all, asking for Heidi, not expecting anything to come of it. Very few households still had land lines. Most people politely informed him he had the wrong number. One man rudely asked who was calling, then hung up on him. He jotted down the guy's address and stuck it in his wallet.

Next he did an internet search on Heidi Barstow.

And found her obituary.

She died from taking the drug Ecstasy a few years after she worked at the Asolo. The notice was brief, listing only a mother as the surviving relative. But her home address was on the same street as the man who just hung up on him.

No mention of a baby.

*

Kat's spirits plummeted at her father's news from Florida. Abbie and Andrew were right. There was no baby. Despite the gloomy news, her dad was sticking around another day or so. There was one more thing he wanted to check out. Kat admired his doggedness. Even if it led to a dead end.

"What's wrong?" Mary asked as they loaded the dishwasher after dinner.

"Looks like I was wrong about Heidi and a baby. I was so sure, Mary. I believed Dad would find that child."

"Why is it so important to you, Kat?"

"I don't know. It just is."

"Don't give up hope. Your dad and Andrew were connected throughout their lives even though they never met."

"What does that have to do with it?"

"Andrew knew for a fact he had an older brother and never stopped looking for him. And your dad once told me a young boy with blond hair haunted him during his childhood. Not literally, of course, but he'd pop into his head regularly. As Nick got older, so did this boy. The boy turned out to be his brother Andrew. So maybe you're just as tuned into Andrew's child. You're both the offspring of your fathers. Maybe you have that intuition. Like your daddy."

Kat stopped what she was doing and threw her arms around Mary. "Thank you."

*

"Me again." Nick stood in front of Principal Platt and produced another photo. "Now I need to find this girl. Joyce Rivers." He discovered Joyce by checking other bios in the Asolo's *LES MIS* program. If they hired one local girl, they probably hired others. Joyce was local, also in the chorus and went to the same high school. Heidi and Joyce had to know each other.

"Joyce." Mrs. Platt smiled. "Very active in our alumni association."

"So you know her?"

"Yes. Why are you looking for her, if you don't mind my asking?"

"I just want to ask her some questions about Heidi."

After pondering a moment, Mrs. Platt jotted down a phone number and handed it to him. "She's a lovely lady."

Back in his car, Nick called Joyce and left a message on her voice mail, not mentioning Heidi. Not knowing the scope of their youthful friendship, he'd get into details when they met. If they met. Besides, spontaneity reaped more rewards. He could tell a lot by body language.

Next he headed to the address of the mystery man who challenged Nick on the phone yesterday, ultimately hanging up on him.

The house was in a rundown area on the outskirts of Sarasota. The wooden frame needed a fresh coat of paint. The front stairs were rickety. The grass needed to be mowed. And the old guy sitting on the porch looked like a pit bull.

When Nick parked in front of his home, the man struggled to his feet and ordered Nick to move his fancy car.

Nick approached, hands out in front of him, indicating he meant no harm. "I'm Nick McDeare, sir. I—"

"I don't care who you are. Get off my property or I'm calling the police."

"Please. I'm looking for anyone who knew Heidi Barstow."

"Get outta here!"

"Did you know her?" Nick persisted, almost at the front steps.

The old man glared with glassy eyes. "Why do you want to know?"

"So you did know her?"

"I didn't say that." He lurched forward, shaking a cane at him. "Get OUTTA here!"

Nick backed off. For now.

As he climbed back into his car, he realized Heidi's address was the house next door, a house even sadder than the pit bull's.

This man definitely knew Heidi Barstow.

*

"I haven't thought about Heidi in years." Joyce Rivers Larson poured Nick some lemonade and joined him at her kitchen table.

Joyce was a petite woman with close-cropped red hair and pale brown eyes. She was dressed in dark gray slacks and a matching silk blouse. Her jewelry was both tasteful and expensive.

The kitchen was well-appointed, as was the entire house. Joyce Larson lived in the affluent section of Sarasota.

"When I got your message last night, I thought someone was playing a joke on me."

21

"Why?"

"Because you're famous. My husband is a huge fan. I've read some of your books, too."

"But you're not a fan," he teased.

Joyce laughed. A musical laugh. It reminded him of Jessie. "No, I am, Mr. McDeare."

"Please. Call me Nick."

Joyce smiled. "My husband Marcus wanted to be here. He thinks you walk on water. Unfortunately, he's out of town on business." She sat back. "So. You said you're here about Heidi."

"Yes. How close were you two?"

"At one time, very close. Good friends in high school. Then we both got cast at the Asolo. That was huge for us. We both wanted careers in the theater. It wasn't meant to be for me. But Heidi was determined."

Nick nodded.

Joyce was watching him closely. "What's this about?"

He met her eyes, watching her just as intently. "My brother. Andrew Brady."

Joyce's expression shifted. "That's what I figured." She took a sip of lemonade. "If you're looking for the baby, I'm sorry to say I don't know what happened to him."

The baby.

There it was.

Heidi did indeed have a baby.

A boy.

He must have been lousy at hiding his surprise. "You didn't know for sure there was a baby?" Joyce asked. Nick shook his head. "I'm sorry. I shouldn't have—"

"I'm glad you told me. I was beginning to think I was wasting my time."

"You're not. Heidi had a baby boy."

"Do you believe this baby was Andrew's?"

Joyce sighed. "Not at first. I knew Heidi had a huge crush on Andrew. He'd flirt with her – He flirted with a lot of girls – and he did seem to single Heidi out at times. When she told me she slept with him, I thought she was fantasizing. I mean, Andrew Brady was from New York. He was one of the stars of *Les Mis*. To be honest, I had my own romantic adventure in the cast and was focused on that."

"Did Heidi sleep around? Sorry to be so blunt about a friend of yours, but it's important. Did she have multiple lovers at that time?"

"She had a boyfriend. But it was on-again, off-again. They fought a lot."

"So that baby might not be Andrew's."

"Heidi insisted Andrew was the father. There was never any question in her mind from the moment she found out she was pregnant. She spent weeks trying to reach him in New York, leaving messages. When he finally called her back, he blew her off. Heidi was devastated."

"But she decided to keep it. She could have had an abortion. A baby can be an impediment for a young girl who has dreams of the stage."

A kitchen timer buzzed. Joyce rose and pulled a tray of brownies from the oven. "Heidi had a rough life. Her father was killed in a plant explosion when she was ten. Her mother was a falling-down alcoholic. The two of them lived off the father's benefits."

Joyce sat down and sliced the brownies, placing them on a plate. "Heidi craved love. She never had it. Until the baby. That's why she kept it."

"So you saw the baby?"

Joyce smiled. "I was with her when he was born. And in his early months. That's when I knew he was Andrew's, not her boyfriend's. Jared was Hispanic. This child had sandy curls and piercing blue eyes that were—" She stared at Nick's eyes "—shaped exactly like yours and Andrew's. He was beautiful and such a happy child. I remember hoping my own children would be like him. He hummed or warbled or something like that before he even began talking. Heidi said he was destined to be a star like his father."

"When was the last time you saw him?"

"He was maybe a year and a half – close to two years old."

"Why was that the last time?"

"I married Marcus, and we moved to Phoenix for eight years because of his work. I heard about Heidi's death shortly after we relocated. So awful. The irony was she wasn't a druggie. Oh, we drank at times, but never drugs. I was told that someone slipped her that Ecstasy."

So Andrew's son wasn't the offspring of a drug-addicted mother. More good news.

"When we moved back to town," Joyce continued, "I made some inquiries, but no one seemed to know what happened to the boy. And right after Heidi's death, her mother disappeared. It's like the whole family never existed. Like I dreamed the whole thing."

"Heidi's obituary made no mention of a son."

"I noticed that."

"It also didn't supply the mother's first name. Just 'survived by her mother.' I've never seen that before. Do you remember her name?"

Joyce shook her head. "I'm sorry, I don't. It was a long time ago." She pushed the brownies towards him. "I read that Andrew had a son with Jessica Kendle. Thank God he eventually had a child, or this would be an even bigger tragedy."

"Anthony isn't Andrew's son. He's Jessie's. Andrew doesn't have any children of his own."

"Oh my God. Oh I'm so sorry, Mr. McDeare – Nick."

"Were there any other relatives?"

"An old uncle lived next door. Not a very nice man."

The man with the cane. "Did you know each other?"

"Yes. But it's been years since I've seen him."

"I had a run-in with him yesterday. Maybe he'd be more cooperative if you were with me." Nick hated brownies, but he reached for one and shot Joyce his most dazzling smile.

*

Larry Williams came out of retirement to stage manage the production of *DIANA* for Quill Llewellyn, one of Broadways premier directors. In his early forties, Larry's long dark curls were now speckled with gray, giving him a distinguished air, but his pale brown eyes were as devilish as ever.

Larry was the epitome of a good stage manager, calm in a crisis and firm when necessary. No one dared mess with Larry Williams. He ran a tight ship, earning the respect of both cast and crew. Once a doting husband and father of two, Larry was recently divorced, his family still back in Manasquan, New Jersey.

Larry and Andrew had been great friends. They had the same sense of humor, something Larry rarely revealed to actors. Andrew managed to pull it out of him, much to Jessie's delight. Larry and his wife Gloria spent most of their free time with Andrew and Jessie, antiquing or indulging in fancy meals or sailing off the Jersey Shore.

This was the third show Jessie worked with Larry, and she was thrilled to have him back. The stateside production of *DIANA* was turning out to be the opposite experience of the London version, and having Larry as the Production Stage Manager made it even better.

Larry and Nora were the only people in *DIANA* who knew about Nick and Jessie's separation. Even Quill Llewellyn didn't know, and he'd worked with Jessie for years. That was how much Jessie trusted her old friend Larry Williams.

They often had dinner together, Nora joining them. Nora had known Larry for over twenty years. He was a god in her eyes. They dined in old favorite haunts, places that would guard Jessie's privacy. It was the only social life Jessie had these days. She religiously avoided all situations that would create any gossip, the kind that sent her into the abyss in London. Occasionally, photos popped up in the local rags of their dinners, but the press merely reported it under 'Seen Around Town.' How could tongues wag about Jessie, Larry and Nora?

Jessie wanted Nick to join them at some point. He'd like Larry's professional demeanor and wry humor. And it would exhibit that the McDeares were still together.

"I notice you don't drink these days," Larry said over coffee one evening in Jessie's suite. They'd ordered dinner from the restaurant downstairs. Nora had eaten and retired to her room for the night.

Jessie took a sip of coffee and looked across the table at her old friend. "Truth? Drinking got me into trouble in London. I …" She looked down at her half-eaten plate.

"We go back a long way, Jessie. Tell me if you want to. Don't, if you'd rather not."

Jessie paused. She hated talking about what happened in London. She hated even thinking about it. But it was the only piece of the Nick/Jessie separation that she'd held back from Larry. It was too embarrassing. "Okay." She set her coffee down and took a deep breath. "I got very drunk one night and slept with someone who reminded me of Nick. I woke up beside him the next morning with no memory of what happened."

Larry registered no reaction at all. Bless him. "Did he drug you?"

"I wish he had. It would have made things easier for Nick." She sighed. "I'm afraid I have no one to blame but myself."

Larry set his own cup down. "Truth? I did the same thing to my wife. Only I wasn't drunk, just stupid. Gloria will never forgive me. She said she married me for my stability. God, stable! Synonymous with boring. In fact, she said, and I quote, 'If I wanted to marry a bad boy I would have married Nick McDeare.' Sorry, Jessie."

She shrugged.

He leaned forward. "So I take it Nick hasn't forgiven you either?"

"If he had, we'd be together."

"It's ironic, considering his past reputation."

"He says he stopped all that when we got married."

"Do you believe him?"

"I have to. If I want to save my marriage."

*

"Mr. Barstow? Do you remember me? Joyce, Heidi's friend?"

Nick and Joyce approached the nasty man cautiously. They'd parked down the street, out of sight, and walked to the man's house.

"Who?"

"Joyce Rivers. Heidi and I used to sit on your porch. We called you Uncle Bo-Bo."

"Uncle …?"

"Our nickname for your real name."

"Beauregard."

"Right. You gave us ice cream," Joyce continued, "and let us play with your train collection."

"Uncle Bo-Bo. Yes." The man pulled himself out of his porch chair and squinted. "I remember you. Joyce. You used to bring treats for my dog."

"That's right."

Mr. Barstow's eyes shifted to Nick. "What're you doing here? I told you yesterday to get off my property."

"This is my friend. Nick McDeare." Joyce laid her hand on Nick's arm as they inched towards the porch. "He's also a friend of Heidi's." They stepped even closer. "Would it be okay if we sat with you for a while, Uncle Bo-Bo?"

The man looked confused, as if he didn't know what to say. "I-I guess so. I don't have any ice cream."

"That's okay." They climbed the stairs. "We just want to visit."

"Well," he shrugged, "sit down, I guess."

Nick sat across from Beauregard Barstow, Joyce beside him.

"Nick and I have been reminiscing about Heidi," Joyce began in a calm voice. "I miss her. It was so sad, what happened to her."

"Heidi was a good girl. So much like her daddy."

"What happened to her mother?" Joyce continued.

Nick was lying low, letting Joyce take the lead for now.

The old man shrugged. "One day she was here. Then she was gone. And that baby, too."

"She took the baby with her?" Nick couldn't resist asking.

Barstow's eyes narrowed. "What's it to you?"

Nick sat back and resumed his silence.

"Did she?" Joyce pursued. "Take the baby with her?"

"Don't know. Never saw that little boy again after Heidi died."

"When did her mom leave?"

26

"The day of the funeral. Left everything behind. Crystal's brain was soaked in booze."

Crystal! Her mom's first name. Nick and Joyce exchanged a triumphant look.

"A horrible woman," Barstow continued. "She hated that child. Heidi did everything she could to protect him from her mother."

"I loved Heidi's little boy. But I can't remember his name after all these years." Joyce glanced at Nick. He could have kissed her. She handled this whole conversation like a pro. "Do you remember it, Uncle Bo-Bo?"

The old man nodded. "Patrick."

*

Nick treated Joyce to dinner in Siesta Key. Despite being anxious to research the new information on his laptop, he owed the woman for what she'd done. He promised to keep her updated on his progress.

Returning to his hotel, Nick immediately searched the internet for Crystal Barstow. Like Heidi, he only found an obituary. The woman left Sarasota and moved a few miles down the Gulf to Bradenton where she finally drank herself to death. There was no mention of Heidi or a child named Patrick.

Next he entered the name Patrick Barstow. Nothing.

What did Crystal do with that baby? Was she capable of killing her own grandson in order to be free of him?

After updating Kat, Nick couldn't sleep. Grabbing a bourbon from the mini bar, he took a walk on the beach. A storm was brewing. Florida was famous for them. They blew up in all their ferocity and disappeared moments later.

Jessie flitted through his mind. That kiss at the theater. Yes, he missed her. He freely admitted he still loved her. But Jessie's reckless behavior in London drove them apart. Could they go back to before? Could they resume their marriage after the destruction of the past few months? Nick wasn't sure.

Patrick.

Unbelievable.

Cue the music from *The Twilight Zone*. Nick's middle name was Patrick. It was also what his birth mother wanted to call him. Chelsea regretted being forced to give him up for adoption and spent the rest of her life searching for him. Nick and Andrew's mother died on an operating table when Andrew was twelve. At the time, Nick was living halfway across the world in Tokyo with his adoptive parents, an Air Force surgeon and his classical pianist wife.

His conversation with Kat replayed itself. She desperately wanted to be here in Florida, making these discoveries with him. He, too, wished she were here. His daughter was smart and intuitive. Too smart at times.

Patrick.

Nick knew he was lucky to have Kat. His son from his first disastrous marriage died of leukemia at the age of ten. Losing Jeffrey nearly destroyed Nick, and only a chance encounter with a stranger prevented him from killing himself. When he met Jessie, he got another shot at both marriage and fatherhood. Nick adopted her son Anthony and loved him every bit as much as he loved Kat.

All Andrew had was five years as Anthony's pretend father. He never got to watch the subtle changes in his child as he grew. Or guide his son as his small world expanded. Or see the boy's personality mingle with the genes he inherited.

Where was Andrew? Was he watching?

His brother had a baby boy at one time. Patrick would be seventeen-years old now. What happened to him?

Tomorrow Nick would check with Child Protective Services.

Someone somewhere had to know what happened to Patrick Barstow.

CHAPTER 3

Helga Piper never heard of Nick McDeare. She didn't have time to read expensive books. So Nick's charm fell flat with the head of Child Protective Service.

The middle-aged frumpy woman was frazzled from the moment Nick sat down across from her. She was constantly interrupted by staff. Her phone rang every ten seconds. Her fax machine buzzed with non-stop inflow. Her desk was messier than anything Nick could create. And she screamed at her assistant incessantly.

"Look," he finally said, shooting the woman's assistant a frustrated look, "I'm trying to find a little boy. I just need five minutes of your time." Her phone rang again. Nick grabbed the receiver and slammed it back down. "Barstow. Patrick."

Annoyed, Helga turned to her computer and typed the name into it. "Nope. Nothing."

"This would have been fifteen, maybe sixteen years ago."

The lady's unibrow shot up. "That long ago? I wasn't here then." She reached for the papers on the fax and signaled for a cup of coffee. In other words, Nick was dismissed.

This woman was in the wrong business. She didn't give a crap about kids. "Nonetheless, it would be in the computer. Right?" Nick was barely hanging onto his temper.

"We only computerized ten years ago."

"Even I know when you computerize you enter all the hard copies, no matter how far back they go." He waited. "Right?"

She glared. "I told you. He's not in the system."

Nick again glanced at the assistant, who smiled an apology. Turning back to the lump in front of him, he asked acidly, "Who was here before you?"

"Who knows? This office is constantly changing." She went back to her fax machine.

Nick could feel steam rising in his lungs. Any moment he'd start to hiss. Slamming his hand down on the copy rolling off the fax he whispered, his voice lethal, "How would I find out?"

"Try Public Records. Downtown."

Now in a rage, Nick stormed outside to his car. They actually paid that waste-of-skin to sit on her ass and do nothing. Typical government bullshit.

Where the hell was Public Records located? He pulled out his cell and searched …

"Mr. McDeare?" Cruella De Vil's assistant jogged towards him "I'm sorry for what happened back there. The office is chaos." The young woman dimpled and stepped closer. Handing Nick a slip of paper with two names and phone numbers on it, she murmured, "These are the people who ran this place around that time. Helga could have found this in two seconds. If she'd bothered."

Nick exhaled slowly. "Thank you, Miss …?"

"Chandler. Lisa Chandler." A full smile now, flirty eyes peeking up at him. "If you need help, I could show you—"

"Thank you." This was turning into a day from hell. "I can take it from here." He slid behind the wheel and closed the door.

A knock on the window. "Mr. McDeare?"

Nick felt like banging his head on the steering wheel. MAKE IT STOP!

Sighing, he cracked the window.

"Prepare yourself. This office has been a problem for years."

"Worse than what I just witnessed?"

Lisa nodded.

Wunderbar.

*

Mary sat with Jessie in the study. It had been too long since they spent time together. "I miss you, sweetie."

"I miss you, too, Mary. I miss being here on a daily basis. I miss all of you."

"How do things stand with you and Nick?"

"I don't know. He came by the theater before he left for Florida. And now he's off doing God knows what. There's always something more important than his marriage."

"He's working, Jessie. Like you are. You and Andrew worked together. You and Nick don't."

"It doesn't help that I hate his investigations, which put him in danger. And it also gives him the chance to— Well …"

"What? See other women?"

Jessie shrugged and looked away.

"Honey, that man hasn't looked at another woman since he married you. When are you going to realize that?"

"I wish he was more like Andrew. Nick slept around for years, and Kat is the result. An illegitimate daughter would never turn up on Andrew's doorstep. He revered women. I've never seen two brothers more different."

Mary wondered, not for the first time, how Jessie could be so stupid when it came to men.

*

Nick sat across from Lorraine Gosling, the director of the private Gosling Adoption Agency. "Our adoptions, Mr. McDeare, are in conjunction with a pregnant mother. Parents are found long before the baby is delivered."

Nick knew all about this system. It was how his own adoption had worked. "What happens when a young child is brought to you for adoption?"

"It doesn't happen. Those children are brought to Social Services."

"Even fifteen, sixteen years ago?"

"Yes."

"I've already been to CPS." Nick tried to hide his disgust.

"They're part of the loop. If a child is brought to them who was abandoned or orphaned, it would be in their records."

"What about hospitals?"

She shook her head. "Those children usually end up with Social Services. But I suppose you could check."

Sighing, Nick got to his feet.

"You might try the churches in the area. They sometimes aid in placing abandoned babies."

"Where would I find a list of churches?"

"The internet."

*

Back at the hotel, Nick went for a swim, then ordered an early dinner from room service. He ate out on the terrace. Florida was finally starting to cool down as September turned to October. The mid-afternoon ocean breeze was refreshing.

He pulled out the phone numbers Flirty Lisa gave him back at CPS.

Herman Stutz sounded elderly. He commiserated about Nick's experience at CPS. Things were even worse when he worked there, he said. They were deluged with cases. Despite their best efforts, children slipped through the cracks. He told Nick to call Georgia Watts, the woman he replaced. "She was fired for trying to tell them how screwed up their

31

system was. A very smart lady. She was my boss for a long time, and I was her temporary replacement. I certainly didn't want the job. Georgia did the best she could with an impossible situation. She was there for over ten years and has a good memory. Here's her number."

Nick jotted it down. Georgia wasn't one of the two names given to him. "Who's Paul Shott?" His second name on the list.

"Never heard of him. He must be one of the pencil-pushers downtown. Now listen. Georgia's hard to reach. She runs an organization in Tampa that places children. She travels a lot, so be patient. That's her private number, so she'll get back to you. You can count on it."

Nick immediately called Georgia Watts and left a message on her voice mail. Next he called the local hospitals, which took a great deal of time. He got the royal shuffle, being transferred from department to department. After three hours, he got nowhere.

Frustrated, Nick fell into bed, sleeping fitfully.

He woke the next morning with an idea. Why didn't he think of this before? When he was trying to find his own birth parents he registered with agencies whose purpose was to reconnect missing family members. That's how Nick and Andrew found each other. The key was having both parties searching for each other. Otherwise, the agency would take Nick's information and hold onto it until Patrick Barstow came looking for his family.

He pulled up the info on his laptop and began the phone calls. As morning turned to afternoon, he gave up. Patrick hadn't registered with a single agency.

Finally, Nick began calling churches, going down the list on the internet. He spoke with priests, ministers, secretaries and volunteers. Many churches weren't involved with children at all. One had an organization, but it was tied into CPS. Another had a small committee, brand new. Another said they ran an orphanage at one time, now long gone. The secretary took his information and said she'd call him back if she found anything in the old records.

His final call was to St. Sebastian's. Nick spoke with a young priest, Father O'Brien. "I wasn't here in those days, Mr. McDeare, so I wouldn't know what the church's priorities were back then. I've only been with this parish for twelve years."

"Only? That's a long time."

"The priest before me was here for over thirty years."

"Sounds like a priest has to die for you to get a good position."

Father O'Brien laughed. "Sometimes. Father Locato was getting up in years and requested a transfer to central Florida where he grew up.

Anyway, I'll be happy to check our records when I have a chance. You said this would have been approximately fifteen years ago, give or take?"

"That's right."

"Everything that's happened inside these stone walls has been written down since the beginning of time. Give me your phone number. I promise to get back to you as soon as I can."

Clicking off, Nick's spirits sagged.

Patrick had vanished.

Maybe he was dead.

No matter what, there were no more avenues to explore.

Which meant it was time to go home.

*

Willie coasted the car to a stop in front of the Promenade Theater. It was opening night of a new romantic comedy. The perfect place for New York's famous couple to be seen. Or so Nick was told by Abbie.

Cameras clicked as Nick and Jessie stepped to the curb. They'd also been photographed leaving Jessie's hotel, thanks to Abbie tipping off the press. Seated down front on the aisle, they held hands and whispered until the curtain went up. Nick was playing his role, though not with great enthusiasm.

Afterwards they went back to Jessie's suite for a late dinner. Once again they were photographed on their way in. The plan was for Nick not to leave until the next morning. When he again would be photographed.

Where he would sleep was the question.

Upstairs, Nick removed his jacket, loosened his tie and rolled up his sleeves. He loathed romantic comedies, and this one was particularly revolting.

"Okay, you hated it. Sorry. It was my agent Jeremy's choice. Not mine. Next time you pick the play." Jessie kicked off her heels and answered the buzzer from downstairs. "Dinner's on the way up."

The waiter who arrived with the serving cart placed lobster dinners, candles and flowers on the table with a flourish before he quickly left the suite.

"Where's Nora?" Nick sat down across from Jessie.

"In Jersey visiting some friends."

So they were alone. Jessie's plan was becoming obvious.

They ate their lobster tails in silence until Jessie suddenly put down her fork and sat back. "Tonight was supposed to be about our talking."

Nick swallowed. "This wasn't what I was picturing."

"What?"

"This whole set-up with the press."

"That was Abbie's doing."

"With your approval, right?"

Jessie looked down.

"This isn't us, Jess. This isn't who we are. Play acting for the press. We like our privacy. This whole thing is starting to drive me crazy."

"We have privacy now."

Nick threw down his napkin and went to the window. "Another set-up." He looked over at her. "Nora's gone?"

Jessie got to her feet. "Nora thought we'd want to be alone to talk."

"To talk?"

"What? You think I'm trying to get you into bed?"

"Aren't you?"

"You know, I'm sick of you thinking every woman wants to screw you. My God, what an ego."

"Look at it from my point of view. Nora's gone. A romantic dinner. Dim lights. Atmospheric music. We could talk anywhere."

"But we don't."

"We don't try."

"I try," Jessie stated. "You resist."

"Because it always feels like you have an ulterior motive."

"Getting you into bed?"

Nick remained silent.

"It's too bad you didn't get a little of Andrew's humility."

"Here we go. Saint Andrew." He turned away.

"Andrew didn't think of himself as a god around women. He didn't go to bed with every woman he met—"

"Really?"

"What's that supposed to mean?"

Nick said too much. "Nothing."

"You think Andrew was like you? Think again, Nick. You may have been brothers, but you are radically different when it comes to women."

"All right, stop. You don't know what you're talking about, Jess."

"How would you know? You weren't around back then. You didn't know how Andrew behaved with me, with all women. He—"

"I can't listen to this—"

"Andrew could laugh at himself. And make women laugh. He didn't have to—"

Nick grabbed his jacket.

"Where are you going?"

34

"Home."

"You can't."

"Why? Because our charade isn't over?"

"You're so damned jealous of your brother, it's pathetic."

Nick turned on her. "I loved my brother. So I'm going to shut up and get the hell out of here before I say something—" He strode towards the door. "Go to bed with your ghost. Saint Andrew."

*

"So what happened with Nick?" Abbie sat down on the couch in Jessie's dressing room.

"We fought. As usual."

"About what?"

"Andrew, believe it or not. But that wasn't all of it. He accused me of getting him over to the hotel so we could sleep together."

Abbie stopped listening at the mention of Andrew. "Why'd you fight about Andrew after all this time?"

"I don't know. I think he's still jealous of Andrew. Of Andrew and me."

The one thing Abbie knew for certain was that Nick was not jealous of Jessie and Andrew. "What did he say?"

"I told him he needed to be more like Andrew when it comes to women, and he got nasty. Nick doesn't like his sexuality being questioned."

Abbie flashed back to her conversation with Kat about Andrew. About women falling all over him.

It was bizarre, so much talk about Andrew after all this time.

Abbie knew all about Andrew's otherworldly spirit still being around. They'd been best friends, after all.

Maybe Andrew was just bored and stirring the pot. That would be so like him.

*

Nick wound down his jog through Central Park, making his way to the exit at Fifth Avenue. It was a chilly October afternoon. Tugging his cap further down on his forehead, he headed home, passing Anthony and Willie walking Monty. Anthony didn't look happy. He kept insisting he was old enough to walk Monty on his own. Nick thought otherwise.

It had been ten days since he left Florida. Despite leaving his cell number with a dozen people, Nick heard back from no one. It was time to give up on ever finding Patrick Barstow.

As he stepped inside the brownstone, his cell thrummed. "McDeare."

35

"This is Georgia Watts, Mr. McDeare. You called me a while back." A deep voice, but soft. Friendly. "Are you the writer?"

Georgia Watts! The woman who once ran Child Protective Services in Sarasota. "Yes. And thank you for getting back to me."

He trotted into the kitchen. Mary stirred a pot of black bean soup. Kat sat in the breakfast nook, her schoolbooks and iPad in front of her.

"Well, I'm honored, Mr. McDeare. I'm a huge fan. Now, your message said you're trying to find a little boy?"

"He'd be sixteen or seventeen by now." Kat's head swiveled, her eyes boring into him.

"Oh, so this is a long time ago."

"Yes. When you were at CPS in Sarasota." Mary, too, looked at Nick. "The boy's name was Patrick Barstow."

A pause. "Doesn't sound familiar. How would he have ended up with us?"

"That's part of the problem. I don't know. His mother died very young, and his grandmother disappeared at the same time. There were no other relatives really. We can't find a trail for what happened to the boy."

"What about his father?"

"The father was my brother. Andrew Brady. He didn't know about the child at the time. I only recently found out myself."

Another long pause. "Andrew Brady. I see. You don't know how much I wish I could help you, Mr. McDeare. What happened to Andrew Brady was a tragedy. It would be fitting if he had a son to carry on his legacy."

"Which is one of the reasons I'm desperate to find him." Nick dropped onto a stool. "So you don't think the child came through CPS?"

"Off the top of my head, no. But I'll check my old notes. I used to keep notebooks on my desk and jot things down before I put them into official files. When I left CPS I should have thrown them away. I don't know why I didn't."

"Cops do the same thing."

"That's what I felt like back then. A traffic cop for kids. Depressing as hell. Anyway, I'll check, but my memory's better than average, and Patrick Barstow isn't ringing a bell. Don't get your hopes up. If I find anything I'll call you back."

"Thank you." Nick clicked off and dropped his head in his hands.

"So?" Kat asked anxiously.

"Another dead end."

He wished he never heard of Heidi Barstow or her son Patrick.

*

Nick retired to his office after dinner. He couldn't stop thinking about Andrew's son. How could he drop the whole thing without a definitive answer?

He sat over a legal pad, intending to jot down every avenue of discovery he may have overlooked.

The page was blank.

His cell went off.

"Mr. McDeare, this is Georgia Watts again. I found something. Now it may or may not be the child you're looking for, and it's not much, but it's worth a shot. And it's in your time frame. A priest brought us a little boy. He'd been abandoned at the church, and all we knew was his name was Patrick. No last name."

"What happened to him?"

"I would need to see my files."

"Where are they?"

"They were computerized after I left, and I wouldn't be allowed access to them."

"But that idiot woman looked for Patrick, and she—"

"She was looking for Patrick Barstow. You're looking for a boy simply known as Patrick."

"And that would make a difference?"

"It might. Now listen. Knowing that branch of CPS, I figured they stuffed the hard copies in the basement and forgot about them. Nobody cleans anything in that place. I talked to an old friend tonight, Herman Stutz, and he confirmed it. They're in the basement."

"I spoke with Herman myself a while back."

"He said. Herman can get me into CPS and the files. After hours. He still has a key. And even if he runs into someone, no one will say anything. They adore him around there. Can you meet us there tomorrow afternoon?"

"We'll fly down in the morning."

"Fly? Where are you?"

"New York."

"Who's we?"

"My daughter and me."

*

"Wow, this place is disgusting." Leave it to Kat to state the obvious.

Nick and Kat were with Georgia and Herman in the dark, dank, moldy bug-infested basement of Child Protective Services. They all wore rubber gloves. Nick wished he had rubber boots. The floor had an inch of water on it.

Georgia Watts was a middle-aged woman with some girth to her. She had a head full of wavy salt-and-pepper hair and soft Bambi eyes. Her voice reminded Nick of his sister Maddie. Gentle and soothing.

Herman looked to be about sixty with a weary face that spoke of his years with Child Protective Services.

It was painstaking work. Sure enough, CPS stuffed the old files in metal cabinets in the basement. In clumps. They'd find fifty or more from one time frame, followed by fifty of a later or earlier time frame. Followed by thirty from … and so on.

After three hours Nick's back ached, and his feet were wet and cold.

"Got it." Georgia raised a cardboard file over her head. "Let's get out of here. I no longer feel my toes. Patience, everyone. Let's get warm and dry before we dive into this."

They went back to Nick's hotel and settled on his terrace. Nick changed clothes, as did Kat. Georgia and Herman sat barefoot, soaking up the last rays of the sun. Nick ordered platters of roast beef sandwiches and French fries, plus large Cobb salads and sodas.

Finally Georgia opened the file and began to read. "Okay. The date works. The baby's name was Patrick. No last name. They figured he was approximately two years old. He was brought to CPS by a Father Locato of St. Sebastian's Catholic Church. Locato found the abandoned boy in the choir loft with a name tag attached. He put a notice in the church bulletin and the local paper. There was no response. That's when he brought him to us. Father Locato was very worried about Patrick's fate, almost reluctant to leave him. CPS assured him the boy would be placed in a good foster home."

"So that idiot woman at CPS missed it." Nick couldn't keep the irritation out of his voice.

"Like I told you, she was looking for Patrick Barstow."

Kat spoke up. "So if she just put 'Patrick' into the computer she might have found him?"

Georgia nodded. "Possibly. It's also possible these old files were never entered. Or they were entered, but they missed this one. Sloppiness."

Kat shook her head and looked at Nick.

Georgia continued to read as they waited. Finally she glanced up at Nick. "Some of this is water-logged. Hard to read." She sighed. "But I remember this case now."

Nick's stomach tightened. Georgia's expression didn't scream good news. "Baby Patrick was placed in a group foster home run by a Jack and Eva Trout, with the assistance of Jack's sister, Carrie. Six other children lived in the house with him. It was supposed to be temporary until a single family could foster him. It never happened."

"Why?"

"The official report here says he was a troubled child. He didn't get along with others and would wander off. But I remember some of the details because it was unusual." She put down the file and removed her sunglasses, rubbing her eyes. "I visited that home. The woman who ran it, Eva, said Patrick didn't talk much. He sang. At the top of his lungs. It annoyed everyone. He'd sing with the TV or the radio or even without music."

"That sounds like Uncle Andrew's son."

Georgia again scanned the report. "Foster homes can be tricky. There are rules to be followed not just for harmony but also for safety. Patrick had a habit of wandering off. Several times he was found in an orange grove all by himself, singing. Another time it took them two days to find him. He was asleep on the beach a mile away."

"How old was he at that time?" Nick asked.

Georgia squinted at the page. "Four or five. Going by the original proximation of his age."

Kat picked at her sandwich. "Maybe he had anger issues. I would have."

"Another time a woman brought him home. She found him in that same grove, singing. Next, a priest showed up at the door. He said he was thinking about inviting the kids for a Saturday picnic at the church and wanted to meet them. This was highly unusual. When an organization or charity wants to do something for the kids, they usually go through the office. Anyway, this priest wandered around the house, chatting with the children, including Patrick, and left. They never heard from him again."

"So what happened to Patrick?" Nick pushed his plate away. "Is he still floating around in the system?"

Georgia shook her head. "One day the boy just … disappeared."

"What do you mean?"

"He wandered off and never returned."

Nick's heart skipped a beat. "Were the authorities notified?"

"Yes. They spent weeks searching. Eventually the case went cold. Their conclusion, not verified, was Patrick found his way back to that beach … and drowned."

39

Nick got to his feet and walked to the edge of the terrace, shoving his hands in his pockets and looking out over the water. "They have no definitive answer, but they close the case?"

"They didn't close it. But they didn't work it."

Nick shook his head. After all his efforts, this was how it ended?

Georgia looked up at Nick. "I'm sorry. Really." She handed him the file. "Keep it. There's more detail in there. At least it will give you a little insight into who your nephew was and what he went through."

Was. Past tense.

Nick felt a kick in the gut.

Patrick was presumed dead.

*

Kat stretched across her bed as she read the file on Patrick. Grabbing a nacho chip and dredging it through the guacamole, she scanned the report again:

Complaints about Patrick:
- *Singing at the top of his lungs.*
- *Rarely spoke.*
- *Had a habit of wandering off. Found in an orange grove several times.*
- *Would strip off his clothes and walk around naked.*
- *Would strike out at anyone who tried to discipline him.*
- *After being punished, disappeared for 2 days. Found asleep on a beach, miles away.*
- *Bit Carrie Trout while being punished.*

Kat tossed the report on the floor. She heard her dad in the connecting room watching a football game. He'd said little since Georgia and Herman left. He was taking the news of Patrick's fate hard.

Kat refused to accept it. Not until she had proof. And she knew deep down her dad felt the same way. He was not a quitter. It was just that this news, on top of whatever was going on with Queen Jessie, was weighing him down.

Her dad's cell went off. Probably Mary checking on the latest news. She heard the low hum of his voice.

As she went back to reading the report, a shadow fell across the page. "That was Father O'Brien at St. Sebastian's," her father said, standing over her. "I talked to him the last time I was here."

"St. Sebastian's is where Patrick was found."

"Right. He said he found the entry about Patrick in their records. A Father Locato discovered him, along with a parishioner," Nick glanced at a slip of paper in his hand, "a Mrs. Tess Cavanaugh. O'Brien had trouble finding the entry because that was a busy day at the church. A rehearsal for the eighth-grade graduation ceremony. A baptism. And a funeral for a young girl. Heidi Barstow."

"Heidi?" Kat sat up straight. "A coincidence?"

"You know I don't believe in coincidence."

"Sooo … you're thinking the mother, Crystal, brought the baby to the church that day before she took off?"

"Yep." Nick sat on the edge of Kat's bed. "Patrick's found in a church by Father Locato. He ultimately takes the boy to Child Protective Services, BUT he's worried about what will happen to him. A few years later, a priest shows up at Patrick's foster home out of the blue and checks out the kids. Then, a little while later, Patrick disappears."

"You think ... maybe Father Locato ...?"

"I'd like to find out. There's something odd here."

"What's the plan?"

"Father O'Brien said Locato is in Mount Dora. Central Florida. Let's pay him a surprise visit."

"Do you have an address?"

"Mount Dora is small. He's a priest. How hard can he be to find?

CHAPTER 4

"You look exactly the same, Mary." Larry Williams helped himself to another crab-stuffed mushroom. "And your food is still the best in New York."

Mary smiled her thanks. She felt nostalgic, having Jessie, Larry and Nora sitting here at the kitchen island. The only person missing was Andrew. "You were always a flatterer, Larry."

"I had to make up for Andrew giving you grief." Larry placed a hand on his heart. "But I only spoke the truth."

Mary winked at Nora. "My very own Eddie Haskell."

"Who?" Jessie asked, her focus on Mary's appetizers.

Nora rolled her eyes. "*Leave It To Beaver?*"

Larry grinned at Jessie. "Before your time."

"And yours," Mary corrected. "You're not that old."

"Forty-two."

"Same age as Nick." Jessie sipped her club soda, still staring at the food.

"Honey," Mary laid a hand on Jessie's arm, "eat something. You're skin and bones."

"Opening night is weeks away, Mary."

Nora pushed the plate of chilled shrimp towards Jessie. "These aren't going to make you fat."

Larry placed the plate even closer. "Starving yourself isn't the answer. You have a demanding role. You need energy to get through it."

"Remember what happened in London," Mary warned.

"That was because I drank on an empty stomach. I'm not drinking anymore."

Larry forced Jessie to look at him. "Don't become a stereotype of the actress who's consumed with her weight. You're better than that. Do you want Quill to put your understudy in for the matinees because you aren't strong enough to handle eight shows a week? Or hire someone to do them?"

Mary could have kissed Larry. He said exactly the right thing.

"Okay, okay!" Jessie took a shrimp and nibbled at it. Glancing up at Larry, she hissed, "You're a tyrant." But her eyes revealed she was teasing.

"Which makes me the best damned stage manager on Broadway."

"Amen." Mary helped herself to a cheese puff and offered one to Larry. "How's Gloria? And the kids?"

Larry chewed and swallowed. "Back in Jersey. We're divorced."

"I'm sorry."

"Me, too."

"I know you retired a few years ago," Mary continued, interested in this old friend of the family. "What brought you back?"

"When Quill called, it was hard to say no. Especially when I knew Jessie was heading the cast. At the time I was directing down at the shore. A small professional theater. The job will be there when I get done here. If I still want it."

"You mean you'd continue to stage manage?"

"It's hard to beat the money. Especially with alimony now in the picture."

"Where are you staying in New York?"

"One of those European residence hotels on the Upper West Side. It's costing me a fortune when all I do is sleep there."

"You know," Mary said, "Nick's half sister and brother share a brownstone in that area with a friend. Plenty of space. Especially now with them being out of town for a while. I'll call Maddie."

"Or you could move into the Galaxy, where Jessie and I are living," Nora suggested. "You'd be near work."

Larry looked from one to the other. "Thanks. I'm fine where I am."

The first lull in the conversation.

"Where's Anthony?" Jessie asked. "And Kat?"

"Kat's in Florida with Nick—"

"He took Kat but not Anthony?" Annoyance crept into her voice.

"Relax, Jessie. Anthony's fine with it," Mary shot back. "He's on his way to Long Island to spend a few days with his old pal Zane. Finn gave him some time off because of his good grades. He'll be down in a minute."

"Why is Kat in Florida with Nick? I thought he was off on an investigation."

"He is." Mary cleared her throat. Time to change the subject. "Let me get some more shrimp."

Anthony came down the stairs with a small leather bag in his hand and Monty at his side. "Mary, where's my athletic bag? Oh, hi Mom." He gave his mother a kiss.

"It's by the front door. Where you left it." Mary passed the plate of shrimp around.

"Anthony," Jessie said, "do you remember Larry Williams?"

Anthony stared at the man. "Did you have a boat?"

Larry chuckled. "Yep. Not a very big one."

"It seemed big to me."

"How old are you now, Anthony?"

"Nine."

"The last time I saw you, you were five. Just before Andrew was—" He shot an apologetic look to Jessie. "I can't believe how much you've grown."

"You have a son, right?" Anthony moved towards the archway.

Larry nodded. "Sammy. He's thirteen now. My daughter's sixteen."

Anthony backed into the hallway, "Sorry. Gotta go. Willie's waiting. Nice to see you again, Mr. Williams." He patted his thigh. "Come on, Monty." The dog followed Anthony down the hall, the sound of his nails clicking on the hardwood floor.

Jessie pushed off the stool. "I need to get some things upstairs. Be right back."

*

The picturesque city of Mount Dora was thirty miles north of Orlando. Parking the rental car in a lot, Nick and Kat strolled around town on a beautiful sunny day. Quaint shops and restaurants were busy. Parks exploded with autumn blossoms. Pumpkins adorned window displays, previewing the coming Halloween.

A few blocks away, the steeple of St. Catherine's beckoned. The Catholic church, with its sandstone edifice and stained-glass windows, was a beauty.

They entered through the side double doors. The interior was cool and dark, the scent of flowers filling the air. Also a hint of incense. Nick could never be Catholic. He hated incense. But his daughter was raised Catholic, so he stayed mum on the subject.

A few people knelt in the pews. A woman vacuumed near the main altar. Another woman dusted. An elderly priest lit candles in an iron bank of red glass holders off to the side.

As Nick and Kat passed the main aisle, Kat bobbed into a quick kneel and made the sign of the cross. Not sure what to do, Nick imitated his daughter. Poorly.

"Wow, Dad. That's the worst genuflection I've ever seen." Kat tried to suppress her laughter.

Shushing his daughter, Nick approached the priest and watched as he stuffed some bills into the offering box.

"So that's how it works," Nick said to the man, who turned at the sound of a voice. "You make the offerings yourself."

"Dad," Kat admonished under her breath.

The priest smiled. "Seeing candles lit inspires others to do the same. They're reminded of loved ones already with God." He looked from Nick to Kat and back again, his face changing subtly as his gaze settled on Nick. The man's stare was so intense it made Nick uncomfortable. If there was a God, this must be what Judgement Day felt like.

"You're new to the parish?" The man finally shifted his eyes to Kat. "Are you looking to enroll this young lady in school?"

"Actually," Nick cleared his throat, "we came to see a Father Locato."

"I'm Father Locato."

The priest was a short, thin man with silver hair, olive skin and dark brown eyes magnified by wire-rimmed glasses. His smile revealed uneven teeth, and his nose looked like it once collided with a clenched fist. "Let's go outside where we can talk." He led them through a side door and onto a patio. They sat around a stone table. "How can I help you?"

Nick decided to jump right in. Not give the priest time to formulate answers. "Fifteen years ago you found a baby in St. Sebastian's. In Sarasota."

A slight pause before the priest nodded.

"The boy was placed in a foster home and later disappeared when he was five. The police believe he drowned."

"Sad." Father Locato brushed a piece of lint from his black jacket.

"I'm not convinced."

"Excuse me?"

"There's no proof of his death. Just speculation."

"I see."

"Before Patrick – that was his name – disappeared, a priest came to the home wanting to plan a picnic for the children. But they never heard from him again." Nick paused, studying the man. "Were you that priest?"

Locato shrugged. "That was a long time ago. My memory isn't what it used to be."

He didn't answer the question. "Was it you?"

The priest met Nick's eyes. "Why are you so interested in this, after all these years?"

"Because the boy's father is Andrew Brady, my brother."

The priest remained still, staring at Nick. "Who?"

Kat finally spoke. "You don't know who Andrew Brady is? A huge star who was murdered in New York?"

Locato shook his head.

"What about my dad?" She looked up at Nick. "Do you know who he is? Nick McDeare, a famous author and investigative reporter?"

"Kat." It was Nick's turn to admonish his daughter.

"I don't read much. Or follow celebrities." Father Locato rose. "I'm sorry for your loss. If you'll excuse me, I have to hear confessions."

Nick placed his card in the priest's hand. "Contact me if you remember anything. My cell number's on the back."

Father Locato slid the card in his pocket and looked down at Kat. "You're Catholic, aren't you?"

Kat nodded.

The priest did something odd, in Nick's eyes anyway. He cupped Kat's chin in one hand and lifted her face. With his thumb, he made the sign of the cross on her forehead. "Go with God, dear child."

With a final glance at Nick, Father Locato hurried towards the rectory and disappeared inside.

Nick turned to his daughter. "What was that about?"

"It's just a blessing. Kind of nice." She looked up at Nick. "He knows more than he's saying, right?"

"Yep. Which means we watch him."

Kat stared at the rectory. "No matter what, I like him."

"Come on. Let's find a motel. We'll pick this up tomorrow."

*

Life in the brownstone continued without Jessie. It depressed the hell out of her. The master bedroom was exactly as she left it, only messier, of course. Meals were prepared and eaten. Homework was done. Nick's books were written. The dog was walked. It all screamed she was superfluous.

Jessie felt odd being in the house without Nick. She sat at the dining room table with Mary, Nora and Larry, trying to enjoy Mary's rack of lamb and new potatoes. Nick's empty chair kept drawing her attention. He should be sitting there, tossing slivers of meat to Monty. Anthony should be talking non-stop about his day.

Jessie wanted to stand up and scream, 'Cut!' as if this were a film, not real life. She wanted her world back. Living in her home. Bantering with her son. Even fighting with Kat. Most importantly, she wanted to spend her days with Nick.

In the car on the way home, Jessie couldn't hold back the tears any longer. "Sorry," she said to Nora and Larry. "I just miss him."

"Go ahead and cry," Larry said. "I did. I hope that doesn't make me less of a man."

"Of course not." Jessie pulled a tissue from her purse as Willie guided the car towards Larry's hotel. "It makes you human."

Nora squeezed Jessie's hand. "Marriage isn't easy. I was with my Chester for thirty-five years. It's hard work. We're flawed human beings, all of us. A husband and wife learn to appreciate the good times and carry on through the bad. And we learn how to forgive."

Jessie sniffled. "Tell that to Nick."

"Nora's right, Jessie. No one's perfect. Not even Nick."

"What about Andrew?" A smile finally broke through.

"Oh, well, Andrew," Larry teased. "We all know he wasn't perfect. He was hell on wheels." He started to laugh. "Remember," he laughed even harder, "remember when he put bubble bath crystals in the washer at the theater during a break in rehearsal? We went down the street for dinner and—"

"—came back to bubbles everywhere!" Jessie laughed through her tears. "The green room—"

"—the dressing rooms," Nora added.

"—the stage," Larry continued.

"—even in the house!" Jessie dropped her head in her hands, howling with laughter.

"It took me hours to clean up that mess," Larry said. "Everything had to be washed or vacuumed."

"Did Andrew ever own up to it?" Nora asked.

"Nope. But I got him back."

"How?" Jessie rubbed mascara from beneath her eyes.

"Itching powder in his dance belt, his shampoo, his socks ..."

The back seat of the car exploded with laughter.

Even Willie was chuckling up front.

*

Father Joseph Locato sat down at the computer in his office. This contraption still confused him at times, but at least he had the basics down. Pecking at the keyboard one-finger-at-a-time, he entered Andrew Brady's name.

The fair-haired man filled his screen. A man with a radiant smile and unusual eyes. Joseph noticed the same eyes on Nick McDeare.

Joseph lost track of time as he researched Andrew Brady. His personal life.

Yesterday Joseph was a man comfortable in his own skin. Content with his orderly and rewarding life.

47

Today everything changed.

Of course he knew who Andrew Brady was. Who didn't?

*

The police car coasted to a stop behind Nick's SUV.

Nick looked at Kat in the passenger seat. "Let me handle this."

A cop approached as Nick rolled down the window.

"License and registration."

Nick handed over his driver's license and the rental car's papers.

"I got a report you've been sitting in this car since six this morning watching the church." He studied the license. "Nick McDeare?" The policeman looked closer at Nick. "Man, you ARE him."

"In the flesh."

"Why are you sitting here, Mr. McDeare?"

"Research for my next book. What it's like to do a long stakeout. I figured sitting near a church would keep me out of trouble."

"And who's this young lady?"

"My daughter. Learning the ropes."

The policeman handed the documents back to Nick. "Okay." He patted the top of the car. "I'll let them know. Next time notify the local authorities."

"I will. Thank you, Officer."

As the police car pulled away, Kat laughed. "That was cool. You're so fast with your stories."

Nick glanced back at the church. "Well, well. Look who finally surfaced."

He started the engine as Father Locato left the rectory and headed down the street.

*

Brianna Fontaine watched the depressing landscape zip by as the Amtrak train sped from Washington to New York City. After two days of interviews, one-after-another, she was no closer to uncovering corruption in the nation's FBI. Corruption she knew existed. The organization was a band of brothers, their motto 'Cover Your Ass.'

Bree needed a diversion. If only Nick was in New York. She felt like eating an expensive steak in an expensive restaurant. She wanted to fill him in on this FBI expose she was working on and get his take on it. But Kat told her a few days ago she was going to Florida with her dad. And no matter how much Bree hinted and cajoled, Kat wouldn't say why. Kat usually told her everything.

So Nick was back in Florida, this time with his daughter, and neither were talking. Strange.

48

*

As Father Locato entered Sacred Heart Senior Healthcare Center, Nick parked the car on the street. "Wait here," he instructed Kat.

"But Dad—"

"I mean it, Kat."

Nick sprinted after the priest and followed him down a long hallway. The padre stopped at the nurse's station before entering a room on the right. Nick halted just out of sight.

Okay. Father Locato is visiting the sick. That's what priests do. This has nothing to do with Patrick.

Nick rejoined Kat in the car and waited. Locato emerged an hour later. They trailed him as he turned down a side street and continued walking. When he entered a small cottage, Nick parked down the street.

The priest only stayed inside for ten minutes before making his way back to St. Sebastian's, Nick following a block behind.

When Father Locato entered the church, Nick made a quick decision. "I want to check out that house," he told Kat. "You stay here and keep an eye on the good Father. I won't be gone long, promise. Try to stay out of sight. If Locato spots you, make up something. You're good at that."

"Got it, boss." Kat saluted and headed into the church. Nick felt confident she'd be okay. After all, it was a church. If she wasn't safe there, she wasn't safe anywhere.

He headed back to the cottage and walked around the tiny structure, peeking in the windows. It was hard to make out the interior. It looked like there was a living room and two bedrooms. One looked feminine. The other belonged to a male, by the look of the mess.

Nick tried both the front and back doors. Locked. Should he break in? As he contemplated what to do, a neighbor spotted him. Nick smiled and waved and hurried back to his car.

He picked up Kat, who said Father Locato was in the confessional the whole time. They sat in the car for the rest of the afternoon, watching as the priest returned to the rectory and stayed there.

Taking up their post the next morning, they were rewarded immediately. This time the priest went to the cottage first, again inside for only a few minutes. He came out carrying a quilt.

"Why would he go to an empty cottage?" Kat asked.

Nick shrugged. "Maybe it's not empty today." They ducked down as the priest passed the SUV. When he was out of sight, Nick said, "I want to check out the place again."

As he started to get out of the car, the neighbor came out of her house, watching him. Damn. Nick got back in the car and made a U-turn, deciding to trail the priest instead.

Nick followed Locato to the hospital and back to the same floor. Again, the priest stopped at the nurse's station. "She was asking for her quilt yesterday. How is she today, Rita?"

"She had a bad night."

Father Locato went into the same room as yesterday. Nick stepped a little closer. With no other options, he decided to see where this went.

Locato emerged quickly, surprising Nick, and headed straight towards him. Nick ducked into a bathroom across from the nurse's station and waited.

He heard the priest stop at the desk. "She's asleep, Rita. I'll come back later." Locato's shoes passed the vent in the door.

Nick counted to twenty. Emerging, he went to the desk. "I'm supposed to meet Father Locato here."

"You just missed him."

"That's what I get for taking a bathroom break."

The nurse laughed. "You look familiar."

He extended his hand. "Nick McDeare."

Shock splashed across her heart-shaped face. "Nick Mc— The writer?"

"Guilty." Nick glanced down the hall towards the room the priest entered. "So Father Locato's already seen ..."

"Mrs. Cavanaugh? Yes. She was sleeping so he said he'd be back later."

Cavanaugh. Nick's heart began to race. As he looked longingly at the open door down the hallway, he formulated a plan. "Thank you. I'll catch up with him at St. Catherine's."

Back in the car he turned to Kat. "First, where did Father Locato go when he left the hospital?"

"It looked like he was heading back to the church."

Nick started the engine. There was plenty of time to put his plan into action. As they coasted forward, searching for the priest, Nick said, "Cavanaugh. Tell me what that name means to you."

"It's the name of the parishioner who found Patrick in the church with Father Locato. I remember because we had a neighbor named Cavanaugh in Lake Placid."

His daughter was already learning the tricks of the trade. Memory association. "You are going to make one hell of an investigator, kiddo."

"Why'd you ask?"

50

"Because the priest is visiting a woman named Cavanaugh in the hospital."

"But Mrs. Cavanaugh lives in Sarasota. We're in Mount Dora."

"Maybe Father Locato brought her with him. Maybe she's a relative of his." He spotted the priest entering the rectory.

Nick pulled the car to the curb and turned to Kat. "I have a job for you. Are you up for it?"

*

Abbie poured herself some coffee and joined Mary at the island. "Jessie's driving me crazy, asking why Nick's in Florida."

"You know Nick. Secretive about his work."

"What's going on, Mary? Please don't tell me he's chasing down Kat's silly theory that Andrew has a child somewhere."

"Your guess is as good as mine."

"Can you imagine Jessie's reaction if Andrew fathered a child?"

"Maybe it would finally force Jessie to see Andrew clearly. Maybe she'd stop throwing Andrew in Nick's face."

Abbie snorted. "Jessie never ever saw Andrew for who he truly was. Not a saint. Just a good guy who meant well but made mistakes like the rest of us."

"Andrew was in love with her for years. She never saw that either."

Abbie added cream to her coffee. "At least they ended up happy."

"But Andrew knew the truth. His was a one-sided love affair."

*

Kat approached the nurse's station, a bouquet of autumn flowers in her hands. The RN who looked up wore a name tag. Rita. "Ooh, aren't those pretty."

"They're for Mrs. Cavanaugh. Where's her room?"

"Are you a relative?"

"Father Locato sent me. When he was here earlier, she was asleep. He's not able to get back to see her today, so he asked me to bring these flowers." Kat and her dad waited a few hours before putting this ploy into action.

"How nice." Rita pointed. "Her room's right there."

"Thank you."

Kat entered the dimly lit room and approached Mrs. Cavanaugh's bed. The elderly woman was asleep. A maze of tubes and wires were connected to her frail body. There were clicks and beeps and monitors with graphs and lights.

Kat had a sudden urge to run. This – all of it – reminded her of her mother's last days in the hospital. As cancer took her life. Kat vowed to never again watch a helpless human being cling to life with the aid of machines.

She closed her eyes and took a deep breath, exhaling slowly.

Setting the flowers on the tray table, she looked around per her father's instructions. A rosary was draped over the corner of the bed. Another was on the tray table. A bulletin board held cards and prayers. A recliner was covered with the quilt Father Locato took from the cottage earlier. A picture of the pope hung on the wall. And near the window, there was a chest of drawers with photos scattered across the top.

Kat stepped towards the dresser and stared.

She no longer heard the machines. The antiseptic odor of the hospital disappeared. Everything in the world ceased to exist. Everything but a large eight-by-ten color photo.

Finally she pulled out her cell. Getting as close to the photo as possible, she snapped several pictures.

"Can I help you?"

Startled, Kat sucked in her breath and swung around.

A nurse stood in the doorway. And she wasn't Friendly Rita.

Kat shoved her phone into her pocket.

"I've never seen you before," the austere RN said, stepping into the room. "Are you a relative?"

"Father Locato asked me to bring those flowers."

"And you are?"

"A friend of Father's." Kat took a few steps towards the door.

The woman remained silent, her demeanor disapproving.

"Anyway, I'm going now." A few more steps. "When Mrs. Cavanaugh wakes up will you tell her Father will see her tomorrow?"

Scooting around the less-than-happy nurse, Kat forced herself to walk normally down the hall. It was the hardest thing she'd ever done in her life.

*

Drumming his fingertips on the steering wheel, Nick waited in the SUV. Kat had been in there for almost thirty minutes. Had she been caught in her lie?

Just as he was about to go in and check on his daughter, Kat pushed through the glass door and broke into a run. She scrambled into the car. "He's alive! Patrick is alive! Look!" Kat pulled up a photo on her cell and handed it to him.

Nick stared at the image on the screen.

52

A young man looked earnestly into the camera, the hint of a smile in his blue eyes. A boy with soft sandy curls, a dimpled chin, high cheek bones …

… and eyes that dipped at the outer corners.

He was a younger version of Andrew Brady.

"Hello, Patrick."

CHAPTER 5

Father Joseph Locato phoned Sacred Heart Health Center and asked for Rita in the Hospice wing. "Good evening, Rita. Would you tell Mrs. Cavanaugh I can't get back over there tonight. I'll see her in the morning."

"The young girl already told us."

"What young girl?"

"The girl who brought your flowers."

Flowers? He didn't— Deflating, Joseph sat back. "What did the girl look like? How old was she?"

"Um, pretty. Blond hair and unusual eyes. Early teens."

The McDeare girl. "Did she see Mrs. Cavanaugh?"

"Well, she brought her your flowers."

She was in the room. She saw—

"Is something wrong, Father?"

"No," he said quickly. "I'll see you in the morning." He clicked off.

"Father Locato?" The church secretary stood in the doorway of his office. "Sorry to interrupt you."

Joseph rubbed his achy eyes. "What is it, Sally?"

"There's a Mr. McDeare and his daughter to see you."

Joseph rose and paced to the window overlooking the church. "Tell them I can't see them right now."

*

Mary sat in the breakfast nook trying not to cry.

Andrew had a son, and she was looking at his picture right now.

Kat texted the photo a few minutes ago, explaining her dad was trying to set up a meeting with him. She also said Mary was to tell no one. NO ONE. Not yet.

Mary sent the photo to her email, then went to the study computer. Two minutes later she held the picture in her hands. Thank God Nick got Kat her own printer. If there had been no ink, Kat would have heard Mary screaming all the way down in Florida.

Mary took the picture to her bedroom, sliding it on top of a stack of books in her bookcase. She vowed it would stay there until she could see and hold the real thing.

Until Andrew's son was home.

*

"I'm sorry, Mr. McDeare. Father Locato can't see you right now. He's working on Sunday's sermon."

Huh-uh. No more delays or excuses. "Please tell the padre I'm not going anywhere until we talk."

"But he—"

"Tell him I know about Patrick."

"But—"

"Patrick. Tell him! Now my daughter and I are going to sit right here in these uncomfortable-looking chairs and wait for him."

Nick sat down and folded his arms, a scowl on his face.

Kat did the same, mimicking him perfectly, as the harried secretary disappeared into the inner sanctum.

*

Joseph Locato knew he was cornered. There was no escape. His secret was about to be exposed.

Joseph spent years fearing someone would emerge who could turn their lives upside down. Now it had happened.

At least he could make this play out on his own terms. He wouldn't allow Nick McDeare to upset or harm anyone. Nor would the man dictate the next step.

After saying a silent prayer, Father Locato went to the front lobby and led the McDeares outside.

*

Nick sat with Kat and Locato at the same stone table in the courtyard. It was past dusk, darkness descending. Small lights around the perimeter snapped on.

Nick punched up Patrick's photo on Kat's cell and slid it across the table to Father Locato.

The priest stared at it until the image timed out. He looked up at Kat. "Please tell me you didn't upset Mrs. Cavanaugh."

"No. She was asleep."

"Tell us about Patrick," Nick exploded. "The truth this time."

"Dad!"

The priest's eyes settled on Kat. "It's all right, young lady."

"No it's not. You're a priest."

"A priest with dirty hands." Nick continued.

Kat shot Nick another look, which he ignored.

"If I did anything wrong, Mr. McDeare, I'll answer to God. Not you." Locato folded his hands on the table. "I'll tell you about Patrick. But not today."

Nick was sick of the game-playing. "No more stalling, Father."

"Meet me tomorrow at eleven." He pulled a piece of paper from his pocket and handed it to Nick. "At that address."

"What is this place?"

"A cottage. Not far from here. I'll tell you everything when we meet."

A cottage? Nick didn't need to look at the address. He knew where it was.

*

Jessie lounged in her dressing room with Larry, gossiping about the day's rehearsal. Nora was in the costume shop, checking on today's shipment from London.

"You know who's going to be really good in this show?" Larry grabbed a cola from Jessie's mini fridge. "Aaron. He's nailed Dodi Fayed."

"He's much better than Moni Mizrahi, who played it in London."

"I know Moni."

"You do?" Jessie's stomach tightened.

"I worked with him in L.A. on *FUNNY GIRL*. Aaron's a better actor than Moni. Also a better singer."

Jessie opened a bottle of water.

"What?" Larry was watching her. "Why'd you go silent on me about Moni? Didn't you like working with him?"

Jessie shrugged, not trying to hide her distaste.

"He's a real lady's man." Larry whistled his disapproval. "Broke up a marriage in L.A."

Jessie peeked up at him. "He may have broken up mine, too."

Larry lowered the can of cola slowly. "Moni was the one you—"

"Yep. So now it's verified I'm the stupidest actress on both sides of the pond."

"Stop it. Moni's smooth. A real snake in the grass. And you didn't fall for him like the actress in *FUNNY GIRL*. You were drunk and thought he was Nick. Big difference."

"God, Larry, thank you. You're such a nice man."

Larry drained the can and tossed it in the garbage. "I'm nice. Synonymous with stable. Synonymous with boring." He lifted off the chair he was straddling.

56

"Don't forget." Jessie smiled. "They called Andrew nice, too."

"But we know the truth, don't we, princess?" He kissed the top of her head. "Got to go. Meeting with the lighting designer. See you tomorrow."

*

"Whose house is this?" Nick asked Locato the following morning, surveying the small living room. This was the cottage he checked out the other day. The room was fussy. Feminine. Doilies and knickknacks.

"Dad?" Kat showed him a framed photo of a young boy and an older woman.

"That's Tess Cavanaugh and Patrick," the priest said. "This house is theirs."

Kat dropped down on an ottoman. "It's pretty clean considering a teenager lives here."

"A lady from the church comes in to clean. You'll feel differently if you see Patrick's room."

"I'd like to." Nick started for the tiny hallway.

"After we talk."

Nick's anger surfaced. This priest would no longer dictate his actions. Catching Kat's imploring look, however, he changed his mind and returned to the terrace doors. The small back yard was sad. Just a stone slab and an overgrown garden. "Where's Patrick now?"

"In Orlando. He has a job as a singing waiter. He splits his time between there and here."

"A waiter? Isn't he underage?"

"Yes. He turned seventeen a week ago. Since Patrick doesn't have a birthday, we gave him one. Just a guess, of course. As for his job, he has ID to prove he's older. I got it for him. And before you get legal on me, Mr. McDeare, Patrick needs the money he makes singing in a restaurant like that. He's supplementing Tess's Medicare and paying rent on this house."

"What about school?"

"He graduated last year. Patrick's exceptional. Highly intelligent."

Patrick apparently had the family genes. Nick started college at fifteen. And his daughter was two years ahead in school. But back to Locato. "Start at the beginning." Nick perched on the arm of a worn couch. Covered with a doily.

"You know the beginning. Patrick was left at the church. I was counseling Tess that day. She'd just lost her son in the war overseas." The priest sat forward. "I did what I could to find Patrick's relatives. No one came forward."

"His mother was a young girl named Heidi Barstow. The funeral in the church that day was for her."

Locato looked surprised. "I didn't know that."

"His grandmother is the one who abandoned him. Before she drank herself to death."

"So he has no relatives."

"He has his father's family. Us."

*

Joseph Locato studied Nick McDeare. "Before we go any further, Mr. McDeare, how'd you put it all together? And why did it take so long?"

McDeare explained the long process, begun by his daughter Kat, which brought them to this living room today.

Joseph researched Nick McDeare before this meeting. His reputation as an investigator was impressive. Now proven by his search for his nephew.

"So how did Patrick end up here with Tess Cavanaugh?" McDeare asked.

Joseph laid his hand on three small diaries on the table beside him. "When Tess lost her son Frankie, I advised her to write down what she was feeling. I thought it might help with her grief. It ended up becoming a habit for her through the years. She didn't write every day or even every week. Only when something special happened."

He picked up the diaries, rubbing his hand over them. "I spent the morning going through these and marking the entries you should read." He extended them to Nick. "When you finish, we'll talk again. And I want them back. They'll eventually belong to Patrick."

"When can we meet him?" McDeare asked.

"Not until you've read the diaries. It'll help you understand what he's been through."

"Tell me," Nick McDeare continued. "Were you the priest who went to Patrick's foster home that day?"

"Yes." Joseph looked down. "What I saw was revolting."

Kat looked at her father. "Georgia didn't say anything like that about the place."

"Georgia?" Joseph asked.

"The lady running Child Protective Services at the time."

"She wouldn't have seen what I saw. My visit was a surprise. Hers was probably planned. I did a lot of research on this subject. You see, the people who foster children get paid for each child they take in. Some of them do it only for the money and don't want to do anything to rock the boat. They clean the place up when they get an official visit."

He shook his head at the memory. "The day I was there it made me physically sick. The house was filthy. Dishes in the sink. Soiled bedsheets. Babies in dirty diaper. The stench! A couple ran the place, along with the man's sister. I'm not saying all foster homes are like this one. I'm sure they're not. This one was horrible."

"Did you see Patrick?"

"I had to look for him. I found him locked in a closet. Singing."

"Why was he in there?" Kat looked horrified.

"My guess? He was being punished. He was sitting on the floor. Naked. There were welts on his back. And cigarette burns on his feet. I had to coax him out. He didn't hear me at first. He was in a kind of trance. His hands were so cold. I looked around for clothes, but there weren't any. Finally a young boy gave me some shorts and a T-shirt.

"I dressed him and told him I'd try to help him. He looked up at me, but he was looking through me or past me. It was like he took himself out of the real world and lived someplace in his mind.

"As I started to leave, he began to sing again. One of the women screamed from the other room to shut the 'F' up. I think she forgot I was there. I'd gone off on my own. Patrick held my hand and followed me outside, singing the whole way."

"What was he singing?" Kat asked quietly. "Do you remember?"

"A song about nothing's going to hurt him ever again. Something like that."

*

Nick rose and turned his back to them. "What's Patrick like now?"

"He's a boy of strong faith. It helped get him through it. Despite his past, he's not bitter." Joseph stood up. "If you want to see Patrick's room, it's down the hall. I'll show you."

It was a typical teenager's room. Messy. But there were aspects that were unusual. A crucifix hung on the wall. A vial of prescription pills was on the dresser. There were photos of stars from Broadway and the West End. Kat listed them off for Nick. "Mary Martin. Howard Keel. Colm Wilkinson. Lea Salonga. Ben Vereen. Michael Ball. Patti Lupone." And Andrew Brady.

Nick turned to Locato. "You knew who Andrew was when Kat asked you."

The priest nodded.

"Why'd you lie?"

"I wasn't sure of your intentions. I wanted to protect Patrick."

They returned to the living room. "We're going to head back to our hotel in Sarasota. Be back in a couple days."

"I have an appointment with the Bishop." Locato checked his pocket watch. "And I'm late."

"Can we drop you?"

"I'd appreciate it. I don't drive much anymore, not at my age. I walked here."

As Nick pulled in front of St. Catherine's, Father Locato turned to him. "Don't judge us, Mr. McDeare. Did we make mistakes? Maybe. But it was done to give Patrick a better life."

Nick watched the priest enter the rectory.

"Do you still not like him?" Kat climbed into the front seat.

"I never said I didn't like him."

"You didn't have to."

*

Back in Sarasota, they ordered room service and sat on the terrace. Nick wanted to dive into the diaries immediately.

Kat sat down beside him. "Can we read them together?"

"Kat, I know this whole Patrick thing got started because of you." He brushed her hair from her face. "And I'm grateful, kiddo. You have no idea how much. But I'm not sure you should read the diaries."

Her face fell. "Why?"

"Father Locato said I should read these to understand what Patrick's been through. Which sounds like it was pretty bad. If there are embarrassing things in these diaries, it could be awkward for you if—when—we meet Patrick. He might resent you for knowing. I don't want to damage any future relationship you might have with him. There might come a time when he shows to you himself. Or tells you about his past. I hope so, anyway."

Nick expected Kat to blow up and pout. Instead, she surprised him. "Yeah. I understand." She got to her feet and kissed his forehead. "I'm going to text Bertie."

Alone, Nick turned off the ringer on his cell, followed the priest's tabs and read Tess's first diary:

When I was doing dishes I heard singing. The voice of an angel or how I imagined an angel would sing. I thought it was Henry's radio out in the garage. Then I realized it was coming from the orange grove behind the house.

A beautiful little blond boy sat against a tree, singing. He was probably four or five. His eyes were closed.

When he saw me he stopped and looked scared. I told him I loved his singing. I promised to keep my distance and sat down in the grass to listen.

When he left I followed him to a house a few blocks away. A woman started shouting and I heard a child crying. I hope it wasn't the little boy.

*

The boy returns to the grove at least once a week. His singing is soothing. I bake cookies for him and bring him a glass of milk. I set them down and back away because he's still afraid of me.

*

Today the boy finally spoke. His name is Patrick. I told him I'm Tess. He let me come closer.

His clothes are dirty. So is his hair. He has no socks. His shoes are too big. There are red streaks on his legs and a bruise on his forehead.

I listen to his singing and applaud, which he loves. His laugh is wonderful. He's gorgeous when he smiles.

He knows so many songs. I wonder where he learns them?

*

I told Henry about Patrick, but he's not interested. I think it hurts too much to talk about another boy. I'm worried about Henry. Except for his furniture-making in the garage, he's not interested in anything. He stopped going to church. He never watches TV anymore. He barely eats.

Today I invited Patrick inside. He was scared but curious. He wandered around, touching everything. He still kept some distance between us, but I think this is a huge victory.

His eyes are unusual. An odd shape. I've seen them before somewhere.

*

Patrick's become a regular visitor. We meet in the grove, then he comes inside and sings for me in the living room. Then we have cookies and milk. He lets me get closer. There was a red streak on his leg and dried blood. When I asked about it he backed away.

His beautiful eyes are hypnotic. As if they can see right into my soul. That's when I realized where I saw them before. Patrick is the abandoned baby in St. Sebastian's. How amazing we meet again. This must be God's work.

*

I lost Henry. He died in his sleep. I think he didn't want to go on without Frankie. My heart is breaking. I'm so lonely. Father Locato comes by and is trying to help. Some days I just can't get out of bed.

I hear Patrick singing out in the grove. He must wonder where I am.

*

Patrick came inside to see where I've been. He was worried. So sweet.

There was a bite mark on his arm. Did an animal get him? I tried to examine it, but he pulled away.

I gave him the fried chicken and mashed potatoes Father Locato brought me. He ate like he was starving.

When I asked about his home, he told me his mom visits. She has dark hair and eyes like his and they sing together. He said she teaches him his songs..

This must all be make-believe. Patrick's lonely and is creating an imaginary mom. Which is okay, if it makes him feel good.

When it started to get dark, I walked him home. I figured they'd be worried. It was the first time I left my house in months! All because of this precious little boy.

A woman came out of Patrick's house and dragged him inside. Then I heard an awful beating and Patrick crying. I wanted to go get him but a man sitting on the porch scared me.

I cried all the way home.

*

Nick closed the book. It was the last entry in the first journal.

He felt hands on his shoulders. "So what are they like?" Kat whispered.

"That poor kid."

She sunk down beside him. "That bad?"

He stood up. "I'm going for a run on the beach."

"You okay?"

He shrugged. "You won't read them while I'm gone? I can trust you?"

"I won't read them. Promise."

As Nick ran in the moonlight. he tried to expel the images of a young Patrick in that awful house. A bruise on the boy's forehead. A bite mark. A red streak with caked blood. And beatings.

Nick had problems with his own childhood, his adoptive parents all about themselves, often forgetting they even had a son. He became a loner at an early age, and the trait stuck into adulthood. His only friend as he grew up was a mutt named Haywire.

But Nick's history didn't compare to what this boy went through.

62

He stopped running and put his hands on his knees, gasping for air.

Would anything have been different if Andrew took Heidi's pregnancy claim seriously? If he'd known about Patrick? It was a tough question. Andrew's career drove him. The stage was home for him.

What would his brother have done with a kid at that point in his life?

For one thing, Andrew would have come up against a brick wall when it came to Jessie, the love of his life. Jessie never really accepted Kat, so Nick could imagine her reaction to learning Andrew had an illegitimate son. It was so damned ironic, considering Andrew loved Anthony like he was his own.

Even more ironic was the fact that Nick, Andrew and Jessie all had children with other people.

Welcome to life in the twenty-first century.

Theirs was the American family.

CHAPTER 6

Nick slept horribly. He was up at dawn and sitting on the terrace, the second unopened diary in front of him. The beach was quiet on this Sunday morning.

The hotel room coffee machine produced only colored water. Nick settled for a cola. At least it was caffeine.

His cell had been vibrating for the last twenty-four hours. He'd ignored all the calls, focused only on Patrick. He checked the messages now. The screenwriter of *THE SILVER LINING* wanting to give him an update. Two calls from his agent Liz, no details, demanding he call her. Bree, wanting to talk. Typical Bree, always mysterious. These calls could wait.

The only message that piqued his interest was from Herman Stutz, the man from CPS who helped them in the basement that day. Nick checked his watch. Too early to call him back.

Opening the second diary, Nick began to read:

Patrick keeps showing up with bruises. One time his eye was swollen shut. I don't question him because he won't answer.

I asked neighbors near Patrick's house about the situation. They told me he's living in a foster home with six other children. The people who run it must be horrible people. I heard Patrick being beaten by that woman. I've seen scars and bruises on him. I can't stand the thought of anyone hurting him.

Today Patrick told me his mother will always protect him. His fantasy life is getting him through. But I pray that God will deliver him from that awful house.
*

I talked to Father Locato about Patrick. He said I'm doing what I can to help the little boy. I'm frustrated and want to do more. I finally introduced Father to Patrick. Patrick was quiet around Father.
*

Father's starting to love Patrick as much as me. Patrick certainly trusted Father faster than he trusted me. He likes having a bigger audience for his songs! He's singing Broadway show songs and pop music now. Where does he learn this music?

Father's seen Patrick's bruises and welts. He took a picture of Patrick and gave me the photo. He told me to hang onto it, just in case.

In case of what?

*

Patrick hasn't come around for three days. I'm worried. I went to his house and asked about him. That awful woman said Patrick was being punished because he ran away. They found him on a beach far away. She wouldn't let me see him.

I went home and called Father. He said he'd see what he could find out.

I couldn't sleep last night because I was so worried. Then Patrick showed up with new welts on his legs. Whenever this happens he doesn't talk, just sings. One of the songs always makes me cry. It's about nothing ever hurting him again.

Patrick was filthy and hungry, poor thing. I fed him and ran a bath. He wouldn't let me undress him, so I left him alone and called Father Locato. When I looked in on Patrick, there were ugly scars on his backside.

I can't take this anymore. I love this little boy.

*

Kat joined Nick on the terrace. She looked like she didn't get much sleep. "How's the second diary?"

Nick closed the book temporarily. "More depressing than the first." He checked his watch. He could call Herman Stutz now. Nick put his cell on speaker.

"I haven't been able to stop thinking about that boy," Herman began. "Georgia mentioning a priest showing up at the foster home finally rang a bell. I went back into my files and looked it up. A Father Locato from St. Sebastian's filed a complaint about the house Patrick was living in. It was just luck of the draw that he ended up at my desk. I took his claim to Georgia. That's what triggered her visit to the place."

"Which changed nothing."

"The people who ran that home must have been tipped off about CPS checking them out. Happens all the time. Anyway, sometime later the priest came back to Social Services. He got the royal shuffle before landing again at my desk. He asked a lot of questions about how to become a foster parent and about adoption. I sent him downtown. I figured they could answer his questions better than me."

"Was that the last you saw of him?"

65

"Yes. I didn't think much of it at the time. But when Georgia told us the other day that Patrick disappeared, presumedly drowned, and you didn't seem convinced, I thought maybe this additional info might help. Maybe the priest has him."

"Thanks, Herman. I'm on it. I'll let you know." He clicked off.

"Father Joe wanted that information for Tess," Kat observed. "She wanted to adopt him?"

"Or foster him."

"It was nice you didn't let Herman know you were two steps ahead of him."

"If Father O'Brien hadn't called me back from St. Sebastian's, Herman would have had the missing clue we were looking for. It would have fallen out exactly the same. We would have gone to St. Sebastian's and tracked down Father Locato, ending up in Mount Dora. I've learned over the years, Kat, that not a lot of people go out of their way to help. When they do, treat them well. You may need them again one day."

*

Mary led the repairman to the cable box attached to the TV in the study. "It might be time to replace it," she explained. "It's pretty old."

The doorbell rang. "Excuse me. I'll be right back." She hurried down the hall and looked through the peephole. Swinging the door open, Bree stepped inside.

"I'm sorry to just drop in," Bree said, "but Ethan said it was urgent."

"Follow me down to the study." Mary did an about-face and hustled back down the hall. She was getting too old for this, but she had a cardinal rule: never leave a repairman alone.

She turned to Bree, out of breath. "Sorry. You were saying?"

"Ethan wants me to take of photo of that painting he did last summer. The one of Nick asleep in the hammock with the two kids. Someone asked him to do a similar tropical painting out in California, but they want to see his work first. It looks like he's getting bored out there and wants to indulge in his hobby again to fill the hours."

"Ethan's an extraordinary artist. But of course there's no money in it."

"Where's the painting?"

"Nick asked me to hang it in my room. He was afraid Jessie would get upset because she's not in it. Go on up. I have to stay here with— Third floor, first door on the right."

Bree hurried out of the room as Mary turned back to— Then it hit her. Oh, dear Lord! "Bree, wait." The woman was already gone.

Mary shouldn't leave the repairman alone but – She took off running.

*

Father's being transferred to a parish in Mount Dora. He asked for the transfer two years ago, before Patrick came into our lives. Mount Dora is his home, so he's happy. But he's worried about Patrick and me.

What will my life be like without Father?

*

This morning Patrick was bruised and limping. I have to get him out of that foster home.

Father looked into me becoming a foster parent for Patrick. It's impossible because of my age and being on my own. The same goes for adoption. I'm so depressed. I'm afraid the people in that house could end up killing Patrick.

So Father has a plan. I'm scared but I want to do it.

*

Ethan's painting hung over a bookcase near the bed in Mary's room. As Bree lifted her cell to take a picture, she spotted a photograph on a shelf below.

Picking up the photo, she stared at the image of a young man.

She heard Mary burst into the room and come up beside her. The woman was gasping for breath. She obviously ran up the stairs.

"This looks like Andrew," Bree said softly, "but it's not, is it?"

Mary dropped down on the bed, trying to calm herself. "No."

"... Is it ... Does Andrew have a son?"

Mary didn't answer.

"Mary? Is this Andrew Brady's son?"

"Yes."

"Is he Jessie's too?"

"No."

Bree nodded. Now it made sense. Nick's silence. "This is what Nick and Kat have been doing in Florida."

"Bree, I'm sworn to secrecy. You can't tell anyone, not even Ethan. And please don't tell Nick how you found out. Promise me."

Bree sat down beside Mary. "Of course I promise."

"This is for your ears only. Nick and Kat went to Florida when they learned that Andrew might have a son, a child even Andrew didn't know about."

"And they found him." Bree stared at the picture, "Look at him, Mary! There's no question he's Andrew's son." Another thought struck her. "Does Jessie know?"

"No. I'm the only one who knows. And it has to stay that way." Mary reached for the photo and ran her fingers over the boy's face. "When I put this picture in here I never dreamed anyone would see it."

Bree met Mary's eyes, the personification of innocence. "What picture?" A lazy smile spread across her face.

Mary returned that smile. "Thank you." She reached for Bree's hand and squeezed.

Bree looked down at the photograph again. "This is going to shake the family down to its core."

*

Today I asked Patrick if he'd like to live with me. He hugged me for the first time. A BIG YES!.

Our plan is set. We're ready. Everything's in place. We can move fast when the time is right. ...

*

I didn't see Patrick for two days. I worried someone learned what Father and I are planning. Then he showed up crying. His clothes were torn. His skin was bright red under his ripped shorts. He raced around the house. His eyes weren't focused and his nose was bleeding. He kept screaming NO.

I kept calling his name but he didn't hear me. I blocked his path and said his name over and over until he finally saw me. He fell into my arms. He was dead weight. His arms and legs were limp. He was sobbing. I laid him on the couch and put a cloth against his nose.

I locked all the doors and called Father. Then I got Patrick into the bath. Father showed up with a van. We loaded my boxes and the clothes I ordered for Patrick from catalogues. Also emptied the fridge and pantry

I helped Patrick dress in new clothes. He was silent, just following my directions. Then I explained what was going to happen. He was my boy now. We were moving to a new town far away and would have our own house. No one would ever hurt him again. He'd go to school and could sing whenever he wanted.

He held onto me. He's come so far from that scared little boy in the orange grove who wouldn't let me come near him.

Today Patrick Cavanaugh was born. He's five-years-old, his birthday's October seventh, and he has a birth certificate to prove it.

When I asked Father how he got the birth certificate, he said it was best I didn't know.

As we headed for Mount Dora, I said goodbye to Sarasota and my beloved Henry and Frankie. They live in my heart, and I take the memories of them with me.

I pray Patrick's memories of his early years will fade. This precious boy deserves a good life now.

*

Jessie's schedule was jam-packed. Media interviews. Costume fittings. Hours in a studio recording the Original Cast Album, which was way behind schedule.

"Is Nick back?" she asked Abbie.

"Not yet."

"What's so important in Florida?"

Abbie shrugged. "He'll be back for opening night."

"I think I'm at the bottom of his list."

"Stop it. Nick wouldn't miss it."

The dressing room door opened. In walked one of Jessie's favorite people in the world. James Lovelock, Master Wigmaster. And trailing behind him, as always, his tiny dancing powder puff of a dog, Cosette.

James was an Asian man with porcelain skin, etched cheekbones and delicate long fingers. His humor was legendary, as were his skills.

James posed on the couch, his posture impeccable. Cosette leapt onto his lap. Today she wore bright turquoise bows above each tiny ear. "So tell me, how are things in Jessieville? And where's your delicious Nick?"

*

Tess Cavanaugh's third diary was all about their life in Mount Dora. They settled into the cottage Nick and Kat visited. Despite his young age, Patrick was enrolled in the parish school, having aced the intelligence tests. And Father Locato presided over St. Catherine's Catholic Church.

They never heard about any fallout from Patrick's vanishing. No one came looking for the boy.

I guess no one cares that a little boy disappeared. How sad. But how fortunate for us. Patrick never explained what made him run from that house that day. I'm just glad he knew he could come to me.

The first few weeks here were difficult. Patrick said very little, just sang. Now he loves it here. He's helping me plant a garden. He loves his school. His teachers rave about how smart he is. His memory is amazing. He can hear a song once and sing it perfectly.

Father found me a job in the rectory. The receptionist is on maternity leave, and Father doesn't think she'll be back. This helps pay the rent on our house. Plus I'm near Patrick at the school.

Despite the lack of news from Sarasota, I'll always be afraid someone will take Patrick away from me. If that ever happened, God forgive me, I'd have no reason to live.

Nick paused in his reading.

He assumed from the beginning that if he found Patrick he would bring him back to New York and integrate him into the family. He never once considered what the boy might want. Or the people who saved his life.

*

Patrick is now in the third grade. The school is doing CINDERELLA and Patrick is playing Prince Charming. He's so excited. And it's a musical. St. Catherine's promotes the arts. They have singing lessons and a dance class, which he loves.

Patrick doesn't like the singing class. He says he has his own style. But he wants to take acting lessons. So I searched and found a coach for him.

*

When Jessie stopped by the house to get her gown for opening night, she pressed Mary about Nick. "What's he looking into in Florida? Is he in any danger?" Jessie constantly feared for Nick's safety when he was involved in an investigation.

"No." Mary poured Jessie a mug of coffee.

"Then what?"

She shrugged. "He's not saying much."

Jessie's instincts were on high alert. "He's being too secretive about this. And the fact that he took Kat with him is truly peculiar."

"Kat wants to learn from the best. And Nick loves teaching her."

"Oh, come on, Mary. You can do better than that! What's Nick really doing?"

Now Mary wouldn't look at her. Nick was definitely up to something.

"When did you become so suspicious?" Mary asked.

"I've always been suspicious where Nick is concerned."

"Which is silly. He's off on a job with his daughter."

Jessie was now more curious than ever. Unfortunately, the only person who could answer her questions was over a thousand miles away.

And he wasn't talking.

70

*

Patrick received honors at the end of the fourth grade. And he helps Father at the church with odd jobs. He's also an altar boy. This boy who suffered so much has such a beautiful spirit. I'm a proud mom.

Patrick is in good health, with the exception of occasional nose bleeds. He won't let me help him when they occur. He can be such a tough guy at times.

*

I'm so proud of Patrick. He's twelve-years-old, good-hearted, polite and a hard worker. And that horrible home in Sarasota is finally a distant memory.

Patrick's really good-looking. He's tall with blond curls and gorgeous eyes. He still sings all the time, my greatest joy. But he's more of a talker now. Mention music and he talks nonstop.

We've become a nice little family - Patrick, Father and me. We finally told Patrick about finding him in the church that day. He said it meant the three of us were supposed to be together. It's God's will.

My father was a tough Irish farmer. He used to say life is a crap shoot. He was right. When Henry and I were raising Frankie we figured our golden years would be spent in Sarasota playing with our grandkids until God called us home.

But here I am in Mount Dora, raising another boy and relying on a very kind priest.

I'm happy.

*

The entries skipped ahead to Patrick's high school years. The boy chose to go to a public high school instead of the one attached to St. Catherine's. The public school specialized in the arts and was known for their musicals.

Patrick was the star in every one of their productions. Billy Bigelow in *CAROUSAL*. Tony in *WEST SIDE STORY*. Jean Valjean in *LES MISERABLES*. Erik in *PHANTOM OF THE OPERA*. Bobby in *COMPANY*. Joe Gillis in *SUNSET BOULEVARD*. And Jesus in *JESUS CHRIST SUPERSTAR*. Tess described Patrick's performances in great detail. She was so proud of him.

And while he was taking on these major roles, he was acing his classes, on a path to graduate early.

The next entry was just a little over a year ago:

I can't believe Patrick's senior year is over. He graduated at 15, such a brain. But he missed out on too many things because of his love for

71

the stage and singing. He's never had a girlfriend, which is astonishing. He's handsome and so sweet. And he missed his prom because he didn't have a girl. I remember my prom. That was when Henry kissed me for the first time.

Patrick's really shy. Maybe that's why he hasn't had a girlfriend. He's also a really good kid, and I hear girls want the bad boys these days. When Patrick's on stage that shyness disappears. He's self-assured and mature. As he's gotten older, he looks more and more like famous Broadway star Andrew Brady, a running joke between Patrick and me. I remember watching PBS when they broadcast HEARTTAKES. Andrew Brady and Jessica Kendle were the stars. When I watch Patrick singing onstage, I always think about how much he's like Brady. So professional.

I've noticed the way girls react to Patrick onstage. They idolize him. If only Patrick could transfer that magic to real life.

*

The last entry was a few months after the last one:

Now I know why I haven't felt well for so long.
I'm in renal failure.

I waited too long to see a doctor, always putting it off. So now I have a choice to make. I either accept my fate and let God decide when to take me and stay home with Patrick. Or I go into a place where I can get dialysis and pray I get a new kidney. At my age, I'm far down on the donor list.

It's a horrible decision because of Patrick, who's devastated by this news. I hate the idea of not being home with him every day. Not making his breakfast or listening to him sing or talk about his day. He pleaded with me to go for the dialysis because it will prolong my life. So that's what I'm going to do.

My time on this earth is limited. Father Joe is in his sixties now. Patrick's relied on us for so many years. Can he make it on his own?

Please, God, please. Watch over my precious boy.

*

Nick and Kat met Father Locato at a small Mexican restaurant in downtown Mount Dora. It was early for dinner, but the place was busy. They weren't really hungry, but they needed to order something to keep the table. Nachos and quesadilla. And a bourbon for Nick, a Scotch for Father Locato.

"First of all," Nick said, passing the diaries to the priest, "what you and Mrs. Cavanaugh did for Patrick was magnificent."

"Thank you, Mr. McDeare."

72

"I think you can call me Nick now."

Locato smiled. "I'm Father Joe to my friends." He looked at Nick, his expression a bit sad. "What are your plans for Patrick?"

"I think we start with a paternity test. Patrick obviously looks like Andrew, but we should verify it."

Father Joe nodded his agreement. "But what are your immediate plans?"

Nick sipped his bourbon, taking his time. "Patrick deserves to know he has family. What he chooses to do with that knowledge is up to him. As much as I'd love to have him come to New York, I have no intention of disrupting his life here. Andrew wouldn't want that either."

"Patrick won't leave Tess right now. She doesn't have long, Mr.— Nick. She was moved to hospice two months ago."

"I wouldn't expect him to leave her."

Father Joe took a moment. "When you first turned up, I was very upset. We've had our life here with Patrick. A good life, and I was afraid of things changing." He cleared his throat and took a sip of his Scotch. "But once I had time to look at the situation realistically ... I'm not getting any younger. My health isn't in crisis, but I feel the aches and pains of my age. A younger priest is about to take over some of my duties. It won't be long before Patrick finds himself alone. Now with you in the picture, I feel easier about it."

"I'd like to meet him. And tell him about Andrew."

"Let's go to Cohan's for dinner tomorrow night. Where he works. You need to hear Patrick sing to understand him. He'll come back with us the next day and stay for his two days off. You'll be able to spend time with him." Father Joe pulled out his cell phone. "The restaurant doesn't close until midnight or later. I usually stay at a hotel next door. I'll make us reservations."

CHAPTER 7

Cohan's was a larger space than Nick anticipated, probably able to seat three hundred. A small orchestra accompanied a young woman singing on the intimate stage. Not many diners paid attention. The chatter level of the restaurant was high.

They were led across the vast room to the next level up by the hostess. Inevitably Nick heard his name whispered. There was nothing he could do except ignore it. This was Patrick's night, not his.

Their table, unfortunately, was in a highly visible area along the railing. Nick put Kat front and center.

He scanned the room, searching for Patrick. Where was he?

Then he spotted him, pushing through the swinging doors from the kitchen.

Lean and lanky with a casual stride, Patrick Cavanaugh was fluid motion. His soft sandy curls bounced with each step. The shape of his eyes verified his lineage, only the color being different. They were bright blue, inherited from his mother Heidi. His smile was dazzling, his teeth a mirror image of Nick's. He was Andrew Brady twenty years younger.

He wore the standard Cohan waiter's uniform. Black slacks, teal dress shirt, black tie, black apron. It suited his fair complexion and hair.

To finally see Andrew's son in the flesh caught Nick's breath.

Patrick said hello to some diners before arriving at their table. Father Joe, who wasn't wearing his collar tonight, rose and hugged the boy. "Patrick, this is Nick McDeare and his daughter Kat."

The name obviously meant nothing to him, which pleased Nick. Kat couldn't stop grinning, a groupie in the presence of her idol.

"Can I get you something from the bar?" He was soft-spoken, his manner casual, his smile infectious.

As Patrick went off to get their drinks, Nick glanced at Kat, who was mesmerized. "It's amazing how much he looks like Uncle Andrew," she said over the laughter of nearby diners.

When the young man returned, he was accompanied by a beautiful black girl. "This is Lena, my partner."

"His runner," she corrected. "You'll see a lot of me. Patrick is popular on Saturday nights and spends most of his time up on that stage."

Nick wanted to sit down with this boy and have a conversation. Instead, he became a spectator, watching Patrick as he took their food order and waited on other tables.

Several people got up and sang, all quite good. Lena, Patrick's partner, sang an emotional love song, her voice both nuanced and powerful. Orlando seemed to have a rich talent pool. Then, as their swordfish was delivered, a chant went up for Patrick.

Lena grabbed Patrick's tray and gave him a playful push towards the stage. Running his hand through his hair, Patrick grinned.

That gesture with his hair … It was a habit of Nick's.

Patrick removed his apron, jogged down the short flight of stairs and leapt onto the stage in one smooth motion. Scattered applause rippled across the restaurant.

Speaking first with the conductor, Patrick took his time, composing himself as he moved center stage. Cupping the microphone, he began to sing 'The Rose' with nothing but the steady repeated chords of the piano behind him. His voice was low and soft at first, building as other instruments joined in. Nick never listened to the words before. Or maybe he did, but they took on new meaning in Patrick's hands.

The applause started before Patrick got to the final note. When the audience demanded more, he sang 'Empty Chairs at Empty Tables' from *LES MISERABLES,* ironically the song sung by Andrew Brady when he was in *LES MIS* at the Asolo. Then 'Maria' from *WEST SIDE STORY.* Patrick's joy was infectious, and the applause wouldn't stop. He seemed almost shy among the cheers, his humility a stark contrast with his enormous talent.

Patrick still had one more song. "My favorite. And his best," Father Joe whispered. "'Gethsemane' from *JESUS CHRIST SUPERSTAR. "*

The diners quieted down as if they knew what was coming, as if this was what they waited for. When there was absolute silence, Patrick began the song, depicting Christ's despair in the Garden of Gethsemane shortly before his Crucifixion. As Nick watched and listened, the writer in him kicked in, his mind taking note of what he was witnessing.

The boy had a gift, not only in his glorious voice, but in the way he used it. He caressed words, elongating consonants, or twisting a vowel with attitude. He'd establish a tempo, then change it mid-stream. Or pause, relishing the silence, before building to a crescendo. Sometimes he softened, his tenor vibrato so pure as to evoke tears. Other times his rich baritone filled the rafters, a sound that elicited goosebumps.

His body became part of the song, his torso and hands adding to the storytelling. Every movement had a meaning. His raw emotions were laid bare on his face, were reflected in his clear blue eyes. His instincts were honed, something that couldn't be taught or bought. He owned the audience.

Nick once dared Jessie to define a great actor in one sentence, what set them apart from the mediocre. She said they inhabited the skin of the character. That's exactly what Patrick did. Whether he was a lone revolutionary who survived a war as his friends died around him or an idealistic young man on the gang-infested New York streets who just fell in love or Christ agonizing about his imminent death, Patrick inhabited the skin of the character.

Andrew Brady left an indelible mark on the theatrical world, no doubt about it. But Andrew's greatest contribution may have been this young man who could reduce a clattering restaurant to dead silence the moment he began to sing.

Andrew was a mega-star.

Patrick was a phenomenon.

*

Lena cornered Patrick after he changed out of his uniform. "I've been trying to talk to you alone all night. Do you know who we've been waiting on? Nick McDeare!"

"Yeah. Father Joe said that was his name."

Lena grabbed him by the shoulders. "Nick! McDeare!"

Patrick's face remained a blank.

"You don't know who he is?" Patrick shook his head. "He's this hot author of a gazillion best-sellers. And he's married to Jessica Kendle."

That got Patrick's attention. "Jessica Kendle? She's about to open in—"

"—*DIANA* on Broadway, right."

"I thought she was married to Andrew Brady."

"She was. But after he died she married his brother."

"Nick McDeare is Andrew Brady's brother?"

"Yes, you moron. You should know this shit. Andrew Brady. Your doppelgänger."

People kept telling Patrick he looked like Andrew Brady. And sang like him. If only. "I'm meeting them next door at the hotel. Want to join us?"

"Are you kidding?" Lena spun in a circle. "No. I couldn't. Could I? No. I'd be tongue-tied. Besides, I have to work my other job early in the morning."

Patrick cracked up. Lena turned into a fangirl!

She shook an exaggerated finger at him. "You listen to me, Patrick Cavanaugh. Don't let this opportunity slip through your fingers. Nick McDeare and especially Jessica Kendle can do a world of good for your career. So go next door and kiss his gorgeous ass."

Patrick grinned. "Not my style."

"Date his daughter. That'll get you in with him. You have to admit she's pretty."

"She's beautiful." He glanced at Lena's finger in his face. "Uh, can I go now?"

*

Nick sat in the dimly lit bar of the hotel with Kat and Father Joe. They'd been waiting for Patrick for almost an hour.

"Nick, I have a favor to ask. Let me tell Patrick. Alone."

Nick took a sip of brandy. "I don't mind your telling him, but I'd like to be there."

"It's going to be a huge shock for him. After his first horrible five years, there were repercussions. It took him time to adjust. I'm worried about how he'll react to such a huge change in his life. He's already scared about losing Tess. Trust me," he added. "I want him to accept the truth as much as you do."

Nick rubbed his snifter between his hands, weighing the priest's words. "What do you mean, repercussions?"

"Here he comes," Kat whispered.

Patrick sat down at their table. He was dressed in jeans and a black shirt. "Sorry. I got held up by a fan of yours, Mr. McDeare."

"Call me Nick. And you're the one with fans."

"I didn't know you're a famous author. I haven't had much time to read." He fidgeted, seeming uncomfortable, and focused on Father Joe. "How's Tess?"

"Good. Anxious to see you."

Nick studied Patrick as he ordered a cola from the waitress. He seemed years younger than the singer onstage. Even younger than the self-assured waiter who took their order. He came off shy and introverted.

Patrick finally looked back at Nick. "You're Andrew Brady's brother?"

Nick nodded.

"People tell me I look like him."

"You do," Kat said.

"Everyone has a double. I loved his work. His voice." He dropped his gaze and chewed on a straw, trying to hide a yawn. The poor kid looked tired. It was a long night for him.

After an awkward silence, Nick asked, "How did you find the job at Cohan's?"

"A guy I went to high school with told me his brother worked there. I had to audition …" As Patrick dove into a long explanation, Nick remembered reading in Tess's diary that Patrick could talk non-stop if interested in the subject. Obviously, he loved Cohan's.

"Did you study voice, Patrick?" Kat wanted to know.

He crinkled his nose. A trait Nick noticed when he was singing. Andrew did the same thing. "I tried. But lessons are more about singing the perfect note than how you interpret the music. A song should tell a story. A monologue set to music." He finished his cola. "Are you a singer like your famous uncle?"

"NOO." Kat laughed. "I mean, I can sing, but not like Uncle Andrew. Writing is my passion."

Patrick looked from Nick to Father Joe. "How did you two meet?"

"Long story." Glancing at Father Joe, Nick drained his snifter. "Come on, Kat. We can pick this up tomorrow." He stood and dropped some bills on the bar check.

The priest took the cue. "Come to my room, Patrick. I want to talk to you."

The four of them rode the elevator upstairs and parted in the hallway, their rooms across from each other.

*

"Sit down, my boy." Father Joe eased himself into a chair in his room.

"Is this about Tess?" Patrick slouched on the bed, rubbing his eyes.

"No. This is about Nick."

"About how you met?"

Father Joe took his time. "Nick came to me a week ago. He was looking for a child." Father paused. "A baby that was left at St. Sebastian's in Sarasota."

"Me? Why?"

Again, Father Joe paused. "Besides being an author, Nick is a renowned investigative reporter."

"What does that have to do with me?"

Father Joe stared at his hands and licked his suddenly dry lips. "Nick discovered that his brother may have had a child years ago. So he

78

used his many skills to find out if it was true. That's what ultimately brought him to my doorstep." He finally looked up at Patrick.

Patrick straightened up. "I'm ... Are you saying ... I'm Andrew Brady's son?"

Father nodded. "Yes."

Patrick's face paled. All expression drained away as he stared at Father Joe, as he absorbed the news. Getting to his feet, Patrick moved slowly to the window.

"Are you all right, son?"

Silence.

"Patrick?" Father Joe went to him, placing a hand on his shoulder.

Patrick shook his head and looked at the priest. "You're sure?"

"We'll need a DNA test to be sure. But Nick's investigation was thorough. And it's obvious. You look like Andrew."

Patrick turned away, running his hand through his hair. He seemed dazed. He walked this way and that, his eyes dancing around the room.

"Once you've had time to think about it, you'll see—"

Patrick bolted for the door.

"Patrick, wait." Father Joe followed, stopping him in the open doorway. "Stay here tonight. We'll talk."

"I need to be alone," he mumbled. "Don't worry about me, okay?" He jogged down the hallway and pushed into a stairwell, the heavy door slamming behind him.

Father Joe crossed the hall and knocked on Nick McDeare's door.

*

Nick's first instinct was to search for Patrick.

Father Joe tried to reach the boy on his cell. It went straight to voice mail. "He lives in a house with some of the waiters. Maybe he went home." Father paced back and forth.

After Nick's initial reaction, he looked at the situation rationally. "Patrick just needs time to let the news sink in. He said he wanted to be alone. We should respect his wishes." Alone. What Nick always wanted when he was overwhelmed. "Why don't you go back to your room, Father, and wait. He may come back there. And you and I will stay in touch."

"Good idea."

*

Patrick took off down the street. His hands in his pockets, his head down, he walked block after block, his mind a jumble.

This was insane. He wasn't Andrew Brady's son. It wasn't possible. They lived in two different worlds.

79

Nick McDeare was wrong. Even great investigators made mistakes.

Someone must be playing a joke on the man, sending him down a rabbit hole. Mr. McDeare was apparently famous. Maybe someone took advantage of his desperation to find a link to his brother, knowing he would jump at the possibility that he might have a nephew. Patrick could understand that. Losing a brother would be painful. He couldn't even entertain the thought of his life without Tess.

Tess. He needed to talk to her. She'd see the situation clearly, like she saw everything. It was always so simple for her. He'd drive to Mount Dora right now.

Sprinting back to his car at the restaurant, he halted.

Something was tucked into the driver's window.

*

Nick sat in the dark, his jacket and tie off, his shirt sleeves rolled up, waiting. Being idle was his enemy.

His cell rang. He jumped on it. "McDeare."

"This is your agent, you bad boy. Why haven't you called me back?"

"Liz, for God's sake, it's the middle of the night."

"I was desperate to reach you. I've left two messages. Now listen to me. Your book will launch early, in two weeks, all because you got the manuscript in ahead of time. Linden Publishing is thrilled and wants to get sales rolling early for Christmas. Which means your book tour is moved up. It starts the first week of November and finishes before Thanksgiving."

The first week of …? "I can't miss Jessie's opening night."

"You won't. But you leave the next day. Plus, they want you to come to London again before Christmas, even though it's not in your contract."

"Email me the details. And no to London." He clicked off. The book tour. The last thing he wanted to do. Or think about. Nick slumped further down into the chair.

Just as the sun was coming up, there was a light tap on his door.

Patrick stood in the doorway. He looked exhausted. Not surprising. He'd waited tables for hours, performed the equivalent of a Broadway show and got slammed with life-changing news.

Nick opened the door wide for him. "Where've you been?"

"Walking. Then sitting in my car." Patrick pulled something from his pocket and handed it to him. Nick's business card? He flipped it over. His address and cell number were written on the back.

In Andrew's handwriting.

"I found it on my car window. Why'd you put it there?"

Nick shook his head and handed the card back to him. "I didn't."

"Your daughter?"

"Kat's been asleep all night."

*

Kat wasn't asleep. She was crouched on the other side of the closed connecting door, listening.

Eavesdropping was her forte. And highly informative. Besides, she was worried about Patrick.

*

"Then who did?"

Now was not the time to tell Patrick about Andrew's ghostly presence. "It doesn't matter."

"Father Joe?"

"Let it go. It's not important."

Patrick slid both the card and his hands in his pockets and paced away from Nick. "This whole Andrew Brady thing. I've been thinking about it. Someone's playing a terrible joke on you."

"It's no joke."

"It has to be. How do you explain Andrew being my father? I lived my whole life in Florida. He lived in New York."

Nick went to his overnight bag and pulled out the *LES MISERABLES* program. He brought it with him in anticipation of just such a moment. Opening to the cast page, he handed it to Patrick and sat back down at the table. "Andrew worked at the Asolo in Sarasota one summer. That's where he met your mother."

Patrick's face changed subtly as he looked at the program. "Which one is supposed to be my mother?"

"Heidi Breen. A stage name. Her real name is Heidi Barstow."

Patrick stared at her picture before tossing the program on the bed. "This is crazy."

"Sit down and I'll explain." Seeing the boy's hesitation, he added, "Come on. You might as well hear the whole story. From the beginning."

Patrick inched down onto the chair across from Nick. "So where is this woman now?"

"She's dead." Nick looked down. "I'm sorry, Patrick."

Taking his time, Nick began with Kat's discovery that Andrew might have a child. He explained the trail of clues, the people he spoke with, the files in the basement of CPS, everything that led him to Patrick. "You have the eyes, Patrick. Everything about you screams Andrew. Even you admit you resemble him."

81

Patrick looked away. Nick realized he hit him with a lot. News that came out of nowhere. He needed time to compute it all. "So … Heidi … who you say is my mother … she died from drugs?"

"Someone slipped her Ecstasy. Her good friend said she wasn't a druggie. She was a girl who dreamed of a career on the stage."

Patrick snorted. "Yeah. Until she got pregnant." He shook his head.

"If the prospect of a career meant more to her than you did, she would have aborted you. She didn't. That's how much you were wanted and loved."

"And then there's Andrew. Who wasn't interested in finding out if he had a kid."

"I won't make excuses for my brother. We were raised separately, so I wasn't around. I've been told that women were always trying to entrap him, so he didn't believe Heidi. At that time, Andrew was on a trajectory that eventually brought him the stardom he craved. That was his focus. But I do know this. He loved kids. If he'd known about you, he would have loved you. Even so, we can't assume you would have had the perfect family: a mom and dad who lived together in a happy household."

Again, Patrick shook his head and sat forward, dropping his face into his hands. "So two people slept together one summer and created a kid. A mistake I had to pay for."

So much for Patrick not being bitter. "I learned the hard way that our lives are often the result of other people's mistakes."

"What do you mean?"

Nick said too much. He didn't want to go there. "Nothing."

"Why do you keep avoiding my questions?"

He was right. Being secretive wasn't the way to earn Patrick's trust. "I was put up for adoption at birth because my father didn't want me. And the people who adopted me were more interested in their careers than in me." God, it sounded trite compared to what Patrick went through.

"But your life turned out okay."

"And so will yours. A new chapter is beginning for you, Patrick. It's a blank page, waiting to be written. You hold the pen."

"You sound like a writer. Pretty words, but what do they mean?"

They sat in silence.

Patrick exhaled slowly. "So what's next? Where do I go from here?"

"That's up to you."

"Really?" Patrick straightened up. "You spend all this time and energy searching for me, you dump the info on me, and then you sit back and tell me what I do with it is up to me?"

"Originally I hoped you'd come back to New York with Kat and me. But that was before I got to know Father Joe and read Tess's diaries."

Patrick looked genuinely surprised. "You read— I haven't even read them." He slouched back and crossed his arms. "Did she write about me?"

"They're all about you. From the first time she heard you singing in that orange grove."

Patrick looked away. "Did she write about … where I lived before …"

"Yes."

The boy's eyes darted to Nick and away again. He was obviously uncomfortable with Nick knowing about his past. Who could blame him? That stuff was private.

Nick stood up. "We should let Father Joe know you're okay."

*

After attending Mass with Father Joe, Patrick agreed to leave his car at the restaurant and let Nick drive the four of them to Mount Dora. He hadn't slept at all and didn't trust his driving.

He was also getting a headache, his vision was messed up and his breathing was labored. He recognized the signs. This hadn't happened in years.

He climbed into the back seat of the SUV with Father Joe, closed his eyes, rubbed his temples and focused on breathing.

"Are you all right, Patrick?" Father Joe whispered.

He nodded.

"Is it one of those attacks again?"

"I'm fine."

Stress brought it on. And exhaustion. He scrunched into the corner, his eyes still closed. But sleep was just out of reach …

He was aware of the voices in the car, snippets of conversation. They talked about him, his songs at the restaurant … how talented he was … just like Andrew … a book tour … writing class … school … opening night … someone named Anthony.

A new voice pushed in … familiar. He couldn't place it … telling him not to panic … things would fall out the way they were supposed to.

Patrick woke up abruptly and looked around. They were at the rectory.

The headache was gone, but his vision was still off.

Father Joe touched his arm before getting out of the car. "Tell Tess I'll come by tonight. And take care of yourself."

"Could you drop me at Sacred Heart?" Patrick asked Nick as the car pulled away. "I want to see Tess. I can walk home from there. It's close."

As Nick pulled under the portico of Sacred Heart, he turned to Patrick. "Get some sleep tonight. Tomorrow we can—"

"I'll be with Tess tomorrow. That's why I come back here on my days off."

"I'd like to meet her."

Patrick got out of the car. "I don't think it's a good idea." It was a terrible idea. "Her health is—" Realizing how rude he must sound, Patrick kicked at a stone on the sidewalk. "Sorry. It's just that I don't want to upset her."

Nick nodded. "How about dinner tomorrow night? Both you and Father Joe."

"Uh, sure." Patrick tapped the top of the car. "Thanks for the ride."

*

Nick called Father Joe as soon as Patrick disappeared into Sacred Heart. "What happened in the car with Patrick? What did you mean, attack?"

"Patrick has occasional attacks. Headaches, breathing spasms. His vision gets blurry. Sometimes a nosebleed. A result of his early life. His terror. The beatings. He repressed it back then. It surfaced later."

"Panic attacks?"

"Something like that."

"Why didn't Tess mention these in the diaries?"

"She doesn't know about them. She never knew. Patrick hid them from her. He never wanted her to worry about him. A doctor gave him pills which seemed to help."

"I didn't see him take a pill."

"He probably didn't have them with him. It hasn't happened much as he's gotten older."

"What brings it on?"

"A combination of things. Stress. Exhaustion. Hunger."

"The news about Andrew?"

"Possibly. Plus, he didn't sleep at all last night. It's the end of his work week when he's tired anyway. And I don't think he ate much in the last twenty-four hours."

"I appreciate your explaining it, Father.

"It's something you should know about."

84

"Kat and I can't stay in town much longer. She's missed too much school. Plus, my wife's opening night is coming up. And my book tour. Patrick agreed to have dinner tomorrow night. We'd like you to join us. What does he like to eat?"

CHAPTER 8

Tess was propped up in bed when Patrick swung into her room. He'd stopped in the public bathroom on the way and splashed water on his face, forcing himself to perk up for her sake.

"You look good," he said, kissing her.

"You don't. What's wrong?" There was no fooling Tess.

"Nothing. Just working too hard."

"You need to take better care of yourself, Patrick. Plenty of rest and good food." She wagged her finger at him but couldn't help laughing. "Don't give me that look. I mean it."

"I know. And I will. Promise." He pulled the chair over and took her hand. "Father Joe came to Orlando last night and brought some friends, Nick McDeare and his daughter."

"Nick McDeare? The author?"

"You know who he is?"

"Sure. I haven't read his books, but I've read about him in magazines and have seen him on TV."

"What do you think of him?"

"He's impressive. He made a name for himself as a reporter for— Oh, let me think a minute. I think it was *The Washington Post*. Also as a best-selling author. He was quite a playboy at one time, but then he married Jessica Kendle and seemed to settle down."

A playboy? Yeah, Patrick could see it. Especially after the way Lena gushed about Nick.

"Imagine. You met Andrew Brady's brother!" It was a joke between them – Patrick looking like Andrew. "How does Father Joe know Nick McDeare?"

"He, uh, came by the church and they got talking." It wasn't a lie. Just not the whole truth.

"Imagine that. So. Did he like your singing?"

Patrick described the evening but said nothing about the possibility of being Andrew Brady's son. He was Tess's son. He would always be her son.

They talked for over an hour. Patrick described the new songs he was working on, Tess always interested in his music. When her dinner arrived, she pushed it away. "Come on, Tess," he urged, feeding her a spoonful of soup. "You need to keep up your strength. Just another spoonful. Do it for me, okay?" He patiently cajoled and teased her, keeping up a steady stream of chatter, until the bowl was empty. Afterwards, he did what she loved best. He sang softly until she fell asleep.

Heading back outside he was surprised to see the McDeares' SUV pull up. Kat leapt out of the front and climbed into the back. "Come on. Get in. We'll drive you home."

Patrick had no choice but to slide into the passenger seat. "You've been waiting all this time?"

"No biggie."

The car was filled with the tantalizing smell of food. Patrick's stomach growled in response.

Arriving at the cottage, Kat handed him a large Take-Out bag.

"We got you some dinner," Nick said. "Thought you might be hungry."

"Starving, actually." Patrick grabbed the bag. "Thank you."

"See you tomorrow night."

Patrick unpacked the bag in the tiny kitchen. Fried chicken and mashed potatoes.

Patrick had loved fried chicken since that long-ago day he fled to Tess's house after— She fed him fried chicken and mashed potatoes …

*

Dinner the next night was at Tokyo Rose in Mount Dora. Father Joe chose the restaurant because it just opened. Neither he nor Patrick had eaten Japanese before, and he was feeling adventurous. "If Patrick ever ends up in New York," Father joked, "he better develop some cosmopolitan taste."

The priest was hesitant about eating raw fish. Not Patrick. He not only tried sushi, he loved it. Buoyed by Patrick's sense of adventure, Nick ordered for all of them. Japanese dumplings. Shrimp and Vegetable Tempura. Negamaki, Nick's favorite, marinated sirloin wrapped around scallions. And on and on.

Shy at first, Patrick loosened up as the meal progressed. He talked about his favorite musical roles and the new songs he was working on. He engaged Kat, asking about her interests. She told him about Bertie, about his being cast in *DIANA*, and the fact that he was only FIFTEEN! They ended up in a long conversation about new singing groups. Out of Nick's league.

Nick was pleased to see them hitting it off. They were first cousins, Andrew's son and Nick's daughter. There should be strong ties between them.

He nixed Patrick's intention to take the bus back to his job the next day. Nick would drive him. He'd already arranged for his plane to relocate from Sarasota to Orlando International Airport. "We have to fly north tomorrow. Kat's tutor called. She needs to get back to her schoolwork."

"I'd rather stay here," she pouted.

"We'll come back down soon for a visit." Nick eyed Patrick, who was focused on his food. He glanced at Father Joe who was also watching the boy.

Nick was quiet on the drive to Orlando the next day. Patrick and Kat jabbered, talking about music and Kat's writing.

As they parted at Cohan's it dawned on Nick he didn't know when he'd see Patrick again. "Look, if you want to come up to New York, you're always welcome. You have my address and cell number. Call any hour of the day or night."

Patrick nodded, looking from one to the other. It was hard to read his expression. He politely shook Nick's hand and thanked him for dinner last night.

Turning to Kat, she clearly surprised him by giving him a hug. He seemed to tense at Kat's touch. "Please come up to New York," she pleaded. "Even if it's just for a quick visit."

Patrick smiled before ducking into Cohan's.

Despite spending the past few days together, Patrick Cavanaugh remained an enigma to Nick.

*

Kat was as quiet as her father on the flight home. She was sad about leaving Patrick. And if she felt this way, how must her dad feel?

She glanced across the aisle at him, sitting like a statue, staring out the window. Usually he made phone calls. Or was busy working his schedule in his day planner.

She wished she could call Bertie. Besides Mary, he was the only one who knew all about Patrick, and he was sworn to secrecy. She trusted Bertie with her life. But Dad didn't know that Bertie knew. And he'd be mad if he knew that Bertie knew.

So she stared out her own window, hoping that Patrick Cavanaugh would come to New York soon so she could tell the world.

*

They'd been back in New York for a week, but Nick couldn't point to one thing he accomplished. Time seemed to just fritter away. He'd sit at his desk and stare out the window, and suddenly it was three hours later. Or join the others for dinner, and the next thing he knew his plate was clean. One afternoon he and Anthony went to the park to hit some balls, and afterwards Nick couldn't remember a thing. Not even their conversation. It was as if his body came home but his brain stayed in Florida.

There was nothing but silence from Patrick. If he had any curiosity about his new family, he wasn't showing it. Nick hated to admit it, but he missed the young man.

Kat, thank God, filled Mary in on their days with Patrick, relieving Nick of that duty. But now Mary was nagging Nick about telling the family. The thing was ... he just couldn't talk about it yet. Besides, they may never see Patrick Cavanaugh again, so why get everyone excited, or in Jessie's case, upset?

So he holed up in his office, brooding and pacing. Andrew haunted his footsteps and invaded his thoughts. The program from *LES MISERABLE* now lived on Nick's desk. He thumbed through it often, rereading Andrew's bio, staring at his brother's publicity photo. At that age, the resemblance between Andrew and Patrick was even more remarkable.

On a whim, Nick scaled the stairs two at a time to the fourth-floor storage room. There were boxes up here filled with Andrew's memorabilia. Nick sat on the floor for hours, pouring over programs and reviews, photos and magazine articles.

A tiny wooden chest held the personal items Andrew was wearing at the time of his death. Jessie said she couldn't bear to look at these things. All they did was bring back the horrible day her husband was shot.

Nick opened the chest. There wasn't much. Nick held his brother's wedding band up to the light. At one time this ring belonged to Jessie's father, Tony. Tony was the only father Andrew ever knew. It meant the world to him to wear it. Next Nick dug out a Saint Genesius medal. Patron saint of actors. Jessie told him the story behind it. Given to both Andrew and Jessie by Tony, a religious man, they always wore the medals when performing. They became superstitious about them, hiding them inside their costumes. Nick flipped the medal over. Andrew's name was engraved on the back.

Nick took the chest back to his office and stowed it in his locked desk drawer.

He decided to surprise Jessie early one evening by bringing her dinner during a break in dress rehearsal. Mary put together a basket, all the things on Jessie's rigid diet.

She seemed pleased to see him. And she looked great. Healthy. Full of energy. Jessie was at her best when she was working. Except for London. "Go ahead and eat. I'm not hungry."

Jessie dug into her salad. "So what took you down to Florida? And for so long?"

He didn't answer immediately. He should tell her about Patrick. Right now. But she was opening in a huge Broadway musical in days. What if the news of Patrick angered her? Or worse, set her back? "Just something I had to look into. Nothing important." As soon as the lie was out of his mouth, he felt guilty.

He'd tell her next week. When the pressure of opening night was over. Damn. He couldn't tell her then. The book tour. The damned book tour.

Nick changed the subject. "Do you still wear that religious medal your dad gave you?

"St. Genesius? No. It was Andrew's and my tradition. It doesn't feel right wearing it. Not without him." She took a sip of water. "What made you think of the medal?"

Nick shrugged. "I was thinking about my own superstitious habits when I write." More lies.

"When does your book tour start?"

"The day after you open. But it's over by Thanksgiving."

"Thanksgiving … What do I do about Thanksgiving? It's always a big gathering for us."

Nick shrugged. "I guess you spend it at the house. With us." Did he really just suggest that? But then, why not? She shouldn't be alone.

A man came through the door. Tall with dark curly hair and wearing a headset, he gave off the vibe of being in charge. If Nick didn't know Quill Llewellyn was the director of *DIANA,* he'd assume this man was. "Jessie, here are the revisions Quill wants—" He spotted Nick. "Oh, sorry." He backed up.

"No, don't go," Jessie said, dabbing her mouth with a napkin. "It's time you two met. Nick McDeare, Larry Williams. Larry is our stage manager and an old friend. Andrew and I spent many happy hours with Larry and his wife Gloria back in the day."

Larry reached out and shook Nick's hand. No male challenge in the grip, Nick noted. And Larry released his hand first. After dropping what looked like several pages of script on Jessie's dressing table, he smiled and left.

"Larry's the best in the business," Jessie said absently, scanning the pages. "He and Andrew were really close."

Andrew. The outgoing brother. Loved by all.

Nick stood up. "Have to get back to work."

*

It was a trying week for Patrick. Torn between a desire to deny any tie to Andrew Brady for Tess's sake and his natural curiosity about the man, he spent hours on his cell, researching everything he could find on Andrew. Also Nick McDeare. It would have been a lot easier if he had a laptop or iPad. Magnifying the print to read it on his old cell phone was a pain.

To make matters worse, there was now an elephant in the room when he was with Tess. And of course she noticed. He tried not to lie, blaming his distraction on other things.

His work suffered, the simple act of getting a dinner order correct suddenly a challenge. His singing, however, was never better, according to Lena. Was he subconsciously playing out his life onstage?

He had another attack. Not while singing, thankfully, but close. He was delivering meals to a table when they told him his nose was bleeding. Grabbing a napkin, he ran to the dressing room. Dizziness hit him. His vision blurred. He couldn't get a deep breath. It took him twenty minutes to get it together again.

When he drove to Mount Dora at the end of the week, he stopped at the rectory before visiting Tess. He needed to tell Father Joe about what was happening to him.

"You're worried about Tess," Father explained. "And you're carrying around a huge secret. That's too much pressure, Patrick. Are you getting enough sleep? And eating?"

Patrick was definitely having trouble sleeping.

"Taking your pills?"

"When I remember."

"Set your alarm on your phone. That will help you remember. Now, listen. I've been thinking about this," Father Joe said. "I think you should tell Tess about Andrew Brady and the McDeares."

"No." Patrick was adamant. "I won't upset her—"

"I don't think she'll be upset. She'll be relieved."

"Relieved that she's being pushed out by—"

"Listen to me." He gripped Patrick's hands. "I know you don't like to talk about this, but we have to. Tess isn't getting better. And she knows it. We had a long talk about it the other day. She's worried about you. She's in a lot of pain. I think she's hanging on because she doesn't want you to be alone."

"Stop it, Father." He shook off the priest's hands. "The dialysis is helping. You know it is. She'll get a new kidney and—"

"She's not going to get a new kidney, Patrick, not at her age—"

"I don't want to hear this!"

"I know you don't, but you must. You have to face reality, Patrick." Father's voice was gentle. "I think knowing that you have a family out there will give Tess peace. And that it's Andrew Brady's family will not only make her happy, it will make her laugh." He grinned at Patrick. "You know it will, after teasing you about looking like him all these years."

"But if I tell her, she'll feel free to die, right?"

Father Joe rose and paced to the window. "I know you don't mean to, but you're being selfish. Tess is suffering now. You have the capacity to bring her comfort." He turned to Patrick. "She won't die. She'll go home to God. Where there is no pain. You've been blessed to have this remarkable woman in your life. She's been the best mother you could have had. But now you have to do for her what she did for you. Set her free. You'll see her again."

*

Kat slid into the breakfast nook across from Mary. She had a few hours before her ballet class. "I'm worried about Dad."

"Me, too." Mary layered the bottom of a casserole with sliced zucchini.

"He won't talk about Patrick."

"Patrick is a bird with a broken wing. That's how your dad sees kids who've had a tough time of it. He wants to fix them. Make them whole. Nurtured and loved."

"Like he did with me."

"And Anthony." Mary added a layer of grated mozzarella. "When Nick first arrived here, Anthony was one sad little boy. The man he thought was his daddy, Andrew, had been murdered. And his mother's grief turned her into a recluse. Nick helped Anthony through some terrible times, including finding out that Andrew wasn't his real dad. And that the man who killed Andrew WAS his real dad. He did the same with you. You were miserable when your mom died and you had to come here to live with a father you didn't know."

"I was horrible to him." Kat hated thinking about those terrible days. She was so angry about losing her mom she took it out on her new dad.

"But he never gave up on you and look at the result. You're Daddy's girl now." She added diced onions to the casserole. "Let your dad brood about Patrick. He'll figure it out." She glanced up at Kat before going back to her casserole. "How do YOU feel about Patrick? Are you jealous?"

"Why would I be jealous?"

"Because of the attention he gets from your dad." Mary focused on her next layer of zucchini.

"No. I'm not jealous. Far from it." Kat glanced out the window. A gorgeous bluebird landed on the sill and looked directly at her. "You were right, Mary. About a special connection between Patrick and me. I don't know if it's because of the bond between Dad and Uncle Andrew, but I felt it right away when I met him." The bluebird was joined by a smaller brown and beige bird. The small bird groomed his ashy breast, puffing it out, before they both stared at Kat. This was getting bizarre.

"And how does he feel?"

"Hmm?"

"Patrick. How does he feel about you?"

"Um, he's hard to read. But he's chatty with me, and this is a guy who clams up more than Dad. He's shy. Really shy. You'll see when you meet him. If you meet him."

"You don't think he'll come to New York?"

"I don't know. We haven't heard from him." The birds continued to stare, sending a chill down Kat's back. Her gaze shifted back to Mary. "Can I ask you something weird?"

"Weird in general, or weird for you?"

Kat rolled her eyes. "Do you think Andrew can manipulate birds?"

Mary finally looked up at her. "Birds? What are you talking about?"

Kat glanced back at the sill.

The birds were gone.

She started to laugh. "Never mind. I think I'm losing my mind."

"What else is new?" Mary winked and went back to her casserole.

*

"There's something I want to tell you, Tess."

They were spending the afternoon together on one of Patrick's days off. She didn't look well but was obviously making an effort for him.

"Let me guess," she teased. "You've fallen in love."

Patrick blushed and looked down. "You're my girl. You know that."

"It's time you found someone your own age. I'm an old bag of old bones."

"Stop it. You're not."

"… What's this about, Patrick?"

He took her hand, playing with her wedding band. She never took it off, not the whole time he knew her.

"You want my ring?" she again joked. "Is that it?"

Patrick smiled. "No. But it's beautiful." He sighed.

"What is it, sweetie?"

He swallowed, focusing on her ring … "Nick McDeare didn't accidentally show up here. He … was looking for me. See, it turns out …" Again he swallowed. "It turns out … I'm Andrew Brady's son."

He watched Tess's expression register surprise. She said nothing, allowing him to describe in his own halting way how Nick put it all together. How Father Joe gave him the news. How kind Nick was when Patrick showed up in his hotel room that night.

When he finished, Tess held out her arms. Patrick laid against her, listening to her heartbeat, like he did when he was a little boy. It always made him feel safe. The tears finally fell.

She stroked his hair and kissed the top of his head. "Oh, my sweet boy, don't cry. This is wonderful news. My prayers have been answered."

*

A Broadway opening was always an extravaganza. For Nick, it was more like a circus.

It began when he went to Jessie's dressing room and discovered the return of James Lovelock, who was fitting Jessie's wig. The man was dressed from head-to-toe in purple satin. A hot pink boa spiraled around his slender neck.

Seeing Nick, James stopped what he was doing, spread his arms wide and shrieked, "Nick, you gorgeous hunk of a man, give me a hug." Before Nick could object, he was tangled in the boa, feathers in his mouth and up his nose. "I still want your yummy locks," James added, fingering Nick's hair.

Nick leapt back. "Where's your partner in crime?"

"Cosette?" James pointed to the floor. There she was, the gnarly little mutt, purple sequined bows above her ears, licking his shoes. The dog had a shoe fetish.

Nick sidled away and approached Jessie, kissing her cheek. "When did Mr. Wiglet return?"

"I thought I told you. I'm thrilled he's back." She dabbed more blush on her cheeks. "It's chaos around here, but you should be used to it by now."

He'd never get used to it.

Jessie was infinitely calmer tonight than she was at the opening in London. But then, the show should be second nature to her by now.

Nora bustled into the room, costumes in her arms. "Hey there, Nick. You look great. Always love a man in a tux." She hung up the clothes and turned to him. "Is the whole family here?"

"All except Anthony." And Patrick.

"He's visiting his friend on Long Island," Jessie explained. "He'll come another night."

Anthony saw *DIANA* in the West End. He would never see the show again. It would always remind him of his stay in London. Which he hated.

A parade of flowers marched through the door and were added to the funereal display along the wall. Nick spotted his lilies on Jessie's dressing table. Next to three other arrangements. He read the cards, knowing his wife was particular about which flowers she kept close.

Mary sent red roses from the whole family. Abbie and Willie chose white carnations. The third vase was a single purple orchid. The card attached said: Glad to be back with the best. Strut your stuff in memory of the good times. Larry.

The director, Quill Llewellyn, hustled into the room. "Nick!" They shook hands before Quill talked briefly to Jessie.

Larry popped his head in the door. "Did you hear the last call, Jessie? Ten minutes." He nodded to Nick before hurrying down the hall.

Nick didn't know how Jessie could hear anything. It was nuts backstage.

Nick sidled over to Jessie and whispered, "I'll see you afterwards. Go. Go be brilliant." What he always said.

*

As Patrick took a quick break, Lena followed him across the restaurant. "Cohan's TV commercial started running today. And you're the star, baby. Take a look while you're on break." She backed up. "I'll grab those steaks for you. Take your time. I got you covered."

Patrick did a search on his cell as he headed outside for some air.

Wow. Lena wasn't kidding. Yes, the interior of the restaurant and the food were highlighted, but Patrick was the only one shown singing. Snippets of three songs. It actually looked okay.

He texted it to Father Joe with the message: Show this to Tess.

*

As he left Jessie's dressing room, Nick spotted Kat and Bertie down the hallway. He gave the young man a bear hug, knowing what a big moment this was. His Broadway debut. "We have to go, Kat."

Kat shyly kissed Bertie on the cheek before they left the backstage area.

"You been hanging out with Big Bird, Dad?"

Irritated, Nick brushed away the pink feathers on his tux. Kat extracted one from his hair.

Father and daughter made their way down the aisle to their seats. Amid the inevitable whispers and finger-pointing.

Just as the curtain was about to rise, a lone pink feather floated over the audience, sending both Nick and Kat into gales of silent laughter.

*

Bertie Castro's heart raced as he stood in the wings, waiting for his featured dance with the girl playing Young Diana. Hearing the cue, Bertie stepped onto the stage and extended his long, graceful arm to his partner.

This was what he lived for, speaking with his body. Lifting the girl high over his head, he glided across the stage. It was three minutes of soaring, of letting the music inspire his legs, his arms, his emotions.

It was over too soon. He wanted to relive the dance, but he couldn't remember it. He'd been so 'in the moment' that his mind took flight and his heart took over.

*

Nick felt his phone vibrating during the first act of *DIANA*. At intermission he hurried through the lobby and outside, checking his texts. Wading through the nonsense, he got to one that made his heart soar.

From Father Joe: Wouldn't Andrew be proud?

Attached was a video about Cohan's.

And Patrick was the star.

*

Patrick lifted the mike onstage at Cohan's. Thinking of Tess and their years together, he began the song 'Memory.'

He took his time, every word hitting home. He sang about his yesterdays and the mystery of tomorrow. It was a song of highs and lows, of fear and hope, of melancholy remembrance. When he finished, his eyes were filled with tears.

The audience roared, their applause refusing to die down.

That's what Lena told him afterwards.

Patrick didn't see or hear any of it.

He'd been lost in the world of the music.

*

In Jessie's final moment as Diana, a specter singing goodbye to her grieving young sons, she drew on the memory of losing Andrew. The devastation of knowing she would never see him again. As she reached the last note, she knew without a doubt it was the best she'd ever sung the difficult song.

The spotlight disappeared. The stage went to black as the curtain call began.

Jessie waited, counting to three before finally appearing before the jubilant audience. She dropped her head, then looked back up, all the way to the upper balcony.

She took two more calls, solo.

What a high to be back on Broadway.

A high like no other!

CHAPTER 9

The opening night party was the usual fare. A lot of lobster and caviar, air-kissing, fake laughter, name-dropping and nobodies pretending to be somebodies. Nick hated it.

Jessica Kendle made a grand entrance, beaming at the applauding crowd, her husband on her arm. Nick did his part, sticking to his wife's side, saying the appropriate things to the appropriate people and answering the media's appropriate questions. Any talk of his marriage was inappropriate.

Kat and Jessie hadn't spoken a word to each other, annoying the hell out of Nick. He was getting tired of this. And Kat was clinging to Bertie, something else that was ticking him off. He wasn't angry with Bertie, who was aware of Nick's annoyance. No. It was his pushy daughter. He needed to remind Kat that she was only thirteen years old.

Realizing his irritability had nothing to do with his daughter, was instead due to the theatrical phoniness and the plastic people surrounding him, he decided to remain silent. Why make things worse?

Nick and Jessie were photographed dancing. Holding his wife in his arms was the only thing he enjoyed the entire night. Jessie was at her best as they danced, her eyes locked with his, her smile genuine. For the first time in months he was sad about the state of their marriage. They'd been more than husband-and-wife. More than lovers. They'd been friends, and he missed his friend right now.

As the dull night progressed, Nick kept pulling out the video of Patrick. It passed the time as he waited to leave. He was stuck here until the reviews came in. Jessie had a tradition. She read the critics' opinions in the back seat of the car with Nick on their way home.

Nick sat at their table, cell phone in hand, keeping an eye on Kat and Jessie. Kat was eating with Bertie. All was well there. As for Jessie, she was dancing with Larry-What's-His-Name. They looked comfortable together. In fact, Jessie looked relaxed, not a word usually associated with his wife on opening night.

Quill sat down beside him, drink in hand, diverting his attention. "Was tonight better than London?"

"Better cast," Nick said.

Quill looked around at the crowd. "I don't know, Nick. This is all becoming so boring."

"What is?"

"This. This whole Broadway thing. Nothing excites me anymore. There are no great new playwrights, no new theaters to break in. And the talent pool is stagnant. They're all the same-old, same-old. Except Jessie, of course," he added.

"Of course."

"I want to be EXCITED again. I want something or someone to INSPIRE me." He was starting to sound drunk. "There is one thing. I have a new musical in development. Kind of an updated or NEW version of *CAROUSAL*, but not really *CAROUSAL*. It was actually Andrew Brady's death that inspired me. A young and upcoming star is murdered at the end of the first act and is a ghost throughout the second. A real love story. But I wouldn't bring it to Broadway to be surrounded by all this HYPE. And where the critics can TRASH it if they're in a bad mood on that particular night. No. I'd go regional theater. Or Off-Broadway. Let it find a comfy intimate home." He slurped his drink. "Ah, who the hell knows, right?" He got to his feet. "Sorry. I'm rambling. Where are the damned reviews? I want to get out of here."

Nick shook his head. Andrew Brady's death inspired Quill? Someone new to excite him? "Subtle, Andrew," he whispered. "Real subtle."

*

The reviews were mixed. *The New York Times* hated the use of a video screen across the back of the stage, calling it a crutch for a bad script, but they loved Jessie. *The New York Post* was lukewarm about everything. "Miss Kendle didn't catapult me out of my seat with her performance, as she usually does." *The Daily News* was a rave for Jessie but a pan of the production.

On top of the so-so reviews, Jessie wasn't able to read them alone with Nick, as was customary. She had to hear her fate in front of Mary, Abbie, Kat and Bertie. They were all in the back of the car as Willie dropped Bertie off at home before heading to the brownstone. The plan was for Jessie to sneak out the back way through Willie and Abbie's place in case the paparazzi were watching. Which of course they were.

Mary and Kat said good night and disappeared up the front staircase.

The reviews put Jessie in a mood. As she walked down the hallway to the back porch, she turned to Nick. "Would you mind if I stayed the night? I don't feel like being alone."

99

Nick hesitated.

Jessie rolled her eyes. "Never mind. I'm going."

"Jessie, wait." He grabbed her hand. "Stay. Sleep in your own bed."

"With you?"

Again, he paused.

"What are we doing, Nick? We live in separate places. We're living separate lives. We might as well be divorced."

"Is that what you want?"

Jessie didn't have the strength to keep up the pretense anymore. Dropping her head in her hands, she started to cry.

Nick's arms slid around her, and he pulled her against his chest. "Jessie, what is it? The reviews? Is that what this is about? Or are you just exhausted?" He stared down at her, those sleepy eyes warm and compassionate.

"It's us, Nick. I miss us."

He cupped her cheek, rubbing her skin with his thumb. "Jess, it would be so easy to go to bed with you tonight. So easy."

"It's what I want. More than anything. But I don't think I could stand your breaking my heart again."

The eyes changed. The warmth dissipated. "Break your heart? What are you talking about? You were the one who—"

"Slept with someone else, yes. I did it. I hated myself. I begged you to forgive me. But you, Nick. You've been rejecting me a little more each day. Death by a thousand cuts."

Now his eyes darted from one place to the other. "Look, Jessie, I miss you, too. I admit it. But—"

"—you're not ready to jump back into our marriage."

He merely stared at her, his eyes now veiled.

"Willie's probably pulled around by now. I better go." She started towards the back porch, her heels clicking on the wooden floor.

He caught her hand again. "I leave tomorrow. Call you from the road?"

She shrugged. "Sure, Nick."

*

It had been a long night for Patrick at Cohan's. He dropped a tray, destroying four pricey prime rib dinners. He spilled a sticky and salty margarita down the front of his shirt. He stepped on a gentleman's foot, who cursed him out with colorful language. And he had to leave the floor when he got another nosebleed.

When his cell rang in the middle of the night, it took him a while to answer it. "Hello?" he rasped.

"You'd better come," Father Joe said. "She's asking for you."

Patrick was instantly awake. "What's happened?"

"She's much worse. It won't be long. Come."

*

Nick usually flew commercial for his book tours. Not this year. He didn't want to be a slave to airline schedules. He'd meet up with his entourage in each city on his own time frame.

His heart just wasn't in it this year. There was a loneliness that haunted him, a feeling of the world swirling around him while he stood by watching. He respected his fans and knew they deserved his attention, but he couldn't concentrate on *BLEEDING BURGANDY* right now.

The Midwest swing was first, six days beginning in Chicago. Nick sleepwalked through it, every city the same. He endured interviews, sat through book signings, did the little extras his bitchy publicist asked of him, treated his driver with the respect he deserved, and schmoozed the VIP's. He couldn't wait to retire to his hotel room each night.

Next was the west coast. Portland, Seattle, Vegas and San Francisco. Then LA for three days. Nick's half-sister and half-brother came from San Diego to see him, a welcome respite. He was surprised when Bree showed up with them. She said it was just luck that she was on the west coast visiting Ethan when Nick's tour came through. Maybe it was. Nick didn't care, one way or another. He was always glad to see his old friend.

Other than briefly visiting with his family, LA was wall-to-wall TV and radio interviews. Up at dawn for the morning shows. Taping Fallon and Colbert and Kimmel in the late afternoon. Book signings. Internet and print interviews. A fan club lunch. It was endless and tiring and boring.

*

"Take a break, Patrick," Father Joe said. "I'll be here with Tess. Go on. Get something to drink."

Patrick was too tired to object. This was the fourth day he and Father Joe sat vigil at Tess's bedside in Our Lady of Peace Hospital. She woke temporarily at times, relieved to see them both, before again closing her eyes. That's when Patrick sang softly to her and held her hand.

Patrick wandered down the deserted hospital corridor. It was almost midnight. A nurse behind the desk smiled as he passed by. He got a Coke from the vending machine and paused in the doorway of the waiting room.

101

A middle-aged couple and a lone woman sat motionless, staring at the overhead TV. Patrick glanced at the screen.

Jimmy Fallon made some kind of joke, and his guest laughed. He—

It was Nick McDeare. Nick was the guest.

Patrick slumped into a chair and stared at the TV. Nick talked about his book. And about some film that was being made from one of his other books. It was beyond strange to sit in a hospital late at night and see someone he knew on television.

"Patrick." A nurse stood in the doorway. "Come with me. Hurry."

*

Nick was exhausted but wired when he returned to the hotel after taping Fallon. He and his driver were stuck in the insane snarled L.A. freeway system for over two hours. Bumper to bumper. Moving a foot every few minutes. Thank God he was getting out of this hellhole tomorrow.

It was past nine o'clock, past the dinner hour. It didn't matter. Nick wasn't hungry. He exchanged his black leather jacket and slacks for his ratty jeans and Mets T-shirt.

Grabbing a bourbon from the mini bar he stepped out on the small balcony. A hot wind whipped his hair. Below, the maze of freeways looked like slithering caterpillars from this distance. How could anyone live in this congested, callous and expensive city? But then, they said the same thing about New York.

The memory of Patrick was fading. It seemed a lifetime ago that he sat at Cohan's watching Andrew's son.

There'd been no word from Patrick since Nick left Florida. It looked like the boy just wasn't interested in pursuing a relationship with his new family.

And there wasn't a damned thing Nick could do about it.

*

Patrick held Tess's hand as she slipped away. As her fingers relaxed. As she took her last breath. Was it always like this? This silent? One minute she was alive. The next, she wasn't.

Patrick swiped at his tears. The world seemed darker. Colder. Emptier. Tess had always been his light.

His breath caught. He cleared his throat and panted for air.

Father Joe took him by the shoulders and sat him in a chair. "Calm down, Patrick. You'll be okay."

Patrick stared at Tess, so still, as his head began to pound and his vision blurred ...

*

Nick was in the middle of a book signing in Dallas when he got a call from Father Joe. "Hold on a minute, Father," He excused himself and moved away from the line of people, his publicist dogging his footsteps. The woman was becoming a pain in the ass.

"Nick, you can't just walk away from your fans—"

"Back off, lady," Nick spat, covering the mouthpiece. He'd had it with her. "This is important." He turned away and went back to his phone. "Father?"

"Am I interrupting something?"

"Not at all, Father."

"I wanted to let you know ... Tess died yesterday."

Nick exhaled slowly. "How's Patrick?"

"Devastated."

"I can imagine." Death flattened you when it came calling the first time.

"He had another attack. When Tess died. It took almost an hour before he was back to normal." The priest sighed. "The funeral is in a few days. Afterwards, I'm going to suggest Patrick get away. Come visit you in New York if it's okay with you—"

"Yes, yes, of course. But I'm not in New York. I'm—" Damn it all to hell! "— on my book tour. He can join me on the road. Maybe camping out in a hotel room would be exactly what he needs. Far away from it all. I'll text you my schedule. Cities and hotels where I'm staying and when. Give it to Patrick."

"Text it directly to him."

"I don't think that's a good idea. I haven't heard from him. If I suddenly contact him right now, it might look like I'm trying to move in fast after he lost Tess."

"You're right. I'll give it to him."

"I'm sorry. About Tess."

"She was a great lady." Father's voice reduced to a whisper. "Patrick just walked in. I'll be in touch."

*

The funeral was tiny. Just Patrick, Father Joe and some people from the church.

Patrick stood under an umbrella in the pouring rain as Father read verses from his prayer book.

Patrick took a pill before the service. He intended to stand tall for Tess. Try to be the man she envisioned. Not a weeping baby. The rain was heaven's tears, he thought. God was doing the crying for him.

He glanced down at Tess's gold wedding band on his pinkie. Father gave it to him that morning. He said it was what she wanted.

Patrick made it almost to the end of the service, to when he had to place his white rose on the casket. His chest heaved, and he laid his head on the shiny wood.

Saying goodbye hurt too much. It just hurt too much. Why couldn't life stay happy? Why did pain always have to intrude? Father put his arm around him and led him away.

A lady from the church dropped him at home afterwards. Father Joe had to go back to the church for a baptism.

Patrick sat on the couch looking around the living room, every inch of it coated in memories of Tess. The only sound was the ticking of the wall clock. Time marched on. The minutes, then the hours. How could time continue as if nothing had changed? When everything just changed?

He got to his feet and wandered from room to room. The loneliness crushed him, the house too empty. Sure, Tess had been in the hospital for months, but there was always his belief she would eventually return home. Now that dream was gone.

Maybe he should go back to Orlando. Maybe he needed to work, to sing. But he didn't want to sing for strangers. He wanted to sing for Tess.

Pulling out his cell, he scrolled to the text from Father Joe. The one with Nick McDeare's schedule on it. Father said Nick would be happy to see him. But would Patrick feel comfortable with the man? They still really didn't know each other.

There was nowhere to go.

No one to sing for.

Curling up on Tess's bed, he pulled the handmade quilt up to his shoulders and closed his eyes.

*

Nick slumped on the couch in his hotel room as he watched the Jets trounce the Dolphins. A good diversion for a boring night in Miami.

When his cell rang he assumed it was Kat, wanting to talk about her writing class that night.

"He's gone," Father Joe said. "Patrick's gone."

Nick sat up. "Gone? Where?"

"I don't know. I came over to the house to see if he wanted to go to dinner. He wasn't here. And his car is gone."

"When's the last time you saw him?"

"Tess's service was day before yesterday. Then I saw him yesterday morning before I had to preside over an elaborate funeral. A big family I've known for years. It was too late to call Patrick afterwards, so I called this morning. It went to voice mail. I kept trying, but he never answered. This afternoon I called Cohan's, thinking he went back there. They haven't heard from him. So tonight I came over here, to the house. He's gone. And I think he's been gone a while. There's a bowl of soup on the counter that looks pretty old. Do you think he's on his way to you?"

"Did you give him my schedule?"

"Yes."

Nick paced, thinking. "Does he have a credit card?"

"Only a debit card."

Okay. A debit card can be traced.

"Where are you tonight, Nick?"

"Miami. I wish I was coming to Orlando, but they scheduled only one city in Florida." Nick's mind was in overdrive. "Father, look around. Can you tell if Patrick's things are missing? Maybe we can gage how long he plans to be gone. Take your time. I'll wait."

When the priest got back on the line, he was even more agitated. "His duffel's gone. And some of his clothes. Also Tess's quilt and her diaries."

"Let me see what I can find out. I'll be in touch. Try not to worry."

"Yeah. Fat chance."

Nick clicked off. He needed to follow Patrick's financial transactions on the debit card. It would be a road map for where the boy went. Willie had a police computer, but Nick didn't want to bring his friend in on this yet, not with Abbie's prying nature. He decided to call Harry Steinmetz, the Desk Sergeant at NYPD's Midtown North and an old friend. Harry said he'd look into it and get back to him ASAP.

The fact that Patrick took some of Tess's personal items with him, things that meant something to him, was significant. It could signal he didn't intend to return to Mount Dora. Nick didn't want to think about the ramification of that.

If he just didn't have this damned book tour!

*

Harry called Nick early the next morning, just as his plane departed for Atlanta. "Three days ago Patrick withdrew two hundred dollars at an ATM in Mount Dora, Florida. The next day he took out another two hundred in Tallahassee. Then yesterday he took out another two hundred in Forsyth, Georgia."

Two hundred was usually the maximum you could withdraw at one time. "Where's Forsyth?"

"Off I-75, south of Atlanta."

Okay. Patrick was on a major interstate, heading north. Maybe he intended to meet up with Nick in Atlanta.

He thanked Harry and asked him to keep an eye on any more withdrawals. Or any word on a missing Patrick Cavanaugh.

Nick spent the day waiting for Patrick to show up in Atlanta. He left a note at the front desk of his hotel for the boy, explaining where Nick was at any given hour. By ten o'clock that night, he gave up.

As Nick's book tour moved up the coast towards New England, the money trail went cold. There were no more ATM withdrawals. And no way to trace Patrick. Nick couldn't focus on the book tour or anything else. All he thought about was Patrick.

Nick tried not to sound despondent in his daily phone calls with Father Joe. Patrick hadn't returned home and hadn't gone back to Cohan's. Nick's calls with Kat were pretty depressing. It was impossible to lie to his daughter.

By the time Nick hit Boston, his last city on the tour, he feared something had happened to Patrick Cavanaugh.

Had Tess's death left him so despondent he took his own life?

*

Kat sat with Mary on the couch in the study on a cold Thursday night. Thanksgiving was a week away. Her dad was finally due home tomorrow morning. He'd called every night from the road, giving them an update on Patrick.

"Try not to think the worst, sweetie." Mary ran her hand through Kat's hair. "I have to believe if Andrew made this whole Patrick thing happen, it's not supposed to end in tragedy."

"But can Andrew influence fate? Some things are out of his control."

"Just keep thinking positively."

"I wish I wasn't going out with Susie on Saturday night. Dad's going to be upset about Patrick and might want me around."

"If I know your daddy, he'll be tired. He always is after a long tour. It's nice of your ballet teacher to invite you out for an evening. And it will be good for you to get Patrick off your mind for a few hours."

*

When Nick arrived home the next day, he didn't try to hide his state of mind. Sensing his mood, Kat and Mary left him alone.

Anthony was excited to see him. Nick roused, spending a few hours with his son in the back yard, tossing a football and catching up. Anthony was leaving for his friend Zane's house on Long Island on Saturday, returning on Wednesday, in time for Thanksgiving. After Kat took so much time off from her studies, it was only fair Anthony got the same treat. Besides, he was an excellent student.

Nick had checked in with Jessie along the road, as promised. Now he called her to let her know he was back.

"You sound down."

"Just tired." It wasn't a complete lie. He was exhausted. More than usual. "I have two days to catch up on sleep before I hit the NYC circuit for the book on Monday. It's finally over on Thanksgiving." He swore this was the last book tour he was ever going to do. At least the kind that took him away for weeks at a time.

"Get some sleep, Nick. I'll see you on Thursday." Nick was glad he never told Jessie about Patrick. If he had, he'd now have to tell her Patrick might be … he couldn't even think those words.

When Nick fell into bed late Friday night, exhaustion overtook him, along with the need to escape his fear about Patrick's fate. He slept around the clock. When he finally woke up early Saturday evening, sleet splattered the dark windows. He threw on sweats and went downstairs. Kat was out with Susie for dinner and a Broadway show.

As he picked at a plate of roast beef and mashed potatoes with Mary, his cell thrummed. "Mr. McDeare, this is Vince." Their nighttime security guard. "There's a kid out front who says he knows you."

Nick bolted from the breakfast nook. Sprinting down the hallway, he swung the front door wide.

Vince stood on the stoop, his eyes on a lone figure at the foot of the stairs.

Patrick Cavanaugh leaned against the black iron railing. His wet hair hung in clumps. Deep circles ringed the apology in his eyes. His jeans and sweatshirt were soaked. A duffel sat on the ground beside him.

"It's okay, Vince. I know him." Nick came down the steps amid the heavy wet drops and grabbed the duffel.

"I didn't know where else to go."

"I'm glad you're here."

*

Mary's heart almost burst at her first sight of Patrick.

He looked like an abandoned puppy left out in the rain. He seemed embarrassed to show up at their door. But as he stepped into the vestibule, shivering, his expression took Mary back in time. This boy was a teenaged Andrew Brady.

"Patrick, this is Mary," Nick said gently. "We'd all be lost without her."

107

Mary smiled at the boy. "Are you hungry, Patrick? Or maybe you'd like to change out of those wet clothes and have a hot shower first?"

He nodded as he removed his sopping shoes, his hair and clothes dripping water. "Sorry about the wet floor, ma'am."

"Don't worry about it. And call me Mary."

"He can use my bathroom." Nick touched Patrick's arm lightly. "Come on."

"I have a room all ready for him," Mary announced.

Patrick's tired face registered surprise. "You knew I was coming?"

Mary exchanged a look with Nick. "We hoped." Mary led them to the third floor, to the back bedroom next to hers. She pushed the door open and switched on the lights. "This was Andrew's room when he was a teenager. We had it redone a few years ago." Going to the king-sized sleigh bed, she pulled back the gray and purple duvet and turned down the pale gray sheets.

Moving on to the bathroom, she flicked on the lights. "Here's your own bathroom. I stocked what I thought you might need. And the closet over there has some of Andrew's clothes, in excellent condition. Make sure you put on one of those sweaters. This old house can get cold." She looked down at Patrick's feet, his socks soaking wet. "Do you have some dry shoes and socks?".

"Socks."

Nick spoke up. "See if Andrew's shoes fit you. If not, we'll get you some tomorrow."

Mary headed for the door. "All right then. When you're ready come down to the kitchen for something to eat."

*

Alone, Patrick Cavanaugh stood rooted in place. He tried to take it all in, this bedroom that was Andrew Brady's, larger and more luxurious than any he'd seen before. The pale gray walls. The shiny wooden floors. The large deep purple area rug. A huge bed. A three-tiered chest of drawers.

Patrick circled the room. Sliding doors led to a small wrought iron terrace. In the corner was a built-in desk with overstuffed chairs on each side of it. A laptop computer waited to be used. Across the room was a built-in modular bookcase with a TV, sound system, books and ... Patrick ran his fingers across shelves of sheet music. Musical after musical. Pop music. Old standards. Other shelves held scripts.

Stepping back, Patrick examined the framed items on the walls. Photos of Andrew Brady. Broadway. Off Broadway. Accepting his Drama

Desk Award for *Hamlet.* Surrounded by gushing celebrities backstage. Politicians gladhanding with him.

Patrick's eyes were drawn to a small glass case on the wall near the bed. He approached it in awe. Hesitating for a moment, he opened it and reached for the statuette.

The Antoinette Perry Award. The Tony. Broadway's highest honor. Andrew Brady. Best Actor in a Musical. *HEARTTAKES.* Awarded posthumously.

He replaced it with care, his fingers lingering. It didn't seem real, all this. How could he be this icon's son? How could he ever live up to this man's legacy?

Ambling to the bathroom, he shook his head, remembering the cottage's ancient bathroom with its clawfoot tub and shower head stuck in the wall. The stand-alone sink, old medicine cabinet and permanently stained toilet despite Tess's best efforts. Here there was a combination bathtub/hot tub and a massive walk-in shower. The long counter held every toiletry he'd ever need.

Patrick hung his clothes on the back of the bathroom door and stepped into the shower.

Letting the steaming water wash over him, he felt warm for the first time since he left Florida.

CHAPTER 10

Nick pressed his cell to his ear. "He's here, Father Joe."

A huge sigh on the other end. "How is he?"

"Hard to tell. Tired. Unprepared for the cold north."

Father Joe laughed. "Do you know where he went? How he got to you?"

"Not yet."

"I'm relieved he's with you."

So was Nick. Relieved beyond words.

"Keep in touch. Let me know how he's doing."

"Of course. I may need your advice."

"I doubt it. You seem to know what you're doing."

"We'll see. At least you can stop worrying now."

"It'll be a cold day in hell when we stop worrying about our kids."

"True."

"Thank you, Nick."

Nick tossed his cell on the island. "Good thinking, Mary. Giving him Andrew's room. And having it ready."

"It's one of the best rooms in this house, and it just sits there as a shrine to Andrew." She began clearing their dinner plates. "Funny. It's as if that room's been waiting for Patrick all this time." She took the dishes to the sink and set a new place. "I almost fainted when that boy came through the door."

Nick agreed. "When you first see him it's a shock."

"He seems shyer than Andrew."

"He is. Except onstage."

Patrick came down the steps hesitantly. He paused mid-way and shrugged, looking down at the sheep's wool sweater he wore.

"That looks good on you." Mary beamed at him. "I remember when Andrew got it. He wasn't much older than you." She nodded towards the breakfast nook. "Come sit down and eat."

He made his way across the room, each step tenuous, and sat across from Nick. "I feel like I'm imposing—"

"You're not. I invited you, remember?" Nick stretched his arm across the back of the bench. "I knew you left Mount Dora. Father Joe called me. We hoped you'd turn up here."

"He must be worried."

"I just talked with him. He's relieved. So am I."

"I'm sorry I worried you both."

"Now that you're here, all is forgiven."

"Where's Kat?"

"Out for the evening. She'll be happy to see you."

Mary set a plate in front of the boy. Roast beef, mashed potatoes and broccoli. "When's the last time you ate?" she asked.

"I don't remember."

"Well, there's plenty more where that came from."

Patrick dug in. It was obvious he was starving, but he maintained his manners. Tess would be proud of him.

Nick was full of questions. But he held off. There would be time for all that later. What Patrick needed right now was nourishment and sleep.

He stared across the table at the young man who tried valiantly to keep his eyes open. Somehow, in the middle of what had to be heart wrenching grief, Patrick found his way to New York. He was safe. That's all that mattered.

*

By the time Patrick climbed the stairs to his room, he was falling asleep standing up. Flipping on the lights, he closed the door and stumbled towards the bed, then halted abruptly.

Was he hallucinating?

His duffel was empty and tucked into the open closet. His few clothes were folded in the open dresser drawers. Sweatpants and a Juilliard T-shirt were stretched across the pillows. Neither were his.

And on the bed, draped over the duvet, was Tess's quilt.

But ... Nick and that nice lady were with him downstairs the whole time.

Did they have a maid?

Who did this?

*

"He's – what? – sixteen or seventeen?" Mary asked. They were in the study with a fire going.

"Seventeen. By just a few weeks." Nick poured a brandy and dropped down on the couch.

"He seems younger."

111

Nick took a sip, the amber liquid burning on its descent to his stomach. "Patrick lived in a fantasy world of his own creation his first five years. Then he was sheltered by a sweet old lady and a priest." His stomach queasy, he abandoned the brandy.

"You haven't told me about those five years, just that it was horrible."

"It was. Too awful to describe. He wouldn't have survived if Tess hadn't gotten him out of there."

"He's like a wounded animal, so young and afraid. He brings out my maternal instincts."

"I didn't know you ever lost them." Nick grabbed a bottle of water from behind the bar.

"But I get the sense he's cautious. Wary of getting close. Maybe he needs to know a person before he's comfortable. He's a lot like you."

"Not Andrew?"

Mary chuckled. "I see both of you in him."

"Two different upbringings."

"We're a combination of our genes and our environment. Look at Kat. She has your genes. She's a mini-you. But there's still a lot of Lake Placid in her."

The front door slammed. Footsteps hurried down the hall. "I'm home." Kat halted between them, looking from one to the other. "What?"

Nick smiled up at his daughter. "Patrick's here."

*

It took Patrick a few seconds to remember where he was when he woke up the next morning. He laid in the big bed under the soft duvet and Tess's quilt and allowed his mind to adjust.

He smelled bacon. And muffins? That nice lady must be making breakfast. What was her name? Mary. It reminded him of waking up in the cottage to the aroma of Tess's waffles.

A photo of Andrew Brady hung on the wall near the bed. He was center stage under a lone spotlight, singing. Patrick hadn't sung since Tess died. It was the longest he'd gone without singing a single note.

Sitting up, he examined the room with fresh eyes. Was he really here?

He pulled on some jeans and last night's sweater and slipped into Andrew's loafers. They fit like a glove. Wandering to the terrace doors, he opened them. It was so cold in the north. Still, he stepped out on the terrace and breathed deeply.

The back yard was carefully tended. Much nicer than what he and Tess created in Florida. Across the way were more buildings. So many

112

structures in this busy city. A woman stood in the window of the ground floor home right behind this one. She stared up at him. A man joined her.

Uncomfortable, Patrick stepped back inside and closed the door. He should go downstairs, but he felt awkward. What was he thinking, bursting into this home unannounced? He wished he was back in Mount Dora with Tess.

*

"Willie?" Abbie stood at the window in their den, a coffee mug in her hand. "Come here."

"What's up?" Willie came up beside her.

"Look. Up there on the third floor at Nick's. Am I seeing a ghost?"

A long pause. "If you are, so am I. What the hell?"

"Are we crazy? That looks like Andrew. Oops. He just went inside."

"I don't think ghosts walk around like us normal folk."

"Well, I'm sure as hell going to find out. Come on."

*

"Hey there, stranger." Kat ran into Patrick on the second-floor landing. Actually, she'd been loitering, waiting for him to come down from his room.

He smiled and dug his hands in his pockets.

"I'm glad you're here. Dad's getting sick of me. He needs someone new to spoil."

That got a little laugh out of him.

"Come on. I smell Mary's orange muffins."

They continued down to the kitchen. Mary sat in the breakfast nook reading the Sunday papers.

"Where's Dad?"

"Still sleeping. Those book tours wear him out."

Kat remembered Patrick didn't drink coffee. "Cola or juice?"

"Uh, juice. Thanks."

Kat grabbed two muffins, handing one to Patrick. "Mary's specialty. To die for. Let's park ourselves on the stools. Mary's taken over the breakfast nook."

"A fine old Sunday tradition." Mary adjusted her reading glasses and went back to her papers. "There's bacon and French toast in the oven."

The back door opened and closed. Abbie and Willie appeared in the archway. They stared at Patrick, both their mouths open. If the situation wasn't so serious, Kat would have burst out laughing.

"Oh. My. God." Abbie mumbled. "Who are you?"

Nick came down the stairs, halting at the sight of Abbie and Willie, who continued to stare at Patrick. Mary looked like she wanted to dematerialize. And Patrick's expression was at best, pained.

This was ridiculous. Kat jumped in. "Patrick, meet Abbie and Willie, close friends who live behind us. Kind of like family."

"And who's this?" Abbie gaze didn't seem capable of leaving Patrick's face.

Nick spoke up. "Patrick Cavanaugh."

"Patrick Cavanaugh?" Abbie asked with skepticism. "Huh-uh. Andrew Brady Jr. would make more sense."

Again Kat took over. "Funny you should say that. Remember our conversation about Andrew working at the Asolo?"

Abbie's expression shifted to shock. "You mean, that girl really was—"

"That'll teach you to listen to me next time." Kat glanced at Patrick, who seemed to be looking for an escape route.

"Have you done a DNA?" Willie asked, grabbing one of his aunt's muffins.

"You don't need one." Abbie moved closer to Patrick. "I mean, just LOOK at him!"

Mary stood up. "How about some breakfast, everyone?"

Abbie turned to Nick. "So this is what you were doing in Florida."

Kat hopped off the stool. "We'll help you, Mary. Come on, Patrick."

"Does Jessie know?" Abbie was now standing next to Patrick.

"Not yet."

"She's going to flip when she sees him."

Patrick slid off the stool and scaled the stairs.

"Nice going, Abbie." Nick took off after him.

*

Patrick was throwing things into his duffel when Nick barged into his room.

"This was a mistake. I never should have come here."

"Patrick, stop. Stop!" Nick grabbed the clothes in Patrick's hands and tossed them on the bed. "Forget what Abbie said."

Frustrated, Patrick strode to the terrace doors, his back to Nick, and ran his hand through his tangled hair. "Why will your wife flip out about me?" He turned to face him. "And where is she?"

Cornered, Nick folded his arms. No more obfuscation. No more dodging the truth. "We're separated. She's living in a hotel near the theater."

Patrick shifted from foot to foot. "I'm sorry."

"I didn't tell her about you because ..." Nick paced away. "In Jessie's eyes, Andrew's a saint. Especially since his death. Andrew was so good, so nice, so funny. He had such a big heart. He revered women." Nick rubbed his brow, a headache coming on. "Andrew having an illegitimate son tarnishes that image."

"If I leave, you won't have to tell her anything."

"No, Patrick. Jessie deserves to know. And you deserve to stay here for now." Nick dropped down in one of the easy chairs. "This was Andrew's home. Which means it's yours, too."

"We don't even know for sure I AM Andrew's son."

"Then let's do the paternity test. It's an easy process." Nick looked up at him. Patrick turned away. "Why are you hesitating?"

His answer was a shrug.

"Are you afraid you AREN'T Andrew's son?"

No response.

Nick got to his feet. "You're his son, Patrick." He couldn't yet tell him that Andrew orchestrated the whole search. It would probably send the boy straight back to Florida. "Look at me."

Patrick hesitantly looked over his shoulder.

"Why did you leave Mount Dora?"

Patrick dropped his gaze and looked back out the terrace doors. "The cottage hurt too much. And I wasn't ready to go back to Cohan's."

"Where'd you end up going?"

"Nowhere. Anywhere. I just drove. I'd never seen the north, so I headed ... My junker of a car died outside Washington, so I got on a bus and decided to come here."

"You got off in Port Authority?"

"What's Port Authority?"

"The New York City bus station."

"Yeah."

Good God, Patrick in that pit with the hookers and pimps and homeless. With his blond hair and blue eyes, it was a miracle he made it out of the place.

"How'd you find your way to this house?"

"I asked people for directions and walked."

"You walked over two miles in the rain and sleet?"

Patrick shrugged.

Nick shook his head. "You know what I think? I think you knew where you were going the moment you left Mount Dora. When you lost Tess, you lost your sense of home and family. So you came here searching for it." Which explained his grit and determination to get here against all odds.

Patrick wouldn't look at him.

Which told Nick all he needed to know.

*

"Mary, Nick has to tell Jessie." Abbie peeled away the paper on a muffin.

"With her opening coming up he didn't want to throw her off her game."

"That's bull."

Kat turned her fire on Abbie. "It's not! That's exactly why Dad didn't tell her. We didn't know if we'd find Patrick. Or even if there WAS a Patrick. Why get Jessie riled if we didn't have to? So we followed the clues and found him right before Dad left on his book tour. When was he supposed to tell her? On opening night? On the phone? Oh, yeah, that would have gone over great. So don't call Dad a liar. And don't you dare give Patrick any grief." She stormed up the stairs.

Abbie looked at Mary. "What was THAT about?"

"Both Nick and Kat are protective of Patrick. There's a whole lot more to his story than you know."

Willie pulled Abbie towards the back door. "Time to go, Abs."

"Make sure Nick goes over to Jessie's tonight and tells her, okay, Mary?"

"Uh-huh."

*

Was Nick right? Patrick thought back over the last week. Did he intend to come here all along? It certainly wasn't a conscious decision. "If I stay for a while, can I keep a low profile? And avoid any more scenes like the one down in the kitchen just now?"

"You can try. But Anthony will be home on Wednesday. And Thursday is Thanksgiving. We always end up with a houseful. Jessie will be here."

"I'll be gone by then."

Nick approached him. "Don't run away, Patrick. Stay until you figure out what you want."

"Who's Anthony?"

"My nine-year-old son." Nick explained Anthony's complicated history. With Gianni. With Andrew. And with himself. "You're not the only one around here who's had to deal with paternity questions."

The idea of Anthony made Patrick feel a little easier. "You said people are coming for Thanksgiving." Images of holidays spent with Tess

116

came back to him. Her special mashed potatoes with cream cheese. Watching the Macy's parade and enjoying the Broadway stars singing. He remembered when Andrew Brady and Jessi— "Do I have to be a part of it? I know that sounds rude, but I—"

"You don't have to do anything you don't want to do. If you want to stay up here in your room, we can fix you a plate. But eventually you'll have to meet everyone."

"Including Jessie? Uh, sorry. I shouldn't call her that."

"Of course you should. That's her name. And don't worry. I'll tell her about you before you two meet."

Nick was being so accommodating that Patrick dared to ask for one more favor. "Today's Sunday. I'd like to go to Mass. If I don't create a scene in the church." He found it bizarre to have to worry about other people's reaction to him. In Florida he was a nobody. In New York he was this Andrew Brady clone.

"Kat will go with you. She's Catholic. And I'll show you my secret for going out without being recognized."

*

Kat clapped her hands and laughed as she walked with Patrick to St. Matthew's a few blocks away. "You look like SUCH a dork in that old-fart golf cap. And the horn-rimmed glasses are hideous! Here, let me fix your scarf." She felt him stiffen as she pulled the navy woolen scarf further up on his neck. "That jacket almost fits you." She didn't know where her dad found the tan suede jacket lined with lamb's wool, but it was very cool.

"Nick said it was Andrew's." He blew on his hands. "It's so cold."

"This is nothing. Wait until January."

"I'll be back in Florida by then."

"I hope not."

He sidled her a look. "Why would you want me around?"

"Our fathers were brothers. I love family. I never had much of it before I came to live with Dad."

"What do you mean?"

"Oh, jeez, I forgot you don't know. You see, Dad and my mom had an affair eons ago. I lived in Lake Placid my whole life with my mom. She died a little over a year ago. That's when she finally told me who my dad was. I didn't take it too well at first."

Patrick halted and stared at her. "You've only known Nick a year? That must have been a shock."

"Kind of like you finding out Andrew's your father, huh? Which is why I get what you're going through."

117

They resumed walking again. "Yeah. I guess you would."

Kat actually enjoyed going to Mass. She hadn't been inside a Catholic church since her mom died. Well, except for St. Peter's Basilica last summer. She quietly observed Patrick throughout the service. He seemed at peace here. And he took communion.

On the way home, she told him about her dad taking her to Italy. "In Rome we visited the Vatican. And we saw the Pieta. The most beautiful sculpture in the world."

"Father Joe went to Rome when he was a young priest. I'd love to see the Vatican."

"Dad will take you."

Patrick chuckled. "I don't think so."

"He will. He believes in showing kids the world. He says traveling teaches as much as books."

"I've never been anywhere. Until I came here, I'd never left Florida."

"Before I moved here last year, I'd never left Lake Placid."

"You're making me feel better. A little less like a hick."

Kat threw her head back and laughed. "Dad's opened up a whole new world for me. He'll do the same for you."

"Was Andrew like that?"

"Ask Anthony. They were really close. From what I've learned, he was a good dad."

"Why will Jessie go nuts when she sees me? Nick said she sees Andrew as some kind of saint, that it will upset her to discover he wasn't perfect."

Kat knew this question was coming. She was walking a tightrope, not wanting to influence Patrick's opinion of Jessie. Not easy. "He's right. See, Dad's reputation before he met Jessie was, well, not the best. He was kind of a lady's man. Scratch that. Not 'kind of.' His reputation was well known, and Jessie knew all about it. He never lied to her. So when I turned up, it resurrected all that. His past. At the same time, she thinks of Andrew as the perfect man. Now here you are, making her realize that Andrew was just like Dad. That he wasn't a saint, and Dad isn't a sinner. They're a combination of both. Which blows that painting to bits."

"What painting?"

"The one in the study of Dad and Uncle Andrew. You didn't see it?"

Patrick shook his head.

"I'll show you when we get home."

"Do you think Andrew was basically a good guy?"

"Absolutely. I'm working on a writing project about him. That's how our search for you began. I found something in his journals that hinted at— Oh, wow, you should read them. In fact, you should go through my research on Andrew. It'll tell you a lot."

"What made you want to write about Andrew?"

Okay, now they were getting into another sticky area. Patrick wasn't ready to hear about Andrew's reach from the other side. How he guided her to look for Heidi's baby. "I realized I didn't know much about him except for his talent. Which blows me away."

"Me, too."

"You're better than he was."

Patrick shook his head and looked embarrassed.

Kat stopped and faced him. "Patrick, your talent explodes on a stage. It's really hard to put into words. I've studied all of Uncle Andrew's shows. And his one-man-concert. Yes, you're like him. Your looks. Your voice. The little quirks, like the way you crinkle your nose sometimes when you sing. And how you use your whole body during a song. But your talent goes way beyond him."

Patrick dropped his gaze and actually blushed.

"I love when you do that."

"What?"

"You look so humble, almost shy at times. It's such a contrast with your talent. It reminds me of something Abbie said about Andrew. She said he was hot, I mean, REALLY attractive to women, but he was completely unaware of it, which made him even sexier."

Patrick laughed. He looked so much like Uncle Andrew when he grinned.

"So tell me about Abbie."

Okay. He didn't want to talk about his talent. Which only made him a better person in Kat's eyes. "Abbie met Andrew when they were seven-years-old at a commercial audition. They were best friends ..."

*

Feeling achy, Nick took a hot shower. It didn't help. In fact, he felt like crap afterwards. He ate a few aspirin and went down to the kitchen. "I thought I heard the front door."

Mary nodded towards the study. Nick wandered across the hall.

Kat and Patrick stared up at the painting of Nick and Andrew.

"It's creepy," Patrick whispered, "how much we look alike."

"Look at your hands," Kat said, pointing. "They're so similar. You both have small waists. Long legs. But your hair's a shade lighter, and it's a little curly. And your eyes are a different color, but the shape is exactly

119

the same. Just like Dad's and mine. Every other aspect of your face is identical." She spotted Nick standing in the doorway.

"The Saint and The Sinner." Nick moved closer.

Patrick wandered around the room, looking at framed photos.

"Have you seen the Baby Grand?" Kat asked. "Come on." She led the way to the living room. "Do you play, Patrick?"

He shook his head. "I always wanted to. But I can read music." He grinned at Kat. "Music Theory. The only music class that taught me something."

"I can teach you piano." Nick joined them. "Or Kat. She plays beautifully."

"Not as well as Dad. He could have been a concert pianist." She turned to Patrick. "How do you learn your music?"

He shrugged. "I just hear it, and I can sing it."

*

Patrick continued around the room, pausing at the fireplace to look at the photos on the mantel. Many were of Andrew when he was young. One photo caught his eye. He picked it up.

The picture was of a woman with dark hair and a young blond boy. Andrew.

Patrick's hands started to shake. His vision clouded.

The closet ... the dark closet ... he couldn't breathe ...

"Patrick?" A voice. Kat. "Are you all right?"

Cold ... so cold ...

He couldn't get a deep breath. Pain shot through his head. The picture slipped from his hands ...

"Patrick." Someone sat him down. Nick. "Patrick!"

Kat sat beside him, tilting his head back and holding something to his nose, which was bleeding.

He tried to focus on Nick, who sat on the other side of him.

Mary stood a few feet away, looking anxious.

Patrick took the cloth from Kat. It was Mary's apron. He ruined her apron. "I'm sorry, Mary."

"It's old. I was going to throw it away. Go ahead. Hold it to your nose."

Kat took Patrick's other hand and rubbed the back of it. Her touch made him uneasy, but he was powerless to pull away. "Your skin is so cold," she whispered.

"I'm better now." He wasn't. His vision was still blurred, and his head ached. But he didn't want to worry them.

*

120

Kat climbed the stairs with Patrick. He still didn't look right. She took a chance and pushed into his room. "Look at all this sheet music." She went to the bookshelves. "We should take some downstairs. I'd love to hear you sing again."

Patrick didn't respond.

"You sure you're okay?"

He nodded. "Your dad … he's being so good to me. Why?"

"Why not?" She wandered around the room."

"That's not an answer."

"Well, he won't admit it, but Dad still resents not growing up with Andrew. That they were separated."

"I'm a stand-in for Andrew?"

"No. But you're a part of Andrew. I think Dad wants to take care of you for him. But it's more than that." She went to the terrace door. "He was a wreck when you were missing. You really got to him. He comes off as this big tough guy, and he is, but he loves his kids." She met Patrick's gaze. "I think he considers you one of us now.

Patrick's expression softened. His eyes were so transparent, so revealing. She could see her words touched him.

"Get some rest, Patrick."

CHAPTER 11

"Sorry, Bree. I should have called you back. I've been distracted since I got home." Nick went into the study, his cell pressed to his ear. "What did you want to talk about?"

"I'm working on something you—"

"Sorry," Mary interrupted him, "but this is important. Jessie's bringing Larry, Ollie, Nora and James Lovelock on Thursday. So you better check the wine in the basement and see if we need to order more."

"Larry and Ollie? Sounds like the regulars at a neighborhood bar."

Annoyed, Mary sighed. "Larry Williams. Old friend of Andrew's and the stage manager of her show. Ollie Farrow plays Charles. And you know James, the wigmaster."

Yes, he knew James. Who would probably come dressed as a turkey. Nick nodded before turning his focus back to Bree. "You're working on what?" He gathered wood from the pile beside the fireplace. This room was too damned cold.

"FBI corruption. Thought you might like to get involved."

A subject near and dear to Nick's heart. "Interesting. Let's talk." A thought struck as he stacked the wood in the grate. "Are you flying out to see Ethan for Thanksgiving?"

"I can't. I have to be in D.C. on Friday for an interview."

"What are you doing on Thanksgiving?"

A long pause. "You know holidays don't mean much to me."

"Come here for the day. We can talk after dinner."

Another pause. "Will Jessie be there?"

"Yes." Jessie invited friends. Nick would, too. "It'll be a large gathering." More like a three-ring circus. "And Kat would love it if you came."

"You're sure?"

"Yep."

"… Okay … See you Thursday. Thanks, Nick."

Nick chuckled as he finished building the fire and lit his masterpiece. He could visualize Jessie and Bree on Thanksgiving. Two cats hissing and spitting at each other. And throwing food. Although that wasn't Bree's style.

Jessie! He had to tell her about Patrick before Thursday. He checked his watch. She was doing a matinee right now. He'd go to her hotel tonight.

Speaking of Patrick ... Nick went to the living room and grabbed the photograph that caught Patrick's eye earlier. Settling into the sofa, he stared at it.

It was of Andrew and Nick's mother, Chelsea. Patrick's grandmother. Nick himself had singled out this picture when he first came to the house nearly three years ago. It had been his first glimpse of his birth mother.

Why would this photo cause Patrick to have another attack?

Because that's exactly what happened.

*

Patrick stood next to Andrew, twin spotlights on them, as they sang a song from *SWEENEY TODD*:

> *Nothing's gonna harm you*
> *Not while I'm around*
> *Nothing's gonna harm you*
> *No sir, not while I'm around*
> *Demons are prowling everywhere*
> *Nowadays*
> *I'll send them howling I don't care*
> *I've got ways*

Andrew faded into the wings, forcing Patrick to continue alone:

> *No one's gonna hurt you*
> *No one's gonna dare*
> *Others can desert you*
> *Not to worry, whistle, I'll be there*

Patrick jerked awake, the music halting abruptly. He sat up, his heart pounding, his eyes darting around the shadowy bedroom. Taking a deep breath, he forced himself to calm down.

The sun had set. He must have slept for hours.

"No one's going to hurt you ever again."

Patrick jumped.

A voice. A man's soft voice. The same voice he heard that day they drove from Orlando to Mount Dora. When he was half asleep.

123

Too many strange things were happening lately. His duffel unpacked. The photograph downstairs. And the song. He never sang 'Not While I'm Around' onstage. It brought back hazy memories, the kind that left him shaking.

That photograph ... The woman with the dark hair.

... the closet ... so cold ...

No! Patrick threw his legs to the floor. This had to stop. He stumbled to the terrace door and opened it. Breathing in the icy air, he released it slowly. The view gave him some peace, the pinpoint ground lights reminding him of Christmas.

Throwing on clothes, he followed an enticing aroma to the kitchen.

Mary sat in the breakfast nook, reading a magazine. "Well, you look better."

The kitchen was cozy, the stained-glass lamp over the nook warm and inviting.

Patrick slid his hands in his back pockets. "Where is everyone?"

"Nick's in bed. Looks like he caught a nasty bug on his book tour." She got up and stirred a pot on the stove. "Kat went to meet her friend Bertie. On Sunday nights their ballet teacher hosts a cabaret on the street front of her studio. SuZee Q's. The kids gather and show off their talent."

"Her ballet teacher?"

"Susie's an old friend of Jessie's. A former prima ballerina. She has a huge studio with classes for all the arts, most of the teachers from Juilliard. In case you didn't know, Kat's a beautiful ballerina. Been studying since she was a little girl. The cabaret raises money for kids who can't afford classes." Mary peeked in the oven. "Hungry?"

Patrick nodded.

"Get something to drink, then sit yourself down."

Mary placed a steaming bowl in front of him. "Seafood chowder. Full of iron and vitamins. I make it for special occasions."

"What's the occasion?"

"You."

Patrick felt his face heat up. He was probably blushing, like some idiot girl.

Mary added a warm loaf of bread and a ramekin of butter and sat across from him. Patrick took a spoonful of the thick, creamy chowder. "This is really good."

Mary smiled. She had the warmest eyes. "What's that ring on your pinkie?"

Patrick glanced at the gold band. "It was Tess's. Tess was … my mom."

"You should put it on a chain so you don't lose it." Mary broke the bread apart and passed it to Patrick.

Patrick smeared the bread with butter. "Kat said she's only been here a year."

Mary nodded. "Hard to believe. It feels like she's always been here. You two have a lot in common. Discovering your fathers after so many years."

"It makes a difference. Kat going through the same thing as me."

"You have a kindred spirit in her. Your fathers were brothers, and you two are so much like your dads."

Patrick remained silent, enjoying the soup.

"You must have a lot of questions about Andrew. He was like a son to me. Jessie's dad took him in as a foster child when Andrew's mother died suddenly. Right before his thirteenth birthday."

"He was a foster child?"

Mary nodded. "He immediately became part of our family."

Part of their family? Hard to imagine foster parents like that. Or a foster home that looked like this one.

"And now you're part of our family." Again, that stunning smile, so much like Tess's.

Patrick paused. "Can I ask you something?" Mary nodded. "Why haven't I met the maid?"

"We don't have a maid. What made you think—"

"When I went upstairs last night, my duffel was unpacked and Tess's— a quilt I brought was on the bed." Mary's eyes shifted away from him. "And a little while ago, I swear I heard a man's voice in my room."

Mary looked everywhere but at him. "You should tell all this to Nick. Maybe he'll have some answers."

*

Patrick knocked on Nick's bedroom door before peeking in. A bathroom light spilled into the dark room, revealing Nick asleep in the big bed.

He placed the aspirin and water that Mary gave him on the bedside table and backed up.

Nick was curled on his side, the blanket pulled up to his neck, his hair covering his forehead. And he was snoring a little.

The room was a mess, clothes everywhere, empty water bottles covering most surfaces. Even the bed held a laptop, notebooks and papers. It looked like Patrick's room at home before the church ladies cleaned.

The sight brought a smile to his face. Despite all the talk about Nick being The Sinner, Patrick thought of him as a near-perfect human being. A successful writer who loved his kids. It was good to know Nick had faults, like being a slob and snoring.

The room grew cold. Patrick shivered.

Someone was watching him. He felt it. He glanced around.

The shadows were deep. The wind howled outside the windows. A clock ticked. And yet, Patrick wasn't afraid. Why wasn't he afraid?

"Feel better, Nick," he whispered.

*

Nick felt like shit. What a lousy time to get sick. Every bug loved him. It had been this way since he was a kid.

It was still dark out when he went down to the kitchen. Mary waited at the island with a cup of broth, crackers, juice and aspirin. "I knew you wouldn't cancel the morning shows. And you better tell those studios to slap on the makeup because you look terrible. Here, eat. Willie's out front waiting, whenever you're ready."

"I'll come home after my book signing and reschedule everything else."

It was a hellish morning, running from network to network, saying the same things. Then he had a book signing up in Harlem. Not wanting to disappoint or infect his fans, he kept his distance and wore latex gloves, explaining he was suffering an allergic reaction to something.

When he got home, the kitchen was chaos. He forgot about the usual Thanksgiving prep. Three days of cooking and baking.

Nick said hello to Violet, Mary's sister and Willie's mother. Also, Abbie, who sidled over to him. Her apron was covered in flour. "You promised to tell Jessie about Patrick last night."

Nick dropped his head. He'd forgotten. "I was sick, Abbie."

"You're making excuses."

"This is her day off. I'll go now."

"You're not going anywhere," Mary interjected. "Jessie doesn't need to be exposed to your flu."

"Besides, you can't." Abbie licked batter from her finger. "Jessie's in Philadelphia taping a Christmas special with Josh Grobin."

Nick pulled Abbie into the hallway. "Has Violet met Patrick?"

"Yeah. Mary just said he was Patrick Cavanaugh. Violet didn't say anything about him looking like Andrew."

"Where is he right now?"

"Upstairs with Kat and Bertie."

*

126

"Kat says you're one hell of a singer." Bertie lounged on the window seat in Kat's bedroom.

Patrick shrugged. He sat on the floor, going through some of Kat's research on Andrew.

Bertie stretched his leg to its full extension over his head. "I'm more of a dancer than a singer."

"Don't listen to him," Kat teased. "He can sing. But his ballet is amazing."

Patrick was impressed with Bertie. Only fifteen and already on Broadway. "Don't you have a show tonight?"

"It's our day off."

"And he always spends it with me. Don't you, Hubert?"

"Not if you keep calling me Hubert."

Patrick watched them. Kat and Bertie were cute together. Their relationship was easy. Comfortable. Were they an item? Or was Bertie gay? Hard to tell.

The Siamese cat jumped to the floor, rubbing against Patrick. He leapt onto his lap.

"Wow." Kat pushed away from her laptop. "Hamlet never does that with strangers."

Patrick's cell jangled. Father Joe. "Excuse me." Lifting Hamlet gently to the floor, he went out into the hallway and closed the door.

*

"What do you think of him?" Kat asked.

"He's different."

Kat's back stiffened. "What do you mean?"

"Don't get crazy on me. I just mean he seems like a nice guy. And shy. I don't remember the last nice, shy guy I met."

"Yes, he's nice. It's refreshing. He's also quietly religious, 'quietly' being the operative word. And he's shy around people he doesn't know well. All qualities I admire." Kat started typing furiously on her laptop.

Bertie moved over to Kat, massaging her shoulders. "It sounds like you have a crush on him."

Kat shook off his hands. "That's disgusting. We're cousins, Bertie."

Bertie dropped down on the floor and took her hands away from her computer. "I'm sorry, Katnip. I didn't know you felt so strongly about him."

Kat rubbed his fingers. "There's something about Patrick that makes me want to protect him. He's the kind of guy kids our age trash. It's so wrong."

Bertie nodded. "As they say, it's ass-backwards."

Kat looked down at their hands. "You're not so different from Patrick. You're not shy, but you're a good person.

"I'm not religious."

"You wear a cross around your neck."

"It was my brother's."

"The one who died in a gang?"

Bertie nodded. "You're right, in a way. Patrick and I are similar. We try to be good people, but there's a lot of shit going on underneath."

"What makes you say that?"

He shrugged. "We both had a messed up childhood. I get it. You never explained about what actually happened to Patrick when he was little—"

"Because I don't know the details."

"That kind of stuff affects you." Bertie continued. "I work mine out with dancing."

"Patrick must work his out by singing." She perked up, squeezing his hands. "We have to take him to SuZee Q's next Sunday. You're going to be blown away by his voice."

"Will I be jealous?"

"Even ANDREW would be jealous!"

*

"I'm sorry I haven't called, Father." Patrick leaned against the wall and ran a hand through his hair. "One day has blended into another."

"I'm just glad you're all right. So. Do you like it there?"

"They're good to me. But I feel out of place."

"Don't. They're your family. Accept their grace."

"They want me to take a paternity test."

"Do it, my boy. It will confirm what we already know."

"I'm scared, Father. This is all happening so fast. First Tess, now—"

"God's hand is in this, Patrick. Trust in Him."

Patrick nodded. "I haven't met Nick's wife yet."

"She'll love you as much as everyone else."

"I don't know. Everyone says she'll be angry at Andrew because he—"

"That's not your problem. You're the innocent in all this. All you can do is be nice to her. And have a blessed Thanksgiving, Patrick. I know you miss Tess but be grateful for your blessings."

*

Nick ran into Patrick on the second-floor landing.

"I was coming to find you. I—" Patrick began.

"Were you in my room last night?"

Patrick looked embarrassed. "Mary asked me to bring you—"

"No, no. It's okay." Nick had the impression he wasn't alone last night. "I just wanted to know if I was dreaming or—"

"That's what I want to talk to you about. While I was in your room, I had the feeling someone was watching me. It was weird.

Nick had his answer. Both Patrick and Andrew were in his room.

"There've been other things. Mary said you were the one with the answers."

Andrew was making his presence known. Nick was going to have to tell the boy the truth. "She was right. We need to talk. Let me lay down for an hour, and then I'll come find you."

*

Patrick lingered downstairs all evening, waiting to talk to Nick. The man never left his bedroom. Nor did Patrick see him on Tuesday. Mary said Nick left at dawn and had a full day of interviews and book signings. "He's so sick he shouldn't be going anywhere," she grumbled.

Feeling useless, Patrick offered to help Mary on Wednesday. She put him to work hand-washing crystal goblets, hauling in wood from the back yard and laying fires in the study and living room. Kat taught him how to build a fire, an education after living in Florida. Together they set the long dining room table, something he knew a little about after working at Cohan's.

"Please change your mind and eat with us," Kat begged.

"I'm not ready for all this yet." Patrick followed her back into the kitchen. Mary was laying out a spread on the island. The others were already eating. Abbie and … Violet? Right. Violet. Patrick was trying to learn everyone's name. He'd be lost with all the names tomorrow.

"We always have a buffet the night before Thanksgiving," Mary explained.

The front door slammed. Nick came into the kitchen.

"You look better," Kat observed.

"I feel better."

The front door slammed again. "I'm home." A young boy appeared, a large black dog at his side.

129

*

Nick looked from Anthony to Patrick. "Anthony, this is Patrick Cavanaugh."

Anthony's eyes were glued to Patrick. "Why do you look like Andrew?"

"Come on, Bongo." Nick put his hand on Anthony's shoulder. "Let's go upstairs and I'll explain."

"Tell me now."

"Anthony." Mary used her stern voice. "Go with your father."

"What's going on?" The boy was rooted in place.

"Excuse me." Patrick disappeared up the stairs.

"Come on, Anthony. Let's talk." Anthony finally followed Nick up to his bedroom, Monty trailing behind.

"Who is he, Dad?"

Nick went to the window and perched on the sill. "Kat discovered something in Andrew's journals. Which is why we went to Florida." He took a deep breath. "Andrew had a son seventeen years ago, a son he didn't even know about. Kind of like I had Kat a long time ago but just recently found out about her."

Anthony slumped onto his bed. "That guy is Andrew's son?"

"Yes."

"Is he living with us now?"

"No. Well, maybe. He's been living in Florida, but the woman who took care of him recently died. Right now he's just visiting."

Anthony looked stunned. His mouth was open, and his eyes darted everywhere. "Is this gonna keep happening?"

"What?"

"Kids showing up. Kids you and Andrew had."

"Of course not." Nick moved to the bed. "You were happy when Kat came to live with us."

"Yeah, but I thought she was the only one."

"Would it make a difference if I told you Andrew's involved in this? He was the one who got this whole thing going. He helped Kat make her discovery. Helped us find Patrick."

Anthony's eyes filled with tears.

"What's wrong, Bongo?"

Nick pulled him into his arms, but Anthony pushed away. "I wasn't enough for him. Andrew wanted a real son. Like you wanted a real kid. Kat. I'm nobody's son. I've had three dads, but I'm nobody's son."

"You're wrong. You're my son, and I love you." He again reached for Anthony.

"No!" Anthony moved further away. "Leave me alone, okay?"

"Come on—"

"I mean it. Leave me alone!"

"I'm not going anywhere, Anthony."

"Then I will." He ran from the room, Nick and Monty on his heels.

*

Patrick heard Nick and Anthony from the third-floor hallway. He knew it was wrong, but he crept partially down the stairs and listened to the conversation.

When Anthony, Nick and the dog rounded the corner, Patrick had nowhere to hide.

"You can have him!" Anthony shouted at Patrick. "Andrew doesn't want me, so I don't want him." His face red, Anthony scooted around him and scaled the stairs, climbing higher and higher. The dog bounded after him. A door slammed.

Patrick was embarrassed. "Sorry. I shouldn't have listened."

"You and Kat have a lot in common."

Patrick stared up the steps. "I don't remember a lot about … but I remember feeling like I was no one's son … until …"

Nick walked in a circle, thinking. "Maybe you should talk to Anthony."

"Me?" Patrick let out a nervous laugh.

"You said you know how he feels. Go on. As a favor to me."

*

Anthony sat on the couch in the fourth-floor luxury suite, crying. Monty sprawled on the floor at his feet.

Someone knocked on the door.

"Go away."

The door opened. Patrick – Andrew's REAL son – came in.

"I really want to be alone, okay?"

"Can we talk?"

Anthony crossed his arms and looked away.

"Your dad asked me to talk to you."

"My dad? That's a joke."

Patrick approached him. "I wouldn't have come here if I knew it would upset everyone else like this."

Anthony rolled his eyes. "Yeah, right."

"I mean it. I'll go back to Florida." He backed up. "This was a mistake." Patrick headed for the door.

"So Andrew isn't your dad?"

Patrick paused, looking over his shoulder. "I don't know. I haven't taken a paternity test."

"What's a paternity test?"

"They take my DNA – my saliva or blood or something - and test it against Andrew's to see if he's my father."

Anthony stared at Patrick. "You look exactly like him."

Patrick imitated Anthony and rolled his eyes. "I've heard that for years. But no one said he was my dad until Nick showed up."

"Don't you want him to be your dad?"

He shrugged and approached Anthony.

"He was a pretty cool dad."

"How old were you when he died?"

"Five. But he's not really dead."

"What?"

"Well, yeah, he died. But he didn't stay dead. If you were his son, you'd know that."

*

Patrick frowned. "What do you mean?"

"He hasn't visited you or you'd know what I mean. And if he hasn't visited you, you're not his son."

Not visited …? Nick said something to Anthony downstairs about Andrew being a part of the search for him … "Explain what you mean."

Monty got to his feet and nuzzled Patrick's hand. Patrick petted his soft fur.

"Monty, come here." Anthony patted the couch. The dog ignored him. "Great. Now my dog likes you better than me." Anthony eyed him. "Why did you REALLY come up here?"

"I thought maybe you could tell me about Andrew. Since you knew him best. As his son."

"I did. I do. And he visits me more than anyone, even Dad."

"Anthony, I don't want to interfere in your life with Nick or Andrew or anyone. I swear. I know what it's like. When Nick showed up in Florida and told me about Andrew, I felt like my world blew up. Please, tell me about Andrew visiting you. I'd really like to know."

CHAPTER 12

Nick sat in his office, waiting. Finally Patrick appeared in the doorway. "How'd it go?"

"Not good at first. But it got better." Patrick sat down beside the desk. "He told me Andrew visits him. And you."

Nick rubbed his brow. Okay. He couldn't avoid this subject any longer. "The other day you wanted to talk about unusual things that happened to you. What were they?"

"The first night I was here? When I went back upstairs my clothes were unpacked, and there were sweats and a Juilliard T-shirt laid out on my bed that weren't mine. Then, when I was in your room the other night, it felt like someone was watching me. And I've heard a man's voice."

Nick nodded. "I know this is going to sound crazy, but—"

"I believe in spirits."

Patrick's words took Nick by surprise. "You've experienced them?"

"The Catholic Church teaches about a place called Purgatory. Somewhere between Heaven and Hell. Where souls go until they atone for their sins. Then they move on to heaven. Or hell if they fail."

"You think Andrew's in Purgatory?"

"It makes sense. That's where ghosts come from. Spirits come back to right their wrongs. Or to help the people they love. That's how they earn their passage."

"Catholicism is more liberal than I realized."

"This is MY belief, not the Catholic Church's. I mean, yes, there is a Purgatory. I just always thought this was the most reasonable explanation for ghosts." He shook his head. "I never even discussed this with Father Joe."

"What about Tess?"

"Tess and I didn't have secrets. She liked my idea. She told me she dreamed about her husband Henry, that the dreams were so real she felt she'd spent time with him again. She said he felt bad because he was selfish after Frankie died, so he visited her to make up for it."

"What about you? Have you ever encountered a spirit?"

Patrick hesitated.

"What?"

"Nothing." He fidgeted.

"Is this about the picture downstairs?"

"Who is she?" Patrick's breathing became erratic.

"Our mother. Andrew's and mine. Your grandmother. Chelsea."

Patrick leaned forward, trying to get a deep breath.

Nick laid a hand on his arm. "I'm sorry I brought this up."

"Why— is this— happening— so often?" Patrick's eyes darted around the room. Blood trickled from his nose.

*

Patrick was back in that closet ... in the dark ... the cold ...

"I'm here, Patrick. Don't be afraid, sweetheart. Don't be afraid." The lady with the dark hair. His grandmother? She combed his hair with her fingers. "Let's sing, okay? Let's sing. 'Nothing's gonna harm you. Not while I'm around. Nothing's gonna harm you. No sir, not while I'm around ..."

Nick physically got him out of the chair and over to a couch, laying him down and holding tissues to his nose.

"You're here, Patrick. In this house. Safe. Do you hear me?"

Patrick tried to focus on Nick. He tried with every ounce of energy he had.

"You're seventeen years old and safe in this house."

He heard Nick. He heard his words. Patrick tried to take a deep breath and focus on the man looking down at him.

"Is he all right?" A young boy's voice. Anthony.

"He will be."

Patrick wanted to be all right. He closed his eyes and thought of Andrew. Help me, Andrew. Please. If you can hear me, help me.

His headache began to fade. The bleeding stopped. His breath wasn't as shallow. Patrick opened his eyes.

Nick and Anthony stared down at him. He looked from one to the other. He didn't know if it was Andrew or his own sheer force of will, but he WAS better. As he pushed himself to a sitting position, Anthony sat beside him. "What's wrong with you?"

"Sometimes I get these ... attacks."

"Did I make that happen?"

"I did it to myself."

"Because I told you about Andrew visiting me?"

"No."

"Are you still leaving?"

Nick finally spoke up. "He's not going anywhere. And neither are you. What would I do without you, Anthony?"

*

Nick dragged himself downstairs for something to eat before turning in for the night. Mary and Abbie sat at the island. "Where's Kat?" he asked.

"Willie took her to her writing class."

Nick lifted a pan on the stove. Chicken noodle soup. Bless Mary. He filled a bowl and joined them.

"Where are the boys?" Mary asked.

"In their rooms."

"Is everything okay between them?"

"They made a start."

"Well, that's good." Abbie took her plate to the sink. "Because I don't think you're going to get a kumbaya from Jessie."

Nick dropped his head in his hands. Jessie. He forgot about Jessie.

"She's the last one to learn about Patrick. How do you think that's going to go over?"

*

Patrick couldn't sleep. He couldn't stop thinking about the woman with the dark hair. His grandmother. Chelsea. He had to see that picture again. Just to make sure.

He snuck downstairs to the living room. The house looked beautiful, all dressed up for Thanksgiving. He smelled bread and pumpkin and a million other things he couldn't identify.

Going to the mantel, he stared at the picture of his grandmother, her arms around a young Andrew. Next to it was a vase of white roses. Their scent reminded Patrick of the stage and orchestras and the joy of singing. They were clean and bright and innocent. Which was why he insisted on white roses for Tess's funeral.

Lifting the photo, a memory surfaced, a good one this time. This woman came to him when he needed her most. She held him. Teased him about his curly hair. Sang with him. Made him laugh when he felt like crying. And she reminded him that he was someone's son.

Replacing the photo, he was drawn to the front windows. Outside, autumn leaves swirled in circles on the windy street. Large, decorated pumpkins lined the stairs of a pristine home across the street. Thanksgiving in New York City. He and Tess fantasized about coming here, seeing the parade in person, shopping at Macy's.

White downy flakes began to flutter to the ground, picking up speed as they were snatched by the wind. Thinking of Tess, he began to sing softly …

Some say love, it is a river that drowns the tender reed.
Some say love, it is a razor that leaves your soul to bleed.
Some say love, it is a hunger, an endless aching need.
I say love, it is a flower, and you its only seed.

Anthony came up beside him. "I forgot.
"What?"
"He sang. All the time. Andrew. You sound just like him. He used to sing me to sleep." He looked up at Patrick. "Don't stop. Please."
As Patrick watched his first snowfall, he continued …

When the night has been too lonely, and the road has been too long.
And you think that love is only for the lucky and the strong.
Just remember in the winter, far beneath the bitter snows,
Lies the seed that with the sun's love, in the spring becomes the rose.

*

Nick awoke on Thanksgiving morning feeling better than he had in days. The aromas coming from the kitchen made his stomach growl. He showered, shaved and went downstairs to devour bacon, eggs, home fries, and an English muffin. He sat at the island eating like a man who hadn't seen food in a week.

Mary checked the bird in the oven. "Did you hear that last night?"
"What?" Nick asked between bites.
"Patrick. Singing. With Anthony as his audience. What a voice that boy has. I stayed out of sight and just listened. Then they sat in the living room and talked."

This day was certainly starting out on a high note. Patrick and Anthony were becoming friends. Well, it was Thanksgiving. And they always got a miracle on Thanksgiving. "What time is everyone due?"

"We're eating at three. They'll get here when they get here, I guess. Including Jessie."

Jessie. He'd forgotten. His jubilation slid downhill. "I'll go to Jessie's hotel when I'm done here to talk to her about Patrick."

"She's at the parade. She and Ollie are doing a song from the show."

His joy evaporated. Damn. Between Jessie's performance schedule, not to mention Philadelphia on Monday and the parade today,

136

when was he supposed to talk to her? He'd have to corner her as soon as she got here.

Finished, Nick scaled the stairs to check on Patrick. "You're sure you won't join us for dinner?"

Patrick shook his head. "I don't want to cause a scene. Kat gave me Andrew's journals to read."

Kat should have asked him first. Still, Patrick should read them. He sat down in the chair beside the desk. "Mary said she heard you singing late last night."

"I didn't mean to wake anyone."

"Anthony was with you?"

"Yeah."

"So you two are getting closer?"

"Starting to." Patrick closed the journal and swiveled to face Nick. "He's a pretty amazing kid. He told me about Gianni. And about Andrew, what he was like as a father. How funny he was. He also told me about the days surrounding his murder. How depressed he was when Andrew died. I understood because of Tess."

Maybe these two boys were good for each other. They'd both been through a lot in their young lives. Anthony never discussed his past with friends. He said it was too embarrassing. But a cousin was different. He was family.

Nick rose. "Well, there's a place at the table for you, if you change your mind." He headed for the door.

"Nick? I've decided to do the paternity test."

Nick walked back over to him. "What made you finally decide?"

"Anthony. He said I should know, one way or the other. I think he wants to know more than me."

"Do you think he'll be okay with it?"

Patrick shrugged. "Do you?"

"Anthony's resilient. Maybe the idea of having an older brother appeals to him."

"Brother? We're cousins. Maybe."

"There was a time when Anthony was Andrew's son. Like you. Maybe." Nick again strode to the door. "I'll get the test scheduled."

He retreated to his office and called Willie. "Do you think the NYPD still has Andrew's DNA on file?"

"I'll check. Is this for Patrick?"

"Yeah."

"I can take care of the test, too."

"Thanks, Willie. See you later." Things were finally falling into place. Now it was time to focus on his next book.

*

Mary was in her element. Thanksgiving was in full swing.

Larry Williams, Willie, Anthony and Ollie Farrow were in the study watching football. With Monty, of course. Ollie was arguing the merits of soccer versus American football. Kat and Bertie were in the living room at the piano. And Jessie, Nora and Abbie were on the back porch. Mary was in the kitchen with Violet making sure appetizers flowed from room to room.

When the doorbell rang, Kat ran to answer it and dragged Bree to the kitchen. The woman held a small planter of mums. "Happy Thanksgiving, Mary."

"Oh, how beautiful. I'll put them on my bedroom terrace. Sit, sit. Help yourself to some food." Mary wanted to keep Bree in the kitchen, as far from Jessie as possible. Unfortunately, her plan didn't get off the ground.

"I heard the doorbell." Jessie appeared in the doorway. Her face fell at the sight of Bree. "Oh. I thought it might be James."

"Hi, Jessie." Bree was cool as a cucumber. "Happy Thanksgiving."

"Happy Thanksgiving." Jessie glanced at Mary. "Where's Nick?"

"Working. I should go get him."

The doorbell rang again.

"That has to be James." Jessie sidled out of the room. "I'll get it."

Mary looked at Violet and rolled her eyes.

James Lovelock skated into the kitchen with Jessie. Dressed in a black silk suit with a pumpkin shirt and tie, he held a bouquet of flowers, a shopping bag and his precious Cosette, whose ribbons matched James' shirt. "Thanks for the invite, Mary. And the house looks beauteous!"

Monty trotted up to James, fascinated by Cosette. The large dog licked his chops.

"Monty, no!" Mary's voice boomed. It did no good.

"What's wrong?" Anthony joined them.

"Call your dog off, Anthony."

"Come on, Monty." He patted his thigh.

Ignoring Anthony, Monty growled and did a little leap, nipping at Cosette's mini-feet. The tiny dog wriggled against James, who had trouble hanging onto her.

The flowers and shopping bag hit the floor, as did Cosette.

138

Terrified, Cosette skittered up the stairs with Monty on her heels. James ran after them, followed by Jessie and Anthony.

*

Hearing a God-awful commotion in the hall, Nick went to his office door. He was in time to see the Cosette train hurtling up to the third floor. Anthony repeatedly shouted Monty's name. Which the mutt ignored.

Nick took up the rear.

In the fourth-floor suite, Cosette was cornered. Everyone tried to nab her, but she became a greased furball. She circled both rooms of the suite, Monty's guttural growls propelling her, before escaping back out the door.

*

Patrick, too, heard the commotion. As he peeked out his door, a tiny white dog slithered through his legs and into the bedroom. This was followed by Monty knocking Patrick down and leaping over him.

An Asian man ran past Patrick and grabbed the little dog, cooing and petting her, trying to calm her down. Nick and Anthony dashed into the room.

As Patrick got to his feet, he was stunned to look into the shocked face of Jessica Kendle.

"Who are you?" Her unblinking stare made him uncomfortable.

Nick moved to his side. "This is Patrick Cavanaugh, Jessie."

The woman was stapled in place. "My God. He's a replica of Andrew. Right down to the dimple in his chin."

Why did she talk about him as if he weren't in the room? As if he were some painting in a museum?

Nick put an arm around her. "Let's go to my office and I'll explain."

Jessie shook off his hand. "Explain now."

"Anthony," Nick said. "Take James downstairs."

"I want to stay with Patrick." He hung onto Monty's collar.

"Anthony, please. Do as I say."

Anthony looked from Patrick to Nick before leading James and Monty out of the room and closing the door.

*

Jessie couldn't believe what she was seeing. This young man was a carbon copy of Andrew. "What's going on, Nick?" She zeroed in on Patrick and asked again, "Who are you?"

139

Nick approached her. "I discovered that Andrew might have had a child. Seventeen years ago. So I went to Florida to see if it was true. As you can see, it was."

Jessie couldn't stop staring at this boy who was the image of her late husband. He took her breath away. "Andrew had a … You're Andrew's son?"

Patrick didn't move. And he didn't answer her.

"Seventeen …? Florida … Who's the mother?"

"It doesn't matter."

"Who's the mother, Nick?"

Nick sighed. "A girl he worked with at the Asolo."

"This happened when he was— Why didn't he tell me?"

"He didn't know."

Stunned, Jessie walked to the terrace door. Andrew had a child years ago, a child Nick just unearthed. This was unbelievable. No, it was a miracle. She walked back over to Patrick. Andrew Brady is murdered, and then a son appears. A boy who could pass himself off as Andrew, with a little aging. "When did you find him?"

"Shortly before my book tour."

*

Patrick shifted from foot to foot. She was doing it again. Talking about him like he was an inanimate object. He wanted out of here, but his path to the door was blocked.

"Your book tour? That was weeks ago." Jessie's face clouded over, her blue eyes hardening, as she turned to Nick. "How could you go to Florida to search for Andrew's son and not tell me?

"We weren't even sure he existed—"

"We?"

"Kat and I."

"Kat. Of course you told Kat."

"Kat told ME. She was the one who found an entry in one of Andrew's journals—"

Jessie's steely gaze flipped to Patrick. "He's living here in the house—"

"Stop talking about me like I'm not standing here—" Patrick interrupted.

"—and everyone knew about him but me."

Nick shook his head. "No one knew until—"

"Secrets. Why are you always so secretive, Nick?"

Patrick suddenly felt like he fell through the looking glass.

"You secretive little brat!"

Jessie continued, "You disappear on a secret mission to Florida that involves me—"

"You disappear for two days—"

"Andrew was my husband. I deserved to know before anyone."

"Answer me, Patrick! Where were you?"

"Did you think you could keep him hidden forever?"

"Did you think you could hide from me forever?"

"You're blowing this out of proportion, Jessie!"

"I was the only one you kept out of the loop. Why? Did you want this boy all for yourself? Is that it, Nick? You didn't get to grow up with Andrew so you'll use his son—"

"You're insane!"

Jessie reared back and slapped Nick hard across the face.

She smacked him hard across the face.

"No!" Patrick lunged for Jessie, knocking her off-balance. She tumbled to the floor.

"Patrick!" Someone grabbed him. He fought back. "Stop it. STOP IT!" A voice snapped him out of it. Nick. It was Nick. What-what happened? Spotting Jessie on the floor he backed up, horrified.

Nick helped Jessie up, but she shook him off. "He can't be Andrew's son. Andrew would never hurt me or any woman. This is a cruel joke, and I hate you for it!" She ran from the room.

Patrick collapsed into the desk chair and dropped his head in his hands.

Nick came up behind him. "What's going on? That's not like you."

"Maybe it is."

*

Jessie hurried down the stairs into the kitchen. Everyone was gathered, and they all stared at her.

"I told them what little I know." James said, standing beside Larry and Ollie and still holding Cosette. "Which is next to nothing."

Jessie turned to Mary. "How could you not tell me?"

"It wasn't my story to tell."

Jessie glanced at Kat, who stared defiantly at her. Even Bertie seemed non-plussed. She looked at Bree. "I suppose you've known about it from the beginning."

Bree's eyes flicked to Mary. That was odd. What was going on?

Then Jessie noticed Abbie and Willie. They wouldn't look at her. "You both knew, too?"

Abbie peeked up at her. "We found out accidentally."

Jessie had heard enough. "Larry. Nora. Ollie. We're leaving." She headed for the hall.

Larry stopped her before she reached the vestibule. "What exactly happened up there?"

"You're not going to believe this. Andrew has a son. A seventeen-year-old son. That's why Nick was snooping around Florida all this time. He was looking for him. And everyone knew. Everyone but me."

Larry pulled Jessie into the living room and closed the double doors. "Start from the beginning."

"I don't want to talk about it. Let's go."

Larry took her arm. "Tell me, Jessie."

She looked up into his soft brown eyes. He was so calm, so solid. The opposite of volatile, unpredictable Nick. Taking a deep breath, she gave Larry an encapsulated version. "And then the kid attacked me."

"What do you mean, attacked?"

"He came after me when I slapped Nick."

"You slapped Nick?"

"He deserved it, believe me. But this kid became a wild man. Typical. All kids defend that monster."

Larry led her to the couch, sitting down with her. "Jessie, you married that monster. You love that monster. So stop with the hyperbole. It doesn't help."

"Why are you taking his side?"

"I'm not. I'm just trying to get to the facts."

"The facts are Andrew has an illegitimate son, just like Nick has an illegitimate daughter—"

"And you have an illegitimate son. Things happen."

Jessie stared at him, her mouth open. "Things happen? How trite."

"Now you're attacking me?"

She stood up. "I want to go back to the hotel."

"And do what? Stew about this and make yourself angrier?" He pulled her back down. "You need to continue the conversation with Nick."

"There's nothing more to say."

"There's plenty more to say. Did he explain why he didn't tell you about Patrick?"

"He was full of stupid excuses—"

"Did he tell you why you're the last one to know?"

"It's obvious—"

"I think your anger is misdirected. Yes, you're ticked off at Nick, but that's nothing new. Andrew's the one you're really upset with."

Jessie again got to her feet. "That's ridiculous." She walked to the windows.

"Is it?" Larry followed her. "Andrew was always a good guy in your eyes. He married you out of kindness, wanting to make your life easier. He was the perfect husband and father. He was a generous actor who always let you take the spotlight, right?"

Jessie didn't answer, not sure where this was going.

"The truth is, Andrew was a guy with flaws, just like the rest of us. He had the biggest ego around. He kept you in the spotlight because it made him look better. And he could be cruel to stagehands and condescending to other actors."

"That's not true! I never saw any of that."

"Of course not. He wanted to remain perfect in your eyes. Yes, he married you to give Anthony a father, but he also did it because he loved you and saw it as his opportunity to have what he always wanted: you. He screwed around, slept with other women before you, just like every other guy who eventually settles down and marries his true love. And one of those women got pregnant, just like what happened to Nick. There are no perfect men, Jessie."

She hated to admit it, but she WAS angry with Andrew. Or maybe disappointed. She thought he was different. But he ended up being exactly like his brother.

"Don't get me wrong," Larry continued. "I liked Andrew. We were good friends, really close at one time. I'm just trying to point out that he had faults, like all of us. It's time you saw him in a realistic light."

There was a knock on the door. "Jess?"

Nick.

"Talk to him, Jessie. Just listen to what he has to say." He took her hand and squeezed before letting Nick in and leaving them alone.

143

CHAPTER 13

Patrick was at the desk, his head down on his folded arms.

"May I come in?"

Mary's sudden voice startled him. He nodded.

She sat down in the easy chair beside the desk. "Are you okay?"

Patrick swiped at his tears. "This has to stop. I don't want to hurt anyone."

"What has to stop?"

"These-these panic attacks, or whatever I keep having."

"What happened, Patrick?"

He shook his head. "I don't know. When Jessie slapped Nick I must have—"

She slapped him so hard he got a headache ...

"Must have what, Patrick?"

The belt ...

"I—She—I was afraid—"

"NOOOO! Stop! Please! ..."

"—she was going to hurt him."

"Jessie was going to hurt Nick?"

She ripped his shorts off ... his T-shirt ... "Please! ..."

Patrick couldn't breathe ...

The belt slashed through the air ... Again and again ... She dragged him away and threw him in a dark closet, striking him again with the wooden hanger ... Cold ... So cold ...

*

Mary touched his shoulder. "Patrick?"

No response. No movement at all.

Thinking quickly, Mary pulled him to the easy chair, cradling him on her lap. He was limp, like a ragdoll. His eyes were glazed. "It's okay, sweetheart," she cooed. "I'm here. You're all right." She rocked him and hummed 'The Rose,' what he sang last night.

It took a minute, but he quietly joined her, singing the words. He stared blankly, nothing moving but his lips. She kissed his forehead, ran her hands through his hair, cupped his cheek. She did what she must to make Patrick feel safe and loved.

144

*

"He didn't mean it." Nick stood a few feet away from Jessie.

"Kids always defend you, Nick. You're a god in their eyes."

"That's not what it was about." Nick walked to the windows, sliding his hands in his pockets. "Patrick was in a foster home until he was five. It was bad, Jess. Really bad. The only details I know are what Tess— the woman who took him in later— wrote in her diary. Seeing bruises and welts. I think his abuse left more than physical scars. When you struck out at me, it must have triggered a memory."

Nick turned back to her. "That's the only thing that makes sense. He's a gentle kid. Religious. Tess and a priest raised him. They kept him sheltered, probably because of what happened to him when he was little. His only release is when he sings. Onstage, he seems years older. And in complete control."

Compassion filled Jessie's eyes. "Is he a danger to himself?"

Good question. "He has panic attacks. Or something like that. They've picked up lately, ever since he learned he might be Andrew's son."

"Might be? You don't know for sure?"

"We're about to do a paternity test. But the truth is obvious. At least to me." Nick sat down beside her. "You have to understand how overwhelming this is for him. A month ago he was just a kid living in Florida. Now he might be the son of a famous star."

"What about Anthony? How does he feel about him?"

She didn't need to know about Anthony's initial reaction. "They're getting to know each other. Patrick's good with him."

Jessie smiled a little. "You're making me feel better about this boy." A moment later, the smile disappeared. "But it doesn't make up for not telling me about this from the beginning."

Nick sighed. "At first, there was no point. I wasn't sure if any of it was true. Then when I realized Andrew did indeed have a son, the clues came fast and furious. There was no time for anything but tracking the boy down. I found him right before I left on the book tour."

Jessie shook her head. "Your memory isn't what it used to be. Have you forgotten we were together on opening night? You could have told me then. Or when you called me along the road."

"At that point I wasn't sure I'd ever see Patrick again. He didn't seem interested in getting to know any of us. When Tess died, he took off. I was halfway through my book tour at that point. No one knew where he was. Should I have told you then? When he might have been dead?"

"So he just showed up here?"

Nick nodded. "Last weekend."

"Why not tell me then?"

"I got sick as a dog, Jessie. Outside of my book commitments, I've been in bed for days."

Jessie paced across the room. "You always have a handy excuse." She turned around, her voice cold. "Secrets were a problem with us from the beginning. You keep everything to yourself, always the loner."

"That's not true and you know it."

Jessie's eyes narrowed. "Actually, you're right. You tell your daughter everything."

Nick leapt up. "Kat again." He ran his hands through his hair in frustration. "You're still jealous of a little girl."

"I am NOT jealous. But I sure as hell resent her. From the moment that girl walked into this house, our marriage has gone to hell."

Nick was suddenly tired. Of the constant fighting. Of the struggle to make things work. "Is that what we have? A marriage?"

Jessie's expression morphed from anger to pain in a split second. "I'll stay for dinner. I don't want to ruin my guests' Thanksgiving. But let's stop pretending we're happily married."

*

Patrick sat up. Mary? He was on her lap? How humiliating.

He scrambled to get up, but she held onto him. "Not so fast."

"I'm too old for—"

"You're never too old for some good old-fashioned TLC. Besides, I was enjoying it. I used to hold Andrew like this. He loved it."

He could see she meant it. Still … "I'm okay now." He slid over to the desk chair. He wasn't okay. But he couldn't continue to be babied. He wasn't a little kid anymore.

"Was that what she did? Your grandmother? Take care of you when you were scared?"

How did she know?

"The way I see it, if Andrew can break through the outer ring, maybe his mama could, too. Is that what she did?"

He looked down and nodded.

"Looks to me like you were taken care of all along. So nothing could happen to you until you found your way home. To us."

Patrick met her eyes. "How do you—"

"You'll soon learn I know pretty much everything that goes on in this house."

He finally broke into a smile. There were things about Mary that reminded him of Tess. Her wisdom. And her heart.

"Patrick, listen to me. No matter what happened to you, no matter what memories surface, it's in the past. You're safe now. You have Nick and Kat and Anthony and me, we're all here for you. And pretty soon, you'll have Jessie, too. And you have one more person, the most important. Andrew." She patted his arm and got to her feet. "Now I better go check on that turkey. I'll bring up a plate in a little while."

He slid his hand into hers. "Thank you, Mary."

*

Kat sat back and enjoyed the fireworks. Also the meal. Roast turkey with rosemary and bacon, glazed ham, mashed potatoes, winter squash, corn, sweet potatoes, Brussels sprouts, brandy-laced cranberry sauce and rye rolls. Kat sampled everything while Bertie inhaled his meal. For entertainment, they kicked each under the table when something in the room amused them.

Her father and Jessie spent the meal sniping at each other. Hit-and-run stuff. Jessie complimented Larry. Dad complimented Bree. Jessie talked about the camaraderie of the *DIANA* company. Dad talked about the camaraderie in the house. Jessie crowed about the many interviews she was doing. Dad announced that *THE SILVER LINING* was still on *The New York Times* best-sellers list.

Jessie singled out Abbie for wearing slacks on Thanksgiving. "You know we always dress up."

"These are Christian Siriano. More expensive than the dress you're wearing!"

Dad singled out James for his conservative attire. "No feather boas?"

"Out of respect for this turkey losing his feathers, no. Don't make fun, Nick. I know how to dress for every occasion."

Larry and Ollie seemed uncomfortable with the hostility between Dad and Jessie. Bree quietly observed the exchanges, like a good reporter should. Mary, Violet and Nora pretended all was well. Abbie and Willie were in their own little world. And Anthony just kept shoveling in the food.

Jessie, Larry, Ollie and Nora left right after the meal. Jessie was the only one who didn't carry her plate to the kitchen. Domestic chores were beneath the pampered queen.

All-in-all, it was an entertaining Thanksgiving.

If only Patrick had joined the fun.

*

Nick looked in on Patrick after everyone left. Kat and Anthony were in their rooms. The house was quiet.

147

Fully dressed, Patrick was asleep on top of his bed. Nick covered him with the handmade quilt and turned out the bedside light.

Grabbing the boy's plate, he returned to the kitchen.

Mary and Bree finished cleaning up. "Thanks for staying to help, Bree. With Violet going home with a headache, and Abbie and Willie driving Jessie and the others home, I was on my own."

Nick placed Patrick's plate on the sink. "He's asleep. He didn't eat much."

"That fight probably shocked him." Mary covered the plate with plastic wrap. "It shocked everyone."

"I'm heading home." Bree backed up. "Thanks for a wonderful meal, Mary."

Nick followed Bree down the hall and helped her into her coat. Grabbing his own, he said, "Come on. I'll put you in a cab."

The night air was bitter. The smell of snow was in the air as they walked towards Fifth Avenue.

"I'm sorry we didn't get a chance to talk about your case." Nick rubbed his hands together.

Bree shrugged, dismissing it. "I'm proud of you, Nick."

"For what?"

"For tracking down Andrew's son. It couldn't have been easy."

Nick pulled up his collar and shoved his hands in his pockets. "You certainly got quite a show today."

"It was just Jessie being Jessie. Dramatic." She looked up at him.

Spotting a cab, Nick whistled. The cabbie screeched to a stop in front of them. Nick opened the back door. "Our lives have always been out of the mainstream, haven't they, Bree?"

"In what way?"

"Traveling the world. Chasing the story. Living out of suitcases. Then we decide to settle down and look what happens. Ethan's in California, and Jessie's in a hotel."

"Yeah, but you have kids to love. That's home for you." She smiled that crooked little smile that made him crazy. "Night, Nick."

Nick leaned over and brushed her cheek with his lips.

He watched the cabbie head for the Seventy-Second Street crossover to the Upper West Side before hurrying home.

He stopped in the kitchen to say good night to Mary.

"I had quite an experience with Patrick earlier." Mary told him about holding the boy while he sang. "It was like he was five-years-old again."

"He probably was. It was strange, what happened with Jessie today. He literally attacked her."

"What did the people who had that foster home look like? Maybe Jessie reminds him of someone."

Interesting. "I'll check Tess's diaries to see if there are descriptions."

Mary nodded and turned out the overhead light. "How are things with Jessie? It was getting ugly at the dinner table."

Nick shook his head. "I think it's over between us."

"Don't give up just yet."

*

"Don't go yet, Larry." Jessie removed her coat and tossed it over a chair. "I don't want to be alone." Nora had gone to bed.

Larry sat down on the couch, stretching his arm across the back. "The meal was great. The conversation? Not so much."

Jessie sat beside him. "I'm so angry with Nick. I can't let it go."

"What did he say when you talked? If you don't mind my asking."

"I don't. I wouldn't have talked to him if you hadn't pushed me." She looked down at her rings, spinning them on her finger. "He made excuses for Patrick. He said the boy had been through a lot when he was little, and it was now coming back to him because of this whole Andrew thing."

"That makes sense."

"Nick is a different person when it comes to kids. He excuses them for everything."

"I don't think he excuses them. I think he understands them. You told me a little about his childhood."

Jessie stared at Larry. "How do you do that? How do you see things so clearly when I can't?"

"You're too close to it. And anger clouds the truth."

Jessie slid her arms around him and laid her head against his chest. "Thank you. I'd be a basket case without you right now." She looked up at him, meeting his eyes.

Lifting up, she kissed him. He tasted of pumpkin pie. And safety.

Larry pulled back. "This isn't a good idea."

"Why not? We've known each other forever. Aren't we allowed to kiss?"

"Not unless we're sure it won't go any further."

She turned away, sitting up. He didn't want her. Another rejection. He rubbed her back. "You're in love with Nick."

"Even if I am, I don't think it's enough. Not for a marriage."

149

"A lot of things go into a marriage. Passion is one of them."

Images of her histrionic fights with Nick flashed through her mind. Of Nick making love to her in his demonstrative way. "What about you and Gloria? Was there passion?"

"We're calmer and more orderly than you and Nick. Which is why my affair ended things so cleanly."

"Do you miss her?"

"Sure. We were together eighteen years."

Jessie nodded

"You know, Jessie, lost in your vitriol towards Nick is how you feel about Andrew's son."

"I don't know how I feel. I didn't spend much time with him. He was too busy beating me up." She chuckled. "I have to think about the situation more."

"And while you think, I'll head back to my hotel." He stood up. "Before we make a mistake we'll regret." Larry grabbed his coat and headed for the door.

"Larry?"

He looked over his shoulder at her.

"Are you sure it would be a mistake?"

*

On Friday morning, Willie showed up as Nick was eating breakfast with Patrick, Mary and Kat. Anthony was still asleep.

"I checked on Andrew's DNA. We still have it," Willie informed Nick. "Now," he said, turning to Patrick, "let's do this test." He swabbed Patrick's mouth with a Q-Tip and dropped it into a plastic bag. "The results should be back early next week."

Nick watched Patrick. He was quiet during the test and as he finished eating. Was he afraid the results would be negative? More likely, he was afraid they'd confirm he was Andrew's son. For a young man who'd been raised by a priest and sweet old lady, this had to be overwhelming.

Nick stood up. "I'm going for a run. Who wants to join me?"

Still silent, Patrick took his dishes to the sink.

"I'll come with you, Dad."

The air was cold, the sunshine bright as Nick and Kat ran their usual route in Central Park.

"I want to convince Patrick to go with Bertie and me and sing at the cabaret Sunday night," Kat said, as they circled the reservoir. "I might need your help."

"What do you need?"

150

"How about if you, Mary and Anthony join us?"

"Sure."

In fact, Nick had an even better idea.

*

As Patrick headed for the stairs, Mary stopped him. "Come over here for a minute. I have something for you." Mary waited for Patrick to sit across from her in the breakfast nook before removing a box from her apron pocket. She slid it to him.

"You don't have to—"

"Just open it." Lifting the lid, he removed a silver chain with a crucifix dangling from it. He looked up at her in surprise. "It was my grandfather's. He wore it until the day he died. Granddaddy was a man of strong faith. I want you to add Tess's ring to it."

Patrick shook his head. "I can't take your—"

"My only children are all of you, Patrick. You're my family. I would have given it to Andrew if he'd lived. Now it's yours. Please. I want you to have it."

*

Nick and Kat sought out Patrick when they got home. He was in his room, as usual, reading Andrew's journals.

"Come with Bertie and me on Sunday night," Kat said. "To Susie's cabaret. You need to get back to singing."

Patrick closed the journal. "Thanks, but—"

"No 'buts.' You're going."

Patrick took a moment. "What kind of accompaniment is there?"

"A piano, base and drums. Sometimes we get a few flutes and horns. It depends on who's available. Or what musicians show up. People sometimes bring their own pianists. Do you want to rehearse?"

"Uh, well—"

"Dad can play for you. He's really good. Or I can fill in." She went to the shelves of sheet music. "Now, what do you feel like singing?"

Nick chuckled. His daughter was a steamroller.

Five minutes later, Patrick and Kat were at the piano in the living room.

Nick ducked into his office to make a few calls before joining them.

As Patrick's beautiful baritone drifted up the stairs, Nick phoned the director of *DIANA*. "Quill. It's Nick McDeare." Amazing how strong the boy's voice was all the way up here. "Remember the opening night party? You told me you were bored, that you wanted something or someone to excite you again?"

151

"A guy can dream, can't he?"

"Well, I may have just the thing—"

"Who's that singing? Nice voice."

"That voice is why I'm calling ..."

*

"So what do you think?" Jessie asked Nora. They sat at the table, finishing a light lunch. Nick had just phoned, inviting her to a place called SuZee Q's on Sunday night to hear Patrick sing.

"I'm dying of curiosity." Nora sat back and crossed her legs. "You saw the kid. I didn't."

"You won't believe how much he looks like Andrew. It was a shock." To say the least.

"I wonder if he sings like Andrew."

"I want to find out. Let's go. I'll ask Larry, too."

"Ah, Larry."

Jessie narrowed her eyes. "What does that mean?"

"Is there something going on between the two of you?"

"Between Larry and me?" She laughed, but she knew it rang hollow. "No. He misses Gloria and I miss Nick."

Jessie became uncomfortable under Nora's scrutiny. "No, Nora. There's nothing going on. It's impossible for two old friends to ever be anything more."

*

When Nick replaced her at the piano, Kat slipped into the dining room and phoned Bree. "We're all going to a cabaret on Sunday night. Bertie and I are singing, and so is Patrick. Can you come?"

"Who's 'we'?"

"The family. And Abbie and Willie. Please come, Bree."

Sensing movement behind her, Kat spun around.

Mary stood in the hallway arch. And she didn't look happy.

*

Patrick was blown away by Nick at the piano. No matter how many deviations Patrick spontaneously made, Nick followed him. 'Gethsemane' was a total rewrite, Patrick making it his own, and Nick never missed a beat.

"You have to play for me on Sunday. I don't think anyone else could follow me like you do. I rehearsed a lot with the pianist at Cohan's, but you just picked everything up immediately."

Kat rejoined them. "I just talked to Susie. She's going to give you a chunk of time on Sunday."

"Why would she do that? She hasn't heard me."

152

"She just heard you through the phone!"

*

SuZee Q's was larger than Nick envisioned, seating maybe two hundred. Tonight it was a less than half full. It covered four store fronts and was two stories high. Susie's classes were on the upper floors.

There was a bar and a food station with pizza, hamburgers, chicken wings and other nibbles. Kat said everyone who worked at the cabaret volunteered their time, all proceeds going to LET THEM SOAR, Susie's campaign to fund kids who can't afford classes in the arts. "Susie calls all her students her little birds," Kat explained. "That's where the idea came from."

They had a large table for ten in the center of the room. Nick sat on one side of Patrick, Mary on the other. Anthony never sat still, always jumping up to take pictures. Kat and Bertie were looking over their music, choosing songs. And Abbie and Willie were over at the food station, getting snacks.

People were beginning to stare at them. Patrick didn't seem to notice. And if he was nervous it didn't show. Nick couldn't remember ever being this nervous. Until now, his gift with the piano was a family secret.

Susie Jacobs stopped by their table, kissing Nick on the cheek. "So Kat finally got you to my place." Seeing Patrick, she gasped. "Oh my God, Kat was right. You look just like him. I can't wait to hear you sing. By the way, Nick. Jessie just walked in. I'll send her this way."

*

As Susie approached, Jessie spotted Bree joining Nick's table. The woman sat down beside Nick. Did Nick really expect Jessie to sit at the same table with his ex?

"You know," Jessie told Susie, "I'd rather sit at a less conspicuous, smaller table."

"Quill Llewellyn is coming tonight. Do you want him to join you?"

Quill was coming? Jessie fumed. Why didn't she know about this? "Yes."

*

"What are you doing here?" Nick asked Bree.

"Kat invited me. Shouldn't I have come?"

"No, it's fine. I'm just surprised to see you." Nick turned to Patrick. "This is a colleague and friend of mine, Brianna Fontaine. Bree, meet Patrick."

"I can't wait to hear you sing, Patrick." No shocked look from Bree. No tired observation about how much he looked like Patrick. Nope.

153

She talked about his singing. As Nick always said, her instincts were impeccable.

He glanced over his shoulder at Jessie. He was met by two sapphire spitfires. So be it.

As the entertainment began, Nick sat back and tried to relax. The acoustics were impressive. There was a hand mike and accompanying stand. Twin spotlights and soft stage gels. Susie had spared no expense. The student singers were all good, including Kat and Bertie. Especially Kat and Bertie.

As Susie introduced Patrick and they made their way to the stage, Nick spotted Quill, hurrying to grab a chair at their table. A murmur spread across the room as Patrick went center stage and Nick sat down at the piano. Either the audience noticed Patrick's similarity to Andrew or they recognized Nick. Or both.

When the room was silent, Patrick looked over at Nick and began to sing 'Last Night of the World' from *MISS SAIGON*, normally a duet but turned into a solo. The room remained quiet, not a cough or a glass clinking as he became an American soldier in love with a Vietnamese girl at the end of the war. This young man once again turned a song into an entire story.

The applause was the loudest of the night. There was a hint of humility in Patrick's smile before he launched into 'This is the Moment,' from *JEKYLL & HYDE*, a piece that built and showed off his ability to belt the high notes. Next was 'Music of the Night' from *THE PHANTOM OF THE OPERA*, a song that displayed Patrick's amazing baritone/tenor range. This was followed by the theme song of *SUNSET BOULEVARD*, Patrick becoming a disillusioned writer in Hollywood. His words were ringed with bitterness, his body language screamed cynicism.

The showstopper was 'Gethsemane,' sung with such passion, such heartfelt pain and resignation. Patrick's talent infused Nick, carrying him along on the high. It had been years since he enjoyed the piano this much.

The audience rose to their feet. They wouldn't stop clapping and cheering. Patrick was forced to sing an encore.

He chose 'The Rose.'

CHAPTER 14

When he got back to his seat, Nick glanced over at Jessie. Her table was empty. What the hell? He caught sight of her hurrying towards the rear exit with her friends. She couldn't stay long enough to say something to Patrick?

Patrick was making his way back. He was stopped at almost every table with people wanting to talk to him. Quill approached Patrick before he could sit down. "You are—I don't have the words to describe what I felt watching you! You have an incredible talent, young man. Sorry. I should introduce myself. I'm Quill Llewellyn."

"The director?"

Quill nodded before touching Nick's shoulder. "Could we talk?" They moved out of earshot. "Who is this boy? And why is he the spitting image of Andrew Brady?"

A smile spread across Nick's face. "I can't say yet. But I'd appreciate your keeping it quiet for now."

"Are you kidding? I won't say a word. I don't want a rival to get wind of him. Listen, I'm on my way to London for a few weeks. Don't let any other director see this kid. Promise me. When I get back we'll talk." He chuckled and patted Nick on the back before jogging towards the door. Quill never walked when he could run.

*

Abbie was on both a high and a low when she and Willie got home from the cabaret. It was the same kind of high she felt after performing. And it was the same kind of low she felt when working for Jessie in London.

She sat with Willie in their living room. "There's something about seeing someone sing who is just so GOOD that words escape you. That kid's going to be a star. He's better than Andrew, and that's saying a lot."

"So what's wrong?"

"How do you know something's wrong?"

"I know you, Abs."

She dropped her head in her hands. "I invited the press tonight. I figured Nick and Jessie would sit together. Good publicity for Mr. and

Mrs. Happily Married, right? Wrong. It was obvious they were fighting. I dread seeing what the vipers write."

*

Jessie sat on her couch, Larry's arm around her. She started crying as soon as they got into her car. She didn't say a word the whole way home, only cried.

"I'm sorry to be such a blubbering fool, Larry."

"I wish you'd tell me what it's about. Is it Nick?"

She shook her head. "It's that boy. Patrick." She dabbed at her eyes. "He was—" her voice cracked, "so much like Andrew. I couldn't believe it. It was like Andrew came back and sang on that stage tonight."

She blew her nose and tried to straighten up. "Everything about him. His inflections. His tone on the high notes. His vibrato. The way he crinkled his nose."

"I noticed that, too. I used to tease Andrew about it."

"It was a signature of his. And this kid does exactly the same thing?" She shook her head and broke down again.

Larry put his arm around her. They settled into the corner of the couch, Jessie tucking her legs beneath her. "It's okay to cry. Seeing Patrick tonight reminded you how much you miss Andrew. It's normal. I've been surprised it hasn't hit you more often lately. You're back where you did your final show with him."

Jessie cried even harder. "I should have told Patrick how good he was. Instead, I ran away. Like I always do. He must think I'm such a bitch."

"I'm sure he's still embarrassed about knocking you to the floor the other day, so it's a two-way street. You can go over there and talk to him privately. It'll be better that way. Less public."

Her tears finally stopped. "Yeah. Good idea."

"Tell him how emotional it was for you tonight. How watching him brought back memories of Andrew. I bet he understands."

She stared up into his compassionate eyes. Lifting up, she kissed him with passion, curling her arm around his neck.

No response.

She pulled back and looked at him. "Should I apologize?"

"Why'd you do it?"

"Because when I look at you I see a good man with a kind heart. No drama. Just humor and truth. You take responsibility for your life. It's refreshing."

"In other words, the opposite of Nick?"

"Nick who?"

Larry uncurled her arm but kissed the top of her hand. "You love Nick, Jessie. And you know you'll always have my complete devotion. Think before you act, princess. Your life will be so much easier if you do that."

*

Patrick stood at the door of his bedroom terrace, staring at the tiny lighted bulbs dotting the garden below.

What a night. Singing at SuZee Q's was the right decision. Tess would have been proud of him, and that filled him with joy. And meeting Quill Llewellyn. He'd read so much about him. Knew the shows he directed, including *DIANA*.

He felt good. He wanted to continue to feel this way.

Patrick had only one moment of panic tonight, but it was serious. It happened when Jessie showed up. He'd fought hard to control his breathing, to not give into a full-blown episode. Both Nick and Mary noticed, but he convinced them he was okay.

When she ducked out afterwards he was relieved. He wouldn't know what to say to her after the incident on Thanksgiving. She must hate him.

He couldn't go on like this, trying to avoid situations or things that might trigger a memory. He didn't want to go through life afraid. He didn't want to see that look of pity in people's eyes when he succumbed to an attack.

He had trouble sleeping that night. When he got up the next morning, he knew he had to talk to Nick.

On his way downstairs, Kat stopped him. "Susie just called me. She wants you back next Sunday, and she's going to promote you."

Wow. He made that much of an impression? "Thank her for me. Uh, can I let her know?"

Kat's face fell. "Didn't you enjoy last night"

"I loved it. Every minute of it. It's just that—I need to talk to Nick about something. I'll find you later and explain."

Nick's office was empty, so Patrick continued down to the kitchen. Nick stood at the island, reading *The New York Post*. Something in his demeanor warned Patrick to wait. He glanced at Mary, who was also watching Nick.

Slamming the paper down on the counter, Nick took the stairs two at a time. His office door banged shut a moment later.

Patrick grabbed the paper, opening to the page Nick was reading. The blurb wasn't hard to miss.

157

MCDEARE MARRIAGE OVER?

Nick McDeare and his wife Jessica Kendle were spotted at an Upper West Side cabaret SuZee Q's on Sunday night – sitting at separate tables. And there was no intermingling. Also spotted was Quill Llewellyn, the director of DIANA, Kendle's Broadway show. Hmm ... He was sitting with McDeare, not with his meal ticket.

It looks like Llewellyn was there to see a new talent. Young Patrick Cavanaugh not only stole the show, he bore a striking resemblance to Andrew Brady. And who was tickling the ivories as the Brady clone wowed the customers? None other than Nick McDeare himself.

Looks like the famous brothers have hidden talents. Nick McDeare with the piano, and Andrew Brady with the ladies.

The article made Patrick sick. It managed to tarnish all of them. Was this what celebrity brought? People following you, writing garbage, trying to destroy any privacy you have? If it was, Patrick wanted no part of it. He could sing anywhere. He didn't need a big audience or a fancy theater.

"Don't let that article upset you," Mary said, refreshing her coffee.

"It doesn't. It's Nick who doesn't need this."

"He's been dealing with it for years."

"It's not right." Patrick scaled the stairs to his room. He'd give Nick some time, then he'd try to talk to him.

*

Nick stared at his laptop. The new book wasn't grabbing him. Maybe he should scrap it and find a new idea. Or maybe it was time to take a year off. He was in a rut, writing all year to get a book out before Christmas. He needed to shake up his routine. He'd talk to Liz, his agent, about it. He was Linden Publishing's most valuable author. He should be able to get whatever he wanted.

He was in a foul mood, all because of that damned article.

There was a knock at the door. "What?" he grumbled.

Patrick looked in. "Sorry. Should I come back later?"

"No. It's okay. I'm just— Never mind. What's up?"

Patrick sat down beside the desk. "I'm thinking about going back to Florida."

Nick's spirits plummeted further. "Why? Did something happen?"

158

"No." Patrick explained his reasoning, why returning to Florida might be important.

Nick sat back in his chair, lacing his fingers on top of his head. "This is a big decision. Are you sure you've given it enough thought?"

He saw uncertainty on Patrick's face.

"Don't rush into this. Not unless you're one-hundred-percent sure."

*

"Abbie, I should fire you for this." Jessie threw *The New York Post* on the couch. They were in her hotel room, Jessie having called her friend, demanding she come over. "How could you screw up this badly?" The article was disgusting. Jessie wanted to scream.

"I thought you'd sit with Nick. I never dreamed—"

"With Bree at his table? Are you crazy?"

"I didn't know Bree would be there."

"It's your job to know these things." Jessie walked in a circle. "You have to fix this."

"How do I explain your sitting at separate tables, Jessie? It's impossible. This is your doing. Not mine. I was doing my job. You keep telling me to make it look like you and Nick are still together. It gets harder by the day. Maybe it's time to end the charade."

"That's my decision, not yours."

"And for God's sake, there's nothing going on between Nick and Bree. She's Ethan's girlfriend, not Nick's!"

"You know nothing, Abbie. Bree is always within arm's length of Nick, waiting for me to—"

"Get over it, Jessie!"

"Get out!"

"Here we go again. London Part Two, starring Jessie the Prima Donna. I don't need this from you." Abbie grabbed her coat. "Today is our day off, a day I always devote to my fiancé because I barely see him the rest of the week." She slipped her arms into her coat. "I'll be at home, planning my wedding. I've put it off long enough because of you and this show."

*

Patrick spent the afternoon thinking about what Nick said. Maybe he was being too hasty. Maybe he should give himself more time here. See if the attacks continued at a rapid pace. He also needed to make sure he took his pills and not let things bother him as much.

He talked to Kat when she got home from ballet. "Tell Susie I'll be there on Sunday. But I'd like to rehearse."

"I'll call Susie right now. Would you mind if I came with you? For rehearsal?"

"No. You can tell me what I'm doing wrong."

*

As Patrick ate breakfast with Nick and Mary on Tuesday morning, Willie dropped by. "I have the results of the paternity test." He placed an envelope on the island. "Patrick is Andrew's son. No doubt about it."

Patrick slumped back on the bench of the breakfast nook. There it was. The truth. There was no denying it any longer.

Andrew Brady was his father.

He stared at his plate, trying to get it to sink in. When he looked back up, everyone was sporting the same syrupy smile as they stared at him. It was actually funny, like a really bad scene from a really bad movie.

"I take it from that goofy grin you're wearing," Nick said, "you're happy about this?"

"Am I?" Patrick asked. "Wearing a goofy grin? You should see your own faces." He dropped his head in his hands and chuckled.

Mary clapped her hands together. "This calls for a celebration. A special dinner tonight. Name your pleasure, Patrick."

"Fried chicken?"

*

Kat was excited about listening to Patrick's rehearsal. When they arrived at SuZee Q's, one of the other singers was just finishing her allotted practice time.

Dressed in tight jeans and a V-neck sweater, Jackie Pomeray was tall with dyed blond hair. Spotting Patrick, she wrapped up her rehearsal and approached him. "You were awesome last Sunday. I was mesmerized."

"Thanks." Patrick looked down and stuffed his hands in his pockets.

"I'd love to sing a duet with you."

Kat stepped in. "Patrick sings alone."

Jackie looked from Kat to Patrick. "Are you his girlfriend?"

"Jackie, you're so obvious," Kat shot back. This girl had always annoyed her. She was so full of herself. "Come on, Patrick."

Jackie stepped closer to Patrick. "What about *THE LION KING*? There's that great love duet we could sing."

Patrick backed up, clearly uncomfortable. "Uh, I—"

"Leave him alone." Kat tried to get between the two.

Jackie prevented it, thrusting Kat out of the way with her hip, accidentally brushing against Patrick's thigh. "What is wrong with you, Kat?"

"Stop it, Jackie."

Patrick mumbled something, taking another step backwards.

Jackie reached out to play with his hair, but Patrick turned away. "You're gorgeous, but you're shy. It's very attractive. And that voice."

He collapsed into a chair, his nose starting to bleed.

Seeing Patrick gasp for breath, Kat swung around Jackie and knelt down. Grabbing a napkin off the table, she held it to his nose.

"What's wrong with him?" Jackie loomed over the two of them. "Answer me, Kat."

"Get out of here, Jackie!" Kat shrieked.

Patrick took the napkin from Kat and dropped his head between his legs. Kat laid a hand on his back, trying to calm him. Jackie, thankfully, disappeared.

When Patrick finally lifted his head, his eyes were dull, and he was shaking. He sat quietly, staring straight ahead, as his breathing returned to normal. "I can't do this. I'm sorry, Kat. I can't. Apologize to Suzie for me." Getting to his feet he staggered up the aisle.

*

Nick and Anthony took off for a few hours that afternoon. The deep-freeze lifted, and the sun's rays were strong. They went to a new photography exhibit at the Museum of Modern Art, indulged in slices of pizza at their favorite hole-in-the-wall, Costello's, and finished up with a trek across Central Park.

"So what do you think of Patrick?"

Anthony swallowed a mouthful of pepperoni. "He's really nice to me. I can talk to him about Andrew and Gianni, and he understands. No one else but you ever understood."

"That's because he knows what it's like to lose someone you love. And to be shocked to learn who your birth father is."

"He doesn't treat me like a kid. He acts like he can learn things from me."

"I don't think he's acting. He wants to learn about Andrew, about what it's like to grow up in our house, and who better to ask than you?"

"I wish he was a little younger so we had more in common."

In Nick's eyes, Patrick's age was all over the place. Sometimes he acted like a seventeen-year-old. Other times, like a little boy. "You know what, Anthony? As you continue to get older, the age difference will mean less and less. And then one day you'll both be adults and the same age."

161

When they got home, the aroma of fried chicken filled the house. Anthony was over the moon since it was also his favorite. Something else he shared with Patrick.

"Are Kat and Patrick back?" Nick poured some coffee and topped off Mary's cup.

"Yep." Mary pointed upstairs as she continued to add chicken to the fryer. "Patrick had another attack."

Nick set his mug down and hustled up the stairs to Patrick's room. He knocked and looked in.

Patrick was stretched across his bed, flat on his back, his hands laced behind his head.

"Mary said you had an attack?"

"Yep."

"Was it bad?"

"I almost passed out."

Nick sat down on the edge of the bed. "What brought it on?"

"A girl. Who got pushy." Patrick sat up. "I have to go to Florida, Nick. This has to stop."

"You're sure?"

Patrick swung his legs over the side of the bed. Clasping both Tess's ring and the crucifix, he stared at the floor. "Will you come with me?"

*

Patrick buckled up as the private jet revved its engines for takeoff. Only twenty-four hours ago he made the decision to return to Florida. They'd be in Mount Dora by early afternoon.

"You've really never flown before?" Nick asked.

"I never left Florida before."

Patrick focused on the interior of the plane to take his mind off his nerves as the jet picked up speed down the runway. A bar. A couch – Were they off the ground yet? – A TV – He hazarded a quick glance out the window. They were ascending.

Patrick closed his eyes and thought of Tess. As they kept going higher, he told himself he was getting closer to Tess in Heaven.

"You okay?"

Patrick nodded but kept his eyes closed. Hearing Nick release his seat belt a few minutes later he opened his eyes a slit. They were above the clouds, leveling off now.

"I don't usually recommend a drink for a seventeen-year-old but go ahead if it'll relax you."

Patrick released his breath. "No, thanks."

The flight attendant approached, asking if Patrick wanted something to eat. She seemed to be flirting. Patrick shook his head.

He peeked at Nick, who seemed calm and cool despite being suspended in a big metal tube over New York City. "So is this what flying's like? Even on commercial flights?"

"No." Nick chuckled. "When you fly commercial, you have a seat designed for a gerbil. And the person smashed against you might not have bathed today. Or yesterday. And you're served stale peanuts and lousy drinks."

Patrick laughed as Nick's list grew. "Even in First Class?"

"It's a little better in First, but not much. Not these days."

As Nick told him about some hilarious flights he'd had to endure, Patrick forgot about his fear of flying. The ride was actually pretty steady.

An hour later they both ate baked ham and scalloped potatoes. Patrick even fell asleep, waking during the bumpy landing in Orlando. Which raised his fear factor all over again.

*

Nick picked up their rental car, and they drove to Mount Dora, checking into a Bed & Breakfast not far from St. Catherine's. The reunion between Patrick and Father Joe was emotional, the priest ecstatic to see Patrick.

The three of them went to dinner at a steakhouse in town. Patrick talked about his time in New York, about the brownstone and Andrew's bedroom. He told Father Joe about Anthony and Mary and how much she reminded him of Tess. He explained in detail the night he sang at SuZee Q's. Nick never before heard so many words tumble from the boy's mouth. Maybe his incessant conversation kept him from thinking about the real reason they came to Florida.

Father Joe came back to their Bed & Breakfast afterwards. When Patrick fell asleep, the priest motioned to Nick to step outside. "I worry this may be too much for him to handle, Nick."

"It was his idea, Father. I insisted he think it through clearly. He says he did. You're sure you don't want to come with us?"

"Patrick needs to rely on you now. It's best if it's just the two of you." He reached into his pocket. "Here are the addresses you asked for."

Early the next morning Nick and Patrick drove west, then turned south on I-75.

Two hours later, they arrived at their destination.

Sarasota.

*

Nick booked them into a resort on Longboat Key, advertised for the rich and famous. Nick didn't care what it was called or what it cost. This was what was needed.

Each guest had their own condo with a private beach. When Nick made the booking there was only one unit left, a one bedroom with two double beds. He grabbed it. The resort boasted five-star restaurants, plus twenty-four-hour room service and a kitchen, including a top-of-the-line coffee machine. Nick needed his morning coffee. And each condo had a piano. He wanted to be prepared for anything, not knowing how long they'd be here.

After settling in, they got back into the car. "Ready?"

Patrick took a deep breath and nodded.

Nick began by driving them out to the sad little house where Heidi lived. "That's it. You lived here with your mother and grandmother the first two years of your life."

"Grandmother? What happened to her?"

"She drank herself to death. After dropping you off at the church."

"So when my mother died, my grandmother got rid of me?"

"She wasn't capable of taking care of you. And she knew it." Whether that was the truth or not didn't matter. Patrick had enough rejection in his life.

Nick spotted old Mr. Barstow on his porch next door. The man heaved his fragile body from his chair and shook his cane at them. "Get away from there."

"I'll handle this." Nick got out of the car and approached the man. "Mr. Barstow? Remember me? Nick McDeare, Joyce's friend? We sat with you and talked about Heidi?"

The man looked confused. "Heidi ... Yes ... You were here with Joyce."

"Right. I'd like you to meet someone." He motioned to Patrick, who joined him. "This is Patrick. Heidi's baby all grown up. Patrick, this is your great uncle. Beau Barstow."

"Come closer." Barstow squinted. Patrick slowly walked towards the porch. "You're ...? Yes. Your eyes. The baby's eyes were odd. Well, I'll be damned." He turned to Nick. "So you found him."

Nick nodded. "With your help."

That pleased the old man. "Happy to do it."

An awkward silence. Patrick looked uncomfortable.

"Well, come on up here and sit." The man motioned and collapsed back into his chair.

Nick guided Patrick onto the porch. They sat in chairs across from Barstow. "Patrick wants to learn about his mother."

"Well ... Heidi was a good girl. Had all sorts of dreams, but that changed when her baby was born."

"How?" Nick steered the conversation for his nephew.

"All she cared about was her baby. Spent all her time with him – er, you." He looked at Patrick. "When she started college she'd leave you with me. Didn't trust her own mother to take care of you." He tried to pull himself from his chair but fell back into it. Patrick helped him get to his feet. "I have something for you." He looked at Nick. "I remembered it after you left last time." He shuffled inside.

Nick exchanged a look with Patrick as the old man returned. "Here." He handed Patrick a pale blue pacifier. "It was yours. Don't know why I kept it all these years. It fell out of your mouth the last time you were here. I washed it and forgot about it."

"Why was it the last time?" Patrick asked.

"Heidi died the next day." He erupted in sudden anger. "Somebody gave her that drug. Heidi didn't do booze or drugs. She saw what they did to her mother." Calming down, he collapsed back into his chair. "Your grandma disappeared the day of Heidi's funeral. I never found out what happened to you. I was afraid that old drunk might have killed you."

"Heidi's mother left Patrick at a church." Nick supplied.

Surprise spread across the old man's face. "I'll be damned. The only decent thing she did her whole life." He smiled at Patrick, then seemed embarrassed. "Well, er, glad you're okay."

Patrick stood up and shook the man's hand. "It was nice to meet you, sir."

"Manners. I like that. Nice to meet you, too."

As they started down the stairs, Patrick looked over at Heidi's house. "Does anyone live there now?"

Barstow nodded. "Go on over and look in the windows, if you're curious. They're not home."

Patrick crossed the yard to the property next door. Nick went to the car, allowing Patrick to explore on his own.

"Young man?" Barstow shouted.

Patrick turned back to the old man. "Yes, sir?"

"Listen here. You have a good life. For both you and your mama, you hear?"

"I'll try. Thank you, sir."

Patrick mounted the front steps of Heidi's former home. He walked the porch and finally peeked inside the windows. Nick tried to imagine what was going through his nephew's mind as he came to grips with where his life began.

When Patrick rejoined Nick in the car, he sat quietly, turning the pacifier over in his hands.

CHAPTER 15

Jessie and Larry stopped by the brownstone on their way to lunch with Ollie Farrow. She wanted to talk to Patrick about his performance.

"They're in Florida again?" Jessie was incredulous. "Why this time?"

Mary pulled a baked chicken breast from the oven. "There were things Patrick needed to do down there."

"Why did Nick have to go with him?"

"Patrick asked him to."

"Of course. The world's perfect dad has to take care of his brother's son."

"Jessie," Larry warned.

"When is Nick going to start telling me when he leaves town? My schedule is tight. His isn't."

"I don't control Nick's comings and goings." Mary started to slice the chicken. "If you have a problem, take it up with him."

"I will."

"Stay for lunch? We're just having chicken sandwiches."

Jessie ignored her question. "Will Nick be back for Christmas?"

"I assume so."

"Well, plan on Larry, Nora and me being here, too."

"Jessie, you should talk to Nick—"

"I have to ask Nick's permission to celebrate Christmas in my own home?"

"That's not what I'm saying ... We're not sure if Ethan and Maddie will come home for Christmas. If Ethan's here, Bree will be here, too."

"No. Bree is not spending Christmas here."

"Jessie ..." Another warning from Larry.

"If Ethan wants Bree here, she'll be here." Mary was now angry.

Jessie was fed up. When it came to Nick, brothers mattered more than wives. She shook her head, exasperated. "See you Christmas Eve, Mary."

*

Patrick and Nick's next stop was St. Sebastian's, where Father Joe was pastor for years. While Nick hung back, Patrick walked around the church and lit a candle for Tess.

A youngish priest approached him. "I'm Father O'Brien. Are you new here?"

Patrick shifted from foot to foot. "I, uh," he began, "I was told I was found here. When I was a baby."

As realization swept the priest's face, Nick stepped forward. "I'm Nick McDeare. You called me and said—"

"Of course. Mr. McDeare. You were looking for a baby." He glanced at Patrick. "And here you are. All grown up." Father O'Brien thought for a minute. "Come with me." He led them up some very old wooden stairs past a choir loft to what looked like a cloak room. "Our official records state you were found here."

Patrick's heart sped up. This was where he first met Father Joe and Tess when he was two years old. Tess said he smiled at her, that he seemed happy. If only Tess had taken him home that day, instead of— But that wasn't fair. She couldn't have known what would happen.

"Father O'Brien?" A voice from below.

"Excuse me. Take all the time you'd like." The priest left them alone.

Patrick tried to imagine what he felt that day, staring up into Tess and Father Joe's faces. Of course he couldn't have known his mother was dead, and his grandmother— This was stupid thinking. He had no memory of being left here. He'd been two years old. Still, he was glad he saw it. He wanted to know every piece of his childhood. Like every other kid.

Leaving the church, they next visited a woman named Joyce Larson, an old friend of Heidi's. She was expecting them.

"I just knew you'd find him," Joyce said to Nick. "If he was out there, Nick McDeare would find him." She turned to Patrick. "I'm relieved to know you're okay. You look just like the baby I remember."

"You knew me back then?"

"Your mom and I were close. I spent quality time with you. She loved you so much, Patrick. And you were such a good baby. Always happy. Never crying. You started singing before you could talk."

They sat in her sunny kitchen and had tea and coffee cake while she showed Patrick pictures of Heidi. She gave him two to take with him. One was of Heidi holding baby Patrick shortly after he was born. The second was Heidi supporting Patrick as he took his first steps.

Patrick couldn't stop staring at the photos. "So you were there when I was born?"

"Yep. You were premature. Lived in the NICU for a while. Heidi was terrified you wouldn't make it. You were born on Valentine's Day. Heidi said it was appropriate because you stole her heart."

An important part of Patrick's past just snapped into place. He now knew the date of his birth. February fourteenth. Which meant he was still sixteen. For a few more months anyway.

"Heidi had copies of that baby picture made. She gave one to everyone. She even sent one to Andrew, but it came back unopened."

For the next few hours, Joyce filled in the blank canvas that was Patrick's mother. He learned that Heidi loved singing and water sports and old movies. She was a star student and the star of their high school productions. An avid animal rights activist, she volunteered at the local pound. And she was a devoted mother.

"Ooh, almost forgot." Joyce dashed into the living room. "The most important things of all." She glanced at Nick. "I went looking for them after your visit." She handed Patrick a small manilla envelope."

He lifted out two items. The first was his birth certificate. It clearly stated his parents were Heidi Barstow and Andrew Brady."

"Heidi was adamant that Andrew's name be on the birth certificate. She believed he'd one day recognize you as his son."

"How did the birth certificate end up in your possession?" Nick asked.

"Heidi wanted it in a safe place. She didn't trust her mother or that house she lived in. I put it in my parents' safety deposit box and of course forgot about it. I found it when they died a few years ago. I didn't think it was right, getting rid of it." She smiled at Patrick. "Divine intervention?"

The second item was a five-by-seven photo of a group of young people. Front and center were Andrew and Heidi, their arms intertwined. Joyce was beside them, holding hands with another young man. "Don't you want this picture?" Patrick asked Joyce.

"It's more important for you to have it. It's probably the only photo of Andrew and Heidi together.

"Where was it taken?"

"At the Sarasota fair. A bunch of us went. Shortly before the season ended."

Patrick ran his fingers over their faces and cleared his throat. "Thank you."

Nick insisted they take Joyce to dinner, where the conversation continued. Patrick enjoyed hearing stories about Joyce and Heidi's childhood adventures. About their time at the Asolo. And about Heidi's embrace of motherhood.

Back at the condo, Patrick stared at his mementos of the day. A pacifier. A birth certificate. And photos. This day alone made the trip to Florida worth it. Who knew what tomorrow would bring?

After a sleepless night, Patrick wanted to see Heidi's grave the next morning. They drove back to St. Sebastian's, to the cemetery attached to the church.

Her grave wasn't easy to find. It was on the perimeter and had only a small flat marker. Just her name and the dates signifying her entrance and exit. Patrick crouched down, brushing away dead weeds.

At this time yesterday, Heidi Barstow was just a name. Now he felt like he knew the woman who brought him into this world. Making the sign of the cross and bowing his head, he said a prayer.

Rejoining Nick, they drove to Tess's old home. As their car pulled into the driveway, Patrick had a flashback of the first time he entered the small white frame house with Tess. It seemed enormous at the time.

Learning that Patrick once lived there, the lady who now owned the property was gracious. She invited them in, offering lemonade.

"We bought the house at a public auction," Mrs. Whitmer informed them. "It was completely furnished. Whoever lived here abandoned it quickly. There were even some clothes in the closets and dry goods in the pantry. It looked like it was taken care of, even loved."

Patrick's memory of the place was hazy. He wandered from room to room as things came back to him slowly. The bathtub where he took his first bath. The living room where he sang for Tess. The kitchen where she gave him fried chicken.

"There was some beautiful hand-crafted furniture in the garage. That table was part of it."

Patrick stared at an end table, made by Tess's husband Henry.

"And this. I found it when we replaced the carpet." She went to a drawer in the tiny dining room and pulled out a photograph, handing it to Patrick. "It didn't seem right to throw away someone else's picture. I figured I'd leave it for the next person to find. Is that you? It looks like you got into a fight with someone." She laughed. "Kids!"

Yes. It was him. He was probably five years old. His long stringy hair was a shade darker because it was dirty. His shorts and T-shirt were torn in places and filthy. His shoes looked to be several sizes too big. And there was a large welt on his leg, crusted in blood.

As Patrick's hand started to shake, he got to his feet, the photo dropping to the floor. He hurried outside, Nick on his heels, and gripped a low white fence.

"Is he all right?" Mrs. Whitmer called from inside.

170

Patrick breathed deeply. He closed his eyes and thought about Andrew. And Tess. "I'm fine. Tell her I'm fine. Please, Nick." Nick disappeared inside.

Still gripping the fence, Patrick spotted the orange grove. Drawing him like a magnet, Patrick wandered over to it, into it, to a particular tree.

He remembered. He remembered it clearly. He came here to get away from … Songs began playing in his mind. He'd sit here for hours, singing. He loved the scent of the trees. Little birds would land on the branches and listen. His prized audience, always wanting more.

This was where he first met Tess. He could see her, sitting right there, a beautiful smile lighting her beautiful face, clapping and encouraging him. A plate of cookies and a glass of milk sat on the grass between them.

He leaned against the tree and cried …

*

Nick said goodbye to his hostess and went back outside. No Patrick. He checked the car. Nope. Where in the hell—? Nick told himself not to panic. Searching the property, he finally spotted him inside the orange grove.

Of course. It made perfect sense.

Realizing he was witnessing a private moment, he backed away and returned to the car.

As he waited, he pulled out the photograph Mrs. Whitmer handed to Patrick. It was hard to believe this pathetic little boy was Patrick. He was the poster child for neglect.

Twenty minutes later, Patrick climbed in beside him. He stared straight ahead.

Nick started the car. "You're sure about this?"

Patrick nodded. But he looked scared.

Following Father Joe's written instructions, Nick drove the few blocks to their next destination, hoping the priest's memory was reliable. There was no physical address.

The houses began to thin out, the few left standing, deserted. Signs indicated the area was scheduled for demolition, a splashy condo complex to be built.

Nick's stomach tightened as they slowed, approaching an abandoned house that sat alone at the end of a road.

Patrick's foster home.

From the outside, it was innocuous enough. Similar to every other sad property in the area. The wood frame structure needed paint. A few shingles had come loose. The yard was overgrown, obscuring the front steps. The windows were filthy. The porch swing hung at an odd angle.

Nick turned off the engine and faced his nephew.

"Will you come with me?" Patrick's voice was low, soft.

"Sure." They got out of the car. Patrick paused on the sidewalk, staring, before walking towards the front porch. He approached it with caution.

Nick followed him into the house. The living room was dismal. Sunlight filtered through the yellowed, broken Venetian blinds. The threadbare couch was missing a leg. The floor was stained. And there was a smell that brought bile to his throat.

*

Patrick's instincts told him to run. But if he did, he'd never be free of what happened in this house. He'd live in fear, a panic attack looming around every corner. He had to know if the memory flashes, those snapshots that came out of nowhere, were true.

He stared at the pitiful front room, smaller than he remembered. A TV used to be over there. He'd sit in front of it and listen to people sing. The man sat on that couch in his underwear, drinking something that stunk and smoking cigarettes.

Patrick moved on to the kitchen, the smell awful. A mouse ran across the floor. Roaches were in the sink. The window was broken, glass on the counter.

He crept into the hallway, Nick following him. He glanced into the bedrooms as he made his way down the hall, pausing at the bathroom. He hated this room. The water rarely worked. The bottom of the tub was permanently stained with rust. The toilet always overflowed. The window was bare, the crusted dirt a poor substitute for curtains.

At the end of the hallway, Patrick halted.

The closet ... the dark closet ...

Nick came around him, staring at the closed door. "What is this?"

"The ... closet ..."

"Where Father Joe found you?" he asked softly.

Patrick nodded.

"Do you want to open it?"

Patrick's inner voice screamed *NO!* "You do it."

Nick reached for the knob and slowly opened the door, the hinges whining in protest.

That sound. The hinges.

172

Empty. It was always empty. Except for the wooden hanger …

"Get in there, you fucking little loser!" She grabbed the hanger and beat him before throwing it at him. The door slammed … it was dark … cold … his clothes … he wanted his—

"Patrick? … You okay?"
Breathe … Just breathe … In … Out.
"Patrick?"
It's just a closet. Nothing to be afraid of. It's just an empty closet.
When Nick swung the door shut, the ancient hinges squealed and came away, the wooden door hanging askew.
That sound again … Patrick backed away from the broken scene from his past. Backed away … Backed into the room across the hall until he slammed into an obstacle. His feet went out from under him, dropping him down hard.
What was he sitting on?
Her bed … Carrie's bed!

"Stop struggling. You know you can't win …"

He fought, but she was too strong …

"Dammit, Patrick, just relax … We're going to have some fun …"

Panic choked Patrick. He struggled to get up. "No," he whimpered, "…No … Don't …"

"Relax dammit!"

"No … please … No …"

"Shut up and—Stop kicking me, you fucking brat. You fucking little BRAT!" Carrie pinched his skin hard as she stripped away his shorts.

Patrick shrieked.

A woman stood a few feet away, watching. Carrie's sister, Eva. "Let him scream. No one can hear him. We're alone. Jack took the other kids to the beach. They'll be gone for hours."

"Give me— I want my clothes." He kicked at the air. "Stop it, Carrie. Stop it. Please!" He looked at Eva. "Help me, Eva. Please. Make her stop. Please!"

"Patrick?" Nick's voice. Far away.

"Stop fighting me. Lay still. I said lay still! Okay, fine." She *reached in a drawer and grabbed the scarves.*

"NO! NO! Don't tie me, please, Carrie, don't tie me, please, please, please, I'll be good, don't, please, Carrie, don't, please, I'll do anything, please." Patrick started to cry. He looked again at Eva. "Tell her not to tie me. Tell her! Please tell her. Please!"

"I said lay still!" Carrie smacked him hard across the face. Continued to smack him. His head hurt. His vision blurred. His nose began to bleed. He fought Carrie as she tried to bind his hands and ankles. "Get over here," she said to her sister. "Help me."
Eva held Patrick down as Carrie ...

He looked up at Eva. "Help me, Eva. Please. Don't let her do it. Help me." He looked back at Carrie. "No, Carrie! You're hurting me. Don't! NOOOO!!"

*

Nick was horrified as Patrick put voice and names to his memory. The boy was locked in the past, reliving it. His nose began to bleed. His eyes lost focus. His protests grew louder. He started to scream. It was the most anguished cry Nick had ever heard.

Frantic, Patrick hurled himself off the bed. He ran blindly, wailing like a wounded animal. In the front room he raced to the window, ripping the broken Venetian blinds away, clawing at the window. He seemed to think it was the only way out. His shrieks continued, his sobs gut-wrenching.

Wanting to break the spell that gripped the boy, Nick lunged for him, pulling him into his arms.

Patrick turned crazed eyes on Nick, staring through him. "NO. NO! Let me go. You're hurting me! P-L-E-A-S-E!!!"

"It's Nick, Patrick! I'm not hurting you."

Patrick pushed him away with such force Nick fell backwards. Free from Nick's grasp, Patrick hurtled to the door and out onto the porch.

Scrambling to his feet, Nick sprinted after him. Patrick raced through the front yard, getting tangled in the tall weeds. Afraid he would disappear or, even worse, remain locked in the past, Nick put on a burst of speed and made a running tackle for the boy, bringing them both down.

Still, Patrick fought him. "GET AWAY! I HATE YOU, CARRIE! I'll run away where you can't find me!"

"I'm not Carrie." Nick raised his voice. "It's me. Nick." He hung on as the boy's bellows echoed across the desolation. Desperate, Nick pulled Patrick towards him and gripped his shoulders, shaking him hard. "IT'S NICK, PATRICK. NICK!"

Finally, FINALLY, Nick got through to him, broke through the memory that held the boy captive. Patrick stopped struggling. His vacant eyes came back into focus. "... Nick?"

"Yeah."

There was silence for a few seconds. Nothing but their breathing, raspy and uneven.

Then ... Patrick covered his face and let out a long wail. "OH MY G-O-D!"

Folding in on himself, he collapsed against Nick, his body shaking with sobs. His breath came in gasps as he faced the full impact of what happened to him years ago.

Nick wrapped his arms around Patrick, his face pressed to the top of his head. Patrick went silent, but Nick felt his heaves, felt him gasping for breath as he cried, his pain so deep no sound escaped his lips.

Time stopped. He didn't know how long they sat there in the blazing sun, the humidity pressing in on them. His entire focus was on this broken boy in his arms.

Gradually, Patrick calmed, his strength sapped. His arms and legs were limp, his shirt stained with perspiration. "She always sang ..." his breath caught again, "that song ... after ..."

Nick had trouble hearing him. "Who? What song?"

The boy swallowed, his lips dry and chapped. "... the woman with the dark hair ... my grandmother ..." Patrick's expression scrunched again. He buried his face in Nick's shirt.

Nick held him, saying nothing, hoping his presence was enough. He understood now.

Understood why Patrick was childlike.

Why he attacked Jessie when she smacked Nick.

Why he never had a girlfriend.

Now he knew why Patrick's singing meant everything to him. It took him out of the real world when he was little. And it saved him from remembering the horror of what happened as he got older.

Patrick was beaten repeatedly, cigarettes stubbed out on his tiny feet, stripped naked and thrown in a closet. A homeless dog had a better life than he had.

But what broke Nick's heart, what made his gut threaten to rebel, went beyond those atrocities.

Patrick Cavanaugh, an innocent five-year-old boy, was sexually abused.

CHAPTER 16

After getting Patrick back to their condo, Nick turned on the hot tub in the bathroom for him. The boy's eyes were red and puffy, his knees and elbows raw from the slide across the weeds. He shivered, his teeth chattering. Not from being cold. From the trauma.

As Nick helped peel away his nephew's sweat-soaked shirt, he spotted pink streaks across his back, disappearing below his jeans. "Are the marks on your back from—"

"You want to see the rest?" Patrick turned to face him, a hint of animosity in his voice, as he started to unzip his jeans—

"Patrick, no ... no."

Patrick looked up at him, his face suddenly desolate. "Sorry," he whimpered. "Sorry."

"You have nothing to apologize for." Nick pulled the vanity chair over. "Sit down." Patrick half dropped, half fell into the chair. "You told me you believe in heaven and hell. Well, now I believe in them, too, because I saw it firsthand. You lived hell on earth."

A lone tear trailed down Patrick's face. "You kn-know everything, don't you?" His voice was hoarse, his teeth still chattering. "All of it. What happened to me."

Nick swallowed before nodding.

Patrick averted his eyes, his shame painful to watch.

Crouching down, Nick took a moment. "I wish I could erase it for you. I wish you grew up with a mother and a father and never knew an unpleasant moment in your young life. That's what you deserved, but it didn't happen, and I don't know why. What I do know is you have to find a way to get past it." Nick stood up. "We'll find the women who did this to you and—"

"No!" Patrick pushed to his feet, frantic. "I j-just want to forget about it. Promise me you won't go looking for them. Promise me." Unsteady, he gripped the counter.

Nick hated making a promise he might not be able to keep. But the manic look in his nephew's eyes forced him to do the right thing. "I promise." Carrie Trout needed to pay. So did her sister. He hoped Patrick would change his mind.

Patrick dropped his head, another tear falling. "People will look at me with disgust. I want to die."

Nick's heart ached for this childlike man. "Look at me, Patrick," Nick whispered. "Look at me." He waited for the boy's tortured eyes to meet his own. "No one has to know about this but you and me. No one. It's your choice who you tell. Whether it's a counselor or a friend or no one at all. It's your choice. I'll go to my grave with your secret. You don't know me well yet, but you have my word. I never go back on my word."

"But you have to feel differently about me now. See me differently."

"No." Nick smiled at him. "What happened only makes me love you more. You're my nephew, my brother's son. An amazing young man with a heart of gold. You'll get through this and come out on the other side intact. We'll figure it out. I promise."

"We?"

"You're not alone in this." Another smile before backing up. "I'll be back. Go ahead and get in." Nick left the room and closed the door to give Patrick privacy.

As he grabbed towels and a blanket from the linen closet, he heard a loud thud, followed by the splashing of water. "Patrick?" Nothing. Nick pressed his ear to the door. "Patrick? You okay?"

"Uh, yeah."

Nick paused, listening. He heard Patrick coughing and moving around in the hot tub. "I'm going to leave more towels outside the door. Holler if you need me. Loudly. I'll be outside for a few minutes."

*

Patrick gripped the ledge of the hot tub, coughing again and spitting out more water. His legs gave out when he climbed in.

Laying back, he forced himself to relax. Every muscle in his body was tense and shaking. The water was hot, but it did nothing to chase away the chill.

He looked down at the scars streaking his body. Nick noticed them, but he didn't see the worst. The ones his jeans covered.

How did he get here? Lying in a hot tub being taken care of by a man who had more important things to do.

He was tired. So tired. Closing his eyes, he gave in to the jets of water massaging his body. Carrie's face floated into the black void, standing over him— No! Patrick's eyes snapped open.

Was this his future? Never being able to shut his eyes without—

178

Maybe he should just end it all right now. Slide down into the water and join Tess. But if he killed himself he wouldn't be with Tess. He'd burn in hell forever.

Tears trickled down his face. There was no hope. This was his life now.

*

As Nick stepped onto the terrace, he took a deep breath of the night air. His stomach was queasy. Perspiration dripped from his forehead. Emptying his pockets, his attention was drawn to the picture of five-year-old Patrick. This kid, so young, used like a worthless piece of …

Nick shucked off his clothes and ran for the water. He dove into the surf and swam out a few yards. Running his hands over his skin, he tried to scrape away the sweat and grit, the images and sounds of that house. Tried to erase the scars he just saw on young Patrick Cavanaugh's body. He dipped his head beneath the surface, hoping to wipe out the ugly tableaus in his mind.

Wading back to shore, he couldn't hold it in anymore. His empty stomach rebelled. Dropping down on the sand, Nick swiped his mouth with the back of his hand. He was determined not to give into his anguish. He needed to hang tough for Patrick's sake.

For the first time in his life, Nick was at a loss as to how to proceed. How did he help this boy who encountered pure evil at such a young age? He'd have to trust his instincts and hope he didn't make any mistakes. Where was Andrew when he needed him most?

Dragging himself back inside, he checked on Patrick before ordering soup and sandwiches from room service. Then he reluctantly made his nightly call to Mary.

*

When Patrick awoke, it was still dark out. He sat up with difficulty, his body achy and tired.

Nick was asleep against the headboard of the other bed, his laptop beside him. He must have been sitting there all night.

This man listened as he relived the atrocities of his childhood and never left his side. He took care of him when the shock of his past left him unstable and lost. It was what Tess would have done, if she could have stomached the truth. Nick gave him privacy when it was needed, held a wet towel to his forehead when nausea hit his empty stomach, and he force-fed him to prevent it from recurring.

Getting to his feet, Patrick made his way to the terrace, his muscles still wobbly. It was quiet, only the whoosh of the waves on the sand breaking the silence. A full moon shone down on the Gulf, turning the placid sea into a blaze of shimmering sparkles.

At a different moment in time, Patrick would be in wonder of God's glorious universe. Not tonight. Tonight he was angry with God, and he ignored any guilt he felt about it. Why did God allow this to happen to him? What did he do to deserve it?

Patrick sat down stiffly at the table.

He shouldn't have come back here. He should have left the memories locked away. Panic attacks were nothing compared to what he felt right now. But ... those images ... for years scenarios flashed before his eyes, snapshots really. They were there one second. Gone the next. He never examined them, never wanted to. He just shut them out.

But now he remembered. All of it. That house. Carrie's bedroom. What she did to him while her sister watched. He could see her long blond hair—

Nick stumbled outside, yawning. Sitting down across from him, he stared at the ocean.

"Why do you stay with me, Nick? I'm a lost cause. Go back to your normal daughter and your normal son."

"First, neither my daughter nor my son is normal. Whatever that is. Secondly, you're no lost cause." He rubbed his eyes. "Not so long ago, you lived in a cottage with a good woman who loved you and took care of you. You had a kind priest as a father figure. You had a job that gave you both happiness and a good income. That safe world exploded when you lost Tess and found out you were Andrew Brady's son. That was enough to knock anyone off-balance. But now ... realizing what happened to you ..."

Nick's eyes were compassionate. As if what happened to Patrick was being transferred to him.

"After you went to sleep I did some research," Nick continued. "Look, I've never been a fan of shrinks. But this is different. You were very young when this happened. I think you should see someone who specializes in this sort of thing."

"No. I can't talk to a stranger."

"My sister – your aunt – is a psychologist."

"I don't want anyone in your family to know. Promise me."

Nick nodded, but he didn't look happy. "I told you earlier I'd keep your secret. Just try to remember you didn't do anything wrong. This was done to you. You were a small child. They were adults."

"Still ..." He didn't want anyone but Nick to ever know.

"Will you do me one favor? Will you keep an open mind about talking to someone? Take a look at my laptop. See what's involved."

Patrick shrugged and looked away. The idea of talking about this with a stranger made him cringe.

*

Mary had a horrible night. She came down to the kitchen before dawn and made some tea. Sitting in the breakfast nook, she stared out the window at the first light of day.

When Nick called late last night, Mary knew. He gave no details, just said it had been a rough day. But she knew. She heard the heartbreak in his voice, realized it was difficult for him to talk. So she got off the phone quickly.

In a way, she knew the moment she laid eyes on Patrick. Patrick Cavanaugh was a teenaged boy held captive by what happened when he was too little to fight back. He craved love, needed someone to guide him, to remind him on a regular basis what an amazing human being he was. All the things a loving parent does for a small child. All the things Patrick missed out on in his formative years.

Mary worried about Nick as much as Patrick. He'd never dealt with something like this before. But if there was one person on this earth who knew how to fix a damaged child, it was Nick McDeare. His own childhood taught him well.

"Can I sit with you?" Kat stood on the stairs, a throw wrapped around her. Two turquoise eyes and a pair of whiskers poked through the blanket. Hamlet was clutched in her arms.

"Sure, honey. Come on." Kat sat across from her. "Can't sleep either?"

Kat shook her head as she stroked the cat. "I heard you talking to Dad last night. It sounded bad."

"It's not good."

"Did something terrible happen to Patrick a long time ago?"

Mary didn't know how to answer her. This was far too disturbing for a thirteen-year-old.

"It did, didn't it?" Kat whispered. She dropped her eyes and pulled Hamlet closer, looking like a little girl, not the 'smart ass' her dad called her in jest. "Why do bad things happen to good people, Mary?"

"A question people have asked for centuries. I wish I knew, sweetie."

*

Nick was in no hurry to leave Sarasota. He intended to stay as long as it took, until Patrick was ready to venture back into the real world. At least, that was his thinking that first morning.

While Patrick got much-needed sleep, Nick spent a fortune in the hotel shops on new clothes for him. Jeans and dress pants. T-shirts and button-downs and sweaters. A three-piece suit. Several ties. A coat, gloves and a suede brimmed hat. Swimwear, underwear and sweats. Shorts and tank tops. Shoes and boots.

Back in the room, he ordered a huge breakfast and made some calls. When Patrick got up, he showed him the clothes, turning a deaf ear to his protests.

"But my old clothes are fine. Tess did the best she could."

"Of course she did. She was a great mom. This is about something else. You need to feel good about yourself. New clothes are a beginning. A fresh start, so to speak."

"I can't let you spend this kind of money on me.

"I'm happy to do it. I'm able to do it."

Still, Patrick stayed in his old sweats that first day. He picked at the meals Nick ordered and slept a lot. When Nick suggested a swim before dinner, Patrick instead returned to his bed.

Later that evening, Nick sat at the piano, playing songs Patrick liked to sing.

*

Patrick laid in the dark, listening to Nick at the piano. Did the man really think music would lure him back to singing? Singing only reminded him of that house …

Patrick covered his ears, trying to plug the memories. Still, he heard the piano. "Stop. Please stop," he muttered. "Andrew, if you can hear me, make it stop."

The music ceased abruptly.

Patrick rolled over and stared into the darkness.

"I don't know if Andrew heard you." Nick stood in the doorway. "But I did. Sorry."

Patrick rolled back over and punched the pillow. Great. He didn't mean to— What was wrong with him? He didn't seem to have any control over what he said or did. Why did he keep hurting the one person who was trying to help?

*

"Jessie's behaving like she did in London," Abbie said to Willie as they folded laundry. "Not as bad, but the spoiled brat is resurfacing again.

"What's going on with Nick and her?"

"She's all hung up on the idea that Nick and Bree are seeing each other."

"That ship sailed a long time ago."

"For God's sake, Bree is living with Ethan now. It's time Jessie and Nick moved on with their lives."

"Together? Or apart?"

"Your guess is as good as mine." Abbie shot him a dark look.

*

Nick walked the beach before turning in, hands thrust into his pockets, bare feet digging into the sand. The sky was overcast, filmy layers obscuring the moon.

Patrick's surly behavior was understandable. Nick knew his darkest secret, and he was mortified. He wanted Nick to give up on him. He wanted to go back to Mount Dora and hide for the rest of his life.

Nick was determined not to let that happen. Patrick had too much to offer. Not just with his talent. With his spirit. Patrick Cavanaugh was an unusual young man in these troubled times of youth-gone-wrong. Kind. Religious. Smart. Patrick won over everyone he met, even Anthony.

Glancing at his watch, Nick headed back to the condo. Patrick should be asleep by now. There would be no more encounters tonight.

When he got up the next morning, Nick found his nephew in the living room, staring at the new clothes on the couch.

"How do I repay you for this kind of generosity?"

"By wearing them." Nick ordered breakfast, and they ate on the deck. Patrick was still quiet, but his appetite was better. "How about a swim?" Nick speared a bite of omelet.

Patrick shook his head. "I'm going to watch some TV." He grabbed his plate and went inside.

Nick didn't object or push. Not yet.

Patrick sat in front of the TV for the rest of the day, channel-surfing. He even ate his fried chicken dinner in front of the tube. When Nick went to bed, Patrick was asleep on the couch.

The next morning, they again met over breakfast. Patrick still wore the same sweats. "Come on, Patrick. Let's go for a swim."

Patrick said nothing, just continued to eat his pancakes.

Frustrated, Nick focused on his eggs.

"I didn't sleep well on that couch. I think I'll take a nap." Patrick started to rise.

"Is this what you're going to do from now on? Hide from the world?"

"What if it is? It's my life." He was sullen, almost angry.

"Sit down for a minute. There's something I want to say to you." Nick waited, his gaze locked on the boy.

Patrick slid back down into his chair. Reluctantly.

Nick put down his knife and fork and laced his fingers against his chin. "There was a time when I was really low. Andrew had just been murdered, right before we were supposed to meet for the first time. And it had been less than a year since, well, since my son died. I drank too much, smoked two packs a day, and my diet was fast food. I had no reason to live, or so I thought." He had his nephew's attention. "I ended up having my stomach pumped after overdosing on sleeping pills. I told the doctors it was an accident. I was lying. Partially. The truth was I just didn't care what happened to me."

Nick remembered that dark period of his life vividly. "When I got out of the hospital, I had two choices. I could continue with my death-wish. Or I could turn it around and start over. I decided I wanted to live. For my son. And for Andrew. I did what I thought they'd want me to do."

"Which was ...?"

"I got rid of the cigarettes and limited the bourbon and brandy. I ate nutritious food and drank more water. Then, and I know this will sound small, I began jogging. It got me moving again. Activity breeds activity. I felt good about myself for the first time in a long time."

"Jogging?" Patrick looked skeptical.

"Okay, maybe jogging isn't your style. Swimming. It's great exercise, plus it's fun." Nick waited. No reaction. "Come on. Give it a shot. You've got the Gulf of Mexico right here in your back yard."

Patrick started to say something, then shut his mouth and slumped down.

"What?"

He picked at the drawstring of his sweatpants. "I don't know how."

"... You don't know how ... to swim?" Patrick nodded. "How'd you get through school without learning to swim?"

"My doctor wrote a medical excuse, getting me out of all my gym classes."

Now that Nick thought about it, he'd never seen Patrick engage in any form of exercise. "Why?"

Patrick shrugged.

A thought struck him. Did those two sisters do something to him— "Do you have a physical disability?"

"No."

184

"Then, what?"

The boy's eyes darted to him briefly. "The scars."

"They're not that noticeable, Patrick."

"You didn't see all of them."

Nick pushed his plate away and stood up. "Come on. Let's take a walk. And I won't take no for an answer."

They set off down the beach. It was early, a breeze cooling the morning air.

"Patrick, everyone has scars. Kids don't get through childhood without scars."

"Most kids' scars aren't from beatings."

"Okay," Nick said. "Yours are from beatings. But think about this. Veterans come back from wars with scars much worse than yours. They lose limbs. And yet they don't let it stop them from doing what they enjoy. Working out in gyms or swimming or catching some rays on a beautiful beach. Hell, they even run marathons, their scars in full view. It wasn't easy for them at first, just like it's not easy for you, but they were intent on not letting life pass them by."

*

Patrick listened to Nick's words, suddenly ashamed of his fear. His scars were nothing compared to what soldiers suffered.

"You have to live your life, Patrick. Stop caring what other people think. You won't believe how liberating it is. It's what Tess would want for you. How would she feel if she knew you were sitting in front of the TV when you could be out here on this gorgeous beach, swimming?"

"I told you. I don't know how."

"So I'll teach you. Come on." Nick headed back to the condo. Patrick had no choice but to follow. "Put on the new swim trunks and meet me on the beach. And use that sunscreen on the bathroom counter, especially on any scars."

"But I—"

Nick was gone, already inside changing.

Patrick went to the stack of new clothes and pulled out the dark blue swim trunks. Going into the bathroom he put them on and examined himself in the mirror. His torso bore faint red streaks, also his shoulders. So did his legs, although most were still hidden. But the cigarette burns on his feet were glaring.

After applying the sunscreen, Patrick stepped outside cautiously, feeling naked.

Nick paid no attention to the scars. "You're built like Andrew and me. You just need more bulk. Come on. Let's get in the water."

There was no one around of course, just the two of them. Still, Patrick hesitantly crossed the beach and waded into the surf.

"Are you afraid of the water?"

Patrick shook his head.

They began slowly, Nick teaching him how to float. His uncle's patience was remarkable considering how many times he sank like a boulder. "I can't do this, Nick. It's hopeless."

"Stop with the negative attitude. Close your eyes and completely relax …"

Gradually, Patrick's sullen mood dissipated as Nick's instruction and soothing voice paid off. He forgot about his scars and started to enjoy the feel of the cool water against his skin.

It took hours, but by the time they stopped to eat, Patrick could not only float, he was starting to swim. He rushed through lunch in order to get back into the water. By dinner time Patrick could swim ten yards, turn around, and swim another ten.

He leapt out of the water in celebration. Running to Nick, they high-fived. Then Patrick threw his arms around the man, jumping up and down. Even a bad sunburn didn't diminish his feeling of accomplishment.

*

Nick read in the resort newsletter that whole lobsters could be delivered and cooked over your own fire pit. He ordered the works that night. They sat around the fire as the lobsters, red potatoes and corn did their job. Then they dug in at the table, butter dripping down their chins and fingers.

Patrick had never tasted lobster before. "We served it at Cohan's, but the staff wasn't allowed to eat it." The kid had a voracious appetite tonight. Nick ate one crustacean. Patrick ate three. Plus a half dozen potatoes and three small ears of corn.

Patrick still wore his swim trunks, but his scars appeared to be forgotten. He looked like a different person tonight, his sunburn a vibrant red against his sandy hair and blue eyes. So much for the sunscreen.

After dinner they watched the sun go down, saying little.

Patrick yawned. He had to be exhausted after all the swimming. "You said you had a son who died." He propped his feet against the fire pit. "What happened?"

Nick didn't like talking about this, but he had to meet Patrick halfway when it came to discussing his past. "Jeffrey. From my first marriage. He died of leukemia when he was ten."

"Wow." Patrick didn't say anything for a bit. "And this happened right before Andrew died?"

"Yeah."

"That had to be tough."

"It was."

Patrick yawned again. "And I felt sorry for myself when Tess died."

"Death's hard, Patrick. For everyone."

"I was taught that death is just the beginning. That the soul goes on to meet God." He shook his head. "It sure didn't feel that way when I watched Tess slip away. All I felt was huge loss."

"It IS loss. For those left behind."

Patrick got to his feet. "I'm heading to bed."

His surprise departure left Nick wondering if he said something wrong. Not for the first time, he felt adrift in handling his nephew's trauma.

"Nick?" Patrick stood just inside the terrace door. "Thanks. For today."

Nick nodded. "Night, Patrick." Gathering the dishes, he put them on the ledge of the fire pit for the crew to pick up in the morning. Heading inside, he pulled out the picture of five-year-old Patrick Cavanaugh. A grim reminder of where this kid began.

But today there was progress. Patrick forgot about his scars, put on his new swim trunks, stepped out into the sunshine and learned how to swim.

A small victory that felt enormous. And perhaps it was. But Nick was no fool. He knew the road ahead was daunting. The visible scars Patrick wore were nothing compared to the emotional scars buried over the years.

CHAPTER 17

The next day Patrick returned to the water, intent on swimming further. He was getting good at it now, each swim instilling more and more confidence. Nick seemed proud of him, inspiring him to work harder. Nick also took the time to explain the dangers of the ocean, what to look out for, what to do if he felt he was in trouble.

His sunburn was morphing into a tan and didn't hurt as much today. "Your skin's like Kat's," Nick observed. "After an initial burn, she tans. You're both lucky, considering how fair you are."

In between swims, he and Nick stretched out on beach towels. As the sun beat down on his skin, Patrick was able to close his eyes without any specters intruding. It was peaceful, the sound of the surf ebbing and flowing, the gulls swooping low over the water for fish or waddling across the sand.

Eventually another sound intruded on Patrick's serenity. Cracking an eye open against the glare of the sun, he stared at the source. Nick was flat on his back, an abandoned book on his chest, snoring.

Patrick threw his head back and laughed. It was the first time he laughed since— It just felt so good.

They ordered platters of cold seafood for dinner. Shrimp and crab legs and scallops. Lobster tails. Oysters and clams on the half shell. Patrick even ate octopus for the first time. It was one of the best days of his life.

The following day Nick rented jet skis. After a lesson on their operation and safety, Patrick gave it a try, Nick hovering nearby. When they both felt confident he knew what he was doing, they spent hours skimming the water, hugging the coast. It was a gorgeous day, the gulf dotted with sailboats and yachts. They even spotted a cruise ship heading out to sea from Tampa. His hair flying, a permanent smile on his face, Patrick relished every moment, the ocean spray cooling the sun's rays.

The tropical music of a Calypso band drew them to a waterfront restaurant for lunch. They dined on a pier that looked down on pools of colorful fish. Patrick immediately covered up with a T-shirt.

"Check out the guy over there," Nick said, scanning a menu. "At the bar."

Patrick glanced over his shoulder. A young man sat on a barstool with his arm around a girl. They both wore swimsuits. A large red scar stretched across the man's back from shoulder blade to shoulder blade.

"Stop caring what people think, Patrick."

Patrick turned back to Nick, whose eyes were still glued to his menu.

Shaking his head, Patrick pulled the T-shirt over his head. "Happy now?"

"The fish and chips sound good."

Patrick smirked. "You're so smug."

"I've heard that a time or two before." A tiny smile flickered across Nick's face.

That night they had reservations in one of the hotel's restaurants. They would be joined by two people who formerly worked for Child Protective Services, something Patrick was dreading.

Before they left the condo, Nick assured him that Georgia and Herman knew nothing about what happened to him in that house. "If they had, they would have had your foster parents arrested. It's up to you if you want to tell them. They can see that the Trouts are prosecuted—"

"I told you I don't want anyone to know."

A frown creased Nick's forehead, but he nodded.

Patrick made an effort, but he was uncomfortable during dinner. Even when Nick explained that Georgia Watts and Herman Stutz were instrumental in locating him, he still couldn't wait to get back to the condo. They reminded him of those nightmare years.

"Did Nick tell you we thought you drowned?" Georgia asked. "He refused to believe it and kept looking. Which is why you're sitting here tonight. I'm just glad this story has a happy ending."

A happy ending? Patrick swallowed his crème Brule along with his disgust.

He was quiet on the walk home. Nick seemed to sense his mood and said nothing. Back at the condo, Patrick went straight to bed. When Nick retired a short time later, the bedroom was still and silent.

"I'm sorry," Nick finally said. "I thought you'd like to meet the people who helped find you. And I wanted them to see their efforts paid off. They don't get many victories in their line of work."

Patrick stared at the ceiling. "I should apologize to you. I was rude tonight. It's just that— they're part of that time in my life. I can't—"

"You don't need to explain, Patrick. I understand."

Patrick rolled over and hugged the pillow. He slept very little that night, but he got out of bed in a better mood the next morning.

After a huge breakfast, Patrick took off with Nick on a hike down the beach. He had to admit it felt good to abandon his bulky clothes, to feel the sun on his skin.

Occasionally, Nick would break into a slow jog, Patrick doing his best to keep up with him. "You're determined to make a jogger out of me, aren't you?"

Nick grinned and stepped up his pace. But when he saw Patrick tiring he slowed to a walk again. The man was definitely tuned into Patrick's shifting moods. Eventually, they went back in the water to swim.

Patrick was falling in love with the ocean. For years he ignored the best part of living along the coast of Florida. How could he have been so stupid?

Dumb question. Easy answer.

He was grateful for these solitary days, and to Nick for providing them. Now that Nick knew the truth about what happened, Patrick felt a new bond with the man.

Their walks and jogs became more important with each passing day. They never retired for the night without first walking the beach, talking about so many things. Everything except what happened to him. Nick was a fascinating man. World traveled. Sophisticated. But also down to earth. Honest. And at times hilarious, his humor droll. He loved to tease and could take it when Patrick zinged him back.

Patrick loved Tess with his whole heart. And he loved Father Joe. But with Nick it was different. Nick became both a father figure and best friend, something he never had before.

*

Jessie sat with Larry over lunch in the suite. "Where's this going, Larry? You and me."

"We're friends. Close friends. Why?"

"I don't know. Stupid question probably. I'm just so... I feel like I'm watching life pass me by. Nick's all involved in Patrick. Anthony's always busy. He has no time for me. They all have their lives, the same as always, even though I'm not there. I'm living in a hotel, doing eight shows a week and not really enjoying it. There has to be more than this."

"Then make a change. Shake things up."

"Like what?"

"Leave the show. Move to Long Island. Get a cat."

Jessie laughed. "Or move back into my own house."

"You'd kick Nick out?"

"I'd give him an ultimatum. Either we have a marriage or he moves on. With his daughter. Who hates me, by the way."

"So what does this have to do with you and me?"

"You're important to me, Larry. I want you in my life."

"Even if you get back together with Nick?"

"Yes. No matter what. I want us to always be as close as we are right now. It's been a long time since I've had a friend like you."

"And on that note, you should know I'm looking for a place in the city." He poured more coffee. "Quill talked to me about a project he has in the works. He wants me in on it. Possibly as the director. A big step up for me. I've always wanted to direct in New York. And *DIANA* will run for years, so I have steady employment until this new thing takes off."

"What's the project?"

"He was sketchy about it. He said it would be different from anything he's done before. A new young cast and theater. Not necessarily Broadway. He piqued my interest."

Jessie flashed back to Quill at SuZee Q's. Did this have anything to do with Patrick Cavanaugh?

*

It was odd, how little Nick thought about Jessie down here in Florida. Every hour of every day was about Patrick.

Patrick's physical scars were faint but substantial. Nick hoped they'd fade as he continued to age and his body developed. His psychological scars were a different issue. Nick felt like he was tiptoeing through a mine field with his nephew. It was tricky.

He was reminded yet again of Bree's words to him years ago: Because of his childhood, Nick related to kids better than adults. He definitely understood them better. Their needs were simple, their outlook innocent and untouched. Until adults intruded. When would parents realize their mistakes had a lasting effect on their children?

Nick kept in touch with Mary and Kat. He also called Anthony every few days. Kat was deeply concerned about Patrick, her worry keeping her awake at night. It was almost as if she knew, but that was impossible. Nick told no one. Being the one who instigated the search for Patrick, Kat's anxiety probably came from feeling responsible for what happened to him. It was typical Kat, her heart peeking through her tough demeanor.

Mary informed him that Jessie came by the house, wanting to talk to Patrick. She got angry when she learned they were both in Florida.

Nick shook his head. Jessie's anger was becoming the norm. It was exhausting.

*

191

Their days in Sarasota passed peacefully. Patrick was in no hurry to leave. He'd stay forever if he could. The walks on the beach. The fabulous food. The swims. And he was starting to enjoy jogging, although he was just a beginner. There was something about finding the rhythm of a run, his hair trailing behind him, perspiration dripping, his mind in a world of its own. It was cleansing in a way, comparable to singing.

On one exceptionally lazy afternoon, Patrick read Nick's book *THE SILVER LINING* as they laid on the beach. He devoured it in hours and afterwards pummeled Nick with questions about the characters and plot.

Nick told him the story behind the book, about his friend Lyle Barton who was tragically killed while helping Nick rescue Anthony from his demon father Gianni Fosselli. Nick's voice softened, and his words were cautious as he spoke of losing his friend. How many times was this man expected to confront death?

Many nights after their walks they'd lie in their beds, continuing their talks. Patrick told Nick about growing up with Tess and Father Joe, about being raised a good Catholic boy and being ridiculed because of it in high school. Nick described his lonely childhood in the Far East, his only friend a dog named Haywire. "Until I hit puberty, I was a tall, scrawny drink of water. No muscles. An academic nerd."

Patrick told him about Lena, his only friend at Cohan's. They were the youngest of the waiters, so they stuck together, an us-against-the-world mentality. Lena was the only girl he allowed to get close, who could touch him or hug him without Patrick freezing. "She always felt safe."

"Do you think it's because she's black, the opposite of those women in your foster home?"

"Maybe. A little. Lena's mother is black, a former Miss Florida. Her father is white and British. I think it's mostly because she's genuine, no pretenses or hidden agenda. She is who she is, so she doesn't scare me."

Nick described his time in Hong Kong with pals Bree and Ozzie, the three of them young and cocky and hungry as they pursued the story or hunted down the bad guys or, in Nick's case, wrote a novel.

Patrick learned he had to pay attention to what Nick DIDN'T say. The man never talked about his marriages. And the name Jessie rarely crossed his lips.

These late-night conversations were cathartic for Patrick. Now that his darkest secrets were exposed, the walls came down, and he wasn't afraid to open up to his uncle. And Nick reciprocated. Patrick stopped thinking of Nick as a famous author, as a man recognized around the world. Nick was family, his best friend, a guy who never judged him, who accepted him for who he was.

No subject was taboo. Not even sex. Somehow Nick even managed to break down Patrick's barrier on that subject. Or maybe it was just easier to talk in the darkness. Patrick had a million questions, all unanswered over the years as he grew up. He could never talk to Father Joe about it. Sex was forbidden before marriage in the Catholic Church, only discussed in pre-marital counseling. He was afraid to go to a bookstore or library for fear someone would see what he was buying or researching. And Patrick never had a close male friend, someone to share his curiosity.

"I feel like a freak," he confessed. "What girl is ever going to want me after this?"

Nick took a deep breath and exhaled slowly. "Look, I can't begin to understand what you went through. But I do know this. Everyone wants to have a normal sexual life. Few people do. After all, what constitutes normal? No one knows what goes on behind closed doors. It's private stuff. Or it should be," he added, sounding bitter. "We all have secrets. Things we're ashamed of."

"Even you?"

Nick didn't respond. Patrick wondered if he overstepped some invisible boundary between them. He heard the man sigh. "For years I went around using women for my own pleasure," he said softly. "How they felt didn't matter to me. If I hurt them emotionally, so be it." Nick paused. "I'm not proud of my behavior. But I own it." He looked over at Patrick. "You don't. What happened to you was against your will. You have nothing to be ashamed of."

Patrick was surprised by Nick's admission. It took guts to confess this. Tucking his hands behind his head, he confided, "When I never had a girlfriend, my friends assumed I was gay. You know, being in musicals and all. It's such a cliché. They learned the truth when they got a waiter at Cohan's to come on to me."

"What happened?"

"I decked him."

Nick burst out laughing. "Sorry. I shouldn't laugh. It's just not like you. Or how I think of you."

"I'm the least violent person I know. But I was tired of the others making fun of me." Patrick flexed his hand into a fist. "I'm lucky I didn't break something. I had to say hundreds of 'Hail Marys' and 'Our Fathers' to atone for that little outburst."

Nick was literally cackling.

"It's not funny. It's wrong to hit someone, even if they deserved it."

His uncle's laughter was extinguished immediately. "Oh God, Patrick. I wasn't thinking. I didn't mean—"

"No, I didn't mean—I wasn't talking about—Sorry. Forget I said that. Anyway," Patrick continued, getting back to the original subject. "I'm attracted to girls. I've gone out. But it was always just a date or two. Nothing ever stuck."

"Not even with Lena?"

"Lena's a friend, not a girlfriend."

"So why didn't anything stick?"

"In the movies the guy is always the aggressor. You know. Pushing the girl to— But that's not true in real life. Girls are, well, they're the ones who want it. At least they did with me. So when things started to get physical, I'd cut and run."

"Is it— Are you able to—"

"Yes." Patrick felt his face heat up. His embarrassment was stupid after what they'd been through together. "It's fear. I'm afraid of … intimacy." He stared at the ceiling. "I'll be seventeen in a couple months. And I've never been with a girl. Another reason I feel like a freak."

"You just need more time. A lot of guys don't experiment until they're older."

"Were you one of them?"

"It doesn't matter what I—"

"How old were you when you first—"

"Fourteen. But I'm a bad example. You have your own inner clock, Patrick." Nick yawned. "Don't feel pressured to follow the crowd. Everyone's different. And as I said, what you do is private. The guys who brag the most usually see the least action."

"You're making me feel better."

They again lapsed into silence.

"Are there books on the subject?"

"Hmm?" Nick yawned again. "What subject?"

"… Sex. Making love."

"There are books on everything. But you won't need them. Your instincts will kick in."

"Really?"

Nick took a minute to answer. Maybe he fell asleep. "Look, I'm not good at this. I've never discussed sex with a son. Jeffrey died when he was ten. And Anthony's only nine."

"I'm sorry. I—"

"No, don't apologize. I just want to explain my awkward or stupid answers."

"I don't think they're awkward. I'm the one who's awkward. And stupid."

Nick looked over at him, an amused smile on his face. "It must be in the genes."

*

Anthony wandered into Kat's room. "Want to see my photos of Patrick? I took them at Susie's when he was singing."

Kat pushed her laptop back and spread the five photos across her desk. "These are awesome, Anthony."

Anthony surveyed his work. Three were close-ups of Patrick singing, two were taken further back. "I have a ton more."

"Look at the emotion on his face. You really captured him. His total commitment to a song." Kat shook her head. "Can I keep one of these? Add it to my research on Andrew?"

"Sure. I can print more. I think I'll put some on Patrick's desk so he sees them right away when he gets home." After Kat selected one, Anthony gathered the rest. "Will Dad and Patrick be back soon?"

Kat stared at the photo in her hands. "I don't know. Why?"

"I miss them. I miss Patrick. He hasn't been here long, but it seems like he's been here forever."

Kat looked up at him. "I feel the same way."

"I always wanted an older brother." Anthony traced Patrick's face on one of the photos.

"Brother? He's our cousin."

"But I was Andrew's son for five years. And Patrick is Andrew's son. So that makes us brothers. And since you're my sister, Patrick is your brother, too."

Kat smiled. "I like the way you think, squirt."

*

On their last evening, Patrick and Nick took their usual long walk. The sun began its slow slide into the ocean. The gulls dove for fish. And the beach was a treasure trove of one-of-a-kind shells. Patrick was collecting the best of the best. To always remind him of the ocean.

As usual, they started out walking in silence.

Patrick now sported a deep tan. Tonight he wore running shorts and a tank top, same as Nick. He hated the thought of heading north and having to bundle up again. Satisfaction crept across his face. Who would have thought he'd ever feel this way? He prayed this newfound freedom didn't disappear in the rearview mirror along with Sarasota.

"What was the song your grandmother taught you? The one you'd sing when you—"

"'Not While I'm Around.'" Patrick picked up a couple shells, skimming one across the water and pocketing the other. "From *SWEENEY TODD.*"

"I've never heard you sing it."

"I don't. Sing it."

"Why?"

Patrick shrugged. "I always felt it was associated with that house."

They were again silent.

"What's the chain around your neck?"

Patrick lifted it, fingering the crucifix. "Mary gave it to me. It was her grandfather's. I added Tess's ring to it."

"Mary thinks a lot of you."

"She reminds me of Tess."

They moved into the surf, wading through the cool water. Patrick was comfortable with their silences, but often the silence brought back memories, especially now that they were leaving. "I can't stop thinking about it. I keep seeing— I try not to dwell on it, but I don't seem to have any control over it." It was the first time he brought up the subject of what happened in that house. He was nervous about how Nick would react.

Nick didn't answer right away. "I don't know how to advise you, Patrick. For some reason, your mind needs to replay it. Maybe the more you see it, the less effect it will have on you. Have you had any panic attacks?"

"No ..." It was the first time he'd thought about it. "Wow. Pretty amazing."

"Before now," Nick pointed out, "the least little thing would bring one on. That's good."

"Yeah. It is. So I shouldn't fight these memories?"

"Have you thought any more about therapy?"

"I hate that word." Patrick dug his toes into the sand. "Couldn't I just talk to you?"

"I'm no psychologist."

"But you understand me. And you went through it with me. How can a stranger understand?"

"They're trained to understand. I'm not."

"But you do."

They were at a stalemate. Patrick stopped walking and stared at Nick.

"What?"

"Would seeing the worst of my scars convince you? Make you realize how hard it would be for me— How I couldn't talk to a stranger?"

"Why would that make a difference?"

"It would show how much I trust you. You. No one else."

"No, it wouldn't make a difference— What are you doing?"

Patrick lowered a portion of his shorts.

Nick's face remained neutral. He swallowed before looking away.

Patrick snapped his shorts back in place. "I'm supposed to describe these scars to a stranger? Or show him? No."

Nick remained silent.

"I used to pray for Tess's health. Now I pray you'll help me ... Will you?"

His uncle stared at the sand, his hands on his hips.

Patrick saw it was futile. "Great. I'm an idiot. I was a fool to show you, to trust you—" Shaking his head, he set off down the beach.

Nick followed him. "Patrick, wait. Your trust is important—"

"Not important enough to make you change your mind." He picked up his pace. "My prayers are useless. And they're selfish. I shouldn't ask for things for myself."

"You're far from selfish."

Patrick halted abruptly and faced Nick. "You think because I had something horrible happen when I was little and because I'm religious that I'm this really good person. I'm not. I told you I hit that guy at Cohan's. And I attacked Jessie. I was mean to those people who helped you find me. And I've been mean to you while we've been here."

"Which proves you're human."

Patrick set off again. He didn't want to hear this.

Nick kept up with him. "Yes, I think you're a good person. I've been around enough crud in my life to know the difference."

"You don't know what crud is until you've met Carrie Trout."

"Then give me permission to find her. Make her pay."

"I told you no." Patrick broke into a jog.

"So you're just going to let her get away with it?" Nick came up beside him, matching his stride.

"I want to forget about it."

"How many more little boys did she hurt? Have you thought about that?"

"Stop it!"

"Maybe she's torturing someone right now—"

"Goddamn it, STOP IT!" Patrick shoved Nick away.

"Good. You're angry. Get it out."

197

"Why are you doing this?"

"You've got a ton of anger boiling inside you. So go ahead. Take it out on me." Patrick didn't react. "What? Now you're afraid to show how mad you are?"

Frustrated, Patrick strode towards the water.

Nick shadowed his steps. "You have a right to be angry, Patrick."

Pacing back and forth in the surf, Patrick fought tears. "Yes, I'm angry, all right? Why did this happen to me? W-H-Y?" he shouted to the heavens. "What did I ever do to—" He clutched his hair, turning away from Nick. He didn't want to cry. He wasn't a baby anymore. He wasn't five-year-old Patrick running to Tess's house, hoping she'd make him feel better.

Feeling Nick's hand on his shoulder, Patrick swiped away a tear. His uncle led him back to the beach, sitting them both down in the sand.

Patrick stared out at the water, the foamy surf sweeping in and out like it had for centuries. The sun was an orange glow on the horizon. The outline of a freighter could be seen in the distance. A tiny green lizard poked his head out of the sand, then disappeared back into the hole he'd dug.

The majesty of the universe was usually a balm, had always reminded Patrick of his place in the world. Of how miniscule he was in this whole mystery called life. Not today. "I hate it, Nick. I hate all these feelings swimming around in me. I don't know what to do with them."

Nick stretched his long legs out in front of him. "I'm honored you trust me," he said quietly. "That you feel you can tell me and show me anything." He looked over at him. "I mean it, Patrick."

Patrick continued to stare at the water. "I DO trust you. As much as I trusted Tess."

"Then trust me on one more thing. All that anger you have needs to be diffused. I just tapped the surface. All those feelings swimming around in you? They need to be sorted out. And that, my dear nephew, is why you need to see a professional."

Patrick turned his gaze on his uncle. Shaking his head, he finally smiled. "You are relentless."

"Thank you."

"And smug."

"I thought we established that days ago."

"God hates smugness."

"God will get me for a whole lot more than smugness. I'll be in your Purgatory for eternity. If I don't go straight to hell." He eyed Patrick, amusement creeping across his face. "How does God feel about cursing?"

Patrick groaned and dropped his head on his chest.

"Better get started on all those Hail Marys and Our Fathers." Nick got to his feet, brushing off the sand. "Come on. Let's go home."

"Home?"

"For one more night. The question is - where's home after tonight?"

"New York." Patrick looked up at him. "Do you mind?"

"Yeah," Nick said sarcastically, "I mind." He headed towards the condo, Patrick hurrying to catch up.

The next morning Patrick stood on the beach one last time and said goodbye to Sarasota. He wouldn't be coming back.

Too much had happened here.

And he was different because of it.

CHAPTER 18

Nick and Patrick spent a few days with Father Joe, staying at the Bed & Breakfast while they cleaned out Tess's house. It was tiring work. And emotional. It was hard to watch Patrick go through Tess's things. Also hard to see how much Patrick would miss Father Joe.

Patrick already had Tess's quilt and diaries back in New York. Now he packed photos and other mementos in suitcases. He also put some special items in a box and sealed it. Everything else would be distributed to the needy.

On their last night in town, Nick and Patrick took a walk. It was a pleasant evening, the temperature in the seventies with a light breeze. "This was a nice place to grow up," Patrick mused. "The people are friendly. And the school system gave me a good foundation in the arts. I enjoyed living here."

"Are you sorry to leave it?"

Patrick shrugged. "There's not much here for me anymore."

"There's Father Joe."

"Yeah." He looked away.

"Do you think he'd like to spend the holidays with us in New York?"

Patrick stopped walking and turned to Nick. "Are you serious?"

"There's no reason for him to be alone down here over Christmas. He said he's retired now."

"Thank you, Nick! Thank you."

*

They stopped at Cohan's on their way to the airport. Nick stayed with Father Joe in the car while Patrick went inside.

The dinner service was about to begin as Patrick headed up to the office.

"Thank God, you're back," the manager said. "Our reservations are off. Everyone's been asking for you. I'll put you in for service tonight."

"I'm sorry, Graham. I'm not coming back."

Graham's smile vanished in an instant. "You're quitting? Seriously? You're a star here, Patrick."

"Thank you for everything. I loved working here. You've been great to me."

"Did someone else hire you?"

"No. I'm moving to New York."

Graham snorted. "You and every other kid with stars in his eyes. Don't be a fool, Patrick."

"Again, thank you." He left the office and hustled down the stairs.

"You'll be back in six months." Graham followed him.

Lena ran over, jumping up and down and clapping her hands. "You're back."

"He's quitting," Graham spit out.

"Really?" Lena asked, her joy fading.

"I'm sorry, Lena. I'll email soon. Promise. I have a computer now. And we'll text. I should have kept in touch, but it's been— I've missed you. Give me your email address."

"Does this have anything to do with Nick McDeare and Andrew Brady?" she asked as she jotted down her addy and handed it to him.

"Why'd you ask that?"

"I called Father Joe a couple weeks ago because I was worried. He said you were in New York."

"Yeah. I've been staying at Nick's. It's, well, it's my home now."

Her eyes narrowed as she stared at him. "Are you ...? Don't tell me you're—"

"I always said you were the smartest person working here."

Throwing her arms around his neck, she whispered, "I'm so happy for you, Patrick. Email and fill me in, okay? I want every little detail!"

*

Hearing the front locks turn, Mary hurried into the hallway, trailed by Kat and Anthony. Nick, Patrick and Willie appeared in the vestibule. Also a priest and a lot of luggage. "You must be Father Joe," she said, ushering him into the hall. "I'm Mary. We're so glad you're joining us."

"What a lovely home. And beautifully decorated for Christmas." Father checked out the living room and dining room. He turned to Kat. "Hello again, young lady. And who's this tough-looking guy?"

Anthony stepped forward. "Anthony. Patrick's brother."

Mary beamed at Patrick. "You have been sooo missed! And look at you. So tanned! Your hair is a shade lighter from the sun. It looks good on you."

"You look like a movie star," Kat gushed.

Mary led the entourage towards the kitchen. "Come on. Let's get you all settled and unpacked. Then we'll have a nice dinner."

"Thanks for decorating, Mary." Nick looked tired. "I couldn't have faced it."

"We worked like dogs to get it ready. And I see what you mean about those Christmas tree holders. I cursed more than I have in my entire life – ooh, sorry Father." She hustled them towards the back stairs. "I put you in a room close to Patrick, Father. Right across the hall ..."

*

Patrick hefted his suitcases onto the bed. It felt strange to be back in this bedroom after Sarasota. Yes, he had a tan and new clothes, but nothing could disguise the fact that he was a different person.

He pulled a seashell from his pocket, fingering its soft surface, reminding him of the condo. Wandering across the room, he found publicity photos of himself spread across the desk. Anthony's handiwork. They were good. Really good. But would he have any use for them? He hadn't sung since— Did the return of his memory mean his days of singing were behind him?

Patrick felt his breath catch. His vision began to blur. He—

What was happening? After everything he went through in Sarasota, after opening up to Nick and starting to talk about—

Patrick stumbled blindly into the hallway and down the stairs, searching for Nick. He found him in his bedroom, unpacking. Nick took one look at him and sat him down on the bed. "What's wrong?"

"They came back," Patrick panted. "The attacks."

"Okay, stop. Take a deep breath." Patrick tried. "Again." Better this time. "They're not coming back, Patrick. You're just nervous about being back here, surrounded by the others. What's that in your hand?"

"A shell. From the beach."

"Keep holding it and close your eyes." Patrick did as he was told. "Take another deep breath."

Patrick inhaled and exhaled slowly.

"Keep your eyes closed and picture the beach down at the condo. Picture it."

Patrick turned the shell over in his hands. He could see the condo. The surf. The sand. The gulls. The peace. Walking with Nick as the sun set.

"Do you see it?" Patrick nodded. "Whenever you start to panic, hold that shell and picture it. Hear it. Feel it." The bed shifted as Nick sat down beside him. "Keep your eyes closed until you feel calm again."

After a few minutes, Patrick opened his eyes.

202

"You okay now?" He nodded. "Patrick, I think you're worried someone's going to figure out what happened to you. They won't know unless you tell them."

"I wish we were back on the beach."

"After the holidays we'll go down to our villa in St. John. It's even better than the condo. In the meantime, focus on taking care of yourself. If you need alone time, take it. You don't owe anyone an explanation."

"What if I need to talk to you?"

"Come find me. If I'm busy, don't be afraid to interrupt. You're not alone, Patrick. You have me. I'm your sounding board."

"There you are." Kat stood in the doorway. "Susie wants you to sing tomorrow night. She's doing a special cabaret before Christmas."

Patrick looked at Nick. "No, but thank Susie for me. I just got back. I need some time."

Kat nodded, her eyes bouncing from Patrick to Nick. "Maybe New Year's Eve?"

"Maybe."

*

Kat was quiet at dinner. She tried to enjoy Mary's veal and gnocchi, but she wasn't very hungry.

She'd caught the last part of Patrick's conversation with her dad up in his bedroom. This time she wasn't eavesdropping. It was an accident. Something was very wrong. She hoped her suspicions were off base, for Patrick's sake.

Mary and Father Joe hit it off during dinner. Father Joe knew how to charm. Kat loved having him here. Even Anthony was chatty with the priest. Her dad was making an effort, but his eyes shifted constantly to Patrick, who rivalled Kat in silence. There was an unspoken conversation going on between her father and Patrick.

After helping with the dishes, Kat asked Patrick if she could borrow Andrew's journals to look something up. She purposely took them all in case he was curious about what she wanted to reread.

Retreating to her room, she rifled through one of the early journals until she found the entry that was on her mind. Andrew was in his first year at Juilliard:

Carlo, a classmate who's become a close friend, burst into tears in Michael's acting class a few weeks ago and ran from the room. I went after him. He was in the first-year dressing room, hysterical. I asked him what was wrong. At first he was embarrassed and wouldn't tell me. When I convinced him whatever he told me was just between us, he told me he'd been sexually abused when he was little. By his uncle. No one knew. Not even his mother. He said his uncle threatened to hurt both him and his mom if he told. The scene he did in class that day brought it all back. I told him to talk to Michael, that he was more than an acting teacher. He cared about us.

Carlo was missing for several weeks. He returned today and thanked me. He said Michael was a big help. I could see there was a new bond between them in class this afternoon. I can't imagine what Carlo went through. Why would an adult prey on a small child? I'm going to tuck this away in case I need to call on this kind of emotion onstage one day.

Was that what happened to Patrick? Kat thought about it … Mary's reaction after talking with her dad that night. She was deeply upset, more than usual … Father Joe's presence. Did Patrick need his emotional support? … Dad and Patrick's conversation, plus their communication during dinner …

Was her dad doing for Patrick what Acting Teacher Michael did for Carlo?

Returning the journals to Patrick, she lingered briefly, making small talk.

Secretly she wished she could hug her cousin and never let him go.

*

Nick sat with Father Joe and Mary in the study. A fire blazed in the grate. They all sipped brandy.

"Maddie and Ethan are staying in LA for Christmas." Mary turned to Father Joe, explaining, "Nick's half-sister and brother."

"Why?" Nick asked.

"The court is letting Maddie have her daughter for the holiday. The case isn't over, but the judge felt Maddie deserved some time with Christine."

"That's good news."

"The bad news is that Bree isn't joining them. Maddie doesn't want to give her ex any ammunition. She wants everything above board and thinks that Bree sleep—" Embarrassed, Mary glanced at Father Joe. "Well, you get the idea." Mary cleared her throat. "Kat doesn't want Bree to be alone over Christmas, so she invited her here." Mary paused. "Jessie will also be here."

Nick's eyebrows shot up. Jessie and Bree would both be here? It was going to be one hell of a Christmas. He slunk further down into his chair and stared at the fire.

"Well." Mary pushed out of her recliner. "I'm off to bed. Goodnight, gentlemen."

*

Kat almost got caught as Mary left the study. She'd been listening at the hallway door. Thinking quickly, she hurried down the hall into the living room, planting herself behind the adjoining door into the study.

*

Nick continued to stare at the fire.

"You never said how it went in Sarasota," Father Joe said. "You were there a long time."

"It was rough."

"I thought so." He swirled his brandy. "I always believed Patrick suffered more than beatings when he was little. The panic attacks. His strong faith, unusual in a young boy. His lack of a girlfriend. And his singing, his escape switch. When he sings, he becomes a different person."

Nick looked over at Father, who stared back at him. Setting his mouth in a firm line, Nick returned his gaze to the fire.

"I admire your silence, Nick. It shows your devotion to Patrick. And the bond you formed in Sarasota. It couldn't have been easy, learning what happened to him."

Nick's eyes swiveled again to the priest. He'd underestimated Father Joe's wisdom.

"I figured it out years ago, but I didn't know what to do with the knowledge. Patrick either didn't remember or blocked it. Who was I to upset his peaceful life with Tess? Now here you are, the answer to my prayers. You took him back to Sarasota, and Patrick is finally facing his past. Sure, it'll be hard, but it will toughen him up. Which is what he needs now. Tess and I got him through childhood. You'll help him become an adult. But make sure Patrick hangs onto the things that make him unique, that matter to him. Like his singing. And his faith."

"I'm not a miracle-worker, Father. Patrick is who he is."

"Patrick will become what you make of him. I know what I'm talking about. I had my own Nick McDeare."

"What do you mean?"

"I was raised by my grandfather. A mean S-O-B. I rebelled. Spent some time in the slammer. Then on the streets. Until a priest found me unconscious, beaten to a pulp. He took me in. Let me sleep in the basement of his church. And he taught me how to fight back. We spent hours in the

205

local Y. Boxing became my reason for living. I was good at it. Never lost a fight."

"How'd you go from being a prizefighter to a priest?"

"Father Carmine taught me more than just fighting. He taught me about a loving and forgiving God. I admired Carmine's grit. But I respected his faith."

"So you turned to the priesthood?"

Father Joe nodded. "Carmine changed the course of my life. You'll do the same for Patrick. Singing is to Patrick what God is to me. His faith serves a different purpose. It gives him a framework for how to live his life. When he came to Tess and me he craved love and structure. A normal existence. We tried hard to give him that."

"Don't sell yourself short, Father. You did a good job."

Father stared into his snifter. "I still live with guilt."

"For what?"

"For not letting Tess raise Patrick from the moment we found him in the choir loft. For turning that sweet baby over to the foster care system."

"We can't rewrite history, Father. No matter how much we want to."

"One of the toughest aspects of my job is when someone asks me why bad things happen to good people. I don't have the answer. I only know that God has a plan for us all, and we eventually reap something positive from it. For me, the positive was Father Carmine. With Patrick, it's you."

Father Joe rolled his eyes. "The brandy's starting to talk. Which means it's time to hit the sack." He pushed to his feet and placed his snifter on the bar. "If you hear a loud noise, it'll be me falling down the stairs. Don't worry. I can sleep anywhere."

*

Kat hurried up the front stairs to her room. Hurling herself onto the bed, she cradled Hamlet and finally let herself cry. It was true. What she feared about Patrick was true.

How could something like this happen to a little boy? A sweet, innocent little boy? How did Patrick survive it?

She knew the answer to that last question. Patrick blocked all memories of what happened to him. Singing was how he survived.

But the memories must have returned when her dad and Patrick were in Sarasota. Which explained Patrick's silence and withdrawal from the family. He was trying to cope, and Kat's father was his rock. Just like Acting Coach Michael was for a Juilliard student named Carlo.

From the moment Kat read about Heidi's possible pregnancy in Andrew's journal, she became invested in the fate of his child. When she came face-to-face with Patrick for the first time, it was as if she'd known him her entire life. They were forever connected in a unique way, just like her father and Uncle Andrew.

She'd keep his secret and honor his privacy. Not an easy task for Kat. But because it was Patrick, it was a no-brainer.

*

Christmas Eve presented itself like a picture postcard. Snow drifted past the steamy windows. A fire blazed in the grates of the living room and study. Candles flickered around the rooms. The trees glittered with lights. Poinsettias were placed strategically. And appetizers were laid out in the dining room, along with Mary's cookies and Violet's dreaded fruitcake. The house smelled of bayberry and pine. Sentimental carols played on the sound system. A Norman Rockwell Christmas with too much kitsch.

Nick had no gifts for anyone this year. Christmas just seemed to creep up on him. He was embarrassed.

When Bree arrived, Kat and Nick met her at the door.

"You look really pretty, Bree." Kat took her coat as Nick stood back to admire the woman. She did look pretty.

Bree Fontaine was one of those women who didn't need makeup or fancy clothes to stand out in a room. Tonight it looked like she made an effort. She wore a dark green silk dress which brought out her hazel eyes. Tiny jade buddhas hung from her ears, a gift from Nick when they lived in Hong Kong. Nick even checked out her legs. Bree always wore slacks, so it had been a long time …

They moved into the dining room, where Bertie and Abbie were grazing at the buffet. *DIANA* was dark for Christmas, a treat for the cast and crew.

Heading down the hall to the study, Nick poured Bree some wine and introduced her to Father Joe. As the others joined them, he remained in the background, sipping a bourbon and watching.

Patrick was quiet, probably overwhelmed by the amount of people. Kat sat on one side of him, Anthony on the other, both silent. Monty spread out at Anthony's feet, looking bored. The entire atmosphere was off.

Around nine, Nick heard the front locks turn. Mary disappeared down the hallway and returned a few minutes later with Jessie and Larry What's-His-Name, who held a stack of gifts. "Merry Christmas, everyone."

The strange evening kicked up a notch. Jessie wore a bright red cashmere sweater dress. Her blond hair was swept back from her face. Tiny rubies sparkled on her ears, and the ruby heart pendant Nick gave her on opening night in London hung from her neck.

Nick watched Patrick and Kat recede further into the cushions of the couch. Anthony decided to download tonight's photographs on his laptop upstairs. Bree sipped her wine, observing.

Jessie approached Father Joe. "I'm Jessie. Merry Christmas. And you are?"

"Father Joe. Patrick's friend."

"And mine." Nick swirled the ice in his glass.

Father Joe rose, giving Jessie his seat. He moved over to the window and perched on the sill. Nick joined him.

"Where's Nora?" Mary asked Jessie. "We were expecting her."

"In Chicago. Her daughter decided to have her sixth baby weeks ahead of time."

It was an awkward evening, to say the least. Gifts were opened as midnight drew near. The stash under the tree was a quarter of its usual size. Apparently, Nick wasn't the only one who came up empty-handed this year.

"You didn't shop, Nick?" Jessie eyed him.

Nick's reply was to refill his bourbon."

Kat spoke up for the first time in hours. "Christmas isn't supposed to be about gifts, Jessie."

Jessie opened her mouth to respond, then shut it with a snap. Her focus moved to Patrick. "Could I speak with you alone for a minute?" She stood up. "In the living room?"

Now what?

*

Jessie sat down on the couch.

Patrick stood a few feet away. "I owe you an apology," he began, "for what happened upstairs on Thanksgiving. I didn't mean to—"

"No, no. It's okay. Nick explained you're going through—"

"Nick told you?" The boy seemed panicked. "When?"

She stared at him, puzzled. "That day. When he and I talked afterwards."

Patrick seemed relieved.

"Please. Sit down." She waited while he joined her on the couch, keeping some distance between them. "I want to explain why I ran out after hearing you sing a few weeks ago." Being so close to Patrick, his face so much like Andrew's, was uncomfortable. "You were wonderful. So

208

much so that it was emotional for me. It was like Andrew came back to life. I couldn't stop crying, and I didn't want to embarrass you."

"I'm sorry I upset you so much."

This boy was unusual. Polite and shy. Not at all like Andrew. "I'd like to spend time with you. I was married to your father. We grew up together. You and I should get to know each other."

Patrick nodded and looked down.

Jessie didn't know what to say next. Patrick certainly wasn't a talker. More like Nick than Andrew. "How about next week? I can show you around the theater and introduce you to everyone."

Patrick smiled. A little. "Uh, that sounds great. Thank you."

This was getting awkward. "Patrick, do I intimidate you?"

"Well ... you ARE Jessica Kendle. I've admired your work for a long time."

Ah, so that was it. It was her fame as an actress. That would be easy to get past, once they got better acquainted. She stood up. "Let's plan on your coming to the theater next week, between Christmas and New Year's. We'll have a late lunch. Then you can watch the show from the wings."

"I'd like that."

Jessie went back to the study. She saw Patrick go into the kitchen. He was definitely odd. Extremely awkward. And he seemed so much younger than the mature young man she saw on the stage a few weeks ago.

She bided her time, waiting for the opportunity to speak with Nick. It finally came as everyone was leaving. He was helping Bree on with her coat. Of course. "Can we talk? Privately?"

As Jessie followed Nick down the hallway, she grabbed Larry's hand. "I won't be long. Wish me luck."

"Just keep your cool," he warned.

*

Kat sat at the island with Patrick, both munching on Mary's frosted cookies. "What did Jessie want?"

Patrick swallowed a large bite. "She wants to get to know me."

Kat bit her tongue and looked down.

"What?"

She peeked up at him. "Why would she want to do that?"

He chuckled. "Why? Uh, maybe because I remind her of Andrew."

"Are you making fun of me?"

"Why would I want to do that?" Patrick mimicked, his blue eyes dancing.

209

Kat grinned. "Okay, okay. But be careful. Your very existence means there was another woman in Andrew's life, and Jessie doesn't—" She forced herself to shut up. "I shouldn't do this. You need to make up your own mind about Jessie."

Her dad and Jessie came through the kitchen and went upstairs to his office. The door shut.

Anthony joined Kat and Patrick, grabbing a cookie.

The house was quiet, the guests gone, the Christmas carols silenced. The only sound was the conversation taking place upstairs.

"Kids," Mary appeared out of nowhere. "Come on. Come back in the study."

Nothing was going to prevent Kat from listening to her father and Jessie. She looked over at Patrick, who remained rooted in place.

"Kids, please."

Anthony turned to Mary. "We're fine here, Mary."

Well, well. The squirt developed a backbone.

When Kat glanced back at Mary, the woman was gone.

*

Nick shut his office door and turned to Jessie, waiting.

Jessie walked to the windows, her back to him. "Do you still love me?"

This again? Nick approached her. "I'll always love you. You know that."

"So can I move back in? Can we resume our marriage?"

Nick didn't know what to say. He hadn't given this serious thought since the discovery of Patrick.

"Should I take your silence as a no?"

"I don't know, Jess. Honestly."

"You've had months to think about it. You still can't make up your mind?"

He looked at her, searching for words.

"Okay, fine. If you haven't made up your mind by now, it's obviously over." She marched towards the door.

He grabbed her hand. "Wait a minute. Slow down. Let's talk."

She shook him off. "I'm tired of waiting. It's been seven months since our marriage blew up. Seven months! And you're still sitting on the fence. Or is it just that you don't want to lose this house and your cushy life here?"

This house and …? Nick started to laugh.

"What's so funny?"

"You. Thinking I'd stay in a marriage just to have some place to live."

"You were living in hotels when we met, Nick."

"When I was traveling for my work, yes! When I wasn't, I had an apartment in D.C."

"A bachelor pad."

Again Nick laughed. "Do they still use that term?" He strode to his desk. "This is a ridiculous conversation."

Jessie trailed him. "I want an answer, Nick. Yes or no?"

"I don't have an answer. Especially when you bring this up out of the blue."

"Out of—?" She started to pace. "Okay. Here it is. I'm moving back in. I have a week's vacation, starting January second. You can either join me and we resume our marriage, or I want you out before I set foot back in this house."

Nick's expression hardened. "You're joking."

"No. I want to get on with my life."

"With Larry What's-His-Name?"

"You love to insult other men, don't you? It makes you feel so virile. No other man can come close to the sex god, Nick McDeare."

"You're behaving like an ass."

"The clock just ticked down. Ding-ding-ding. Time's up. Make your decision. Either we have a marriage, or you move out and we divorce."

"And what about the kids?"

"Kat will go with you. Anthony stays with me."

"Anthony and Kat are inseparable."

"Oh, please!"

"They'll hate being apart."

"No they won't. Anthony resents the time you spend with Kat."

"How would you know? You barely spend five minutes with him."

"Don't you dare try to steal my son! Or Patrick."

Now Nick was angry. "Don't YOU dare talk about Patrick. You don't even know him."

"He's underage. I heard Mary say tonight he's actually sixteen, not seventeen. Which means he needs a guardian. He's my dead husband's son. I have as much right to him as you do."

"Bullshit!" Nick exploded. "You're no relation to him. And why would you want him anyway? So you can pretend your god, Andrew, is still alive? You're not going to live vicariously through Patrick, Jessie. That kid deserves better."

Jessie's eyes filled with tears. "Why are you so cruel, Nick? I don't know you anymore."

"Ditto, sweetheart."

She brushed away her tears and straightened up. "January second I'm moving back in. If you're here, I'll know we have a marriage. If you're not, I'll file for divorce."

"On what grounds? You're the one who—"

"All right, dammit, you file. I don't care as long as this sham of a marriage is over. And don't think you can run to the villa because that's mine, too." She threw the door open.

"Wrong. There is no 'yours' or 'mine.' It's all ours. Fifty-fifty, remember? It was what you wanted when we got married. We were going to be 'Till death do us part.' You aren't my Sugar Momma like you were with Andrew. We both brought money and assets to the marriage. So I'll go wherever the hell I want to go!"

CHAPTER 19

"Damn you, Nick. Damn you to hell!" Frustrated, Jessie started down the stairs. Halting, she was stunned to see the kids in the kitchen.

"How can you be so hateful?" Kat asked, her eyes slits. Nick's office door slammed in punctuation.

"I'm staying with Dad," Anthony's lips formed a firm line, a haunting imitation of Nick.

Jessie felt like she'd been body slammed. "Anthony … sweetie …"

Anthony sprinted past her up the stairs. A moment later, another door slammed.

Jessie glanced at Patrick, who was as white as a ghost. He stared at Jessie in shock. "I'm sorry, Patrick. You turned up at a really bad time. I-I'm sorry." Hurrying to the living room, she clung to Larry. "I lost it. I completely lost it."

*

Mary sat in the dining room. It was a tough decision, allowing the kids to hear the fight upstairs. In the end, she decided she couldn't shield them anymore.

Nick and Jessie's marriage was over, which was sad. The destruction began when Kat came to live with them, followed by Jessie's miscarriage. Her reckless behavior in London was the final nail in the coffin. Nick, for his part, too often focused on his job or the kids instead of his wife. And he couldn't forgive her for cheating on him, for never being able to trust him.

Everything happens for a reason. Mary's guiding principle. Right now she couldn't see anything good coming out of this debacle.

Jessie paused in the dining room arch, her face streaked with tears. Larry was at her side. "You heard?"

Mary nodded.

"You'll stay with me, right? Here at the brownstone. I need you, Mary."

Mary stared at the woman she helped raise. "Honey, I've loved you since you were a little girl. But this last year has me scratching my head. What is going on with you?"

"You didn't answer my question."

"I'm all about the kids. I'll go wherever they go."

"What if they're split up?"

"You can't split these kids. They need each other."

Furious, Jessie turned on her heel and disappeared down the hallway.

Mary locked eyes with Larry, who looked frustrated. "I'll see what I can do," he said quietly. "For what it's worth, Merry Christmas, Mary."

*

Patrick's instincts were to talk to Nick, but Kat stopped him. "Give him a little time to cool down."

"But he's always the first one to jump in when one of us is upset."

"It took me a long time to know when to back off. Mary clued me in. She gets Dad better than anyone. When Jessie pushes his buttons he needs some time alone."

It didn't seem right. But then, nothing seemed right tonight. Including Anthony, who outright rejected his mother. "Would Anthony really choose Nick over his mom?"

"Yes."

"Why?"

"Because Dad's always there for him. Always. Like he is for you and me." She climbed the stairs. "Some Christmas, huh?"

Father Joe suddenly appeared in the kitchen. "Is it safe to come in now?"

Patrick shrugged, embarrassed Father was a witness to what just took place.

"Is that typical around here?" Father Joe sidled up to him.

"I don't know. Jessie hasn't been around much." He glanced up the stairs, concerned for his uncle. Nick's anger and language stunned him.

"Come on. Let's get some sleep. Tomorrow is the birth of our Lord. The true meaning of Christmas."

*

Nick sprawled in the darkness of his office. The house was quiet. He heard the kids come upstairs a while ago.

His marriage was over. Nick was now a two-time loser. He didn't intend to make it three. He'd never marry again. Bree pointed out a few years ago that neither of them were the marrying kind. She was right.

Where was Andrew through all this? He was uncharacteristically silent.

Nick heaved his tired body out of the chair and went down the hall to check on Anthony. A plastic Santa glowed in the window, his son's yearly Christmas decoration. Monty was stretched beside Anthony, who was sound asleep. The heavy quilt was almost on the floor, Anthony having tossed it off in his sleep. Nick tucked it back around his shoulders.

Jessie wanted her son. Nick couldn't bear the thought of not having Anthony with him.

A framed picture of Andrew sat on his bedside table. It had lived there since Nick first set foot in the house. And on the opposing wall was a large oil of Andrew, Jessie and Anthony. It originally hung over the mantle in the downstairs study. Until The Saint and The Sinner replaced it.

Nick kissed Anthony's forehead and quietly left the room.

*

Usually this was Mary's favorite moment of Christmas. When everyone was in bed, she'd sit in the study and enjoy a fire in the grate and the multi-colored bulbs of the old-fashioned Christmas tree. Not tonight. Tonight she couldn't wait for Christmas to be over. She hadn't felt this low since Andrew died.

"Mary?" Patrick came around the couch, holding a box. "Am I interrupting? Would you rather be alone?"

"No. No, sweetie." She patted the couch. "Join me."

Patrick sat down, setting the box on the floor between them. "I have something for you. I didn't want to give it to you earlier because, well, I don't have anything for the others." He opened the flaps on the box. "I'm sorry it's not wrapped."

He lifted out an ancient wooden cigar box and opened it, revealing some jewelry and a tiny velvet box. "These were Tess's. She didn't have much, but what she had meant a lot to her. Most pieces she got from her mother."

He opened the velvet box, revealing small diamond stud earrings. "These were a wedding gift from her husband Henry. She wore them every day. Tess said nice things shouldn't be saved for special occasions because every day you're alive is special. I want you to have these things. If Tess knew you, she'd feel the same way."

Mary stared at the earrings in his hand. "Oh, Patrick. I am so touched." She looked up at the sweet young man. "Are you sure about this?"

Patrick nodded. "Now I have your grandfather's chain and cross, and you have Tess's jewelry."

Mary was far too emotional tonight. "Well, Patrick Cavanaugh, your Tess was a wise woman. I'm going to wear these earrings every day, just like she did. So I can honor her." She reached over and cupped his face. "And you."

"There's more." Patrick showed her the rest of the items in the box. "These are Tess's aprons. She used to brag she had one for every holiday and one for every day of the month. They're all handmade. And this is Tess's recipe file. It goes back generations. Her mashed potatoes are my favorite. And her corn souffle."

Mary had been sitting here feeling so sad, and now… "Thank you, dear boy. Thank you."

She pulled Patrick into her arms, hugging him. He didn't tense or resist her touch anymore. No, his arms slid around her, and he hugged her back.

*

Nick climbed the stairs and looked in on Kat.

"Daddy?"

"Why are you still awake?" he whispered into the darkness.

"I was worried about you."

"You heard?"

"We all did."

He sat down on the bed.

"Is it true? We have to move?"

Looking down at his daughter, he nodded. "I think it's for the best."

She sat up and reached for his hand. "I never liked Jessie, and I don't think that will ever change, but I'm sad for you."

Nick remained silent, rubbing his daughter's fingers with his thumb.

"We'll be okay," Kat whispered. "You, me, Patrick, Mary and Anthony."

"Jessie wants Anthony."

"He won't go with her. You should have seen him in the kitchen tonight. The squirt stood his ground. I was really proud of him."

"Then we're in for one hell of a battle."

*

"I don't know what happened." Jessie sat with Larry on her couch. "He just made me so mad, and all these words came flying out of my mouth."

"Do you want to take them back?"

"Some of them."

"The divorce?"

216

She stretched her feet across the coffee table. "The divorce is inevitable. We bring out the worst in each other."

"But you still love him."

"I think once you love someone, truly love them, it doesn't just fade away. It's ironic. I loved Andrew, but I wasn't 'in love' with him. We'd known each other too long and too well for that. We were more like an old married couple. But it was a solid marriage. We rarely fought, and when we did it was resolved quickly. We were both focused on raising our son in a loving home."

"And with Nick?"

"It was out of control from the beginning. But it was also fun." She leaned back and closed her eyes. "Nick is a strong personality, and I went along for the ride. God, we were so much in love." Her eyes slid open. "It was his past I had trouble accepting. I worried he'd screw around on me, and that's no way to live."

"But you ended up screwing around on him."

"Thanks for reminding me."

*

When Nick checked on Patrick he was surprised to find him at his desk, writing in a leather book. "What are you doing?"

"This was on my desk when I came upstairs." Patrick closed the book and held it up. In the upper left corner of the cover were the initials *AB*. In the lower right corner, *PC*. "Is it from you?"

Nick shook his head. "Looks like Andrew left you a Christmas gift. You've read his journals. And Father Joe advised Tess to keep a diary when she lost her son. Maybe Andrew's saying this will help."

Patrick looked down at the book. "I'm describing tonight in it."

Nick's face fell.

"Can Jessie really take me away from you?"

"No. You're no relation to her. But if she tried, I'd fight like a man possessed."

Patrick fingered the crucifix on his chain. "Your argument with Jessie—"

"Argument? More like World War III."

Patrick slipped the journal into the top desk drawer. "Was it always like that? Between you and her?"

"No." Nick thought back over the last few years. "At one time we were happy."

"What happened?"

Nick sat down and blew out his breath. "A long story."

"Tell me. I really want to know."

217

"You don't need to hear about a marriage gone wrong. You should talk to people who are happily married."

"Where are they?"

Nick snorted. Good question.

"You know the worst about me," Patrick pointed out. "Why can't you tell me about your marriage?"

Nick eyed the young man, his expression a mixture of curiosity and compassion. Yes, Nick knew the worst about Patrick. Would hearing about Nick's marriage help him realize everyone had big problems?

And so he told him. Beginning with their first meeting right here in the brownstone on a chilly April night three years ago, Nick explained how he and Jessie fell in love as he tracked down Andrew's killer. When he described their over-the-top celebrity wedding, Patrick's laughter was infectious.

But as Nick reminisced, sadness crept into his narrative. They'd been so much in love. Until Kat turned up, shining a spotlight on Nick's sordid history with women. Then the miscarriage, striking a deadly blow.

Patrick listened quietly, reacting as Nick reacted. "And that's what ended your marriage? Losing the baby?"

"Pretty much."

"What aren't you telling me?"

Nick looked away and took a deep breath. "I don't want to influence your opinion of Jessie. You need to have a relationship with her because of Andrew."

*

Bree stood in the darkness of her living room, staring out the window at the white flakes drifting to the ground.

It didn't feel like Christmas. Not that she knew what a traditional Christmas felt like. Most Christmases she was on the other side of the world, not even aware of the holiday. The only Christmas that was memorable was the one she spent with Nick and Ozzie in Hong Kong. There was no tree. No special dinner. No gifts. They had each other, and that was all they needed.

The scene at Nick's tonight was a train wreck. Jessie sashayed into the fray in her pricy neon-red cashmere dress, scattering what little Christmas cheer existed. And dragging with her a man who spent the evening looking for a trap door to fall through.

And the kids … Since when are kids mute on Christmas Eve? Kat hardly said a word all night. The same was true of Anthony and that boy, Patrick.

Bree watched Patrick during the evening's events. Watched dread creep into his expression when Jessie called him into the living room. Watched the protective air Kat assumed around Patrick. Watched Anthony look to him for approval.

There was a lot going on in Patrick's transparent eyes. Something happened to him, something serious, and Nick was tuned into it.

Bree smiled. Nick and kids. His one soft spot. He was a different person around kids. He was loquacious and engaged. It made Bree love him even more.

And she did love Nick. Would always love him. She knew he loved her, too, in his own way. The relationship they developed over the years was rare. They could think as one. Could communicate silently. Knew each other completely. It was better than a love affair, which is where they began. Nick was her best friend. She would trust him with her life. Would she like a little sex thrown into the mix? Sure. But it would probably ruin everything.

Jessie and Nick were high drama and histrionics and shouting. They were the symbol on top of a wedding cake. All show and hollow on the inside.

Speaking of Jessie, what went on in Nick's office after Bree left? She'd find out tomorrow over Christmas dinner when 'The Nick and Jessie Show' continued.

*

"I can't believe Mary would abandon me for the kids," Jessie said. "But the worst part of the night was when Anthony said he wanted to live with Nick. My little boy doesn't like me." She looked up at Larry, tears in her eyes. "From the time Nick came on the scene, Anthony was enamored of him. It was the same with Andrew."

"Little boys need their dads more than their moms. Sammy was exactly like Anthony at that age. Gloria would get so mad at me, but it wasn't my fault."

"So what do I do? Just let Anthony live with Nick?"

"If that's what Anthony wants, yes. Otherwise, he'll resent you even more. The more you push, the more Anthony will dig in, and your relationship will continue to go downhill. You can work out those details in the divorce agreement."

"Nick's and my second anniversary is in a week, and I'm talking divorce."

*

"Why does everyone try to protect Jessie?" Patrick asked. "First Kat. Now you. Why can't you just tell me what happened?"

219

"It's adult stuff."

"I'm almost seventeen."

"You're a sheltered sixteen-year-old."

Patrick got to his feet and paced. "How can I grow up, how can I learn about life outside a small town if you won't help me? If I continue to stay, as you call it, sheltered? I live in New York now. It's time I learned about the real world." He sat back down at the desk, frustrated. "I thought we trusted each other."

Nick was quiet. Patrick figured he was angry and would probably leave after what he just said.

"I'll make a deal with you."

Patrick glanced over at him. Nick stared back. "I'll tell you the truth about Jessie if you promise to talk to a professional."

Sighing heavily, Patrick collapsed against the back of the chair.

"I'm doing this for your own good, Patrick. I think it will make a difference."

The last thing Patrick wanted to do was talk to a stranger about ... "Would you come with me? Be there in the room with me?"

Nick, too, slumped back. "If I'm allowed, yes."

"If you're not, game over."

*

"I have no one, Larry. Not even Mary. I've never felt so alone."

"You need a fresh start, Jessie. Blow the cobwebs away and start clean. But first you have to be sure you want a divorce. And that you want to move back into the house."

Jessie thought about the brownstone, so full of family history. For the first time she pictured living there without Nick. Or Mary. Or Anthony. It would be strange. She'd been her daddy's little girl in that house. Andrew's goddess. Anthony's mom. And Nick's wife. All in that house.

Where did she go to just be Jessie?

*

"Jessie cheated on me. In London," Nick began, keeping his part of the bargain. "I was in Italy with Kat at the time, chasing down my brother Ethan." He was uncomfortable talking about this, but he had no choice. "She said she was drunk and doesn't remember it."

"Then how—"

"When she woke up she was—" This was getting tricky.

Patrick rolled his eyes. "After Florida I think you can say just about anything to me."

Nick scrubbed his hand over his face. "When she woke up she was in bed with him."

220

"And her excuse was she didn't remember?"

"Yep. That, and— She said she always expected me to cheat on her, because of my history. Bree was working with me in Italy, so Jessie assumed we were ..." Nick refused to finish the sentence.

"Had you ... been with Bree before?"

"A long time ago. When we were younger."

Patrick nodded, an ornery smile creeping across his face. "You left that part out when you were going on and on about your adventures in Hong Kong with Bree and Ozzie."

"You're enjoying this, aren't you?"

"Kind of."

"You're starting to sound like Kat." Nick shook his head. "Anyway, I found out about Jessie, got angry and came back to the States. When Jessie came home she moved into the hotel so the kids could have the house." He stood up. "End of story." He headed for the door.

"None of this is your fault."

Nick paused in the doorway.

"Kat turned up in your life, just like I turned up in Andrew's. Sins of the past, not the present. And you weren't the one who cheated. You stayed true to your vows."

Nick smiled. Patrick was attempting to make him feel better. "But I couldn't forgive her. And that was the deal-breaker."

"Did you try to forgive her?"

"I'm still trying."

"Then that's that. Thou shalt not commit adultery. It's one of the Ten Commandments. And it's a big deal in the Catholic Church."

"You certainly know your theology."

"I was raised by a priest."

Nick chuckled. "Goodnight, Patrick."

"Nick? I miss our late-night talks in Florida."

"We just had one."

*

Christmas Day dawned dark and snowy. Patrick put on his new charcoal suit, his calf-length black wool coat, his black suede brimmed hat, his lined gloves and walked the few blocks with Kat and Father Joe to St. Matthew's. Despite his layers of clothing, he felt the cold down to his bones. After living in sunny Florida, would he ever get used to frigid New York?

Just as the Mass began, Bree joined them. Their little Catholic group was growing. Patrick couldn't help eying her throughout the Mass, now knowing her history with Nick. She caught him staring at one point and grinned back at him. There was something warm and approachable about her smile.

Bree left them outside the church, saying she'd see them later.

"How'd she know we'd be here?" Patrick asked as they walked home.

"I told her." Kat beamed. "You should get to know her. She's a fabulous lady. And so smart."

"Nick said she writes for *The New York Times.*"

"Yep. And has a Pulitzer, just like Dad."

"Nick has a Pulitzer?"

Kat nodded. "Bree interviewed Pope Francis when we were in Italy. You should ask her about it, Patrick."

"I'd like to know about that myself," Father Joe spoke up.

Patrick couldn't get used to being around so many celebrities. And yet, once he got to know them they were just like anyone else.

Everyone arrived in the early afternoon for dinner. Everyone but Jessie. Patrick wasn't surprised. After what happened last night, how could she just show up for dinner? But she rapidly became the hushed topic of conversation.

*

Under Mary's watchful eye, Abbie put together a large basket of homemade rolls and breads at the kitchen island. "It's really over between Nick and Jessie?" Abbie added five little ceramic pots of sweet butter.

"Looks like it." Mary thickened the gravy, put the sweet potato casserole on the warming plate, and checked on Violet, who was mixing the Waldorf salad. She needed the arms of an octopus today.

"I'm not surprised. My last conversation with Jessie was heated. She's reverting to the old Jessie."

Mary hefted the standing rib roast from the oven to the stovetop. "Violet, can you grab that casserole in the upper oven and put it on the warming plate? And Abbie, chop those chives for me."

"Already done." Abbie handed her the chives. Mary added them to the potatoes, along with cream cheese, before whipping the mixture into thick peaks.

Violet stared at the casserole in her mitted hands. "What is this? I've never seen it before."

"Corn souffle."

*

Jessie and Larry met at The Unicorn, a favorite restaurant that was serving dinner on Christmas. The place was fully booked but found room

222

for Jessie in the late afternoon. Once in a while her celebrity came in handy.

"I feel like getting away," she said, perusing the menu. "Maybe to the villa. Want to come?"

"What's the villa?"

"Don't you remember? Andrew and I bought a place on St. John."

"Oh, right! That was a couple years before he died. You were trying to get Gloria and me to come down, but it never worked out. When do you plan to go?"

"Next week. When I have vacation. Can you get the week off, too?"

"Jessie, you're supposed to move back to the house next week."

She put down the menu. "After you left last night, I called Nora and asked if she'd like to live with me at the brownstone. She said she wouldn't live there without Mary, that Mary sort of comes with the place. Apparently, the brownstone is everyone's home but mine."

"You're a busy lady. Mary runs the house for you."

"That got me thinking. To be honest, I didn't get much sleep because I couldn't stop thinking about the house and the kids and ..." She took a sip of water. "I love that house of course. I grew up there. But in a way, it's more Mary's than mine. She makes it function. I haven't added a thing to it over the years. Oh, I had rooms redesigned, but most was done with Mary's eye. Even Nick added his own touch by turning a large storage area into his office."

"You're thinking of giving it up, aren't you?"

"Maybe."

"Well, for what it's worth, that house down in Manasquan? I had it for years before Gloria and I got married. When we had the kids, I added on. And on. And when we divorced, I gave it to her."

"Why?"

"Because it made sense. I'd outgrown it, in a way. And it was the only home the kids ever knew. They had their school. Their activities. It seemed heartless to throw everyone out so I could live there alone. Besides, it's kind of nice starting over. Finding a place that fits who I am now."

"You have more common sense than anyone I know." She lifted her sparkling water in a toast. "Merry Christmas, Larry."

"Merry Christmas, princess."

*

Father Joe sat with Patrick on the back porch, admiring the wicker furniture and Tiffany lamps and plants. "This is a beautiful home, Patrick. Makes you forget you're in New York City."

"Yeah. It's like a cocoon."

Father turned his attention to Patrick's classy suit. "You were born to wear clothes like that." He flashed back to the little boy in Tess's house, his clothes dirty, his shoes too big."

"I have to pay Nick back for the clothes. Get a job somewhere."

"Nick is happy to do it."

"I want to pay my own way."

The perfect opening Father Joe was waiting for. He glanced through the window into the kitchen, catching Nick's eye, before turning his attention back to Patrick. "Why don't you get another job as a singing waiter? There must be a dozen places like Cohan's in New York City."

Patrick shook off his jacket and hung it over the back of a chair. He was obviously avoiding the subject.

"I don't hear you singing around here."

"I haven't sung much lately."

"Why not?"

Patrick shrugged.

"Tess would yell at you."

The boy's gaze swiveled to Father Joe. "Please don't say that."

"Nothing made her happier than hearing you sing."

Patrick played with a thread on his shirt.

"Kat told me you've been asked to sing at a cabaret on New Year's Eve. Why don't you do it? I'll stay to hear you."

Another shrug.

Father Joe glanced at Nick again and shook his head.

*

Kat and Bertie were up in her room, watching videos on her laptop.

"What's wrong, Katnip?"

"Nothing."

"Don't lie to me. You've been down all morning. What's wrong?"

Kat ambled to the window. The snow was coming down hard, the sidewalks and trees coated. "I found out something awful happened to Patrick when he was little. Something hard to get past."

"I figured."

She faced him. "How?"

Bertie shrugged. "After what I went through, I can recognize it in other people. How bad was it?"

224

"I can't tell you, Bertie. It's hard for me to keep anything from you, but this isn't my secret."

Kat went to Bertie and slipped her arms around him. "There's something else." She laid her head on his shoulder. "I can't shake the feeling that change is coming."

"It's the move. That's what you're feeling."

"It feels bigger than that."

"Trust me. It's the move."

"Yeah. You're probably right."

But her gut told her Bertie was wrong.

And her dad taught her to always listen to her gut.

CHAPTER 20

Bree sidled up to Nick, two eggnogs in her hands. "Here. It's Christmas. We're required to drink eggnog on Christmas."

"Just straight eggnog?"

"Would I do that to you?"

Nick grinned. "Good girl."

They wandered down the hallway towards the living room, relatively alone.

"Father Joe and Patrick cornered me earlier. They wanted to know about my interview with the pope. Patrick asked all the right questions. He's a smart kid. But shy. On anyone else Patrick's age, 'shy' would be off-putting. But it works for him."

"Because it's genuine."

"I caught the exchange between you and Father Joe a moment ago. I think you've become fond of that man. Nick McDeare and a priest. Now I've seen everything."

"He's good for Patrick. That's what matters. But, yeah, I like the guy."

Bree took a sip of the thick drink. "It's all about Patrick now, isn't it?"

Nick's expression was hard to read.

"I can't stop watching him," Bree continued. "There's something about Patrick that just sucks me in. I want to open him up and see the components inside, the ones he's hiding. I bet I'd find things that can't be talked about in polite society. Things that would infuriate a man like you and put you back in fighting form."

Nick met her eyes.

"Patrick's wounds aren't his fault, are they? Which is why you're in Papa Bear mode."

They stared long and hard at each other.

"Do you ever stop being an investigative reporter, Bree?"

"I guess you just bring out the snoop in me." That crooked little smile inched across her face.

It was met by the barest hint of admiration in Nick's eyes.

*

Dinner was subdued. Nick scanned the faces at the table. Bertie sat next to Kat, their heads together. Bree chatted up Father Joe as they enjoyed Mary's rib roast. Mary and Violet were deep in conversation. Abbie and Willie were whispering. Anthony fed Monty as much beef as he himself was eating. And Patrick was his usual quiet self.

The empty chair at the other end of the table hit Nick hard. Last year Jessie sat there, pregnant with their little girl, Lyla Mary. Who would have thought both the baby and Jessie would be gone this year? And with the thought of Jessie, Nick's mind flipped to Andrew. He, too, seemed to be missing, only making his presence known with Patrick's journal. Why the silence? What did it mean?

Nick again looked over at Patrick. The boy stared back at him, his eyes a reflection of Nick's thoughts. A small smile passed between them.

*

Patrick took it all in. The hushed conversations around the table. Father Joe fitting in with everyone. A fantastic feast. The New York Philharmonic playing Christmas carols over the sound system. And Mary, wearing Tess's earrings and Christmas apron.

On the table was a roast with all the trimmings. Including Tess's mashed potatoes and corn souffle. This would now be Christmas for him, today and for all of his tomorrows. A blend of the past and the present. Mary caught his eye and winked.

Patrick glanced at Nick. Despite a valiant effort at hiding his feelings, Nick was depressed today. Patrick guessed he was missing his wife. At that exact moment, his uncle looked at him and smiled. The smile never reached his eyes.

*

After the dishes were done and the guests gone, Nick layered up in double sweats, a knit hat and gloves and went for a run. It was snowy and cold, but he needed to breathe the invigorating frigid air. He had a lot on his mind and a lot of tasks before him tomorrow. Starting with looking for a new home.

He made it only as far as Fifth Avenue when his cell went off. Nick dug for it, buried in his pocket.

Jessie?

Peeling off his glove with his teeth, he clicked on as he slowed to a walk.

"Nick?"

"I'm here."

"Surprised to hear from me?"

"Shocked."

She laughed. That musical xylophone laugh he loved so much. It had been a long time since he heard it. "It's good to keep you on your toes."

"No one does it better than you." Nick pumped his legs up and down to stave off the cold. "What's up?"

"I want you to know ... you don't have to move ..."

"Excuse me? What did you say?"

"I know. After my behavior last night, it's a surprise. Hear me out. After spending the last twenty-four hours thinking of nothing else, I ... I've decided to give you the house."

Nick couldn't believe what he was hearing.

"Actually, the house is Anthony's. Don't you remember?" she continued. "Andrew and I put it in Anthony's name when he was born. For tax purposes. But also so we could be sure it would remain in the family. It's his outright when he's twenty-one. You agreed to keep the ownership in place when we got married."

Yeah, Nick remembered now. "Does Anthony know about this?"

"No. We decided not to tell him until he was much older."

"But why are you giving up—"

"Let me finish. After talking with Larry I realized I need a fresh start—"

"Is Larry why you want a divorce?"

"Larry? No. He has nothing to do with it."

Maybe. Time would tell.

"Anyway, I realized I've lived in that house my entire life. There are too many memories of my dad and Andrew and even Gianni - and most of all, you in that house. I want to find a new place and start new memories. A place I can fix up to my own taste. Something that's all mine ... Do you understand?"

"What about Anthony?"

"We'll work it out. Hopefully split time with him. That house is his home. It's always been his home. It doesn't seem right to yank him out of it. He can come stay with me for weekends. Or ... maybe I'll take him on trips. I want him to be happy, Nick. He's happiest with you." She sounded sad. And resigned.

"Jessie, he loves you. He's just at that age where—"

"I know." Was she crying?

"Are you sure about this?"

"... Yes ... I don't want to fight anymore, Nick. When we get together, we end up screaming at each other. Which is why I called instead of coming over. How did we get to this point when we were once so deeply in love?"

"I don't know, Jess."

"Maybe we'll be better friends than lovers." She sniffled.

Nick took a chance, memories of their antics in bed flashing before his eyes. "I don't know, Jess. We'd have to go some to beat that."

It was good to hear her laugh again, even if it was through her tears.

"You're blushing, aren't you?" His own laugh was throaty.

"Probably. Thank God no one can see me." Again a sniffle. "I promise to never eat chocolate chocolate-chip ice cream and crunchy peanut butter without you." Their post-sex treat. Feeding each other among fits of laughter.

There was silence for a few seconds as Nick was filled with melancholy.

"I'll get my things out of the house when I get back from vacation."

"Where are you going?"

"The villa. We'll work the villa out, too. We'll have to share it. I love that place. So did Andrew."

More silence.

"Well," Nick said softly, "I was just going for a run, and I'm freezing."

"Bye, Nick."

*

Patrick knocked on Kat's bedroom door.

"Entra."

Patrick peeked in. "What language is that?"

"Italian. I learned it before we went to Italy last summer." She was sitting on her bed, her laptop in front on her.

"I always wanted to learn Italian. Maybe you could tutor me?"

"Absolutely. Come on in."

"I brought Andrew's journals back." He held up the stack of books before setting them on the desk.

"You finished them?"

"I learned a lot. Thanks." He rubbed Hamlet's head and sat down on the bed. "Are you happy about the divorce?"

Kat slumped. "You're determined to get me to talk about Jessie, aren't you?"

Patrick said nothing, merely smiled. They stared at each other for a moment.

"Okay, yes." Kat closed her laptop. "I'm happy. I can't stand Jessie. She was horrible to me from the day I arrived. And she was jealous of my relationship with my father."

"Were you jealous of her relationship with Nick?"

"No! I want Dad to find someone. Someone who deserves him."

"Like Bree?"

"I'd be thrilled if they got together."

"Are you okay with my relationship with your dad?"

"Why wouldn't I be?"

"Because of the amount of time he spends with me. I don't want to come between you and Nick."

Kat pushed aside her laptop and scooted over to sit beside him. "Dad and I are just fine." She took his hand. "I know you need Dad right now while you adjust to all this new stuff in your life. I think Dad needs you, too."

"Why?" Patrick looked down at their hands. Normally he was uncomfortable with a girl's touch. Of course, Kat was his cousin, which made a difference. A touchy-feely cousin. He was starting to get used to it.

"He and Jessie are divorcing. When Dad goes silent on a subject, you know it's bothering him."

"I'm the same way."

"No matter what, I'd never be jealous of you, Patrick. You belong in our family. You're more like my brother than my cousin."

Patrick felt himself blushing. He envied Kat's ability to just say what she felt. The only time he was able to do that was when he sang.

He squeezed her hand before moving to the door.

"You know you can tell me anything." Kat eyed him, stroking Hamlet as the cat crawled onto her lap. "I may be thirteen, but even Dad says I'm much older."

"I noticed that about you right away, Kat." He found her insistence on being treated like an adult amusing.

Then she took him by surprise. "Could I come to you, if I needed help or advice?"

"Yeah. Sure."

"That's what sisters and brothers do."

Siblings. Another first for Patrick.

"You know, Kat, you're the reason I'm here. If you hadn't unearthed Heidi and Andrew's story I, well, I would be ..." He turned to leave.

"Do you feel it?"

"What?"

"The sadness tonight. For some reason, this house feels sad."

*

Anthony was at his laptop, editing his Christmas photos. Monty was stretched under the desk.

Ever since he'd earned praise for his photos of Patrick, he was focusing on shooting people. He got some nice ones.

"Those are good, Bongo."

Anthony looked up. "Thanks, Dad. I think so, too." He flipped to the next screen and dropped his head on his fist.

"Is something wrong?" His father sat down in the chair by the desk.

"I don't know. I just feel sad tonight."

"Is it because of what's happening between your mother and me?"

Anthony shook his head.

"Kat told me you stood up to your mom last night."

Anthony remained focused on his photos. "I told her I wanted to live with you."

"Well, you're going to get your way. I talked to her a little while ago. She said you could stay with me. And we don't have to move."

Anthony finally forgot about the photos and stared at his dad. "Really?"

"Really. She's giving us the house and getting her own place."

Anthony smiled for the first time in hours. "Good."

"Are you at all sad that your mom and I are splitting up?"

He looked out the window, thinking about it. "She's my mom, and I love her and all, but I think everyone will be happier."

"You only get one mom, Anthony. Don't throw it away."

"I get one mom. But three dads?"

"Yeah," his father chuckled, "but the third one's the charm."

*

"Jessie gave you the house?" Kat wasn't convinced. "She has to be up to something."

"Kat, stop." Nick stood near his daughter's desk, overflowing with her research on Andrew. "She wants a fresh start in a new place."

"She'll change her mind in a year."

"We're not moving. Enjoy it." He looked at Kat's papers covering half the room. "How's it going?"

"Okay. I've written almost fifty pages."

"Isn't that a little long for a short story?"

231

"It's going to be a book. And I'll take my time with it. I want to get it right. For both Andrew and Patrick." She stopped what she was doing, the air going out of her. "I feel sad tonight. And it's not because you and Jessie are divorcing."

"Anthony said the same thing."

"Maybe it's because Christmas was so … not Christmas this year."

*

Even though it was late – and Christmas night – Nick called an old friend, a psychologist who worked with the NYPD. Dustin Clarendon was single, married to his work, and didn't mind the interruption.

After giving his pal the briefest of information, Nick was supplied with a name and phone number. "He's a huge fan, Nick," Dusty said. "We've talked about you and your books often. I guarantee he'll take your call. Let me give him a heads-up first. Wait five minutes, then call. If I can't reach him I'll call you right back."

Why not? Nick was willing to use his celebrity or money or bribery, just about anything to get what he wanted. So he waited five minutes and called the man.

Dr. Benjamin Brody picked up on the first ring. "Mr. McDeare?"

"Yes."

"Dusty said you needed my assistance."

"Yes. For my nephew. Andrew Brady's son. I'd appreciate your seeing him as soon as possible."

Twenty minutes later Nick filled out Dr. Brody's paperwork, describing Patrick's history, and emailed it back to him.

*

After speaking with Nick, Jessie wandered around the hotel suite, looking for something to do. She wished Larry was here, but after their dinner at the Unicorn, Larry went back to his hotel. He was expecting a call from his kids and wanted to be alone when he talked to them. She knew he would have spent Christmas down at the shore if he didn't have to work tomorrow.

Tomorrow she'd call a few real estate agents and get them started on looking for a new place for her. She should be excited about this new venture in her life. Why wasn't she?

Missing Nora, she called her in Chicago. After asking about her new grandson, she told her about the latest developments with the brownstone. "So will you come live with me in my new place, Nora?"

There was a long pause on the other end of the line. "I'm contemplating retirement, Jessie. And a move to Chicago so I can be near my daughter and grandkids. With Chester gone, they're all I have."

Retirement? Jessie couldn't imagine doing a show without Nora at her side. "Won't you be bored?"

"I'd sure like to find out." She laughed. "I've worked hard my whole life, Jessie. It's time to kick back and enjoy my family. But don't worry. I'll finish my contract with *DIANA* and make sure I find a top-notch replacement for your future shows."

Jessie mumbled something about Nora deserving a rest and what a great city Chicago was and … Finally, she was able to get off the phone.

She quickly dialed Larry and told him about Nora.

"Good for her. She's earned it. But Broadway won't be the same without people like her. We're losing all the old-timers. The backbone of what makes the Great White Way work."

"You're depressing the hell out of me, Larry."

"Sorry, princess. Just stating the facts."

"I talked to Nick."

"I'll bet he was shocked by your news."

"He was."

"You okay?"

"I'm fine. Just tired and anxious to get away. Have you decided about coming to the villa with me?"

"Actually I'm going down to the shore for that week. Gloria said the kids miss me. And you know I miss them. It's the first generosity my ex has shown me, so I better jump on it."

"Oh. Well, that's good."

"Yeah. And when I got back to the hotel tonight there was a message from Quill. He wants to meet in the next few weeks about this new project. He definitely wants me to direct. I finally get my shot."

"Fantastic." Jessie hoped she sounded enthusiastic. "You deserve it."

"With so many changes happening on Broadway, I'm glad Quill's offering this new opportunity. Anyway, now's my chance to take care of my personal life before I get really busy."

His personal life. Nora's daughter and grandchildren. "I'm happy for you, Larry. And for your kids." She did her best to sound upbeat.

"It looks like things are starting to work out for both of us. There is life after divorce. Next we have to find our own places."

Places. Plural. "Yep."

"See you tomorrow, princess."

*

"So we're not going to have to move." Nick sat in the breakfast nook with Patrick, everyone else in bed. They were polishing off the pumpkin pie and washing it down with milk.

"You must be relieved."

Nick loved this house, partly because Andrew grew up here. "You, too." He pushed the remnants of the pie towards Patrick. "Finish it."

"I'm getting used to living here now. It's full of Andrew, which helps me understand him." He scooped the last bite.

Nick stared at Patrick's chain, the crucifix and ring intertwined. "You never refer to Andrew as your father."

"I don't?"

"What's wrong? You seem down."

He shrugged.

"Are you worried about starting therapy tomorrow?"

"I'm freaking about it. But if you're there—"

"I'll be there. Dr. Brody agreed to it. So is that what's bothering you?"

"I don't know what's wrong. I just feel sad tonight. This house feels sad." Patrick stood up. "I want to write in my journal before turning in." Halfway up the stairs, Patrick paused. "Merry Christmas, Nick."

"Merry Christmas." Nick put their dishes in the sink, turned out the lights and climbed the stairs.

He felt the same as Patrick. The same as Kat and Anthony.

There was something in this house tonight …

*

Andrew Brady watched the exchange between Nick and Patrick. They both sensed what was coming. Everyone felt Andrew's infinite sadness. No surprise. They were all connected to him in ways that defied explanation.

Did Jessie sense it? Or had she extricated herself from the past, no longer in tune with her former husband?

*

Jessie curled on her side, willing sleep to come quickly. It was a horrible Christmas, a day she would always look back on with pain. A horrible year, starting with the miscarriage and ending in divorce. Nick was gone, really gone, no longer part of her life.

Her eyes filled with tears as she replayed her conversation with Nick on the phone a little while ago. It had been like old times. Nick was funny and thoughtful. Almost loving. She could picture him going for his jog afterwards, then returning to the house. A fire would blaze in the study.

234

He'd check on the kids, then pour himself a brandy. Life would go on for Nick.

There was no going back for Jessie. The divorce was her choice, not Nick's.

It was done.

Jessie buried her face in the pillow and cried.

*

Andrew stood over Jessie's bed. His former wife was still a beauty, her soft flaxen hair spilling across the pillow, her features like fine china, her tears drying on her cheeks.

If only she could have trusted Nick's love for her, trusted his fidelity to her. If only she could have seen Kat as an addition to her family instead of a detraction. If that baby, Lyla Mary, had lived … If any or all of these things happened, Jessie would be wrapped around Nick right now instead of moving on with her life, solo. Jessie was used to life going her way. This time, when it didn't, she sabotaged her own happiness.

He sat down on the bed. "I'm worried about you, Jess. You managed to alienate everyone over the past year. Even your own son. I'm not going to be around anymore to balance out that selfish streak in you. You have to clean up your own messes now." He brushed her hair from her forehead, ran his fingers down her arm.

"I've loved you since we were kids, Jess. Before I even understood the concept of love. I slept with a lot of girls in my youth, but the one in Florida? I chose her because she reminded me of you. So I guess I should thank you for inadvertently giving me Patrick."

Andrew leaned over and kissed her soft lips. "I wish you peace, Jess. I pray to God you find it."

CHAPTER 21

Andrew Brady wandered into the brownstone study. He was in no hurry. There was plenty of time.

The Christmas tree was lit, it's candy-colored lights reflecting on the ceiling. Rudolph stood guard in the window, his nose glowing red, just as he had since Andrew was a young boy. Boxes of opened gifts were stacked neatly atop Mary's prized holiday blanket. The room smelled of bayberry and cinnamon and a traditional rib roast. It had been the same down through the years.

Andrew loved this old house. It was too cold in the winter and too hot in the summer. It needed constant attention and loving care. It had seen great joy and too much sorrow. Andrew lost his virginity in this house. Got married here. And it was here where he silently watched Jessie and Anthony grieve when he was murdered.

He stared up at the painting over the fireplace. The two brothers. Such a long history, full of twists and surprises. Raised apart but bonded like twins.

Despite his window on this world closing, Andrew had time. Time to remember. And to see them one last time …

*

Kat was obsessed with her book on Andrew. As she curled up in bed with Hamlet, she thought about the next chapter, working out its details. She was just at the point where Andrew worked at the Asolo. When he met Patrick's mother. She needed to talk with Patrick about Heidi Barstow. He told her before he left for Florida that he wanted to learn more about his mother. Kat wanted to make Heidi a living, breathing character.

She closed her eyes and prayed her Uncle Andrew's guidance would help her write his story. She was asleep in minutes.

*

Andrew approached Kat's bed as the frightened cat galloped from the room. "You are your daddy's girl, Kat. You have his instincts. Watching you relate to Patrick has been a joy."

He watched her sleep, her face so much like Nick's. "Keep an eye on your dad, Kat. But never let him know. Nick likes to think of himself as a tough guy, a man who can walk away from a divorce without a scratch.

He did the first time. But this time is different. He fell hard for Jessie. He's going to need you. He's going to need all of you." He brushed Kat's hand with his fingers. "I'm glad you and Patrick have each other. He needs a little sister with your wisdom. And you need an older brother with a moral compass. There is so much you can teach each other."

*

Mary turned out the light and climbed into bed. She'd felt like crying all evening. At first she thought it was the impending divorce. Or Patrick. How would that boy get past what happened to him?

Too many things pressed on Mary in the darkness.

But there was something else … something that made her want to drop her head and cry.

Sighing, she drifted off, hoping for better days ahead.

*

Andrew sat down in Mary's rocker near her bed. So Mary sensed it also.

How many hours did he spend in this room, spilling his guts about Jessie? She'd listen while he complained about Jessie's callousness. She watched as Jessie took Andrew for granted, even after they married. Her arms were always open for his tears, for his heartbreak. Mary was the only one who knew the depth of Andrew's love for Jessie.

But then, Mary knew and saw everything. Mary instinctively realized what happened to Patrick and gave him the love he craved, the maternal gene missing in his life since he lost his beloved Tess. She understood how to handle Kat's thirteen-going-on-thirty individuality, understood that this girl was a mirror image of her father, saw that her edgy exterior hid a vulnerable interior.

Mary loved Anthony from the day he was born, became the strict but affectionate grandma the boy needed, gave him the structure missing in his life because of having an actress-mother. And she knew Nick better than anyone, knew who he was, where he'd been, what made the man tick. She considered him her son, just as she had with Andrew.

"You are the heart of this house, Mary. It couldn't function without you. You get everyone through the good times and the bad. They need you and love you."

He stood up and pressed his lips to her forehead. "But no one loves you more than me, Mary."

*

Anthony stared into the darkness. Monty was passed out alongside him, sound asleep, his chew toy in his mouth. Shadows moved on the walls, more mesmerizing than scary.

237

His gaze moved to the framed picture on the bedside table. Andrew. It had been there since he died. For a long time, Anthony never went to sleep without saying goodnight to his former dad. But that was when Andrew's spirit was around. He'd sit on the bed and they'd have long talks, just like they used to when he was alive.

Andrew had been silent for a long time. Anthony missed him.

Yawning, he whispered, "Night, Andrew. Merry Christmas."

*

Andrew stroked Monty. The dog was calm, remembering Andrew from past encounters.

Anthony looked so innocent, curled on his side, his breathing a steady rhythm. Andrew couldn't count the nights he'd spent watching this boy sleep.

He took a deep breath. This one was difficult.

He'd seen Anthony into the world and cherished him for five years. Taught him to ride a bike and hit a ball with a bat. Sang him to sleep at night and dined on Gerber mashed carrots and pureed bananas to get baby Anthony to eat. "I did the best I could, Anthony. So did Jessie. Don't shut her out. You're always going to need your mom."

Andrew looked down at the bedside table. A tiny wooden chest now sat in front of his framed photo. Inside was Andrew's wedding band. "It's yours now, Anthony." He leaned over and kissed Anthony's cheek, lingering. "I love you, Bongo," he whispered. "Forever and ever."

*

Patrick closed his journal and put it in the top desk drawer. He'd written about Andrew. He wished he could have just one conversation with him. To hear him speak. To see his eyes up close. Nick said Andrew was around, watching over them. And the journal was proof. But why didn't he show himself the way he used to?

Patrick went to the terrace door. Snow floated to the ground, reminding him where he was. In New York. In Andrew's house. He should be grateful, not wishing for the impossible. He said a quick prayer and slid into bed.

*

Andrew stood over his son's bed. Patrick lay on his stomach, hugging the pillow. His mop of fair hair covered his forehead.

"Oh, Patrick," he whispered. What a wonder he was, this precious boy who endured so much. Who found a haven in singing, his only safe place.

Wandering to the window, Andrew perched on the sill. "Patrick?"

Patrick stirred and burrowed further into the bed.

"Patrick."

He lifted his head, his back to Andrew.

"I'm here."

Patrick looked over his shoulder. As realization registered, he turned around and stared at Andrew.

Andrew returned his gaze, finally able to look into the face of his son.

"I just wished for this," Patrick whispered, swinging his legs over the side of the bed. "To see you."

His sandy curls were a mess, sleep still clung to his blue eyes, his T-shirt was bunched, and his chain was twisted around his neck. But he was the most beautiful sight Andrew had ever seen.

"Is that why you're here tonight? You knew I needed to see you?" Patrick asked.

"I wanted to see you, too." He couldn't tell him the truth yet. Why he was really here tonight.

Andrew rose and ambled around the room. "If these walls could talk. I had so many dreams. I wrote them all down in my journals in this very room."

"Like I'm doing."

Andrew nodded as he approached his Tony Award. "Do you want one of these, Patrick?"

Patrick shrugged. "I don't think about awards or being a star or things like that."

"But you've been given an incredible talent."

"Singing's how I work out what I'm feeling. I don't know. I've just always sung."

Andrew walked back over to the boy. *"Whereof what's past is prologue; what to come, in yours and my discharge."*

Patrick got to his feet. "From *THE TEMPEST*."

"You know your Shakespeare."

"It's one of my favorites. About a storm and shipwreck survivors."

"Like the storm that swept through your life."

Patrick dropped his eyes, those blue beacons extinguished.

"Do you know what it means?"

"Sure." Eye contact again. Andrew loved his son's eyes. "Everything that came before was in preparation for what's to come."

Andrew nodded. "Everything you endured was to prepare you for what's to come. Everything I was, everything I achieved, was to pave the way for you." Andrew's voice caught. "I'm sorry, Patrick. So sorry for what you went through. No child should have to—"

239

"Don't blame yourself. I don't. And I don't blame Heidi either."

Andrew's brow furrowed. How could this boy not blame his parents?

"Did you love her? My mother. Even a little bit?"

Andrew stared at the floor. "I wish I could say yes. For your sake. She was a summer fling. It was what you did back then. When you were young and hungry. You went out of town for a job and found someone to have fun with. She lived in Sarasota. I was going back to New York at the end of the season. I was honest with her."

"It sounds like you're blaming her for everything."

Andrew continued to pace his old bedroom. "Things changed. She wanted more. She wanted to move to New York in the fall. She was obsessed with it, talking about all the things we'd do together in the city. She became clingy, showing up at my place late at night. I used to play ball with some guys in the company at a local park. She started showing up there. When Abbie came for a short visit, Heidi even intruded on that."

"She just wanted to be with you."

"Patrick, she was suffocating me. Sure, I wanted to be with her, but with limits. About a week before the season ended, a bunch of us went to the local fair on our day off. She dragged me off to get a lemon shake-up." He shook his head. "Weird, the tiny details you remember … So while I'm trying to drink this lemony thing and batting away the hordes of bees who were attracted to the sugar, Heidi came right out and asked if she could stay with me in New York until she found her own place. That's when I knew I had to end it." He looked at Patrick, trying to gauge his reaction. The boy's face was impassive. So much like Nick.

Patrick went to his desk. When he returned he handed Andrew a photo.

Andrew couldn't believe what he was looking at. "This is us at the fair that day. Where did you get this?"

"Heidi's friend Joyce gave it to me." Patrick folded his arms. "What did you say to her? When you ended it?"

"Nothing." Andrew stared at the photo. Heidi had her arm looped through his. Their hands were clasped. "I took the coward's way out. I avoided her during performances and didn't answer my door when she showed up uninvited after the show."

"It wasn't cowardly. It was cruel."

"Maybe. But it was who I was back then." He handed the picture back to Patrick. "Getting involved in a serious relationship wasn't in the cards for me. At least … not with Heidi."

Patrick returned the photo to the desk. "Heidi tried to reach you in New York. To tell you she was pregnant. You didn't believe her."

"You read that in my journal?"

"I read all your journals."

"No, I didn't believe her."

Patrick approached Andrew. "Joyce said Heidi sent you a picture of me. After I was born. It came back unopened."

Andrew's head shot up. "I never got it. I swear. If I'd seen a picture of you I—" What would he have done if he'd known he had a son at that time in his life? He didn't want to answer that question. "You're a much better person than I am, Patrick. You never would have abandoned your child."

"So you did know about me."

"No. I never got a picture of you. I was on tour with my class. We went to Europe. And then we graduated."

"Did you know Heidi's home life was awful? I think she just wanted to be loved. But she didn't know how to go about it."

Andrew stared at his son. "How do you know that?"

"I learned a lot about her when Nick and I were in Sarasota." Patrick shoved his hands in the pockets of his sweatpants. "I've learned a lot about you, too. Some say you're the nicest guy in the world. Fun. Easy-going. Others say you have a monster ego. That you'd mow down little old ladies to get what you want."

"Both are true."

Patrick looked puzzled. "I read in your journals that you sabotaged Jessie's affair with Gianni, Anthony's father. That you lied to her for years about it. It took Nick to uncover it."

"And it got me killed."

"You wrote in your journals that you slept with lots of girls. But everyone says you were obsessed with Jessie from the time you were kids." Patrick stepped closer. "So what's the truth?"

"All of it."

"How can it all be true?"

Andrew smiled grimly. "Nick likes to say I'm the saint, and he's the sinner. We're neither. We ricochet back and forth, but most days we fall somewhere in between. We're just two guys who try hard but mess up."

Patrick watched him, remaining silent.

"You want to know who I really am?" He paced to the bed. "I'm a guy who dreamed his whole life of being an actor, of earning that Tony Award over there. I was driven to 'make it,' to be a huge star. Like you, I used to sing all the time. In this room. For hours. But unlike you, I wanted it all. I wanted to be the best actor, the best singer, and I worked hard to get there. I wanted fame and everything that went with it. BUT – and this is the big 'but' – I also wanted love."

Andrew rubbed his eyes as he thought back to his youth. "You're right about Jessie. I was in love from the moment I laid eyes on her. She wasn't interested until Gianni was out of the picture. I didn't mean for things to fall out the way they did, but in the end it got me Jessie. When she married me I thought my dream had come true, that I had it all. But the truth was she never loved me, not the way I wanted to be loved. Not the way she eventually loved Nick. So maybe Heidi and I had more in common than I realized. Anyway, I paid for my selfishness. And I have no one to blame but myself."

"You sound like Nick. He said he owns his behavior."

Andrew laughed and sat down on the bed. "Nick. The bad boy. The loner. Thoughtless. Heartless. I could go on and on. He can be all those things. And yet … Did Nick cheat on his marriage? Did Nick turn his back on his illegitimate daughter? Did Nick give up on finding you when everyone believed you drowned? See what I mean? Neither saint nor sinner."

"Nick's been good to me."

"He's been a better father to you than I could ever be." He snorted. "Parenting. The hardest job in the world. And I had the best role model in my mom."

Patrick sat beside him. "She came to me when I was— She taught me songs. Made me feel …"

"She knew you needed her." He shook his head, picturing her. "She was something else. I dragged her from audition to audition, and she never complained. She kept losing jobs because of my auditions. We were dirt poor until I started making commercials, but I didn't know any of this until much later. She was all about me and my future. I don't know if I ever thanked her."

"Tess was like that. All she cared about was me. I felt the same way about her."

"She saved your life. You gave her the greatest joy."

Patrick dropped his head. Was he crying?

"Tess is the past, Patrick. This," Andrew rose and looked around, "this house, Nick, Kat, Anthony and Mary, they're the future." Andrew felt the clock ticking. Time was passing quickly. Too quickly. "Look at your chain."

"My ...?" Patrick untwisted his chain and examined it. He glanced up at Andrew. "Saint Genesius?" The medal hung with the crucifix and Tess's wedding ring.

"Patron saint of actors. Jessie's dad gave it to me. I never went onstage without it, even if I had to pin it in my costume. It's yours now." Patrick's eyes shifted from Andrew to the medal and back again. "Look on the back."

Patrick flipped it over. "Our names are engraved."

Andrew nodded.

Reaching out, Andrew cupped the back of Patrick's head and pulled him into his arms. He held him close, breathing in his youthful scent, rubbing his face against his hair, trying to memorize this moment. "Time is running out for me, Patrick."

Patrick let go of him. "What do you mean? ... You're leaving?"

Andrew stared into his son's eyes, so like his own, one more time. "Nick once told you our lives are often the result of other people's mistakes. It was true for Nick, and it's certainly true for you. Heidi and I were a colossal mistake, and you paid for it. I'm sorry, Patrick. But I'm not sorry you were born. Now it's up to you to make your own future."

"Will I see you again?"

"One day."

"In Heaven?"

Andrew brushed Patrick's cheek with his thumb. "Sing on New Year's Eve. If not for me, for Nick." Andrew swallowed. "You fill my heart, Patrick."

*

Nick looked around the master bedroom, shared with Jessie until now. Tonight he felt the emptiness. The loneliness.

Guilt crept into Nick's psyche. What happened to his marriage wasn't solely Jessie's fault. If only he could have forgiven her. Ironic, considering his past. After his legendary treatment of the opposite sex, he couldn't forgive the one woman he truly loved for doing what he'd done for decades.

Sitting down on the bed, he dropped his head in his hands.

*

Andrew spotted his brother in the darkness, the picture of despair. "Nick?"

Nick's head jerked up. He sucked in his breath. "God, you scared the crap out of me."

"My specialty."

"I've been wondering where you were."

243

"I came to say goodbye."

"Didn't we do this before?"

"It didn't take. This time it will."

Nick pushed off the bed. "Why now?"

"I accomplished what I had to."

"Which was?"

"Remember our deal? Back when you first came to this house? If you'd find my killer, I'd take care of family for you. You held up your end of the bargain, and so did I. Kat. Ethan and Maddie. And Patrick. So it's time for me to move on."

Nick's smile was tinged with sadness. "Patrick's description of Purgatory. You're stuck in a place until you right your wrongs. Is that where you've been?"

"If that's what you want to call it."

"And now you go to – in Patrick's words - Heaven?"

"No matter where I'm going, this is goodbye. For real. And don't denigrate Patrick's faith. It helps define him. A defense against his past."

Nick sobered. "Have you seen him?"

Andrew nodded. "Just now." He walked over to the window, looking down on the quiet street. He loved the view from this window. It was the essence of home to him. "I told him the truth."

"What truth?"

"About me. About my history. About who his dad really is."

"How did he react?"

"Better than expected." Andrew faced his brother, an ironic smile creeping across his face. "I want to be just like him when I grow up."

"What's wrong? Something's off with you."

"What's wrong?" Andrew ambled around the room. "I'm a failure with Patrick. And there's nothing I can do about it."

"You didn't know—"

"DON'T say I didn't know about him!" Andrew's anger exploded. "I could have known. Heidi tried to tell me. I ignored her." He shook his head and squeezed the bridge of his nose. "Why is it we learn what's really important in life when it's too late?"

"Andrew, stop it. Stop the pity party. Patrick's happy you're his father. And the past is the past. What's important is his welfare. He'll be okay. With time."

Andrew continued to pace the room. "I saw Jessie earlier."

Nick remained silent.

"Maybe this was meant to be," Andrew continued. "You here in the house with the kids. Maybe that was the master plan all along, and I never knew."

"Whose plan?"

Andrew stared long and hard at his brother. "What you did for Patrick in Sarasota … It wasn't easy … You have the instincts, Nick. You know how to reach kids."

"I was flying blind."

Andrew continued to stare. "It's my fault. What happened to him. Patrick says it isn't, but it is. I stand here wondering what my life would have been like if I'd believed Heidi. Would I have had a career? Would I still be alive?" He turned away, frustrated.

"Andrew, you—"

"Let me have my say, Nick. Please." He shook his head. "That poor kid. He may be damaged for life because of my selfishness. I'm some saint, huh?" He looked over his shoulder at Nick. "You always saw me realistically. You're the only one." He smiled, but it was ringed with sadness. "And Mary. She always knew exactly who I was."

"What about Jessie?"

Andrew snorted. "I even managed to screw up Jessie. My murder changed her. And not for the better."

"You're blaming yourself for who Jessie is today?"

"You should have known her before. She was centered. There was a glow about her. Sure she was spoiled, but that only made her more fun. And she didn't throw it around like she does now. She could laugh at herself."

"Maybe she could laugh because you made her laugh. When you died, she was lost. Getting involved with me didn't help. I'm the opposite of you."

"Are you, Nick? The opposite of me? I'm not so sure anymore. I think we're more alike than either of us realized. And where we differ, you end up being the saint, and I'm the sinner."

"For God's sake, Andrew, where's this maudlin talk coming from?"

Andrew licked his lips and looked down. "This is the last time we'll be able to talk like this. It's time for some truth … Time … There's so little time … The clock is ticking …" He began to pace in a circle. "So much more I need to say …"

Nick grabbed his arm. "Andrew, stop. Just stop."

"I can't, Nick. Don't you see? The seconds are ticking by and I— Take care of Patrick. I know you will, but I— He loves you, Nick. Promise me. Promise you'll take good care of my son."

"Of course I will. Andrew, slow down—"

"I can't. There's no time. Dear God, there's no time left!" In a panic, he threw his arms around Nick. "I don't need to say it, right? You know how I feel, have always felt, right?"

Nick gripped him tighter.

Andrew hung onto his brother until time ran out.

*

The dark bedroom came back into focus. Nick swiped his cheek and stared down at his wet fingers. What the ...?

Andrew.

The hint of musk was in the air. His brother's scent. He was here.

Andrew came to say goodbye. For good this time. Nick was holding his brother, and then he was gone. He said he saw Patrick—

Nick took off, sprinting up the stairs. After a quick knock, he pushed into Patrick's room. The boy sat on his bed, his back to him. Nick came up beside him.

Patrick's hand was clasped around the chain Mary gave him. "He was here."

Nick nodded. "He came to me, too."

"He gave me this." The St. Genesius medal somehow made it from Nick's locked desk drawer to hanging from Patrick's neck. Nick never questioned Andrew's ghostly powers. He made things happen.

"I didn't know him before, like you did. Now, in a way, I feel like I do." Patrick's eyes wandered, his face unreadable. "He's different from what I imagined."

Nick sat down beside him. "How?"

"He was an icon in my eyes. Some huge star who had it all."

"And now?"

Patrick shrugged. "He's just a guy. A huge talent, sure, but just a guy. He could be mean. He hurt people. But he was also hurt."

"Who hurt him?"

"Jessie. She didn't love him. Not like she loved you." He looked at Nick. "He's different from you. When you found out about Kat, you brought her here." Patrick's gaze drifted again. "I don't think Andrew would have done the same, even if he believed Heidi."

"You don't know that."

"I think I do." He again looked at the medal. "You know what? I'm not angry. Or bitter. I should be, but I'm not. Why?"

In an odd way, Nick understood. "Andrew and Heidi created you. Just like my birth parents created me. We spent our lives never knowing them. Tess and Father Joe were your true parents. Parenting has nothing to do with blood."

"Sometimes it does." Patrick shifted his focus to Nick.

The boy had an uncanny knack of seeing into Nick's very core.

Rising, Nick moved to the window. He stared down at the back yard, at the twin plum trees growing from a single seed. Andrew planted the original plum when he was thirteen.

"Will you stay for a while?" Patrick asked.

"Funny. I was just going to ask if you'd mind." He sat down in the rocker and leaned back, suddenly tired.

Patrick slipped back under the duvet, curling on his side and watching Nick. "It was hard, wasn't it? Saying goodbye to your brother."

Nick nodded.

"You'll see him again. One day."

For a brief moment Nick wished he had Patrick's faith.

"I've decided to sing on New Year's Eve."

Nick looked up, surprised. "What changed your mind?"

"Andrew." A smile crept across Patrick's face. "I want to sing for my dad."

EPILOGUE

Nick and Patrick met with Dr. Benjamin Brody at an address only a few blocks from home. It was a comfortable space, more like a study than an office. A fire blazed in a stone grate. The furniture was unassuming and comfortable.

Brody looked to be around Nick's age. He was of medium height, trim, with close-cropped brown hair. He had a congenial, laid-back demeanor.

"Before we begin, let me explain a couple things. We go on a first-name basis here, so call me Ben. We'll continue to meet in this space, which is in my home. I keep an office here for patients who require anonymity. No one will see you coming or going from the back entrance. My main offices are attached to Mount Sanai Hospital."

Ben looked at Patrick and smiled. "Next week I'd like you to see my medical associate, Dr. Jack Mint. He'll give you a complete physical in his private clinic. For the next few days, we'll just talk, you and me."

"Nick can stay, right?" Patrick sounded anxious.

"Yes. Parents often want to be here—"

"I'm not a parent," Nick interrupted.

"Yes, you are," Patrick said quickly.

Nick not only saw Patrick's fear, he felt it. Was he doing the right thing, bringing him here?

"Okay. Let's start at the beginning. Take your time, Patrick. No pressure …"

For the next three days, over eighteen hours, Nick listened while Ben gently got Patrick to talk about life in that foster home. It was an art, the way he eased Patrick's anxiety, the way he'd jump subjects if Patrick began to panic. At times, Ben would stop the session and they'd have a soda or a snack.

Starting with generalities, Ben guided Patrick carefully, winnowing down to greater and greater detail. Nick was impressed. Ben handled Patrick with compassion, sensitivity and intelligence.

When the time came for Patrick to describe in detail what the Trout sisters did to him, Nick struggled to keep his temper in check. Occasionally Patrick couldn't get the words out, overcome by tears or anger or shame. He'd grip Nick's hand or pace like a caged animal or crumble into the corner of the couch.

When they returned home each day, Mary never asked questions, but Nick saw concern in her wise eyes. Often Patrick asked Nick to come upstairs with him. Usually he said nothing, just took comfort in Nick's presence. He never talked about that day's session, and Nick didn't bring it up.

When Patrick fell asleep, Nick would disappear into his office, full of rage, bourbon his only escape from the ugly images he couldn't chase from his mind.

Kat knocked on his door the second night. "You okay, Daddy?"

Nick shrugged.

"What about Patrick?"

"What about him?"

"I'm not stupid. I know he's seeing a shrink."

Nick's eyes swiveled from his daughter to the glass in his hand.

"Okay, you promised not to tell anyone. So I won't push. I just wanted to check on you. I won't bother Patrick."

Nick reached for Kat and pulled her onto his lap. She was sweet and innocent, the opposite of that house of horrors in Sarasota, Florida. "I love you, baby girl."

*

SuZee Q's was packed tonight. The place was done up for New Year's Eve. Bottles of champagne were brought in. Party hats and paper horns were at every place setting.

Nick had his same table in the center of the room, every chair taken. The whole family was here, with the exception of Bertie who had a performance of *DIANA*. Bree even turned up, courtesy of Kat.

Tonight was Nick and Jessie's anniversary. Two years ago, they were the celebrity wedding of the decade. Last year the kids threw a surprise party for them. Now they were headed for divorce court. Here he sat, surrounded by people but very much alone. And Jessie was onstage at the Crookston Theater, working.

Nick tried to suppress his gloomy feelings and concentrate on Patrick. His nephew stood in the far corner, preparing for his turn onstage. He kept catching Nick's eye, his expression impossible to read.

Father Joe sat across from Nick, anxious to hear Patrick sing again. Early that morning, Nick invited the priest to stay in New York a little longer. Father Joe immediately said yes. Without being told, the priest understood what was going on. Patrick was struggling with his therapy sessions. Who wouldn't? Nick could never do what Patrick was

249

doing, talk about— describe what— Having Father Joe around would be a comfort. For both Patrick and Nick.

Nick scanned the crowd, looking for a particular face. He was rewarded. Dr. Ben Brody sat along the wall with his wife. Nick told him he had to see Patrick onstage to understand his patient.

Quill Llewellyn turned up at Nick's side. "Remember that project I told you about? The one on the back burner? Well, it's cooking now. And I wondered if you might be interested in coming aboard."

"In what capacity?"

"As the playwright. We all need a new challenge these days."

"I've never written—"

"I've never done something like this project either. Created something from scratch. Based partly on an old standard musical and partly on what happened to your brother. You'd be perfect for this."

Write a play? It was true Nick was bored with churning out a novel every year. Still …

"I'm starting my own production company. And I've asked Larry Williams to direct. It will be a musical of firsts for all of us. Of course I want to work with Patrick. Where is he?"

"Getting ready to sing."

"He's Andrew Brady's son, isn't he?"

Nick flashed an enigmatic smile. "You'll have to ask Patrick."

Quill dashed off to talk to Patrick.

Bree, sitting beside Nick, whispered, "He's determined to make Patrick a star. Like his father."

"Patrick's not Andrew."

*

Patrick waited to hear his introduction. He spent the afternoon working with the musicians, which tonight would include a violin, sax and flute. The pianist was good, able to follow him beautifully, freeing Nick from accompanying him.

"Excuse me. Patrick?" Quill Llewellyn stood beside him. "Sorry to interrupt. I know you're about to go on. Would you come and find me afterwards? I want to talk to you about something."

"Sure."

Quill lingered. "Would you answer a question for me?"

"If I can."

"Andrew Brady is your father, isn't he?"

Patrick stared at the man. "Why is it important?"

Quill contemplated his question. "I don't know. Maybe it's not. Your talent can stand alone." He started to leave but turned back again. "Please. I have to know."

Patrick slid his hands in his back pockets and eyed the man. "I've been blessed to have more than one father. Andrew Brady was one of them." Patrick looked over at Nick. He was talking to Mary, his arm resting across the back of her chair. "Now if you'll excuse me..."

"Uh, sure ... sure."

Amused by the look of confusion on Quill's face, Patrick turned his attention back to his prep for going onstage. Checking himself in the full-length mirror, he was glad he chose to dress in black. He wanted his singing to be highlighted, not how he looked or who he resembled.

It had been a rough week. His sessions with Ben took a toll, leaving him drained and feeling raw. He'd use it tonight. Like he always did. Just go out and sing what he was feeling.

Hearing his introduction, Patrick moved center stage. Two spotlights hit him. He couldn't see the audience, which was how he liked it. It was just him and his music. He closed his eyes and began ...

Each song was chosen for a personal reason. 'I Dreamed a Dream' from *LES MISERABLES* turned into a story of his childhood with Tess, and of how scared he felt when he lost her. 'The Rose' took him back to the night he stood at the living room window with Anthony watching his first snowfall. It represented his new home, his new family and how much he loved them.

Next was 'Gethsemane' for Father Joe. Also recognition of his faith. Patrick became so submerged in the story that sweat poured down his face and his heart raced. Towards the end he spotted movement in the audience and realized they were on their feet clapping. As he belted out the last word, a word he held until his breath ran out, a roar went across the room, cheers that sounded like one voice. Surprised and humbled by the outpouring of love coming at him beyond the spotlights, he tried to start singing his quirky "Sunset Boulevard,' but had to wait for the audience to settle down.

He added a few new songs to his repertoire and finished with 'Empty Chairs at Empty Tables,' from *LES MIS*. For Patrick, this song represented the missing people in all their lives.

When the applause again wouldn't stop, he had to make a decision. Should he do the encore he rehearsed but dismissed? Could he sing it?

Patrick took a deep breath and nodded to the pianist.

This one was for his grandmother. The woman with the dark hair who chased away a five-year-old's fear and sang with him.

It was also for Nick.

As the musicians began the beautiful but haunting intro, Patrick cupped the microphone. Inhaling slowly, he took his time and sang sotto voce ...

Nothing's gonna harm you
Not while I'm around
Nothing's gonna harm you
No sir, not while I'm around ...
*

Nick's chest tightened as he listened to the lyrics, as he realized what Patrick was singing. Glancing across the room, he caught Ben Brody's eye.

After a week of hell, of spilling his guts about the atrocities he endured as a little boy, Patrick walked back into that closet tonight.

By himself.

In front of a couple hundred people.

If he was strong enough to do this, he was strong enough to release Nick from the promise he made in Sarasota.

Nick McDeare intended to go after Carrie and Eva Trout and make them pay for what they did to five-year-old Patrick Cavanaugh.

Hell would seem like paradise when he finished with them.
*

A few blocks away in an elegant co-op apartment on West Seventieth Street, a woman took five-year-old Dylan Leicester into the luxurious master bathroom. His parents were out for the evening, not due back for hours.

He was such a beautiful child, his strawberry curls highlighting his blue eyes. Born with a damaged larynx and rendered mute, the boy learned at an early age to use his hands to communicate.

Cathy loved this job. Loved all her jobs. She babysat for three affluent households in Manhattan.

Smoothing back her hair, she placed Dylan in the spacious bathtub, pulled a scarf from her pocket and bound the child's hands.

Watching fear creep into the boy's eyes, she smiled. Dylan couldn't yell, so neighbors wouldn't overhear their special time together. There were no baby cameras in this room. And she had all the time in the world.

Cathy Tractman, formerly Carrie Trout of Sarasota, Florida, said to the gorgeous little boy, "Remember, this is our secret. If anyone finds out, they'll take you away from your mommy and daddy and lock them up. You'll live in a dark, cold room ..."

***

About the Author:

Deborah Fezelle has a vast background in the arts. She began as a professional actress, training at the Juilliard School in NYC, and worked on Broadway, Off-Broadway, the Kennedy Center in Washington, and other regional theaters around the country. She later moved on to directing and coaching while simultaneously embarking on a writing career. With writing partner Sherry Yanow, Deborah penned five plays, two web series and the first two McDeare novels, THE EVIL THAT MEN DO & A WALKING SHADOW. Continuing the series on  her own, she wrote FULL CIRCLE, DISCRETION & now WHAT'S PAST IS PROLOGUE. After spending twenty-five years in her beloved Manhattan, Deborah now makes her home in North Carolina.

Printed in Great Britain
by Amazon

78980727R00149